It was all Dylan could do █████████████████████
as he ran them up and dow██████████████████████
heart had been in his throa████████ D0175770 ████
putting himself through mo███████████████
mit, where was that iron control he used ▓▓ ▓
on?

"Dylan?"

As Jamie's soft voice pulled him from his crazy, reckless thoughts, he moved his gaze to her face. And lost his battle. Her eyes were heated, filled with a want that echoed within him. With a groan of surrender, he lowered his head and took her mouth. He softly teased her lips, her taste sweeter than every fantasy he'd ever had. When he felt her hands on his shoulders, pulling him closer, he licked at her lips, seeking a sweeter, deeper taste. The opening of her mouth took his breath. There was no hesitancy in her actions. Her tongue met and dueled with his, drawing at him.

Lowering his body over hers, careful of his weight, he propped himself on his arms, allowing only his lips to touch her. Angling his mouth, he pressed deeper, withdrew, and plunged again. Thrusting and retreating, over and over, mimicking the motion for what another part of him ached to do.

Soft, insistent hands tugged at him, pulled him closer. Dylan lowered himself until he lay on top of her. Still mindful of his big body over her much smaller one, he tried to keep most of his weight off her. Jamie was having none of it. Pulling him harder, she spread her legs and allowed him to settle between them. Dylan nudged his erection against her mound. They groaned into each other's mouths at the delicious contact.

Warm, soft hands moved beneath his shirt. Needing the same contact, Dylan slid a hand under her sweatshirt and felt the soft, supple skin he'd dreamed about for months. Silky and firm, she was every man's fantasy . . . and Dylan's only dream.

A dream that couldn't come true.

ALSO BY CHRISTY REECE

No Chance
Second Chance
Last Chance

Rescue Me
Return to Me
Run to Me

Sweet Justice

Sweet Revenge

A Last Chance Rescue Novel

CHRISTY REECE

BALLANTINE BOOKS • NEW YORK

Sweet Revenge is a work of fiction. Names, characters, places, and incidents are the products of the author's imagination or are used fictiously. Any resemblance to actual events, locales, or persons, living or dead, is entirely coincidental.

A Ballantine Books Mass Market Original

Copyright © 2011 by Christy Reece
Excerpt from *Sweet Reward* copyright © 2011 by Christy Reece

Published in the United States by Ballantine Books, an imprint of The Random House Publishing Group, a division of Random House, Inc., New York.

BALLANTINE and colophon are trademarks of Random House, Inc.

This book contains an excerpt from the forthcoming book *Sweet Reward* by Christy Reece. This excerpt has been set for this edition only and may not reflect the final content of the forthcoming edition.

ISBN 978-0-345-52405-8
eBook ISBN 978-0-345-52406-5

Printed in the United States of America

www.ballantinebooks.com

9 8 7 6 5 4 3 2 1

Ballantine mass market edition: October 2011

Fabulous teachers can make
such a difference in a child's life
and two very special
English literature teachers
made a huge difference in mine.

Thank you, Betty Howton and Professor Pace.

And to a very special teacher named Kara—you rock!

Sweet
Revenge

prologue

Bustarviejo, Spain

The night was silent and still. The air, thick and humid, held a feeling of expectancy—as if aware that rescue had finally arrived. Stooped behind a low brick wall, his eyes narrowed into a squint behind powerful binoculars, LCR operative Dylan Savage surveyed the perimeter of the massive property owned by Stanford Reddington.

The house in front of him held Jamie Kendrick—a young woman who'd been abducted by a maniac and then sold to Stanford Reddington. Purchased for what purpose, Dylan didn't even want to consider. Their mission was clear: rescue. Their plan: a soft entry. Grab Jamie and get the hell out, hopefully without firing a shot.

"Everyone in place and ready?" Noah McCall asked quietly. The Last Chance Rescue leader kept his voice calm and low, his tone revealing none of the tension Dylan knew he must feel.

On missions, McCall acted as though ice ran through his veins. That was an attitude Dylan had adopted long before he'd joined LCR. Never let them see you flinch. He'd learned that lesson as a child. Staying expressionless had saved his ass more than once.

Dylan answered with a soft "Ready."

Adrenaline surged as the three other people on the op answered in the affirmative. Any second now . . .

"Go," McCall whispered.

Staying low, Dylan and McCall ran toward the back door that their informant, Raphael, had promised would be unlocked. Noah eased the door open . . . Dylan peered inside. Scanning the large kitchen, he briefly noted that not only did the room look like a pigsty, it stank of old food and stale alcohol. The messy space had one thing in its favor: no people.

Dylan entered first, McCall behind him. Dim light filtered from a greasy bulb over the stove revealed the remains of last night's dinner and four dirty plates on the counter. Four here, including Jamie?

In the middle of the kitchen, the men stopped . . . waited . . . listened. On cue, a loud, thudding knock sounded at the front door. A moment of dead silence, then lights came on as someone stomped toward the door. The instant the front door opened, Dylan and McCall moved.

Guns at the ready, their steps silent, they made their way to the next room. At the entrance to the living room, McCall went in one direction, Dylan the other. Sticking his head into a small den and a bathroom, Dylan found nothing other than furniture and more evidence that slobs lived here.

One minute later, they met in the middle of the living room. The loud protestations coming from the front of the house reassured them that the home owner would be occupied for several more moments.

His black eyes glittering with cold determination, McCall mouthed silently, "Anything?"

Dylan shook his head.

Both men turned and headed up the stairway. Halting at the top of the stairs, they assessed the area. Bright lights from the first floor allowed them to see three rooms to check on this floor. McCall jerked his head at the stairs to the third floor.

With a quick nod, Dylan headed upstairs. At the top of the small landing, he stopped and listened. The only sounds were the distant mumblings of Reddington as he argued with the Spanish police. Two rooms to check here. The door to one of the rooms stood open. Easing his head in, he looked around. A storage room, filled with furniture and boxes.

Swiftly, silently, Dylan moved across the hallway, toward the closed door of the other room. His ear to the wood, he listened and heard a soft, trembling sigh.

He put his hand on the doorknob. Locked. Pulling a small tool from the belt at his waist, he inserted it into the keyhole. At the sweet sound of a click, he twisted the knob, eased the door open, and stepped inside. The room, midnight dark and deathly quiet, held the musky scent of sour sweat and felt heavy with fear, confirming what he already knew: she was here.

The softest whisper of sound put him on alert; half a second later, a small body leaped onto his back. Not wanting to hurt or frighten her further, Dylan dropped to the floor with Jamie Kendrick hanging on to his shoulders.

She ground her knee into the small of his back and spoke in a harsh, raspy voice, "Touch me and I'll kill you."

Admiration and compassion slammed into him. She was tough. Good. She would need to stay that way. "I'm here to rescue you, Jamie."

With a soft, laughing sob, she said mockingly, "Yeah, my knight in shining armor."

"I'm with Last Chance Rescue."

After a long pause, she whispered hoarsely, "What's that?"

"A rescue organization."

Another long pause. Finally, a shaky, tear-filled voice asked, "Are you for real?"

"Yes." He waited two heartbeats, giving her time to absorb the information. Then, since time was of the essence, he said, "We need to get out of here."

Her slight weight eased off his back, and he felt her shift away from him.

Getting to his feet, Dylan took a flashlight from his utility belt and clicked it on. His heart thudded and crashed as he got his first glimpse of slender, petite Jamie Kendrick. Perched on the edge of a bed, she'd snagged a sheet to cover herself. Untamed, golden-brown hair draped over her bare shoulders. Gray-blue eyes shimmered with tears; white teeth bit at her lips as if to control their trembling. The thin sheet covering her nude body couldn't hide her uncontrollable shaking. Despite his reassurance, she was terrified that this was a trick.

"Found her," he whispered softly into his mic.

"Get her out," McCall answered softly. "Reddington's still at the door, arguing. I've got one bastard down, two more on the run."

"Affirmative," Dylan answered.

There was no time for more reassurance. They needed to get their asses out of here . . . now. He took a step toward her. "Let's go."

She lifted a hand to tighten the sheet around her, and he saw the handcuff dangling from her wrist. Pulling a standard key from his belt, he reached for her. Admiration grew in him as he watched her stiffen but refuse to back away. He unlocked the cuff from her bruised, raw wrist and then let her go. The last thing she probably wanted was for a man to touch her. Unfortunately, he was going to have to do more than just touch her if they were to get out of here in one piece.

With a sweep of his flashlight over the room, Dylan took another quick scan. No clothing. He pulled his black cotton T-shirt over his head and handed it to her.

"Put this on." Giving her a brief moment of privacy, he went to the door to peer out. Still quiet.

At the sound of a small, relieved sigh, he glanced over his shoulder. She was ready. Her feet were bare, and her body swayed as she tried to stand. The T-shirt swallowed her, landing just above her wobbling knees.

"It'll be easier for both of us if you let me carry you out." He wasn't asking for permission, but he didn't want to scare her by just lifting her without warning.

"I can walk."

"You're barefoot and weak. We need to get out of here as fast as we can." Giving her no time to argue, Dylan reached for her and scooped her into his arms. Her body was shaking with terror, but she didn't fight him, and that was all he needed.

He made a rapid exit from the room and strode quickly toward the stairway. As they got halfway down the stairs, the distant blast of gunfire ramped up the tension. *Shit!* No way was he not getting her out of here alive. Holding her tighter against his chest, he whispered, "Hang on, sweetheart."

Lowering his head, Dylan ran like hell.

One month later
Charles de Gaulle Airport
Paris, France

"Ladies and gentlemen, flight 231 to Atlanta, Georgia, U.S.A., will begin loading in ten minutes."

A bright, sunny smile plastered on her face, Jamie turned to her sister, McKenna. This stiff-upper-lip thing was a lot harder than she'd thought it would be. This wasn't goodbye forever, but still . . . "I'll see you soon again . . . I promise."

McKenna's face, so similar to Jamie's, revealed the

same turmoil. "You're sure you don't want me to go with you? It's not too late for me to buy a ticket."

The lump grew in Jamie's throat at the offer. McKenna's anxiousness was sweet but unnecessary. She wasn't nervous or worried. After everything that had happened the last few months, she felt insulated from the trivial stuff. And she'd been given a miracle: her sister. Her biggest concern was being separated from McKenna again.

"I'll be fine. I just want to get this behind me so I can move forward."

"Will you have to see him?"

Funny, even the thought of seeing her ex-husband again didn't cause the thud of dread it once had. "I don't think so. My attorney assured me I'd just need to appear before a judge."

"You know I'll be there for you if you need me. Right?"

Jamie hugged McKenna again. After her rescue, they'd spent almost a month together and had gotten even closer than they'd been as kids. Having both survived their own hell, being together again made them appreciate each other so much more.

She pulled away and smiled through her tears. "You need to go see Lucas."

At the mention of Lucas Kane, a breathtaking expression came over McKenna's face. Never had Jamie seen anyone more in love. And just from the short amount of time Jamie had spent with Lucas, she knew he felt the same way. Other than her parents, she had never known a couple who loved each other like that.

"You promise to come back to Europe soon?"

"Cross my heart. And if not, you can always come see me." She gripped McKenna's hand and held tight. "We'll never let each other go again."

Tears sparkling in her eyes, McKenna nodded fiercely. "Never. I promise."

"Jamie? McKenna?"

They both whirled around at the sound of the familiar masculine voice approaching them. A gasp escaped Jamie before she could stop it. She hadn't thought she'd ever see him again, and yet here he was. *Dylan.*

"Hey, what are you doing here?" McKenna asked.

"I heard Jamie was headed back to the States. I've got some business to take care of there, so I thought I'd tag along." His emerald gaze turned to Jamie. "That okay with you?"

It had been almost a month since she'd seen him. Dylan had been the one to carry her out of that house, the one to rescue her from hell.

Her rescue had been as dramatic as any television drama, with Dylan and the other LCR operatives swooping down in the dead of night and rescuing her from Stanford Reddington and his vile son. Jamie barely remembered the event other than Dylan's gruff, reassuring voice, his strong arms carrying her out of the house, and him saying, "You're safe now, Jamie" as he handed her over to the EMTs.

Then she'd been lifted into a helicopter and taken to the hospital. She'd gone from abject misery and terror to comfort and safety in a matter of seconds. And she had thought Dylan was the most wonderful of heroes.

For the first couple of days after her rescue, he'd been kind and wonderfully attentive. Then something had happened, and for the life of her, she didn't know what. The day of her release from the hospital, Dylan had turned noticeably cooler. She'd tried to tell herself she was just imagining it, but when he'd given her a barely perceptible nod after she'd thanked him once more for her rescue, she had known it wasn't her imagination.

Those words of thanks were the last ones she'd thought she'd ever get to say to him, and now here he was, going to the States with her.

Realizing that both McKenna and Dylan were looking at her strangely, Jamie knew a deep blush covered her fair skin as she stammered, "Yes . . . of course, that's okay with me."

"Ladies and gentleman, flight 231 to Atlanta is now boarding."

As the airline personnel gave boarding instructions, Jamie forgot everything other than the knowledge that she was saying goodbye to her sister. Throwing her arms around McKenna's neck, she whispered in her ear. "I love you, Kenna."

Her voice thick with emotion, McKenna answered softly, "I love you, too. See you soon. Okay?"

Unable to speak for the giant lump in her throat, Jamie nodded and tightened her arms around her sister one last time . . . then made herself let go. McKenna didn't need to see the uncertainty and dread that had suddenly swamped her. After everything she'd been through, what was there to fear?

McKenna's eyes glittered with emotion. "Call me as soon as you land. Okay?"

She nodded again. "I will."

She wasn't surprised to see McKenna hug Dylan—he seemed to have an affectionate rapport with her sister. Something that was sadly missing with her.

With her carry-on gripped tightly in her hand, Jamie headed to the ticket agent. At the door, she turned back for one last glance. McKenna waved and blew a kiss. Jamie gave her the best smile she could muster and turned to walk down the narrow tunnel to the plane.

"Want me to take your bag?"

Despite the massive willpower she thought she had, tears were flooding her eyes. Not looking at Dylan, she shook her head.

"You okay?"

"Yeah, just hate saying goodbye." She straightened

her shoulders, determined to get past her weepiness. "Where are you sitting?"

"First class, row two, seat A."

Startled, she jerked her head up. "I'm in row two, seat B. How'd you manage that?"

He shrugged as if it was nothing and stopped at the entrance to the plane, allowing her to go first. As she passed by him, his closed expression told her he wasn't going to explain anything. Not why he'd arranged to sit with her, and probably not why he'd just shown up, out of the blue, to travel with her. Telling herself she didn't need an explanation, Jamie settled into her seat and watched as the most handsome and infuriatingly mysterious man she'd ever known dropped into the seat next to hers.

Would nine hours of sitting beside him give her any insight? Like why he'd made the effort to travel with her but still treated her as though she'd done something to offend him?

Dylan stretched his long legs out and cursed himself once more for coming. She would've been fine traveling on her own. He hadn't seen her in almost a month, and during that time, she'd obviously recovered. So why the hell was he here, like some sort of guard dog? Hell if he knew.

She looked healthy. No, not just healthy . . . she looked beautiful. When he'd rescued her from that hellhole, Jamie's golden-brown hair had been almost to her hips. Now it was shorter, just past her shoulders, and highlighted with golden blond streaks. The bruises and swelling on her face and neck were completely gone, and her silky, fair skin glowed. Even the dark, haunted look in her eyes had vanished.

This morning, he'd been at LCR headquarters giving a review of his last op. After his meeting with McCall, he'd anticipated going back to his apartment and healing for the next few days. The job had had gotten a little dicey, resulting in a couple of bruised ribs and a deep thigh bruise. A long soak in a hot tub and about ten hours of uninterrupted sleep had been his only plan. The instant McKenna had called Noah and mentioned that Jamie was headed back to the States, alone, his plans had changed. Dylan had shot out of his chair and, on the way to the door, asked his boss to arrange a seat on the same flight. If he hadn't been in such a hurry, he would've stopped to snarl at McCall's amusement.

Had anyone asked him why he felt the need to be with her, he wouldn't have had an answer. He'd rescued dozens of people for LCR. And while he wished them well, not once had he felt any real desire to see them again, much less accompany them home.

What was it about this woman that made him react in a way opposite to what was normal for him? Nothing could happen between them. She was going back home to live in the States. He lived in Paris.

Yeah, like that's the only thing keeping you from pursuing something.

"What kind of business are you going back for?"

Jerked out of his dark thoughts, he shrugged. "Family stuff."

"Where does your family live?"

He didn't hesitate with his answer: "Florida."

So what if "live" wasn't exactly the right word? While he was in the United States, he figured he might as well visit his mother's and grandmother's graves in Florida. He could rent a car and be in Jacksonville in a matter of hours. And he'd be visiting the only family he'd ever wanted to claim.

"Are you flying out of Atlanta to Florida?"

Dylan shook his head and asked, "What about you? You headed to Louisiana?"

"Yes, I have a connecting flight to Baton Rouge about an hour after I land."

"You going to have to see your ex?"

She grimaced. "You know about him?"

"I know that he hurt you."

Her chin came up in a defensive gesture. "Just once. He never got the chance again."

"Will you have to see him?"

"I don't think so. My attorney seems to think that I can just file another complaint against him and then appear before a judge. He was only in jail for a few days. . . . He deserves a longer sentence."

"You want me to go with you?" The words were out before he could pull them back. Hell, what was it about her?

If Dylan was surprised, Jamie was apparently stunned. Her eyes widening, she blushed a crimson red and stuttered, "Oh . . . I . . . well . . . that's so swee—" Thankfully she stopped before she got the word out. Even when he'd been a baby, "sweet" was one description that had never been attributed to Dylan. She swallowed and said, "I appreciate the offer, but I need to handle this myself."

He shrugged. "Yeah, that's what I figured." He was relieved she'd said no, so why did he have this odd letdown feeling? Damn weird.

"Besides, I'd hate to take you away from your family."

He looked away from her, to the flight attendant headed their way with the drink cart. "Yeah, they'd be disappointed."

"How long are you going to be in the States?"

He shrugged, not really wanting to go back to that discussion. "Just a day or so."

"Wow, you came all the way from Paris just for a day? Won't your family—"

"You want something to drink?"

Looking startled at his abrupt question, she said, "Oh . . . yes. Hot tea. Thanks."

Dylan gave the order, hoping that once Jamie had her drink, she'd forget what they'd been talking about. Discussing his family—or, for that matter, his life—wasn't something he liked to spend a lot of time on.

There was an awkward silence while Jamie accepted her hot tea and Dylan chugged down his black coffee. By the time she'd sweetened her drink to her taste, his cup was empty. Though a slug of bourbon or a Scotch neat would have been his preference, coffee was the only drink he could allow himself. Maintaining his wits would keep him from uttering another dumb-ass comment. Offering to go to Louisiana with her had been stupid enough.

She took a sip of her tea, and Dylan felt his mouth twitch with a smile. Everything Jamie did was feminine and . . . what was the word . . . dainty. She even made drinking a beverage a feminine action. Where he swallowed in gulps, she sipped like a delicate sparrow.

Mentally rolling his eyes at the stupidity of his thoughts, he said, "You and McKenna enjoy your time in Paris?"

Her eyes glowing, she nodded. "It was wonderful. I've always wanted to visit, and Kenna knows the city so well. We did all the touristy stuff, along with lots of things people who have never been to Paris might not know about."

"You probably had a lot of things to get caught up on."

Her eyes dimmed for an instant, and Dylan felt like an ass. Bringing up the past meant reminding her about all the crap she'd been through. Not only had she been brutalized by the now-dead scumbag Damon Hughes, she'd been held captive by the human slime Stanford Reddington and his son. Of course, it wasn't something she'd ever be able to forget, but his comment sure as hell hadn't helped. This was just another reminder that he needed to stay away from her. His late wife had told him more than once that he had the tact of a water buffalo.

Thankfully, Jamie's smile returned. "We had years to get caught up on. Our lives have been completely opposite."

"What was it like, living with your aunt?"

Her pretty mouth twisted in a wry smile. "The best description I can come up with for Aunt Mavis is a cross between an elderly drill sergeant and Miss Manners. My aunt had an opinion on everything and felt it her duty to share that opinion with everyone."

"Doesn't sound like a lot of fun."

"It wasn't." Slender shoulders lifted in a delicate shrug. "But I was safe and warm, had good food to eat and a place to sleep. Kenna didn't have those things."

"Are you going to see your sister again soon?"

She nodded. "I haven't told her because I wanted to surprise her, but as soon as I settle things in Louisiana, I'm going back there to live."

Dylan felt a kick to his gut. "In Paris?"

"Yes. I fell in love with the city, and being so far away from Kenna isn't something I want to do again. Family is so important, don't you think?"

Since everyone in his family was dead and most of them hadn't been worth much alive, he didn't have an answer that wouldn't cause more questions. He settled for a vague nod and another question: "Are you going to continue teaching?"

For the first time since he'd known her, he saw a flicker of secrecy in her expression. She shrugged and took another sip of her tea. "I'm not sure yet. There're a lot of possibilities out there."

That was about as vague as one could get. "McCall

has a lot of contacts," Dylan said. "He could probably help."

Yet another slight flicker, but all she said was "That's a great idea. I'll give him a call as soon as I get settled."

The seat-belt sign went off, and Dylan used that as an excuse to get up and walk around. He needed a few minutes away from Jamie not only to come to terms with these damn odd feelings of protectiveness but also to deal with the news that she was moving to Europe. It'd been easy enough to stay away from her the last month. He'd been working ops, and Jamie had been recovering. What was he going to do now that they would be living in the same city? How was he going to stay away from her when he hadn't gone a day without thinking about her since they'd met?

Hell!

Jamie took one last sip of her now tepid tea and grimaced. Aunt Mavis had been a hot-tea drinker, and it irritated her that she'd instinctively requested what her aunt would have expected her to order. Though she'd only lived with the woman for five years, her aunt had worked hard to fit a lifetime of strict lessons into that time. Aunt Mavis had been gone for several years—she had died peacefully in her sleep. Jamie couldn't help but wonder if she'd just decided to die that day and had then done it. The woman had had that much iron-willed discipline.

"You want to get up and stretch your legs?"

Swallowing a gasp, she jerked her head to gaze at the man standing beside her. He moved so quietly, she hadn't heard him. "Quiet" was a good description for Dylan Savage. He didn't talk a lot, and when he moved, he barely made a sound.

She smiled her thanks. "No, I'm fine."

As he eased into the seat beside her, she noticed a slight wince, as if he were in pain. "Are you okay?"

"Yeah, just a couple of bruises."

"From a job?"

He nodded.

"Did I ever thank you?"

For the first time ever, Jamie saw a small smile at his lips. "Yeah, about twenty times that first day."

"I wanted to send you something, but McKenna said that wasn't necessary."

He looked over at her, a slight softening in his eyes. "I don't think anyone's ever done that before. What were you going to send?"

"For saving my life?" She laughed, pleased that she actually found some kind of humor in referring to those dark days before her rescue. "I was torn between a fruit basket and a bottle of Scotch. McKenna said Scotch was your favorite drink."

"You didn't need to send anything. It's my job."

She ignored the sting of his comment. Of course that's what she was to him: a job. How silly to think he'd be attracted to someone he'd rescued. "Are you married?" Oh God, had she just asked that question?

"No."

Feeling like she'd opened a giant hole and was teetering on the edge, she added, "Me neither."

"Yeah, I know."

Jamie fought to control the blush she could feel spreading over her entire body. She had worked so hard to overcome her tendency to glow like a beacon when she said stupid or inappropriate things. With Dylan, all of that training and discipline vanished. And this had to be one of the stupidest comments she'd ever made. Of course he knew she wasn't married; they'd just talked about her ex-husband. Besides, there was little the man didn't know about her life. Whereas she knew next to nothing about his.

She looked up as Dylan stood again and pulled something from the overhead compartment. He handed her a small pillow and then, sitting back down with a pillow of his own, reclined his seat, put the pillow behind his head, and closed his eyes.

And just like that, all conversation stopped. Not that it was his responsibility to entertain her. Still, she couldn't deny the sting. His response to her single status wasn't exactly encouraging, even if it had been an inane statement.

Jamie looked out at the bright blue sky. Okay, so what if he had no interest in her. She had more on her mind than starting a relationship that could go nowhere. The news she'd received this morning before leaving—news she hadn't shared with McKenna—was going to occupy all of her thoughts. Because if things progressed as they looked like they might, she was going to have to figure out how to not only hunt down and capture a fiend but also find a way to stay alive.

one

"Do you take this man to be your husband?"

A pregnant silence filled the ancient church, as if it, along with the one hundred plus guests, waited breathlessly for the bride's response. No one doubted what the answer would be, but still, there was excited anticipation as McKenna Sloan said, "I do" and became Lucas Kane's wife at last.

At those words, Jamie let out a long, silent sigh of delight. Standing to the right of her sister, holding a spray of roses along with the bride's bouquet of orchids, she could barely contain the joy that swelled within her. Seeing McKenna marry the man she adored was a dream come true. No one deserved happiness more. And Lucas was equally in love. His handsome face held an expression of tender reverence as he repeated the same vows McKenna had just recited.

While the minister continued his instructions, Jamie's gaze shifted to the guests. It was a small group by most standards, especially for a man of Lucas's wealth and stature, but McKenna and Lucas had wanted in attendance only those who meant something to them. For Lucas, that included a handful of friends, and for McKenna that meant as many operatives of Last Chance Rescue as could get there.

Noah McCall had the honor of walking McKenna down the aisle. Jamie knew only a few of the other operatives. She recognized the stunning face of Skylar James, a woman who'd been on the covers of numerous fashion magazines and was the wife of LCR operative Gabe Maddox.

Shifting her gaze slightly, she saw a beautiful auburn-haired woman and a man with long golden-blond hair and a scar on the left side of his face. McKenna had introduced them to her last night as Shea and Ethan Bishop. To their right sat Cole and Keeley Mathison and their adorable twin daughters, Hannah and Hailey.

In front of that group were LCR operatives Eden and Jordan Montgomery, whom she'd met this morning at breakfast. Sitting beside Eden was a little boy of about five, their newly adopted son, Paulo. On the other side of Jordan were Noah; his wife, Samara; and their son, Micah.

Sitting one row back, she recognized the blond head of Aidan Thorne. Though things had been blurry the night of her rescue, she vaguely remembered seeing him there. In a pew behind Aidan was a dark-haired, exotic-looking woman named Angela, LCR's receptionist. According to Noah, she was the one person Last Chance Rescue could not live without.

Her attention moved back to the people standing at the front of the church with the bride and groom. Jared Livingston, Lucas's best man, looked almost frightfully grim. Jamie had seen him several times at Lucas's home, and each time, he'd seemed to grow more forbidding. McKenna had mentioned that his marriage had ended; she hadn't needed to say more. The end of a marriage was like a death in many ways.

The man standing beside Jared was Conrad, Lucas's butler. No one had questioned why the wealthy Lucas Kane had asked his butler to stand up with him on the most important day of his life. Anyone who knew Lucas knew that Conrad was much more to him than an employee. Having stayed with Lucas and McKenna since her rescue, Jamie could attest to that. The man was both amazingly efficient and wonderfully kind.

Drawing a breath, but having no other choice, she let her eyes travel at last to the one man she'd been studiously avoiding not only talking to but even acknowledging: the new bane of her life, Dylan Savage.

How could one man be so gorgeously handsome, so wonderfully heroic, so seemingly kind, but so incredibly obnoxious, rude, and, well, just generally an asshole?

When he'd shown up at the airport to travel with her to the States, she'd started to reconsider her opinion. Had thought maybe she had imagined his animosity. And though they'd shared some conversation at the beginning, it had ended quickly, with Dylan dozing for the rest of the flight. About an hour before they'd landed, he'd woken, but he had been noticeably cooler. Every question she'd asked had been met with a grunt or a one-word answer. Jamie had finally given up and sat beside him alternating between hurt and anger.

When they'd arrived in Atlanta, he had silently walked with her to her connecting gate. Thankfully, she'd had only a few minutes to spare before her flight had begun loading. Standing beside him while he kept his gaze on everyone else but her had been just another frustration. When she'd suggested, somewhat sarcastically, that she could manage to get on the plane by herself, if he wanted to be on his way, he'd turned and given her a heated look that'd almost melted her insides. Then he had looked away again and continued to ignore her until her flight was called. The second she was able to board, she'd almost run from him with a barely audible "Have a good visit with your family."

Before she could take more than a couple of steps, he

had caught her arm to pull her around to face him. Jamie had lost her breath. The intensity of those emerald-green eyes seared her. She'd waited, breathlessly, for him to say something—sure that whatever it was would be monumental and meaningful. But what had he said? Nothing magical, nothing monumental. Beautiful mouth straight-lined and unsmiling, his hold on her arm tight, he'd growled, "Stay out of trouble," and then turned and disappeared into the crowd.

She had spent the entire flight from Atlanta to Baton Rouge coming up with one-line zingers she should have hurled back at him.

Last night, at the rehearsal dinner, was the first time she'd seen him since she'd returned to Europe. Not that he'd said anything to her. She'd gotten a hard, searching look and a nod of acknowledgment. Nothing more.

As if he knew that her eyes were on him, Dylan moved his dark head slightly and looked directly at her. Eyes, glittering like shiny jewels in his starkly handsome face, stared coolly at her. Then, as she continued to look at him, he arched one brow arrogantly. Refusing to back down at the unspoken challenge, Jamie decided to arch her own brow. Unfortunately, she had never mastered the art of a one-brow arch; she figured she looked more surprised than defiant. And, as usual, she could feel her blush deepen, which she was sure made her face glow fire red. Still, she was proud of herself for keeping her eyes glued to his.

"May I present to you Mr. and Mrs. Lucas Kane."

Jamie jerked her attention back to the wedding proceedings, mortified that she'd been daydreaming and had missed the rest of her sister's wedding. Appalled at her selfishness, she exploded into applause, startling everyone. Thankfully, the entire room followed suit, everyone joining in exuberantly.

McKenna gave Jamie a loving smile and a wink.

Relieved that she hadn't ruined anything, Jamie pulled herself together and followed the newly wedded couple down the aisle. Today was Lucas and McKenna's day. Her preoccupation with a man who frustrated and irritated her beyond reason didn't belong here.

Nor did she want to think about the phone call she'd received an hour before the wedding. Unsurprising news, but nevertheless devastating. Soon she'd go back to considering what lay ahead of her. For now, she wanted to celebrate and be thankful for what she had. The hard stuff would be here soon enough.

She was doing that thing with her mouth again. Dylan had watched Jamie during the entire ceremony. Did she know that every emotion she experienced revealed itself on her face? Did she know that when she was nervous, she nibbled on her lower lip? Did she know that it was as distracting as hell?

He stood in a corner of the small reception hall, his back to the wall. He'd congratulate the bride and groom later. For now, he wanted to watch her—the maid of honor—the loveliest creature he'd ever seen in his life.

The hell of it was, she didn't know it. He'd never seen anyone so incredibly artless and unaware of her own appeal. She thought she had offended him somehow, and while he regretted her hurt feelings, he couldn't change his attitude toward her. He'd much rather see disdain in her eyes than fear.

Jamie had been through hell, and though she had adjusted better than any victim of abuse he'd ever seen, she was still vulnerable. If she knew his thoughts, she'd be wary, maybe even terrified. And what good would it be for her to find out the truth anyway?

So he'd be the jerk, something he had a lot of practice with, and she'd never know that his heart thundered like a herd of stampeding rhinos when she was near or that another body part hardened at just the thought of her. These were secrets he'd take to his grave.

"We need to talk."

Dylan turned to see Noah McCall standing beside him, the grim expression on his face not a sign of anything good. "What's up?"

"Let's go outside."

With an ominous chill zipping up his spine, Dylan followed his boss out the door to an enclosed courtyard. Both men remained silent until they stopped at the other end of the small area.

"What's wrong?"

"All charges against Reddington have been officially dropped."

Dylan didn't even have a curse vile enough to spew. "I thought at least a few of them were going to stick. What happened?"

"I don't have the details yet. I've got a call in to the prosecutor's office."

"Jamie know yet?"

"Yeah, apparently she got a call earlier today."

And she'd stood at the wedding, looking beautiful and happy, as if all was right with her world. Dylan hadn't thought his admiration could get stronger.

"What are we going to do about it?"

"I'm going to get the details; then we'll go from there. With what she's told us she overheard while she was in his house, there's got to be a way we can get inside his organization and stop the bastard."

Dylan gazed around the peaceful serenity of the private garden. Peace was only a façade—he'd learned that painful lesson long ago. But, dammit, if anyone deserved to have that illusion, it was Jamie.

He turned back to McCall. "Whatever it takes to get to him, I want the job."

"I figured you might. Jamie's asked to see me tomorrow . . . I'm assuming about this."

"Don't bring up my name . . . okay?"

McCall paused for a second and then said, "You know, it's not a sin to be attracted to her."

The hard glare he gave his boss would have stopped most people from treading further into dangerous territory. Of course, Noah McCall wasn't most people.

"At some point, you have to put the past to rest."

"Let it go," Dylan bit out.

Having made his point, McCall started back to the church. "I'll let you know when I learn more." He stopped and looked over his shoulder. "You coming?"

"In a minute." Dylan turned his eyes back to the darkness. Put the past to rest? No, some things couldn't be put to rest or forgotten. Like a stench that never leaves your memory or a vile taste you can never forget, some things are meant to stay with you forever.

"You're missing all the fun."

The soft, almost melodic voice hit his ear like a wind chime—the last voice he wanted to hear.

Without looking at her, he said, "Then why are you out here?"

"I wanted to ask you what I've done."

Turning, Dylan faced her and felt his heart do that damn thudding thing again. Beautiful, delicate, with the face of an angel and a smile like sunshine.

"Done?" Dylan asked mildly.

"To offend you."

"You've done nothing."

"Then why are you so cold to me?"

Dylan raised one brow. An affect he'd practiced and perfected as a kid to show everyone he didn't give a damn. This time he used it purely for self-defense. "I wasn't aware I was anything. Last night was the first time I've seen you since you returned."

"And when I saw you, you acted as if I'd done something I shouldn't have."

He shrugged. "I don't usually see the people I rescue after it's over."

"I see."

Regret hit him, and he wanted to snatch the words back. As if her importance were only relegated to being a victim. Hell, what was it about her? With anyone else, he would've come up with something acceptably vague. With Jamie, not only did he not know what to say, but when he finally did speak, it came out either garbled or so damn blunt, even *he* winced.

This time was no different. As he watched hurt shadow her face, he made the determination that he just needed to get away from her and stay away for good. He couldn't treat her like anyone else because she wasn't like anyone else. It was that simple.

She turned away from him. "Fine. I won't bother you again."

The instinctive need to offer comfort had Dylan reaching out his hand. A second later, he pulled away, allowing her to leave. What could he say? Nothing that would do a damn bit of good. She needed to get back to her safe, secure life, and he needed to return to the one he'd chosen.

Her movements swift and agitated, she almost ran to get away from him. Unable to look away, Dylan watched her silver-and-gold gown shimmer like a graceful, beautiful butterfly until she disappeared from his sight. And then, once again, he was alone.

Last Chance Rescue headquarters
Paris

Noah McCall's black eyes were penetrating and cool as he shook his head. "We're not in the revenge business, Jamie. You know that."

Sitting across the massive cherry desk from him, with every muscle in her body almost spasming with tension, she carefully watched the man's face. She'd known him for a few months and had only ever seen the compassionate side of the LCR leader. As she had explained her position, his expression had grown noticeably harder.

Unwilling for him to think her plan was so self-serving, she said, "Revenge isn't my only reason."

"But a large part. Correct?"

"Do I want to punish the man who purchased me like a toy for his son's entertainment? Of course I do. But Reddington's done and will continue to do much worse things than what he did to me. He has to be stopped." She gave a nonchalant shrug, not feeling nonchalant in the least. "Revenge is merely a by-product. The icing on the cake."

The black eyes narrowed and turned flinty, no doubt trying to pierce the thin veil of bravado she had going for her. Little did Noah realize that he could cut straight through her till he saw daylight and she wouldn't change her mind. Yes, she was terrified, and yes, she knew she had a long road ahead of her, but that didn't mean she was any less determined.

"I still haven't talked to the prosecutor's office," Noah said. "And I know Lucas has got a call in to them, too. There're still avenues that haven't been explored. Don't give up hope that he can't be—"

She snorted softly. "Let's not lie to each other, Noah. Reddington's claim that he and his son found me in a ditch and nursed me back to health wouldn't fly for most people. Stanford Reddington is not most people. He's got so much power and influence in Spain, even if the charges did stick long enough to go to trial, there's no way he'd ever be convicted."

The grim set of Noah's mouth told her he wanted to argue with her, but she knew he couldn't. Despite having the police there when she'd been rescued and even though two people, one of whom was her sister, had been shot, Reddington had finagled the telling of the story so well that, on the surface, he looked like a cross between a fairy godfather and the Good Samaritan. He'd only been trying to do the right thing, and look what it'd gotten him. Poor, misunderstood bastard.

The things she'd heard while she was in that house of horrors had been amazingly detailed but, in the end, pointless for the prosecution. Her word against his. And Reddington's held a hell of a lot more weight.

The phone call she'd received yesterday, before the wedding, had confirmed what she'd long suspected was going to happen. *"We're so sorry, Ms. Kendrick. Without actual, physical proof, there's nothing more we can do."*

The man was not only going to get away with what he'd done to her, he was getting away with so much more—horrendous, vile things that had been going on for years. He had to be stopped. Despite the fear, the knowledge that she wasn't trained for this, she had to be involved in bringing him to justice. There was no other option.

"I can't be the only person LCR has rescued who's asked to work for you."

"Is that what you're asking . . . to be an LCR operative?"

Was it? She didn't know. She hadn't thought that far ahead. "Do you ever train people to be operatives and then, if they decide it's not for them, let them go?"

Though he didn't smile, she saw a spark of amusement in his expression. "Working for LCR isn't a prison sentence, Jamie. I've had a couple of people who chose different paths after a year or so. And several of our operatives came from successful rescues." All amusement gone, he leaned forward. "What I do insist is that my operatives are focused solely on the well-being of others, not their own agenda. Rescuing will always be our primary reason to exist."

"But in this case, there are people to be rescued."

"Then we can find them, without your help."

She raised her chin determinedly. "I want to be involved."

"Having an operative go after their abuser or abductor is asking for trouble. Personal involvement can screw up your thinking."

Jamie took a silent, bracing breath. Might as well go for broke. When Noah refused, which she now had no doubt he would, she could get up and leave, and go on to her second choice. "I'm giving you an opportunity, Noah."

"What do you mean?"

"With or without your help, I'm going to get what I need to stop the man. If you want to be involved, this is your chance."

Only by a small, subtle shift in his body could she tell that she had surprised him. "And if I don't agree . . . ?"

"LCR is my first choice, but there are other organizations and people who would be more than happy to assist me. I wanted to give you the first right of refusal." She leaned forward and said, "What's it going to be?"

Jamie watched coolly as McCall pondered her challenge. Hiding behind a mask had been her way of life for years, so she wasn't worried that he could see the emotions jumping through her like popping corn in an overheated popcorn machine. Dylan Savage was one of the few people who had the ability to destroy her carefully built façade. Thankfully, he wasn't here to challenge her.

Her ability to hide her thoughts from others was one of the biggest reasons she knew she could do this job. Being someone else would be no problem. Defending herself if something went wrong was most certainly an issue. She was just hoping that Noah would see fit to offer her a solution.

As she waited for his answer, her sister's face came to her mind. McKenna was going to kill her. Okay, probably not kill her, but she was going to be very upset. Her sister had risked her life to save her. How was she going to react once she learned that Jamie planned to pursue the devil in his own backyard?

Noah thought she wanted to do this for revenge. No way would she deny that she wanted revenge. That would be disingenuous; plus, she was human enough to want to make sure the bastard paid. But what he'd done to her was barely a ripple in the man's dark pool of evil.

"Tell me what you're suggesting." McCall's grim voice was a reminder that she still had some major hurdles to jump before she could even get to that point.

"I have no real concerns about being able to get inside or about getting the information I need. My biggest problem is, if I'm caught, I need to know how to survive. I've had no training. If I had, I probably wouldn't have been taken in the first place. I need LCR to teach me what I need to know."

"You're not afraid that he'll recognize you?"

"No, he only saw me a few times, at the beginning. My face was so bruised and swollen, even I didn't recognize myself." Odd that she could speak of something so painful and humiliating as if it had happened to someone else. Though the memories lingered, they were covered with a determination so strong, a need so fierce, that the hurt was buried. And if she achieved her goal, she could bury it so deep with satisfaction that anything remaining would be like a bad dream.

"What about his son Lance? He saw you after you healed, didn't he?"

She didn't even flinch at the sound of the disgusting name. "The prosecutor told me he's been sent to live with a distant relative in Germany. He's going to school there and has apparently been told not to return for a long while."

"You've already told me you're untrained, so what makes you think you can get anything? What qualifications do you have to get inside and get this information?"

The truthful answer would be "None." However, she had something that trumped experience. She had inside information that could get her into the midst of Reddington's family. She spoke fluent Spanish and had no doubt that she could play her role well. Last, and probably the most important: she had the sheer determination to do this job. To anyone else, it might be just another mission. To Jamie, it was her life's goal.

"My lack of experience is a plus."

"How's that?"

"Who would suspect someone who looks like me of coming in to spy on such a powerful, wealthy man? La Femme Nikita I'm not."

"Maybe you should tell me exactly how you think you can get inside and how you plan to get the information."

She wouldn't fall for that. "Not until after my training."

"Why?"

"Because if I tell you, you'll pat me on my head, tell me to go back home, and then you'll do this on your own."

"We *can* do this on our own, Jamie. Never doubt that for a minute."

"I have a way inside that no one else . . . no other operative, would."

"Are you willing to risk your life and risk failure if this doesn't work?"

"I won't fail." Brave words, but she spoke the truth.

"What about McKenna? What would you tell her?"

She lifted her chin higher. Funnily enough, she'd rather face ten Noah McCalls than have to explain her plan to her sister. McKenna wouldn't like it, but if there was anyone who could understand why she had to do this, it was her sister.

Before she could answer him, Noah spoke again, and this time, he went straight for her heart. "She almost died saving you. Putting your life on the line like this is a hell of a way to show your appreciation."

The barb went deep, as he'd intended. Jamie refused to let the hurt show or the sting deter her. There were a lot more painful things coming her way. "McKenna will understand."

"Will she?"

"Yes." She glanced down at her watch—a defense mechanism she'd learned while living and surviving with Aunt Mavis. The tactic had worked with her aunt, since if Mavis didn't look like she was getting a rise out of Jamie, she usually shut up. Though it probably wouldn't work with Noah, the familiarity of the habit soothed her.

"Let me think about it. I'll get back to you."

"No. I either have your agreement now or I'll leave and not bother you again."

Yes, she knew she was on shaky ground, and she felt like crap for being so hateful to the man who'd done so much for her. Noah didn't deserve this treatment, but if she didn't stand strong, he'd never agree to her proposition.

His stare almost melted her, that Jamie withstood it. Determination and sheer adrenaline kept her from falling to the floor in a mass of nerves.

"All right."

Instead of her nerves making her fall to the floor, the shock of his agreement almost did. Oh sweet Lord, he was agreeing. She took a moment to steady her heartbeat, which was now rivaling a runaway freight train for speed.

"Thank you, Noah. You won't regret it."

He gave her a final warning: "Be very sure this is what you want, Jamie. You get into this kind of life, it changes you in ways you could never imagine."

As she was about to reply that she was willing to take the risk, Noah added an ultimatum of his own: "Before you start training, I need an assurance from your therapist that you're ready to go through the challenges you're going to face."

Once again, before she could answer, he said, "That's not up for debate. I have to know that my operatives are mentally tough enough to handle what's expected. You're no different. If you can't agree to that, then we need to scratch the entire thing."

Jamie wasn't going to argue. The sessions had helped. Four days a week for the last two months, she'd been in therapy. The nightmares had lessened considerably. Her therapist, Dr. Sophia Schooner, would attest to her progress. Whether she would agree that Jamie was mentally sound enough to be an LCR operative was another matter. But having convinced Noah McCall, Jamie was sure she could convince anyone of anything.

She nodded. "I'll have Dr. Schooner get in touch with you."

"Does McKenna have any idea what you're planning?"

"Not yet. I didn't want to mention it before the wedding."

"Tell her before she and Lucas leave for their honeymoon. I'm not going to proceed further until she knows."

As much as she dreaded that moment, Jamie agreed. She wouldn't keep the truth from her sister.

Noah stood. "As soon as you speak with her, have her call me."

Recognizing dismissal, Jamie got to her feet. "Thank you, Noah. I'll make sure you won't regret it."

His expression not changing from its grimness, he walked her to the door. "Once we're set with McKenna's and your doctor's approval, I'll have Dylan contact you."

The heart that had just settled into a normal rhythm went through the roof. "Dylan?"

"Yes, he'll be your trainer."

"But . . . I thought . . . I mean, isn't he too busy?"

"No, he's one of LCR's best trainers. He'll get you prepared."

Noah opened the door for her, and Jamie, stunned into silence, wordlessly walked past him.

Dylan was going to be her trainer? The man who acted as if he couldn't stand to be in the same room with her? The man she couldn't stop thinking about?

Oh sweet heavens, what had she gotten herself into?

Noah closed his office door. Took a lot to surprise him, but Jamie had achieved that and then some. Actually, it wasn't surprise as much as shock. No way in hell had he ever anticipated that she would ask of him what she was asking. What he'd told her was true: LCR had many operatives who'd come to them through successful rescues. But most of them had arrived with a gritty toughness. Just how tough was Jamie? He would soon see.

She not only looked a lot like her sister, McKenna, but she obviously had the same strength and determination to overcome huge obstacles. Only McKenna was a trained operative; Jamie was an elementary school teacher. Could she be trained to be an operative? Maybe. But no way could she handle the job she was proposing. And no way could he allow it.

Though he'd tried to downplay it, she was right about Reddington. He was still waiting to talk to the prosecutor, but last night's email from her had offered little hope. Even the police chief, who'd been a supporter in the raid to rescue Jamie, had backed down and apologized to the bastard. The officer who'd been shot during the rescue was on an extended leave of absence. Convenient as hell.

Noah understood revenge. He'd felt that need himself. But if what Jamie had overheard while she was in Reddington's house was correct, any kind of revenge or personal vendetta had to be wiped out by the sheer necessity of stopping Reddington from what he'd been getting away with for years. LCR would do whatever it took to get the evidence to put him away. That couldn't include involving one of his victims.

He wasn't proud of what he was about to do. Rescuing and protecting innocents had become his way of life long before he'd created Last Chance Rescue. And the phrase "It's for your own good" never made anyone happy. With Jamie, he had no choice. After what she'd been through, it was understandable that not only would she want revenge, but she'd also want to be involved in seeing it come to fruition. Letting her sacrifice herself in the process wasn't something he was willing to risk.

Picking up the phone, Noah punched a speed-dial number.

"Savage," a deep male voice answered.

"Can you come to the office? I have an unusual assignment for you."

"Be there in about an hour."

Noah replaced the phone and released a resigned sigh tinged with sadness. No, he wasn't proud of his plan, but damned if he would do anything else. Now, on to the hardest part of all: convincing Dylan that he was the man for the job.

two

Booted feet propped up on the wooden rail, Dylan took a giant swallow of his first cup of coffee for the day. The steam bathed his face in warmth, then threatened to freeze as he lowered his hand.

Going to be a cold one today . . . highs in the mid-teens. A few feet of snow already blanketed the mountains. More would arrive before tomorrow morning, cocooning the cabin in for a good week, if not more. Jamie had better arrive before the big snow hit or she wouldn't make it at all. And that would be just fine with him.

He took another gulp of coffee and reviewed the plan that he despised but had taken on because he agreed with McCall—there was no other way.

His mind went back to the day he'd entered his boss's office and gotten the worst assignment of his life. Anxious to get back to work, he'd been feeling almost good for a change. Despite his encounter with Jamie at the wedding, he'd been all set to put that behind him. She would forget about her hurt feelings once she got back into a normal routine and would probably never think of him again—which, he'd told himself, was what he wanted.

When McCall had told him about Jamie's intent to go

after Reddington, that good feeling had crashed to the ground like a giant meteor.

He'd stared at McCall in disbelief. "Did you tell her that LCR would do this without her help?"

"She's insistent that she's going to do it on her own if we don't help."

Unable to sit still, he paced around McCall's office. Incredulity and fury bubbled, threatening to explode. "I can't believe you're letting her call the shots."

"I'm letting her think she's calling the shots. Big difference."

The grim tone in McCall's voice told Dylan that the man didn't like it any more than he did. Returning to the chair he'd jumped from moments ago, he leaned forward. "You think she has something on Reddington she hasn't told you about?"

"Yeah, I do. Or at least information on getting inside his walls. We already know it's going to have to be an inside job. If she's got an inside edge, we need to know what it is."

Dylan snorted his disgust. "The man knows what she looks like. How does she expect to fool him?"

McCall shrugged. "She made a good point that Reddington didn't see her after she healed. Her face was so swollen from the beating she got before he purchased her, she was unrecognizable."

"That doesn't mean he hasn't seen her since. Hell, for all we know, he's got people following her, making sure she doesn't cause him more trouble. And what about Reddington's son? I know he saw her after she healed."

"Lance Reddington has been sent away to live with a distant relative. I'm assuming Reddington did that to get him away in case any charges stuck."

"And that's for sure not going to happen?"

"Reddington's deep pockets bought his way out." McCall lifted a shoulder. "Jamie's right. The only way to get to him is to obtain irrefutable evidence of his slave-trading market."

"You got a plan to do that?"

"I've got three investigators working night and day. The info's coming in at a snail's pace, though. If we try to get inside without being assured of a good cover, we'll fail. The man will be on the highest alert for a while, so we're going to have to go slower than I'd like. He knows we were involved in Jamie's rescue, and he knows our reputation for going undercover to bring monsters like him down. He won't trust anyone new for a while."

"What about that kid who helped us get inside Reddington's house?"

A small smile twitched at McCall's mouth. "Raphael just received a full scholarship to a university in the States. He won't be available to help."

Already knowing the answer, Dylan said, "Your doing."

"Yeah. The kid won't stay out of it, and I can't let him risk his life again. We were damn lucky he didn't get caught before. After the hell he's been through, Raphael deserves a life free of danger. Not that he was all that happy about it, but I promised him that if he still wants to work with LCR after he graduates, he's got a job."

Dylan had met Raphael Sanchez only one time, and that had been right after LCR operative Cole Mathison had been rescued. The kid had been abducted, just as Cole had, and even while incarcerated, he'd done everything he could to help Cole escape. Raphael had spunk and then some.

"He's going in the middle of the semester?"

McCall shrugged. "He's going to get his apartment set up, find a job, and then start next fall."

Though Dylan agreed that Raphael shouldn't put himself in danger again, having no easy way inside Reddington's organization was problematic. It was going to take time and finesse. "When we do find a way to get in, I still want to be the one to go."

"When we find it, the job's yours. For now, you'll have your hands full with this new assignment."

McCall was right. Saving Jamie from herself might be the toughest assignment he'd ever been given. Staying away from her while being with her wouldn't be easy, either.

"Does Jamie know I'll be her trainer?"

"Yeah. She had an unusual reaction."

Yeah, he could only imagine. Diplomacy wasn't a skill he'd ever acquired; every time he opened his mouth around her, he offended her in some way. Yesterday, he'd decided the best thing he could do was to just stay away from her completely. And now look what he was about to do.

The meeting ended abruptly with Dylan getting up and going to the door. "I'll wait for her to contact me. Maybe she'll change her mind."

McCall's expression had been one of doubt—for good reason. Jamie would be arriving very soon. And it was up to Dylan to not only train her to defend herself but to make her realize there was no way in hell she would ever be qualified to go undercover after Reddington.

The crackling of gravel underneath heavy tires gave him his first warning. Training day had finally arrived.

Jamie rounded yet another ice-slicked, jagged curve. She'd started out early this morning from the hotel, nervous but sure of her course and what lay ahead. And now, three hours later, with those jittery nerves on edge, she was questioning if she would even reach her destination alive. Learning to drive in Louisiana didn't exactly prepare one for driving on mountainous snow-ridden death traps.

She'd called Dylan when she'd gotten in last night,

and in his usual blunt manner, he had given her the sketchiest of directions. She'd gotten the point: if you can't find your way, how the hell do you expect to do this job? So she'd taken the directions, planned out her course, and felt confident. That is, until she'd hit that first patch of ice and slid to the edge of a mountainside. As Aunt Mavis would've said, that had taken the starch right out of her bloomers.

Despite the near-death experience, she found the scenery almost overwhelming in its beauty. She'd lived in Nebraska until she was fifteen, and then Louisiana after that. She'd never imagined anything so awe-inspiringly vast or stunning. With the steering wheel twisting in her hands as she hit another patch of ice, she added "deadly" to the description.

Silly, but she had thought explaining her plan to McKenna would be her toughest challenge. Having just saved her little sister from death or worse had definitely brought out McKenna's protective instincts, but when Jamie had told her, her only response had been to ask how she could help.

And when McKenna asked how she could help, she'd meant it. Her sister had told her that the self-defense part would be the easiest to learn. McKenna had shared some stories with Jamie that had not only shocked her but had put her even more in awe of her sister. And Lucas, bless him, had showed her a few lethal moves. Between the two of them offering their help and advice, she'd come away feeling more confident. Yes, she knew she had a long way to go before she was ready, but she was on her way. And she anticipated surprising the hell out of Dylan.

Dylan. How could a man so damn good-looking be so damn infuriating? When he'd rescued her, he'd treated her with the utmost gentleness. His behavior since then had waffled between sarcastic and mocking to downright rude. Why did he treat McKenna like a sister and Jamie like the enemy?

Was he disappointed that she wasn't more like her sister? Even though she and McKenna could pass for twins, much of their resemblance stopped there. McKenna walked with an air of self-confidence; Jamie faked much of hers. Her sister never seemed to lose her cool and rarely said anything inappropriate or silly. Jamie often used sarcasm as a defense mechanism and could be a smart-ass on occasion. And Aunt Mavis had told her more than once that she could stick her foot in her mouth faster than anyone she'd ever known.

Admittedly, Jamie hadn't had the best of luck with handsome men. Her ex-husband had been all looks and no substance—something she'd learned only a few months into their short marriage. Jamie had stubbornly hung on, determined to make it work. Finding out about his affairs had hurt, but the beating she'd received when she'd demanded a divorce had been the final blow— literally. Much to his surprise, it had landed him in jail.

When she'd returned to Baton Rouge a few months ago, she had surprised him once again. He had apparently been under the assumption that the matter was settled. He'd spent only a few days in jail and hadn't expected to have to do more. Jamie, along with her savvy attorney, had seen to it that he spent more time behind bars. He was out of jail now, and it was her sincere hope that she never saw the cretin again.

She rounded another curve and blew out a giant, tension-filled sigh of relief. The rusted mailbox at the edge of a gravel road had the correct address. A glance at her watch told her she was going to be ten minutes early. Satisfaction and an odd tingle of anticipation at seeing Dylan again caused her to overshoot the turn. Cursing breathlessly, Jamie twisted the steering wheel and started up the long, winding, steep drive. Five minutes later, when no house had yet come into sight, she wasn't feeling quite as smug. Dammit, where was the—

She almost missed it. Snow-laden and deeply hidden within the forest, the cabin looked as if the giant trees were part of it. Such a strange house should have been ugly, but somehow, it wasn't. There was an old-world charm in its weathered wood and giant wraparound porch. The man lazed back in a chair on that porch, with his size 13 boots propped up on the railing, took much of that charm away.

Shifting the SUV into park, she took a shaky, bracing breath. One hurdle out of the way—she had arrived. The second hurdle, much bigger than the first, gazed down at her with that infuriating blank expression he seemed to save especially for her.

The next few weeks were going to be tough, but she'd been through much tougher ordeals than anything Dylan Savage could throw out at her. With that comforting thought, Jamie grabbed her purse and opened the door.

She put her feet on the ground and stood. The dark expression on Dylan's face was as unmoving as his body.

Longing to erase that look, she felt the need to say something smart and clever. Her mind scrambling for something brilliant, she opened her mouth and said, "I'm here." Clever and brilliant were apparently beyond her.

Jamie took a step toward the porch and felt the world tilt as her feet slid on a patch of ice. A small shriek became a large yelp when strong hands gripped her waist and pulled her against a hard body. She looked up at the too handsome face and breathed, "How'd you get here so fast?"

Green eyes blazed down at her. "I was on my way down when you made your graceful exit."

With anyone else she would have laughed and made a

similar comment, but Dylan's mocking amusement irritated her. Pushing away from him, she found herself in the same predicament, with her feet again sliding. This time she grabbed the car door and held on.

"You're going to need sturdier shoes."

She looked down at her simple, pretty flats and sighed. He was right. She also needed to get over this useless resentment she had toward this man. So what if he treated her like a cross between an irritation and an amusement? She was here to learn how to defend herself, and he was going to teach her. Being her best friend wasn't a requirement.

"I have better shoes in my luggage."

"Let's get your luggage." He looked up at the sky. "Winter storm's rolling in . . . it's about to get cold."

Since it was barely in the teens, she really didn't want to know what "cold" meant to him. She watched as he lifted a large duffel bag and a suitcase from the backseat and turned to the house.

"I have another one in the trunk."

Without turning, he grunted and said, "Be careful bringing it in."

Figuring she was lucky he was helping at all, Jamie opened the trunk and pulled one more bag out. She slammed the trunk and turned, letting out another shriek when Dylan was there once again.

"How the hell do you move so fast?"

He took the bag and said, "Better get ready to learn how to move just as fast."

"Not sure that's possible."

"Too bad. Moving slow will get you killed." And with that, he turned his back on her and headed into the house.

Dylan dumped the last of Jamie's luggage in her room. He hadn't said anything about the amount she'd brought with her. Apparently, she believed that she was going to be here for months, and that a large wardrobe would be required, too. He didn't plan for her to be here for more than a couple of months, if that, and sweats and running shoes were the only clothes she'd need.

He had told her nothing about her training sessions or how to prepare. Shitty of him, he knew, but it was all part of his shitty plan.

"This place is beautiful." She tilted her head back. "I love all these exposed beams. Is this your cabin?"

Dylan shook his head. "It's McCall's. We train a lot of our new recruits here."

She took a deep, audible breath and said, "Okay. So where do we start? What should I do?"

"Eat."

"Pardon?"

"You've lost weight since I saw you last, and you were bone skinny then. You're going to have to keep up your strength."

Her full lips trembled, and he knew she was struggling to keep from replying with a smart comment. Having her hold back on her temper was important. Exploding with anger could be dangerous. However, if she had something to say to him, he wanted to hear it.

"What?" Dylan arched a brow, knowing that'd piss her off. "You got something to say, say it."

"I had a stomach virus a couple of weeks ago and couldn't eat."

Okay, so what if he now felt lower than a slug. By the time he was finished, he figured he'd feel a hundred times worse. He turned to go out the door. "Lunch will be ready in about twenty minutes."

"Dylan."

He glanced back at her. "Yeah?"

"Why are you doing this?"

"And *this* would be what?"

"Why did you agree to train me when you clearly don't want the job?"

"Who said I don't want the job?"

She straightened her shoulders and took another deep breath, determination glinting in her eyes. "Your attitude."

This was the Jamie he wanted to see. Not the polite Jamie, or the treading-carefully-to-keep-from-offending-him Jamie. He wanted to see the spirited woman who would stand up for herself. The woman who'd jumped on his back when he came to rescue her and threatened to kill him if he touched her.

He might not want to see her put herself in danger, but one thing he could do for her was make sure she was never a victim again. That included not putting up with any crap, from him or anyone else.

"There's a big difference between wanting to teach you to kick ass to protect yourself and training you to put yourself in danger again."

"But you're going to do both. Right?"

"I'm going to teach you how to fight." He turned and walked from the room. "What you choose to do with that knowledge is entirely up to you."

She followed him into the living room. "You think I should just let this go? Do you know what Reddington is doing? What he's been doing for years?"

"Yeah, human trafficking, rape, murder."

"And you think I shouldn't do something?"

"I'm not arguing about whether the bastard needs to go down. Having you be the one who does that makes no sense."

"Because I'm too weak and untrained?"

"There is that, but that's not the biggest reason. Victims going after their violators never works. There's too much emotion, too many personal needs. Staying detached is imperative."

"But it can be done."

"Rarely."

That stubborn, determined expression he'd become familiar with crossed her face. He mentally shrugged. He hadn't expected to convince her on the first day.

Little did she know that he was just as determined. The next couple of months were going to be interesting. Had it been anyone else but Jamie, he might even have looked forward to the challenge. Problem was, it *was* Jamie. A woman who not only could turn him on with just a smile but made him feel things he'd never felt before.

So, did he look forward to it? No. Did he want to be anywhere else than where he was right now? Hell no.

three

Jamie spooned creamy potato soup into her mouth and eyed the huge ham sandwich Dylan had placed beside her bowl. Since she didn't have McKenna's metabolism—her sister could eat like a thirteen-year-old boy and never gain weight—she wasn't too keen to gobble down the entire meal, no matter how delicious it might be.

The stomach virus she'd had a couple of weeks ago had played havoc with her appetite, and she had lost a few pounds. Funny, but she'd been proud of the weight loss until Dylan's blunt comment.

"When you're through with lunch, I want to do a physical exam."

Her head shot up. "What?"

His mouth twitched slightly, as though he fought a smile. "Thought that'd get your face out of your bowl."

So what if she hadn't looked at him since they'd sat down to eat. Looking at a grumpy man across the table wasn't exactly appetite-inducing, no matter how handsome the face.

"You weren't serious, then?"

"I'm very serious. I want to test your physical stamina before we get started. Pulse rate, blood pressure, reflexes. I'll put you on a treadmill and see what we've got to work with."

"Do all LCR people have to do this?"

"You're not an LCR person, Jamie."

For some reason, the comment hurt. No, she wasn't officially an LCR person, but she was going through the same kind of training.

As if he hadn't just stomped on her feelings once again, he added, "Everyone has to go through an evaluation before starting their training. Few operatives come to LCR fully trained."

"Did you?"

"Hell no. Took me months to get trained."

"How long do you think it'll take me to learn what I need to know?"

For once he didn't bother to hide his thoughts—the doubtful look said he didn't think she'd ever be ready.

Since she was sure she would argue with any answer he gave her, Jamie quickly switched subjects. "How long have you worked for LCR?"

"About five years."

"Where did you live before you came to Paris?"

"The States." He stood and went to the sink.

Though his reluctance to share anything personal was obvious, Jamie nevertheless continued. "Where in the States? Florida?"

He turned and leaned back against the sink . . . two hundred and ten pounds of hard muscle and prickly, secretive masculinity. "Lots of different places." Barely pausing for a breath, he asked, "You did several months of counseling. Right?"

She nodded. "Four days a week, for almost three months." In case he doubted her, she added, "My therapist released me. She gave Noah a full report of my progress. Why?"

His face went granite hard. "Because once we get you into halfway decent shape, there's going to be a lot of hand-to-hand combat. I need to be able to touch you without freaking you out."

A thousand retorts to his insensitivity came to her

head. Jamie eyed him carefully. She still didn't know a lot about this man, but she knew that his comment had been deliberate. He had wanted to provoke a certain response. Fine, she would give him one. Lifting her chin, she faced him with a resolute stare. "It won't work."

One of his dark brows arched. "What won't work?"

"There are only two reasons you would have said that. One, you're the most insensitive moron this side of the North Pole. Or two, you're hoping to make me so angry, I'll say, 'Forget about this' and leave."

"I need to know how tough you are. If that remark bothers you, that's your problem."

Jamie stood, and though she knew it was a defensive gesture, she couldn't prevent her hands from going to her hips. "If what you know about me doesn't convince you I'm tough, I don't know what will."

"I know that you've survived a lot. That's not my concern." He came close . . . closer than he'd ever been before.

Wishing her legs weren't shaking, Jamie raised her head and met his gaze head-on. "Then what is your concern?"

"Are you going to be able to kill a man?"

She gasped and took a step back. "I'm not planning to kill anyone. I just—"

"Yeah, I know, you just want to expose Reddington for a sleaze, bring him to justice, and get a little revenge while you're at it. Problem is, Reddington's been getting away with this shit for years and making a boatload of money to boot. If he discovers who you are, you think he's going to just pat you on the head, tell you that it's okay, and let you go? You're going to have to fight for all you're worth. That might include killing someone to save your life." He got closer still . . . leaning down, his nose within inches of touching hers. "You got that kind of grit inside you, little Jamie?"

Rattled, but refusing to back down, she thrust her chin even higher. "Do I want to kill? No. Will I kill to save my life? Yes." Tired of the intimidation tactics, Jamie took the extra step. With their bodies now touching, his heat making her burn even brighter, she glared up at him. "That answer your question . . . big Dylan?"

With the warmth of his breath coating her face, he stood for several seconds, unmoving. Then a change she'd never expected came over his face. The mouth that always looked so grim and unyielding turned up in a full-fledged, sexy smile. "Yeah, that answers my question."

Backing away from her, he glanced at her empty bowl and half-eaten sandwich. "You through?"

Overheated, her heart pounding, she nodded. Speaking right now was well beyond her ability. She could barely think. Holy hell, she had just been turned on by a scowl, a challenge, and a beautiful smile.

"Get changed into some sweats. We'll take a quick tour of the grounds, do your health eval, and then go over the training schedule."

Still unable to form the right words in her mouth, Jamie turned and marched out of the room. Five minutes later, in between muttering obscenities to herself for her foolishness and to Dylan for his arrogance, she dressed in thick fleece sweats, two pairs of socks, and hiking boots. She threw on her heaviest coat and returned to the living room.

Dylan stood in the middle of the room wearing the same coat he'd been wearing before. In his hands was a smaller, similar coat. "Put this on. That thing you're wearing is for looks, not warmth."

Arguing would do no good. If she went outside and froze to death, what exactly would that prove? Still, she bit the inside of her jaw to keep from spouting off a smart comment as she took the coat and shrugged into it.

He threw some gloves at her. "Wear these."

Before she could say, "Thanks," he turned to the door. "Try not to get lost."

There were so many things on the tip of her tongue, and though she knew he was only trying to get a rise from her, it was infuriating not to respond. She stepped out onto the porch and promptly forgot her anger. A wonderland of whiteness awaited.

She'd been so involved with what was going on inside the cabin, she hadn't bothered to look outside. Just in the short amount of time she'd been here, it had snowed at least four inches. Everything was coated in fluffy whiteness . . . her Jeep was completely covered.

"Looks like it'll have to be a short tour. Snow's coming faster than I thought it would." He had been standing beside her, but now he went down the steps and held out his hand. "It's slippery."

Jamie looked at the big hand in front of her and swallowed hard. Stupid, but somehow she felt, as she put her hand in his, that they were making some sort of pact or a special connection.

Even through the gloves, she could feel the warmth and the strength of him as his hand closed around hers. The look in his eyes was one she had never seen before. Solemn, almost gentle, but still so damn secretive.

What secrets lay behind that mysterious dark green gaze? And would she ever know them?

She was actually doing better than he'd thought she would. As soon as she'd gotten out of her Jeep this morning, he'd made a necessary adjustment in her training program. Hell, she'd looked like the mildest of breezes would whisk her away.

His plan had been to spend no more than a couple of

months teaching her self-defense. And during that time, he'd delve as deeply as he could to uncover any information she was keeping to herself about Reddington. While the latter agenda was still a go, the self-defense training would have to wait. It was going to take at least a couple of weeks of good meals and sleep before she'd be capable of what he was going to put her through.

And knowing what he knew about her, she wasn't going to like the delay one little bit.

Sprawled in a chair a few feet from the treadmill, Dylan watched as Jamie kept up a brisk pace on the treadmill. A glowing sheen of perspiration on her face told him the workout was probably a little more exertion than she'd had in a while. He'd stop her in a few minutes. Some muscle soreness was inevitable, but he didn't want her so uncomfortable that it would cause her pain. She had a hell of a lot ahead of her . . . no point in overdoing it on the first day.

Training in between ops was a normal course of events for all LCR operatives. And helping to train each other went with the territory. Most times he enjoyed the challenge of helping someone meet the next level of fitness or skill.

"What was your fitness routine back home?"

She replied breathlessly, "When I lived in Louisiana, I belonged to a gym. I haven't had a regular fitness routine in a while."

Yeah, he'd figured that. After what she'd been through, he was surprised her fitness level was as good as it was. Wouldn't take more than a month or so before she'd be ready for more intensive training.

"Okay, that's enough. Let's check your pulse rate. I need to do some things outside the cabin before the blizzard hits."

"Blizzard?"

"Yeah. Was just supposed to be a winter storm, but

looks like it's going to be a heavier one than they expected."

"So that means . . ."

He got to his feet and went to stand in front of her. "It means you're stuck here for at least a week. So if you were thinking of changing your mind, it's too late now."

She pressed the Stop button on the treadmill with a hard, telling punch. With that delicate, stubborn chin at an all-time high, she snapped, "I wasn't, and I won't."

"Give me your arm."

Her hand shot out, barely missing his face. Dylan didn't mention the near miss as he checked her pulse. He frowned at the rate. "You pulse is higher than I thought it would be."

"Then stop pissing me off."

"You're too easy."

"Excuse me?"

"If you get angry every time I say something you don't like, you're going to be wasting a lot of energy being mad instead of learning what you need to learn."

"How am I supposed to react?"

"Like you don't give a damn."

She huffed out an exasperated breath. "Couldn't you just try to be more agreeable?"

"Now, what would be the fun in that?" He threw a towel at her. "Make sure you're dry. Don't want you getting sick again."

With that slow, lazy walk that Jamie found almost mesmerizing, Dylan sauntered out of the room. Gripping the towel he'd thrown at her, she fought the need to throw the damn thing back at him. He said things to deliberately infuriate her and then chastised her for getting angry.

From the age of fifteen, Jamie had diligently practiced stifling emotions and not showing her thoughts. On her best days, Aunt Mavis had been manipulative and overbearing; on her worst she'd been downright mean. Jamie had learned to survive by never allowing her aunt to see behind the calm mask she'd adopted. School had been an additional challenge. As the awkward and too quiet new girl whose parents had been murdered, she'd been the talk of the small school, and that had given her even more training in hiding behind a façade.

So how was it that with a small quirk of his mouth or a mocking glint in his eyes, Dylan could bring out these bubbling, boiling emotions that had once been so easy to contain? She didn't know the answer, but she had to admit he was right about one thing. She did need to act as if what he said didn't faze her—like she didn't give a damn.

Wiping her face, neck, and arms until they were completely dry, Jamie threw the towel in a laundry basket beside the door. After swallowing the entire glass of water Dylan had put on a table for her, she took a few slow breaths. Anger hadn't made her breathing any easier. She hated how out of shape she was. Not that she'd ever been an exercise queen, but at one time, she'd been in decent shape.

How long would it take her to get where she needed to be physically? Though she had no plans to have to fight anyone or run for her life, she knew the possibility of danger existed.

Fortunately, most of what she planned involved things she already knew how to do. The training LCR was providing would be needed only if things didn't go as planned. She hoped she wouldn't have to use these new skills, but having them would give her an extra dose of confidence . . . and she could definitely use more of that.

Dylan's short tour of the grounds had given her a good idea of what to expect once the weather cleared. He'd pointed out several trails, one so steep that part of it had a rope for climbing. There were also three obstacle courses with varying degrees of difficulty. The comment that it'd be a while before she'd be using any of them had been clear. He either thought she'd never be in good enough shape or he expected her to quit. She was determined to prove him wrong on both points. Not knowing what came next was bothersome, but worrying about it would do no good. She would do what she had to do. It was as simple as that.

With Dylan busy outside, she saw no harm in taking a quick tour of the cabin.

The gym covered the entire basement level and contained numerous exercise machines, including some she was familiar with and others she'd never seen before. Along one wall, free weights of varying sizes and shapes were stacked. The opposite wall was mirrored, with a large cushioned mat running the length of it.

She headed upstairs, to the main floor. They'd eaten lunch in the kitchen, which seemed amazingly well equipped, with every modern convenience, including a gigantic freezer. Made sense if they were going to be snowed in for a while.

Just off the kitchen was a small dining room with an oak table and a large picture window that looked out onto the back. She peeked out and spotted Dylan driving her Jeep into the garage. That act struck her as kind and gentlemanly—completely incongruent with his attitude toward her.

Shaking her head at the man's oddities, she continued her exploration. The living room had a large rock fireplace, with a luscious-looking, colorful rug in front of it. If she were here for pleasure, she'd love to lie in front of a blazing fire and sip hot chocolate.

The furniture was sturdy, with two oversized leather sofas and several comfy-looking recliners. The high ceiling, with exposed beams, made the entire area seem huge but still cozy.

Knowing Dylan might come back anytime, she hurriedly peeked into his bedroom, unsurprised to see his bed neatly made and minimal evidence that the room was even occupied.

She closed the door and turned to her bedroom, across the hallway. A hot shower after getting so sweaty would be heavenly. Closing her door, Jamie stripped and headed to the bathroom. Her cellphone buzzed just as she passed the nightstand where she'd placed it and the charger.

She grabbed the phone, knowing that it could be only one person: her sister. "Hey."

"Hey, yourself. Are you there yet?"

Jamie sat on the edge of the bed, grateful for the good heating and insulation in the room. "Yes, got here a couple of hours ago. I've already been on a short tour outside and had a physical."

McKenna made a sound between a snort and a snicker. "Dylan gave you a physical?"

"Just my pulse and blood pressure. Nothing invasive. He said everyone had to go through something similar."

"Is that right?" McKenna's amusement was obvious. "You didn't?"

"Well, no, but to be fair, I was already trained and working ops for LCR before Noah officially hired me."

That seemed like a reasonable and simple explanation. However, with Dylan, nothing was ever simple.

"Is he always so irritating and confrontational?" Jamie asked.

"Actually, no, he's one of the more easygoing of us. The confrontational part comes with the territory, though."

So he was just being irritable for her sake, trying to get her to quit. Well, that wasn't going to work. Dylan Savage was about to find out just how tough Jamie Kendrick could be. And she'd learn to deal with the confrontational part.

"Any news on your front?" Even before she'd started training, she knew that LCR had begun working several angles to get to Reddington.

"No more than we had before. By the time you're trained, I'm sure we'll have more."

The stomping of feet at the front door told Jamie that Dylan had returned from his chores. Figuring he'd have a new assignment for her, she hurried to say goodbye. "I hear Dragon Man coming back in. Gotta go."

"Okay, well, don't kill each other the first day."

"I can promise that; maiming is another thing altogether."

Jamie closed the phone on her sister's laughter.

The knock on the door shouldn't have startled her. "Yes?"

"You ready to go over your training agenda?"

Suddenly remembering she had meant to take a shower and was still nude, she eyed the doorknob nervously. "Do I have time for a shower?"

"If you shower every time you get sweaty, you're going to be showering every few hours. Put on some dry clothes and let's get started."

Resisting the urge to stick her tongue out at the closed door, Jamie grabbed another pair of sweats and some underwear. The fact that what he said made sense didn't help. She wasn't here to smell fresh and clean as a daisy; she was here to work. Besides, Dylan was so damn blunt, if her odor offended him, she was sure he'd let her know.

Halfway dressed, she swallowed a small yelp when he pounded on the door again. "You about ready?"

Muttering obscenities, she pulled the sweatshirt over her head, finger-combed her hair, and pulled it up into a ponytail. Grimacing at the unattractive, frazzled girl in the mirror, Jamie headed to the door. This man would not defeat her.

An hour later, she wasn't feeling quite as confident. When Dylan handed her the one-page sheet, her alarm grew with each line she read. She had expected the regimen to be difficult, not impossible. "I have to be able to do all of this before my self-defense training begins?"

Without glancing up from the wicked-looking gun he was cleaning, he answered with a nod and a grunt.

Jamie stared back down at the list. In her best shape, she would never have been able to perform half of these: thirty push-ups, seventy-five sit-ups, ten chin-ups, and an eight-minute mile.

"Why do I have to be able to do all of this?"

"Because if you're not at least at the minimum required fitness level, you'll never be able to complete the final exam."

"Final exam?"

"Yeah. You don't leave here until you pass."

She shook her head. "Noah never mentioned—"

"Noah's not your trainer . . . I am."

Biting back a sarcastic reply, she asked, "What does the final exam consist of?"

He shrugged. "Just one thing."

"And that is . . . ?"

He raised his head and looked directly at her. His expression was characteristically blank, but his eyes held a dead seriousness. "Bringing me down."

four

Madrid, Spain

The thousand-dollar Gurkha cigar puffed like a chimney from his mouth; Stanford Reddington sat in his leather recliner and observed the new merchandise. As each item was hauled out of the darkened storage room, in mere seconds his experienced eye evaluated it with the expert precision of a true connoisseur of human flesh.

He was going to miss this aspect of his business. Every other Tuesday, for the past six years, had been market day. Deciding which newly acquired piece of merchandise would go where was a tradition he'd only begun to train his son in when the shit had hit the fan. And now, because of one little bitch, he had to put his profitable business on hold until things settled down.

Why the hell hadn't he killed her when he'd had the chance? Second-guessing himself wasn't something he did often. Usually when he made a decision, he knew it was the right one. But how was he supposed to know that a piece of merchandise he'd picked up on a whim would end up costing him so much? Hell, she'd been so bruised and battered, he'd seen himself as doing her a favor. No one else would've touched the bitch.

Who could've known that Jamie Kendrick was not only the sister-in-law of one of the wealthiest men in the world, but that she'd be rescued by Last Chance Rescue, an organization that could bring his entire financial kingdom down if it had its way?

Between the legal maneuvers from Lucas Kane's attorneys and the concern that Last Chance Rescue would try to infiltrate his organization, he could now trust only his closest associates. LCR had a reputation for destroying flesh-trading organizations. He refused to get caught in its net.

Able to compartmentalize between business woes and business at hand, Stanford gestured with his head toward the line of females. "Tell the third one from the right to stand up straighter."

He waited while Armando went over and whispered something in the girl's ear. Whatever he said worked like a charm. The skinny, slumped-over girl straightened her shoulders immediately, her previously sullen expression turning to wild-eyed terror. He nodded his approval as the man returned to stand beside him. Taking another puff of his cigar, Stanford reflected on what a treasure his employee was . . . he always knew the right words.

Dissatisfaction grew within him as he continued to study the merchandise. This was one of the worst batches they'd had in years. And to think he wouldn't be having any more for a while. It sickened him to think of all the prime flesh he was going to miss. "Where the hell did you come up with these skanks?"

Armando shrugged his brawny shoulders. "You told us to stay low-key for this last shipment. We got the ones no one will miss."

Dammit. Yet another reason he'd like to have those LCR idiots strung up by their balls. The demand was high for young, nubile girls, but there were risks involved. Risks he couldn't take until the heat was off his ass.

Making the decision quickly, Stanford said, "Dispose of one, two, four, five, and six as domestics. Take noth-

ing less than a thousand for each. What's the story behind three and seven?"

"We got the blonde from a middle-aged couple in
Lima. They've used her as a sexual third for the past
couple of years but want to go younger. I told them we'd
give them a deal on their next purchase."

"Better not make it too good of a deal. This one looks
like she's seen and done it all a few thousand times."

"She's still got some juice in her." The man smiled
smugly. "I got a sample on the way home. Girl's got
some damn fine skills."

"She using?"

"No drugs and they swear she's never even touched
alcohol."

"Clean her up and send her to me tonight. Now tell
me about number three."

"Found her outside Barcelona . . . mother was selling
her for a fix."

Knowing that the man never left loose ends, Stanford
asked, "And the mother is . . . ?"

"She got more than the fix she wanted. She never
made it home."

Taking one last puff of his treasured cigar, Stanford
ground it out in the dish beside him and stood. "If I'm
pleased with the blonde, I think the Goddess House
could use her."

"And the kid?" Armando asked hopefully.

More than aware of Armando's secret cravings, Stanford eyed the sad, homely-looking child. "How old is
she?"

"Her mother said she was sixteen."

Stanford snorted. "She's not a day over ten. Otherwise you wouldn't be nearly as interested."

The other man's eyes skittered away guiltily. Stanford
knew his friend fought his sickness daily, which was one
of the reasons he allowed him to sample as much of the

adult merchandise as he wanted. The fact that he'd brought the girl here instead of taking her for himself showed Armando's strength of will.

"Take her to the orphanage and drop her off."

Though his mouth tightened in disappointment, the other man nodded. "Very well."

"I'm going home tomorrow; I'll stay there until I feel it's safe to resume business. Once you've made arrangements for everyone, feel free to join me for a few days."

They both knew it was not an invitation but an order. Stanford enjoyed his power over people. He no longer gave orders. What he said, in any manner he wanted to say it, would be done.

"I'll be there in a couple of days."

"And your family . . . ?"

Another tight-mouthed look and then a nod. "They'll be there as well."

"Excellent."

Stanford received no small amount of satisfaction from encouraging family time for his employees. His own family sustained him. Except for his elder son, they knew nothing of his businesses, legitimate or otherwise. That was the way it should always be . . . the way his own father had taught him and the way he would teach his son. When he'd started training Lancelot, the kid had stared wide-eyed as Stanford explained his legacy. But there had been the gleam of excitement in his eyes. An excitement Stanford still felt even after all these years.

Only now all of that was on hold. His son, the light of his life, had been sent away. Protecting him from all the nastiness of the investigation had been of utmost importance. How long would Lance have to be away? How long would Stanford have to curtail his business practices? It was hard to say. One thing he knew for sure: if he ever had the chance to repay Jamie Kendrick for all the trouble she had caused him, she'd be begging for mercy days before he put her out of her misery.

West Virginia mountains

Feet going at a good clip on the treadmill, impatience in her voice evident, she shouted, "How much longer am I going to have to work out like a demon before I learn anything?"

Not bothering to lift his head from the magazine he was reading, Dylan asked, "You've not learned anything in the two weeks we've been training? I'm crushed."

"I've learned that you're an ass."

His mouth twitched only slightly. "Took you two weeks to figure that out? You're slower than I thought you were."

For once ignoring his baiting comment, she asked, "When do we start the self-defense training?"

"When I say so."

He heard the slap of her hand as she slammed it against the treadmill to stop it. Another smile that he couldn't allow tugged at his mouth. She would think his amusement was because of her frustration at him. However, it was the result of her frustration that he found amusing. For someone who looked like a spun-sugar fairy, Jamie Kendrick, he was learning, had a toughness he'd never anticipated. He could help her achieve a higher level of physical fitness and teach her self-defense skills, but Jamie had something that couldn't be taught. She had an innate determination and resiliency.

Each day, he put her through intense and grueling workouts. At night, she watched training videos, and during dinner, they discussed them. She was physically stronger than she'd been when she'd first arrived. Not only did she have a healthy glow, she'd gained muscle and a couple of pounds. She'd been soft and too slender before; now her body was becoming toned and tight, and the inevitable one-on-one training was going to have to begin. At that thought, his amusement disappeared.

"What kind of answer is that?"

Lowering the magazine, he glowered. "Just what I said. When I say so."

He watched warily as she jumped down from the treadmill and headed toward him. Since the day she'd arrived, he hadn't been within two feet of her. Looked like that was about to change.

"Do you want me to die?"

"Now, why the hell would you ask that?"

"Because if I leave here without learning what I need to, I won't be able to defend myself if something goes wrong. Can you live with that on your conscience?"

Dylan got slowly to his feet. "Let's get two things straight. First, unless you storm out of here like a two-year-old, when you do finally leave, you will know how to defend yourself. Second, if you think I'd feel guilty for you getting yourself killed, then you're sadly mistaken. If you die, that will be your fault, not mine."

"Then when are you going to teach me?"

"You think you're ready?"

"I've been ready."

"Then turn around."

"What?"

"You heard me. Let's see if you're as ready as you think you are. Turn around."

As she stumbled awkwardly around, showing him her back, Dylan gritted his teeth. He had known this day was coming but had somehow hoped that when it did, his attraction to her would have burned itself out from lack of fuel. Unfortunately, this kind of desire required no fuel and no encouragement from her. It was just there, like a never-ending and hopeless entity.

Dammit, he had agreed to this job, and no matter how physically painful it would be to touch her, it'd be a million times more painful if something happened to her because she wasn't trained. Yeah, he'd lied about that. Not his first lie, and it sure as hell wouldn't be his last.

Jamie almost stopped breathing in anticipation of Dylan's touch. For two whole weeks he'd done nothing but growl out orders or tell her when she was doing something wrong. How the hell she could want him even within touching distance was a mystery to her, but her entire body felt alive, tingling with excitement, at the thought of his hands on her.

A hard hand wrenched at her shoulder, pulling her around. Jamie forgot who was behind her, forgot that she was in the middle of a training exercise. She only knew that the hand felt like a threat. Whirling around, she threw her hand up, but it was caught and twisted behind her back. Panting and close to panic, she found herself slammed up against a rock-solid chest. A chest that held a heart that was thudding almost as hard as hers.

She jerked to pull away and couldn't. She spoke against his chest, her voice muffled: "Okay, you made your point. Let me go."

"Like hell I'll let you go," Dylan growled above her. "Get out of the hold."

She jerked again. His hold was just as firm as before. "Dammit, how am I—"

"Calm down, Jamie, and think."

Determined to stop panicking and prove that she could do this, Jamie took a steadying breath. The DVDs she'd been watching for the last few nights . . . they'd showed step-by-step how to get out of these kinds of holds. *Do it, Jamie!*

With her arms locked at her sides, her only recourse was to use her legs. Lifting one leg, she kneed toward Dylan's groin, but he quickly blocked her. Grunting her frustration, fury lending her skills she didn't yet have, she stomped her foot on top of his, kicked his shin, and then, when he shifted back, she kneed him hard in the groin.

Hissing a curse, Dylan dropped his arms and backed into the chair he'd just left.

Horrified at the pain on his face, Jamie went to her knees in front of him. "Oh my gosh, are you okay?"

Instead of growling at her or retaliating, Dylan did something she'd never thought would happen. He burst out laughing as he pulled her into his arms and then did the most astonishing thing of all—he dropped a quick kiss on her mouth. And though he released her before she could even consider responding, she felt the touch throughout her body.

Scooting away slightly, she said again, "So you're okay?"

The twist of his mouth was more of a grimace than a smile. "Not the first time I got kicked in the balls . . . won't be the last. Gotta say, though, you surprised me."

Delighted, she said, "I did?"

"Yeah, I thought you'd stomp on my other foot or try to use your head against my throat." He blew out a breath, and then he did that amazing thing with his mouth again . . . he smiled. "I'm proud of you, Jamie."

The thudding of her heart had little to do with the physical exertion and everything to do with that beautiful smile and the most wonderful words she'd ever heard from him . . . Dylan was proud of her!

"Does that mean we can start some self-defense training?"

"We'll start a few things, but you'll still have to do all the other workout stuff, too."

She nodded, understanding suddenly that if they'd started training right away, not only would she have been too weak, she would have been even more panicked than she had been today. But now she was more than ready to move forward.

"The sooner I can get trained, the sooner I can put Reddington behind bars."

She saw immediately that she'd said the wrong thing. The smile disappeared, and that cold, ominous expression she'd thought was a permanent look returned.

"Why are you so dead set against me doing this?"

His good mood gone, Dylan stood, causing her to have to back completely away from him. He could deal with sore balls. Even handle the self-castigation of doing something so out of character as kissing her. However, her reminder that she still planned to go after Reddington surpassed everything else. Especially when he still planned to make sure she did nothing of the kind.

"Because no matter how much you train or how hard you try, you will never be ready to do what needs to be done. That's why."

She rose gracefully, a cloak of dignity wrapped around her in obvious self-protection. Yeah, he knew he'd hurt her feelings again. Her expression clearly revealed her thoughts. Another reason she didn't need to get involved with Reddington and his shit. The woman couldn't hide an emotion for more than a few seconds. How the hell did she think she was going to go undercover with the sleaze and not reveal everything?

"If I'm not ready, it won't be my fault. It will be yours. I'll do everything you tell me to do." She gave him a stiff nod and added, "Put that in your pipe and smoke it, Mr. Savage." Then, turning her back to him, she headed toward the stairway.

"Uh, Jamie."

Without turning, she snapped out "What?"

"I don't smoke."

Watching her shoulders stiffen even more in outrage almost made him forget his anger. She was just so easy. And so damn beautiful.

As she disappeared from sight, Dylan turned away and blew out a ragged sigh, disgusted with himself. He'd kissed her . . . holy hell, he'd kissed her. He could lie and tell himself it was the shortest and least romantic kiss on record. He'd barely felt the warmth of her mouth before he'd pulled away. But when she'd surprised him with her kick and then looked so horrified that she'd hurt him, he'd reacted with pure instinct. Two weeks of keeping his distance by doing nothing more than growling orders at her had been totally demolished.

Now he had to reestablish that distance, because if he didn't, the next time he touched her, he wouldn't be able to stop with a quick, chaste kiss.

The buzz of the cellphone in his pocket steered his mind back to his mission. A few days ago, McCall had said there might be some information soon. He pulled the phone out but before answering, he ran up to his room and closed the door. When he spoke, Dylan's words were an indication of his mood: "I hope to hell you're calling with some news."

McCall snorted. "Sounds like your day has been as good as mine."

"Don't tell me you have no news."

"Oh, I have news. Unfortunately, none of it's good."

"What?"

"Reddington's gone off the grid."

"What do you mean?"

"Just that. The man can't be found."

"How the hell does a man with so many businesses and contacts just disappear?"

"Money helps, I would imagine. My sources tell me he's gone home, to wherever he keeps his family stashed. We knew he had a secret hideout . . . Jamie got that information for us. Problem is, so far, we haven't been able to find that location."

"So if he's gone, I guess that means he's not kidnapping and selling human beings."

"There is that, but unless we catch him in the act, or find a way to get inside his organization, we're stuck twiddling our thumbs."

"And we're sure he's not trading?"

"As sure as we can be about a man we can't even find. Word is, he's going low-profile until the heat's off. We knew he'd probably curtail his auctions for a while. I just didn't expect him to disappear, too."

"As much as I hate for him to resume business, if he doesn't, it's going to be a damn sight harder to get to him."

"Yeah . . . but he won't give it up. It's too profitable, and my sources tell me he likes it too much. We just need to be ready when the time comes. How's the training going?"

"Let's just say I'm going to be walking funny for a couple of days."

"She got the drop on you? I didn't know anyone could do that."

Dylan snorted. "It helps when my opponent looks like she couldn't swat a mosquito." He added grudgingly, "She's got good instincts."

"You find out what she's hiding?"

"No. We're not exactly on speaking terms yet. Getting her to open up with me is going to take some time." He shrugged and added, "Still not sure she knows anything significant."

"Maybe, but if she's got anything, it's more than we

have right now. At least with Reddington shutting down for a while, you'll have the time to find out."

Dylan looked out the window at the white blanket of snow that still covered the ground. The sudden desire to get some fresh air made him cut the call short. "Yeah . . . that's true. Listen, let me know if anything changes on your end. I'll see what I can find out here."

"Will do."

Dylan closed his phone and grabbed his jacket. Wouldn't hurt to have more firewood. The fact that he had enough stored up for another week didn't matter. Getting some fresh air but, most of all, getting as far away from Jamie as possible felt imperative.

Shrugging into his jacket as he crossed the living room, he slid his feet into his boots, grabbed the ax from the wall and his gloves from his pocket, and opened the outside door.

"Where are you going?"

After an imperceptible sigh, he answered, "Need to chop some firewood."

"Can I come with you?"

"No" trembled on his mouth, but he'd heard the plea behind the question. Hell, she'd been locked inside this cabin for days, too. And she'd had it harder . . . being cooped up with a surly grouch was no one's idea of a good time.

Without turning, he growled, "Get the heavy coat I gave you and your snow boots. I'll be out back."

He was barely down the steps before she was on the porch and following him. He glanced back to see that the coat almost swallowed her and the boots she wore were now knee-deep in snow.

"Can you walk?" He wasn't planning on carrying her, but if she couldn't get through the deep snow, maybe she'd turn around and go back to the cabin.

As usual, that stubborn little chin jutted out and her

mouth took on a mutinous line. "If you can, then so can I."

Resisting the urge to go to her, cover her delicate pink lips with his mouth, and taste her sweetness, Dylan turned around and kept on walking toward the tree stump.

He heard her struggling behind him and knew she was having a hell of a time making it through the snow. Damned if he'd ask if she needed help. Still, he made the pretense of looking up at the sky so he could see her out of his peripheral vision. Yeah, she was having trouble, but she was making it.

With the decision to pretend that she wasn't within feet of him, Dylan took a dead tree limb, placed it on the stump, and swung the ax. The loud *whack* was startling in the midst of the white dead silence. Grabbing another limb, Dylan set to work, hoping for relief from this never-ending need he could do nothing about.

Jamie hugged herself for warmth as she watched the surly man working in front of her. Breathing the icy air into her lungs was almost painful, but damned if she would go back to that cabin. This was the first time she'd been out in days. She couldn't face those walls again . . . at least, not yet.

The fact that Dylan didn't want her out here with him was evident. She had thought she'd ceased being hurt by his more than obvious resentment of her presence. But after their little training interlude today, she had hoped the ice had been broken. Not only had Dylan laughed— something she hadn't believed was even possible—but he'd kissed her. Holy guacamole, he'd kissed her!

Okay, so it'd been barely a peck and was over before her brain could even register it was happening . . . still, it had happened. She told herself it didn't mean any-thing. Just a spur-of-the-moment reaction to what she'd managed to do. She had almost brought Dylan to his knees.

At that thought, Jamie started worrying. That kind of injury could incapacitate a man. Maybe that was why he was so surly again. Had he been limping when he'd walked outside? Was he still hurting?

"Are your testicles okay?"

In the midst of swinging the ax down, he missed the wood completely. The blade lodged with a thud into the tree stump. He whirled around, his expression one of incredulity. "Excuse me?"

A fire-red blush heated her cheeks. Okay, so it was probably an inappropriate question. No, not probably . . . it *was* an inappropriate question. Aunt Mavis was probably doing triple spins in her grave. Still, the question was out there. There was no point in pretending she hadn't asked it.

"I know that kind of blow can be really painful for a man. I was just wondering if you were still hurting."

He shook his head, and Jamie could swear his mouth twitched as though he fought a smile. "My balls are just fine. Thanks for asking."

"Because if they're not, I thought maybe an ice pack might help."

He turned his back, and she saw his shoulders jerking. He was laughing at her. That didn't bother her in the least. Making Dylan laugh, even if he was laughing at her, felt like she'd won the lottery.

Surprising her, he turned back around, and yes oh yes, that beautiful, usually grim mouth was smiling again. "The thought of putting an ice pack down there sounds a hell of a lot more painful than being kneed."

She laughed. "I guess that would be uncomfortable."

Shaking his head as if he couldn't believe their conversation, he turned back to chopping.

No longer occupied with her worry about Dylan or

embarrassment over her question, Jamie suddenly realized she was freezing. Expecting the man chopping
wood with the ferocity of a lumberjack in a speed contest to speak to her again was hopeless. Even with his
back to her, she recognized that he'd closed himself off
again.

"I think I'll head back inside."

Dylan's answer was a barely distinguishable nod.
Blowing out a sigh at the foolish wish that some of the
ice surrounding him had melted, Jamie turned and
trudged toward the cabin. She barely got two steps before Dylan called out "Put on your workout clothes.
We'll get in a quick self-defense lesson before dinner."

Maybe something significant *had* happened . . . perhaps not ice breaking, but a breakthrough all the same.
At this point, she would take what she could get.

Feeling ridiculously happy, Jamie picked up her pace.
Finally, her self-defense training was about to begin.

five

"No, allow your feet to move your whole body." Dylan stood in front of her. "Watch."

In wide-eyed awe, Jamie watched as Dylan's entire body twisted in one seamless, graceful movement as he turned almost completely around. How could someone so big move with such precision and grace?

"How long did it take for you to be able to move like that?"

"Each person has their strengths. When I was a kid, I used to pretend I was a jungle cat. I practiced moving slowly and stealthily." He shrugged. "I think that helped."

Thrilled that he'd shared a piece of his childhood, no matter how minute, Jamie asked, "What about your speed, though? Your movements are so slow and deliberate, but when you need to, you can move like a cheetah."

His eyes glinted with a slight amusement. "Not cheetah speed, but again, cats move fast when they need to."

She shook her head. "I don't think I'll ever be able to move that fast."

"Moving fast is helpful, but while we're training, you'll identify your strengths and we'll work them to their highest potential. Strengths can minimize weaknesses."

"Do you have any weaknesses?"

"Lemon pie."

"Excuse me."

"That's my weakness. Put lemon pie in front of me and I'm the weakest man alive."

Disappointed but not surprised that he wasn't willing to reveal any more personal information, she tilted her head and smiled. "Guess I'd better keep an eye on my lemon shampoo or I'll find you guzzling it someday."

For some odd reason, known only to Dylan, his eyes darkened and an intense look flashed across his face. An instant later, it was replaced with another one of those granite expressions. If it had been anyone else, she would have sworn there had been desire in his eyes. But Dylan attracted to her? No, he was surly, grumpy, and downright rude. There was absolutely no indication that he felt the least bit of attraction to her. Well, there had been that surprise kiss earlier today, but that had been an anomaly. Or had it? For the first time ever, Jamie began to wonder if maybe the attraction she felt for Dylan might not be one-sided after all. A shiver of excitement zoomed up her spine at the thought.

"You cold?"

Dylan's abrupt tone pulled her from the absurd fantasy; she shook her head.

"Okay, try it again."

Remembering his instructions, Jamie went to the mat and once more tried to move her body the way he'd showed her. She whirled around, stumbling a bit. At his command, she repeated the move. And again, and then again. Though breathless, Jamie felt more confident with each successive try. When, at last, she nailed it, she threw him a brilliant smile, waiting for his praise.

Instead, he grunted and said, "That's one move. You've got about a thousand to go." He went to the middle of the mat. "Watch me."

Feeling like a silly, immature twit for wanting a compliment when she had so far to go, Jamie watched as

Dylan added arm movements to the body twist she'd just mastered. A one-two punch that would block an opponent and deliver a blow almost simultaneously.

In awe once again of his graceful but lethal-looking moves, she went to stand beside him as he showed her the arm movements and made her practice them over and over, and then several more times. In those hours, Jamie began to have serious doubts that she could pull this transformation off. Oh, she still believed she had a surefire way inside Reddington's private domain, and once in, she could get the information she needed. However, defending herself if she had to wasn't going to be as straightforward as she'd hoped.

McKenna and Lucas had made it look so simple . . . effortless. And the training films she'd watched made the moves seem uncomplicated and easy. Getting her body on board with the easy and uncomplicated part was the problem. Could she really make this happen?

With each minute that went by, Dylan could feel Jamie's doubts increasing. Those white teeth were nibbling at her lip—something she often did when she felt uncertain. Also, her eyes had taken on a darker, more somber color. She was beginning to wonder if she had it in her to succeed.

He told himself he had no reason to feel guilty. Keeping her safe was his number one priority. Besides, it wasn't his intent that she leave here without being fully prepared to protect herself against a predator.

As he watched her complete yet another jerky arm motion, Dylan acknowledged that he was walking a fine line. Giving her the confidence to defend herself without the assurance that she could go after Reddington was going to take the delicacy of a true diplomat. Since he had a tendency to be as blunt as a mallet, he might have had his own doubts about whether he could pull this off—if it wasn't for the fact that he couldn't fail.

With that thought in mind, Dylan moved behind her and prepared himself for the torture of touching her. The thought of this woman being hurt in any way again cooled his desire to the freezing point.

"Let me hold your arms and we'll go through the motions together."

Standing behind her, he watched her face in the mirror as he held her slender arms and took her through the movements. A fine sheen of perspiration covered her entire body, and the desire he had hoped he'd squashed refused to leave. Her hair, slightly damp and smelling like the lemon fragrance he associated with her, was in an untidy ponytail, with loose strands falling around her delicate face.

Able to make the movements without much thought, Dylan gave in to a rare fantasy.

What would happen if he turned her in his arms and covered her mouth with his? Though he'd barely touched her lips earlier with that too quick kiss, he remembered their softness and the sweetness. Desire pumped through him as he imagined how she would open for him and his tongue would enter that sweet cavern. How the slender arms he held would wrap around him as he pulled her closer and how his hands would cup her beautiful butt as he pressed her against the aching, painful arousal that only her heat could satisfy.

Growling his frustration, Dylan dropped his arms and backed away. "That's it for today. We'll pick it up in the morning, after breakfast."

Her eyes wide with surprise, she said, "But can't I—"

"Your muscles are going to be sore if we keep this up. Let's have dinner, and then you might want to consider a hot bath."

Before she could question him further, Dylan stomped up the stairs, headed to his room. A cold shower in the midst of winter was a damn stupid thing to do. Since today had been full of damn stupid things already, he figured one more wouldn't matter.

Her steps light and quick behind him, Jamie asked, "Want me to start dinner?"

The last few days, they'd been sharing kitchen duties. Being in the too small room, with Jamie brushing up against him every so often, wasn't a torture he was willing to put himself through tonight. Dylan nodded. "Yeah, thanks."

Before she could say anything else, he closed the door to his bedroom, shutting himself inside and away from the biggest temptation of his life.

Jamie woke the next morning only a little sore from the previous day's workout but a lot confused about Dylan. During dinner, he'd uttered exactly three words: "Pass the salt."

Once they'd finished her hastily prepared beef stew and corn bread, he had insisted on cleaning up, since she'd made dinner. She didn't even think about protesting. Trying to carry on a conversation with a man who obviously had no desire to talk was exhausting. She'd said a quiet good night and had done what he'd suggested earlier—taken a hot bath and gone to bed. And she had slept almost dreamlessly. In the middle of the night, she'd woken with her body on fire and an ache between her legs. She had a vague recollection of Dylan lying on top of her, kissing her as he moved inside her. A sex dream about Dylan? She shook her head at not only the insanity but also hopelessness of it all. That was never going to happen.

Stretching carefully, she noted that she was glad she had followed Dylan's advice. There was a small amount of tightness in her muscles, but nothing painful. A hot shower should take care of that, and then she'd be ready to try those moves again.

A glance at the bedside clock told her she had at least another hour before her normal routine had to begin. Since she'd gone to bed earlier than usual, she'd woken early. The thought of practicing without Dylan's critical eagle eye was too tempting to pass up. Wouldn't he be surprised if he walked in and found she'd finally managed to master the move?

With that incentive, Jamie bounded out of bed and took a quick shower. Though she would have liked to stand under the pounding hot water much longer, she couldn't. Getting to the gym before Dylan arrived was her biggest priority right now. Drying hurriedly, Jamie brushed her teeth, slapped some moisturizer on her face, pulled her damp hair into its usual ponytail, and then slid into sleek spandex pants and a T-shirt.

She opened her bedroom door and stuck her head out. Relieved that Dylan's door was still closed, she decided to forgo coffee and headed down the steps to the gym. She was at the bottom step before she realized that the room was already occupied. Her disappointment at not being able to practice quickly disappeared. Her legs collapsed silently beneath her and she quietly dropped to the bottom step . . . in awe.

His handsome face one of concentrated intensity, Dylan went through a series of slow, graceful movements. He wore only a pair of old khakis; a fine sheen of perspiration covered his skin. Jamie swallowed hard. This was the first time she'd seen him without a shirt. To describe a man as beautiful seemed odd—especially when Dylan was so incredibly masculine—but "beautiful" was the first word that came to her mind.

He was so tanned and smooth; his skin looked like bronzed silk. Yesterday, she'd felt those hard arms around her, but she hadn't been able to appreciate how muscular and well defined they were. His broad chest had a slight sprinkling of hair that traveled down his long torso and disappeared beneath the waistband of his pants. Jamie watched a drop of sweat roll from that beautiful chest, down his hard, flat stomach. Her mouth watered, and a strange sensation went through her entire body.

She mentally shook her head at the incredulity and oddity of life. Her experiences this last year had left her wondering if she'd ever have the normal sexual desires she'd once had. The dream last night and now the delightful sensations zooming through her dispelled the worry. She had known she was attracted to Dylan, and now she knew it was more than just attraction—she wanted him.

And this wasn't just the normal kind of want. She knew what sexual desire felt like, and before she'd learned what a mistake she'd made in her marriage, had experienced sexual fulfillment. This heat and need went beyond the bounds of anything she'd ever known.

Much too soon, he finished. He had to know she was there, but he didn't acknowledge her presence as he grabbed a towel from the shelf against the wall and dried off, his back to her.

Feeling like an interloper but unable to leave and pretend she hadn't seen him, she broke the silence. "I've never seen anyone do tai chi in person."

Giving no indication that he'd heard her, Dylan pulled a T-shirt over his head and then guzzled down a bottle of water.

She waited for several more seconds, but when it was apparent that he was going to ignore her, Jamie got to her feet. If he planned to act as if she didn't exist, then she'd just get on with her day and pretend he didn't exist, either.

Finally he spoke, his tone and words an indication that he'd woken up in his usual state of grumpiness. "What are you doing down here so early?"

"I thought I might practice the moves you showed me yesterday."

"Any muscle soreness?"

"Not really. I took a hot shower and feel fine."

He nodded and headed for the stairs. "I'll get breakfast ready while you practice."

Out of the corner of his eye, Dylan saw the expression on her face and heard the soft sigh. Both indicated extreme relief. Hell, who could blame her? When he wasn't hurling instructions at her, he was grunting one-word answers.

He'd woken this morning with the clear knowledge that his attitude was going to have to change. She might trust him with her training, but he wanted more—he needed her to trust him enough to tell him what she was hiding. Behaving like a caveman only made her warier.

Hell of it was, he was damn good at cover-up and subterfuge. He should've had her eating out of his hand and telling him her secrets within days. Instead, he'd let his desire get in the way of his job. A damn foolish and stupid thing for him to do. Jamie's well-being trumped his inconvenient lust to hell and back.

At the bottom of the stairway, he stopped and turned. "I'll let you know when breakfast is ready."

She gave him a tentative smile, as if she realized that a truce of some kind had been called.

Dylan stomped up the stairs and headed to his room. Maybe a shower would put him in the agreeable frame of mind he needed. He turned the shower on full blast and stripped down to nothing. Holding his head under the deluge of water, he closed his eyes and prepared himself for the challenge ahead. Not the agreeable part, although being an asshole was a comfortable attitude for him; but that wasn't the part he dreaded.

For years, he'd practiced being anyone other than who and what he was. Last Chance Rescue was the perfect fit for him. Not only did he find enormous satisfaction in saving lives; being anyone other than the dirt-poor Ohio boy with the guilt of the world on his shoulders was like being given a new life. Weeks, sometimes months would go by without him remembering the sheer misery of those years. The terror, the beatings, the loneliness . . . all of those things had molded him into the man he became. And though his grandmother had saved him from a lifetime of abuse—or death—Dylan knew that much of the man he was today had been formed in those early years.

He'd been on numerous undercover missions. Been everything from a fake hit man to a sleazy pimp. When he'd agreed to take this current assignment, he had known it wouldn't be easy. Training a new operative could be rewarding or a pain in the ass, depending on the person. But Jamie wasn't an LCR operative, and never had he encountered an assignment where he had to ferret out secrets from a woman who was . . . hell, he might as well admit it . . . so damn lovable.

Dylan turned off the water and stepped out of the shower. Whether he liked the job or not, he had to do it. If Jamie was withholding valuable information, it was irresponsible and selfish of her. And since she'd made it clear yesterday that her plans hadn't changed, it could also get her killed.

The thought of something happening to her was enough to shut out those whispers from his conscience. He refused to question why he had such a strong need to protect her. No use denying something he had known from the moment he'd carried her out of that house. Jamie was special, and he'd do anything he had to, including lying and abusing her trust, to protect her.

He tugged on a pair of sweats and a T-shirt and, with barely a glance at the mirror for his still wet, tousled hair, headed to the kitchen. Spending any more time on his dread and regrets would get him nowhere. Now he had to concentrate on feeding Jamie the line of bullshit she would need to hear to trust him with her secrets.

For the first time in a long time, Dylan wondered if he wasn't more like his trashy, low-life family than he wanted to admit.

six

Breathless but triumphant, Jamie stood in front of the mirror and watched herself go through the motions Dylan had shown her yesterday. Though not as smooth and graceful as she wanted it to be, nonetheless, the sequence looked so much better than yesterday's effort.

"Lower your right arm a little."

She jerked around to find Dylan standing only a few feet from her. Dammit, the man *did* move like a cat.

"How long have you been watching?"

"Not long. Your movements are better, more certain."

A compliment from Dylan? A glow glimmered through her body.

"Come eat breakfast and then we'll work on another move you can combine with that one."

Almost afraid that there was a trick involved, Jamie eyed him suspiciously as she went up the stairs. She was used to Dylan being surly, condescending, and occasionally hateful. And though his attitude might not be called nice by most people's standards, considering his previous behavior, for Dylan, this was downright friendly.

Jamie washed up and headed to the kitchen, from which delicious fragrances were emanating. Her stomach rumbled as she sat at the table and admired the mini feast he'd prepared. Scrambled eggs, bacon, biscuits, and orange juice.

"Looks delicious."

"Figured you'd be hungry. Working out before breakfast always increases my appetite."

Jamie knew she was gawking and did nothing to hide it. "Okay, what's going on?"

She caught him with his mouth open to take a bite of biscuit; he shoved half the biscuit into his mouth, chewed, swallowed, and said, "What?"

"You haven't been this nice to me since you rescued me."

Though his face was in its usual shutdown mode, his mouth twisted in a wry smile. "Figured we'd get a lot more accomplished if I stopped being an ass."

She didn't bother to point out that behaving this way from the beginning would have been helpful. She was just grateful for the change of heart.

Digging into her breakfast, Jamie continued to be surprised as Dylan continued to talk.

"The weather's supposed to warm up by the end of the week. We should be able to use one of the obstacle courses."

Jamie gulped, her appetite suddenly diminished. When she'd first arrived, he'd showed her those courses. As much as she wanted to meet all the challenges he put before her, she couldn't deny the dread. Climbing over walls, crawling through tunnels, swinging on ropes—those things were completely out of her realm of understanding and knowledge.

"Don't look so worried. I won't time your first couple of tries."

Had he thought that information would reassure her? The dread only increased. Of course timing would be involved. From what she could tell, there was little in her training that didn't include doing it either as fast or as quietly as possible.

She took a breath and lifted her chin. Fear wasn't going to stop her. "I look forward to the challenge."

Though that damn eyebrow he was so fond of raising shot up, he didn't comment on what sounded, even to her own ears, like thin bravado.

Moving her attention back to her meal, Jamie took several more bites. The silence wasn't the one she'd gotten used to over the last couple of weeks. This was the kind of silence that was bound to be broken. And once again, Dylan didn't disappoint.

"What do you know about Reddington you're not telling us?"

The question so surprised her, she swallowed a bite of biscuit too soon. Grabbing her orange juice before she choked, she drank half the glass to unclog her throat and then shook her head. "I've told Noah everything I know about his operation."

"Everything?"

She'd never realized how penetrating a green-eyed stare could be. Didn't matter. She had told the truth. All the information she'd gleaned about Reddington and his horrific slave trading had been given to Noah McCall the day after her rescue.

"Tell me again, then."

"What?"

"Humor me . . . tell me again."

Her lips trembled with the need to say something sarcastic. But this was the most Dylan had talked with her since she'd been here. Creating goodwill by reviewing what she'd learned wasn't a big deal. She was hiding nothing useful about Reddington. At least, nothing useful for LCR.

"The first time I heard him, he was discussing a business transaction about a young woman he'd purchased in Seville. He said he wanted her included on the next market day."

"And how was it that you heard this?"

Jamie forced herself to view her memories objectively. Those dark days had been some of the scariest and most humiliating of her life. If she didn't allow herself to get drawn into the emotions, it was much easier to recall what she'd heard.

"As you know . . . since you were the one to find me . . . I was locked in a room on the third floor. I was handcuffed to the bed most of the time, but when my meals were delivered, I was free to eat, go to the bathroom . . . whatever. Sometimes hours would go by before they'd remember to come back and lock the cuffs. They weren't really afraid that I'd try to escape. The only way out was through the door, which was always locked, or through the window. Since I was about thirty feet from the ground, I'm sure they figured I wouldn't jump."

Little had they known that'd she'd contemplated that very thing. The jump would have killed her, but at her lowest point, she had been desperate. But then blessed anger had returned and, with it, the determination that the bastards would not win. If she had jumped out that window, no one would have blinked an eye. She would probably have been thrown into a hole in the woods, and that would have been that.

Realizing she had gone where she had promised herself she wouldn't, Jamie took a breath and made herself continue: "One day when I was free and looking for a way out, I found a heating vent on the floor. I managed to pry it open. There was no way I could escape through it, but I could hear voices. That's when I realized my room was right above Reddington's office. I heard numerous phone conversations—all one-sided—but he had no regard for what he said. He conducted a lot of business in that office."

"And that's how you learned that he's into slave trading and human trafficking?"

"Yes."

"Did he ever suspect that you knew anything?"

"No. I only saw him a couple of times, and that was in the beginning."

"Did he say names, locations, dates?"

"No names, other than a man's name—Armando—who I think works for him. He was very open in his conversations with both his son and Armando. The people he sold were discussed as if they were cattle. Sometimes he'd refer to them by number or hair color. I remember he referred to one as 'the old hag.'"

Dylan nodded. "That's consistent with what McCall's sources uncovered. He's not just into slave trading for sex. He sells humans for every possible market out there for human beings."

"I heard him say something about a promising young man he had his eyes on. That was the only time I heard Reddington and his son argue."

"What did they argue about?"

"About this promising young man. His father said he thought the young man had potential. The son was resistant."

"You tell McCall about this?"

"Of course."

"What else did you hear?"

"Market day is every other Tuesday. He told his son Lance how . . ." Her breakfast lurched up her throat. How could she have forgotten the one conversation that'd made her throw up the small amount of food she'd ingested the day she'd heard it?

"What?"

Though his eyes were as hard as ever, Dylan's voice had softened noticeably. He knew how hard this was for her. That one kindness helped her to say, "He said that one of the ways Lance could become a prime judge of . . ." She grimaced. "Sorry, I won't repeat the word he used."

"You don't have to. Just give me the gist."

"Reddington said that once Lance had experimented with me in all the ways he could, he'd have a good idea what to look for."

"That didn't happen, though."

Dylan's words were a statement of fact. And something for which she was exceedingly grateful. No one, other than her therapist, knew what had happened. Having anyone else know the truth would benefit no one.

She acknowledged his statement with a slight nod, saying, "Thanks to you."

"Can I ask you a personal question?"

Jamie nodded hesitantly—the fact that he'd asked permission worrisome. She had thought the questions he'd already asked were personal and could have sworn that not by the slightest flicker had she revealed that she wasn't being entirely truthful.

"You've recovered incredibly well in a short period of time. How did you do that?"

She knew he didn't mean physically. The bruises and surface injuries she'd received at the hands of Damon Hughes had healed within a couple of weeks of his attack. No, she knew he meant, *How did you recover from the terror and fear that accompany a brutal assault?*

"I don't think I have an easy answer to that. I thank God every day that I can't remember Hughes's attack. The doctors called it selective amnesia. Said I might never remember anything about it, which is exactly what I want. I remember being held in his house and how terrified I was, but the actual attack is a complete blank." She shrugged and added, "And maybe the fact that he's dead helped in some way."

"Thanks to Lucas Kane."

She smiled and nodded. "Thanks to Lucas."

"But your experiences with Reddington. You remember all of that?"

"Yes, those memories are, unfortunately, all intact. After I was rescued, I had nightmares for the first few weeks . . . still do occasionally."

"As anyone would."

She could explain it away by saying that concentrating on going after Reddington had helped, but that was only partially true. Jamie knew there were extenuating circumstances that had helped her heal faster than she might have.

"After my rescue, I had two options: be bitter and full of fear or realize what I'd been given. My sister, the one person I'd thought I'd never see again, was returned to me. And not only that, I got to see what a remarkable person she is. McKenna went through so much more than I did, but instead of allowing it to destroy her, she used her pain as an impetus to help others.

"Having McKenna to talk with was a blessing. She knew exactly what I was feeling. Then, when I went through counseling, getting everything out in the open— all of my pain, fear, anger, resentment—was a tremendous help." She shrugged helplessly, realizing she'd basically been rambling. "Does any of that make sense?"

He gave a quick nod in acknowledgment of her question and, as if she hadn't just bared her soul, continued his interrogation: "What else did you hear while you were there?"

She blew out a sigh, suddenly exhausted. "He talked to his wife on a daily basis. Actually seems to be a very devoted family man. Once I heard him defending his son . . . saying that she shouldn't worry . . . that Lance was a perfectly normal young man." Something Jamie knew wasn't true.

"And he gave no indication of where his family lived?"

"No. I never heard him discuss any kind of location. All I remember is that once I heard him talking to Armando. I think a customer wanted some information about one of their purchases. Reddington said that the man would have to wait until he went to his family's home to get that information, since that's where all his sales records were kept."

His stare was harder and more direct than she'd ever seen it. She knew what he was trying to do. He thought she was hiding valuable information. She wasn't . . . not really. The only information she hadn't shared wouldn't be helpful to LCR at all. The organization could do nothing with it. For Jamie, it was the most important piece of knowledge she had on Reddington. Information that was not only going to get her into the man's private life but give her access to his secrets.

When Jamie was through with him, Stanford Reddington would never see freedom again. She'd love to have that punishment extended to his perverted excuse for a son, but when she'd decided upon this course of action, she had known that might not be possible. However, she would take what she could get, and that would have to be enough.

Either Jamie was getting better at lying or she really didn't have more information to share.

Dylan stood on the porch, waiting. Jamie was changing into warmer clothes so they could go over the obstacle course once more before she tried it out tomorrow.

Her answers to his blunt questions had been clear-cut

and direct. He'd seen no deception or hesitancy. Could McCall be wrong? No, he didn't think so. Jamie might not be withholding vital information, but it was clear she thought she had a way inside to Reddington. That was the information she was hiding. And that was the information he needed to get. It might not help them get to Reddington, but knowing her plan would give him an opportunity to make her realize how dangerous and ridiculous it would be for her to try to infiltrate the man's organization.

Learning to kick the shit out of someone did not qualify a person to go undercover.

"Okay, I'm ready."

Dylan turned and had to work like hell to keep from smiling. Covered from head to foot, she looked like she'd barely be able to breathe, much less move. The only visible parts of her body were her eyes and the tip of her nose. Everything else was covered in layers.

"We're not in subzero temps, you know."

"Yesterday I almost froze, and I was only outside for a few minutes. I figured if we're going to be walking a distance, I needed to stay warm."

"Warm, yes. Smothered, no."

Before she could respond, Dylan reached out and began to unwrap the scarf around her head and neck. As he worked to uncover her, an unexpected surge of arousal hit him hard. The thought of being able to fully undress her and reveal all the delicacy and beauty beneath the clothes caused an unwelcome reaction. He had done so well for the first two weeks by not talking to her or being close to her. Yesterday had broken that routine. Problem was, he could do nothing about it. He wanted her . . . he couldn't have her. There was no leeway, no solution.

Glad that his jacket hid the unwanted reaction, Dylan

stepped away from her. Pointing to the yard, he said, "Supposed to get up into the low fifties today. The snow's still deep in some areas, but I cleared a path to the easiest course yesterday." He glanced down at her clothing again. "You're not going to be able to do much in that getup, though."

Her eyes went wide. "So I'm going to run it today?"

"We're going to run it together."

"Oh."

The little gasping breath she made with that one word almost did him in. Furious at himself, he turned and stomped down the steps. "Try to keep up."

Not waiting to see if she followed, Dylan went to the side of the house and started down the trail to the small obstacle course. The property had three courses. This one was so easy, a child could finish it within minutes. He had considered showing her only the most difficult course, in the hopes that she'd realize that this kind of training was too rough for her. That had been only a brief consideration. Not only did he intend to honor his commitment to train her; he knew Jamie well enough to understand that she wouldn't have backed down no matter how difficult the course.

With the weather on a warming trend through next week, his plan was to run this course each morning. Tomorrow afternoon, they'd go to a more difficult course and walk through it together. The last course would have to wait a few weeks. It would take her that long to perfect the first two.

He heard her shallow breaths behind him and was pleased that she'd been able to keep up. The daily runs on the treadmill had increased her fitness. He stopped at the entrance to the course. Now it was time to see if she had the physical strength to go along with her improved stamina.

She came to a stop beside him. "So how fast do I need to be able to do this course?"

"As fast as you can."

"Why is it that every time I think I've made progress with you, you take a step back?"

Surprised at the confrontation, he looked down at her. "Progress with me? I thought you were the one who was supposed to be clocking progress. Not me."

"You're right, but would it kill you to stop being nasty?"

"What did I do that was nasty?"

Jamie rolled her eyes, not even dignifying his question with the smart-ass answer that trembled on her lips. She had mistakenly believed they'd crossed some sort of invisible bridge with their earlier conversation. Now he was back to the gruff one-sentence answers. She had to get over the need for him to like her. It was obviously not going to happen.

"How long does it take for you to run this course?".

"My best time was forty-three seconds."

She gulped. "Forty-three seconds?"

At his nod, Jamie felt a quick moment of panic as she took in the obstacle course once more. What had appeared to be a small child's playground with some fun diversions now looked more ominous. She had expected an answer of maybe four minutes. Forty-three seconds was insane.

"That's my time, Jamie. Not yours. That's why I said 'as fast as you can.' You're not competing with anyone but yourself."

She blew out a sigh. He was right. Odd, but she never considered herself argumentative or even that competitive. Every time Dylan said something, though, she took it as a challenge. The comment he'd made her first day here was right. She was expending a lot of useless energy. Dylan was who he was. He wasn't going to turn into Prince Charming. And that wasn't why she was here, anyway. She was here to learn.

"You're right."

She saw a flicker of surprise before his expression went back to the blank one she was used to. And why shouldn't he be surprised? She hadn't exactly been the most agreeable of students. Jamie made a silent vow to change that. From now on, she'd be the epitome of agreeability.

"So, let's get started," she said. "What do I need to do?"

"Watch me." With those words, Dylan pulled off his jacket and dropped it onto a wooden bench. Dressed in a thin navy blue T-shirt and a ragged pair of navy sweatpants, he looked powerful, determined, and competent.

Wide-eyed and suddenly breathless, Jamie watched as he took a running start and jumped over a wooden hurdle. Then, with seeming effortless ease, he grabbed the high bar and swung himself over, landing on the other side of a small sand trap. His expression one of intense focus, he ran through a row of tires and then leaped up to a low wall and climbed over it. And without stopping, he turned and ran toward her.

Her heart pounding hard and her mouth desert dry, she watched him come closer. There was something beautiful about Dylan. Not effeminate and not pretty, but the grace and incredible strength in his body was magnificent to watch.

"You ready to try it?"

She nodded and walked with him toward the first hurdle. Why did her body suddenly feel like an ox's? Never had she been more aware of her limbs and lack of grace.

"Hey, it's fun. Enjoy yourself. There's no time limit

today. Just a chance to try it out a few times and see how it feels."

Putting on the mantle of determination she had adopted to get through tough times, Jamie took a deep breath and began running.

seven

Canary Islands

The sun blazed down on Stanford as he walked along the beach. The heat should have warmed him, but his insides felt cold and empty. Almost a month had gone by without him leaving his home. To others, this might look like paradise. As a man who thrived on staying active, he felt imprisoned.

He had known that scaling back on his marketing business would eat into his profits; he just hadn't realized that it would also eat into his soul. Stanford not only truly enjoyed his chosen trade, he was an expert. He had a sterling reputation in the flesh-trading market, and because of one poor choice, he was paying a high price.

"Are you troubled, Stan?"

With a small frown of confusion plastered on his face, he glanced down at Sarah, his wife of twenty-four years. "What makes you think I'm troubled?"

Still as lovely as the day he'd married her, Sarah smiled up at him. "I know when you have something on your mind. Are you so eager to end your vacation with us and return to Madrid?"

Yet another reason for him to be angry. His beloved wife was worried. For years, he had protected his entire family from the necessary nastiness of the world. Stanford was an old-fashioned family man. As the head of the household, he treasured and cosseted his loved ones. They had no real knowledge of how he made his wealth . . . and they didn't need to know. Though Sarah probably suspected, they of course never discussed anything so mundane or crude as business.

It rankled him that when he'd made the decision to bring a family member into the business, allowing him to see his future legacy, the plan had failed miserably. Now Lancelot was in a far-off land, away from his loved ones. Away from his family, who missed him desperately.

Still, he couldn't let on that anything bothered him. He had pledged to her when they'd first married that Sarah would know only happiness. And he had done everything in his power to keep that promise.

"There's nothing on my mind other than making sure our daughter chooses the right man to marry."

She gasped and jerked to a stop. "But Giselle is only seventeen. You promised to give her time to grow up before she has to decide upon a mate."

He heard the fear in her voice and fought his irritation. Had he not done everything to ensure Sarah's happiness? To have her question him indicated that, even after all this time, she still didn't trust him. Stanford worked hard to keep from revealing his frustration. "I'm not saying she has to marry immediately. However, she's at an age where young men should be catching her eye and she, theirs. She has no prospects here."

A slender hand grabbed his arm. "You're not thinking of sending her away, are you?"

He patted his wife's hand. "Of course not. That's never going to happen. She will always be here with you. However, there are no young men on the island. Giselle needs more than just exposure to young men— they have to be the right kind."

Her mouth tightened, and Stanford wondered if she

thought to argue with him. Then, after several seconds of silence, she drew in a long, resigned breath and asked, "What do you propose, then?"

"I have invited a young man here to stay with us. He should be arriving shortly."

"But you can't force Giselle to fall in love."

"Did I say anything about force?"

When she took a small, subtle step away from him, Stanford realized he'd allowed his anger to show. He took a calming breath. "Of course we can't force her to fall in love, but we can give her the opportunity to see the kind of man we would like to have join the family."

Her expression still wary, she said, "Tell me about him."

"He's a young man Lance introduced me to several months back. An enterprising young fellow who wants to work for me. When I told him that I don't hire people just because they are friends of my children, he assured me that he would like to start at the very bottom, learning as much as he can."

"And did you hire him?"

"I was going to. Before I could, he announced that he was leaving for the U.S. Apparently, he obtained a scholarship for his last two years of college."

"But how did you persuade him to come here if he's in school?"

"It wasn't difficult at all. I made the invitation, thinking he'd refuse. Instead, he indicated that he'd rather learn business with me than go off to a foreign country and study dry statistics and data." Stanford chuckled at the memory of the boy's eagerness. "That young man might well run the company someday."

"But what about Lance?"

"There will always be a place for Lancelot." Remembering with fondness some of the explicit conversations he and his son had shared while discussing the flesh trade, Stanford already knew where his son's talents lay. "My companies need diverse leaders. I already see many of my own characteristics in our son."

She was quiet for so long, he thought the discussion was over. They walked in silence for several more minutes, and then she said, "And you promise to allow Giselle to fall in love on her own?"

"Of course I will. This is merely an opportunity for her to meet the right kind. If there's no spark there, I won't encourage it further."

Her mouth trembled into a weak smile. "So when does this young man arrive, and what is his name?"

"He'll be here the day after tomorrow, and his name is Raphael Sanchez."

Madrid

Raphael stared at the cellphone in his hand. He had put off making the call about as long as he could. Very soon he would be at Stanford Reddington's home. If he didn't notify Noah now, it would be too late.

Noah would be furious, at first. That was a given. Instead of heading to the States, enjoying the free education he had been offered, he was doing the exact thing he'd been told not to do. He was going to put himself in the midst of Stanford Reddington and his family. And he was going to get the information LCR needed to put the man away.

Disappointing Noah McCall wasn't something Raphael took lightly. He owed his life to Noah and Last Chance Rescue, and that wasn't something he planned to forget.

A few months back, he'd been able to infiltrate Reddington's tight-knit organization by befriending Lancelot Reddington, the man's slimy offspring. In doing that,

Raphael had been able to assist in saving Jamie Kendrick from God only knew what. And though that had felt good, the fact that Reddington and his son hadn't been prosecuted was unacceptable.

He had seen the dedication of the LCR operatives. They were real-life heroes, and their mission of rescuing victims was one he wholeheartedly embraced. McCall had promised to one day consider Raphael as an LCR operative. He knew Noah McCall was a man of his word, but he also knew that the LCR leader wanted to protect him.

It wasn't as if he hadn't intended to do what Noah wanted and get his education. Attending university in the States was a dream come true. But when Stanford Reddington had called and asked him if he wanted to come for a visit to his home, Raphael hadn't been able to resist. This was an opportunity LCR had been waiting for . . . how could he turn down the offer?

After being treated like he was garbage for most of his life, having so many LCR operatives interested in his future meant everything. Cole Mathison, the LCR operative he'd been held captive with, had invited Raphael to his home. Cole had even asked Raphael to attend his wedding to Keeley. He treated Raphael like family.

And Noah had offered to look for any remaining family Raphael might have. Since his mother was gone and he'd never known who his father was, Raphael had declined the offer. He hadn't wanted to know if there were others. His mother had turned him against meeting any more of his blood kin.

LCR's people had been kinder to him than anyone he'd ever known. They'd given him a chance. It was his dream to work for them someday, and he trusted Noah to give him that opportunity. But now he had a chance to repay them for their kindness by helping bring Stanford Reddington to justice. How could he not take advantage of it?

With a sigh, Raphael pressed a speed-dial number and waited for Noah to answer.

"McCall," Noah said.

"It's Raphael."

Last Chance Rescue headquarters
Paris

A grin lifted Noah's mouth at the sound of the voice of the young man he'd come to admire and love. "You packed and ready to go?"

"Yes."

"Good. Massachusetts is chilly this time of year, but you'll enjoy the—"

"Uh . . . there's a slight change of plans."

"What's that?"

"I'm not going."

"What do you mean, you're not going?"

As Raphael began his explanation, Noah got up on his feet. By the time the kid had finished, Noah was pacing the length of his office. "Dammit, I told you to stay out of it."

"I know, and I was going to, I promise. I didn't solicit the invitation . . . he called me. This is too good of a chance to pass up."

Grimly, Noah had to admit that Raphael was right. Every lead he'd had on Reddington's home location had dried up. As much as he didn't want the kid to take this risk, how many lives might be saved if he actually succeeded in helping?

"Has he given you any idea how long he wants you to stay?"

"No. He just said he liked that I had taken the initiative to go after what I wanted. Said if I would come stay with him at his home, he'd give me more education than any university ever could."

Noah closed his eyes. He could only imagine the kinds of things Reddington wanted to teach an impressionable young man. What would he expect out of Raphael? Would he have to prove his worth in some horrific way?

"I'll be fine, Noah. I promise. And I'll find a way to get in touch with you."

Making a decision he didn't want to have to make, Noah began to strategize. "Okay, where are you now?"

"At my apartment."

"Reddington may be having you watched. Can you be at the coffee shop on Murat Street in exactly two hours?"

"Yes."

"I'll have a new phone delivered to you. It'll be too dangerous to carry any bugs, but the phone I'm giving you will have a long-distance GPS device. Once you get it, throw away the phone you have now. Don't make any calls that can be traced. Samuel, the man who will meet you, will show you how to use it."

"I know you're not happy about this, but it'll work out."

Since there was nothing more he could do but pray that it did work out, Noah sat down and, in a half hour's time, gave Raphael a quick lesson in deep cover and, most important, staying alive.

West Virginia mountains

Jamie eased into the steaming-hot tub and moaned at how wonderful it felt. Dylan had told her not to overdo, but she'd been having such fun, she had insisted on one more run on the obstacle course. Falling over the wooden hurdle had at first damaged only her pride, but the longer the day went, the more she realized that something else hurt more—her bottom felt as though she'd been kicked.

Thankfully, Dylan hadn't given the lecture she had expected. Though there'd been a small curve to his mouth and an unusual twinkle in his eyes when he'd helped her up.

She refused to let his amusement or even her soreness bother her. She felt triumphant and excited. The obstacle course had frightened her because she hadn't been sure she could do something so athletic-looking. And what had she done? She'd overcome her fear and then some. Even Dylan had praised her.

"Jamie?"

At the sound of his voice, Jamie sat up, then winced. "Yes?"

"I'm putting some ointment outside your door. It should help with the aches."

Since she'd walked back to the cabin like an octogenarian on her last breath, she wasn't surprised he knew of her aches. What he might be surprised at were the words that sprang to her mind: *Want to rub the ointment on for me?*

What would he say if she asked him? He'd refuse, of course. Probably be embarrassed for her when he realized that she was attracted to him. Maybe even feel sorry for her. Because if there was anything that was clear at all, it was that Dylan wasn't the least bit attracted to her. She was a job and nothing more. How foolish of her to want anything else.

Jamie eased back against the tub. Becoming involved with Dylan would be pointless. She had a job to do. Any and all personal relationships would only get in the way. Besides, the man disapproved of her plans. If they did start a relationship, he'd only try to talk her out of them. That couldn't happen.

She had two more months before she had to implement the first part of her plan. Whether she would be ready when she got the call she expected, she didn't know. She just knew she was going for it. This was her one and only shot.

Sometimes, late at night, when she couldn't sleep and the silence became too much, she would remember. She had told herself and everyone who'd asked that this wasn't about revenge. But during the dark stillness of the night, when her memories haunted her, she knew that it was a large part of her need. The things he'd planned to do and the things he had done. How could she forget? How could she not want retribution?

Water splashed over the tub's side as she sat up abruptly. No, she wouldn't think about those things. Replaying those dark days in her mind was a useless endeavor.

Pulling herself from the bath, she dried quickly and dressed in jeans and a sweatshirt. Then, wiping the steam-filled mirror with a towel so she could see her reflection, she gave herself the same lecture she'd been using for years. She could endure any and all things because of who she was inside. She'd had the best, most loving parents in the world. They had instilled within her a core of steel that had often been dented but had never been, would never be, dissolved.

To others, her soft gray-blue eyes might look vulnerable and innocent, but she knew what lay beyond them. She had endured some horrific events in her life, and though they'd punctured and sliced into her soul, they hadn't destroyed her.

"Jamie, dinner's ready."

Dylan's voice pulled her back from the dark, as it had

so many times before. Would he be surprised about that?

"I'm coming."

And with those words, Jamie gave the determined nod she'd learned long ago and headed out the door.

Dylan placed the Crock-Pot filled with pot roast, potatoes, and carrots on the table. About to take the rolls out of the oven, he stopped abruptly when Jamie entered the kitchen. How the hell did someone who'd just gone through a grueling day of training look as though she'd spent a relaxing day in a spa? She had to be exhausted and aching in every muscle. Instead, she offered him a sunny smile as she sat at the table.

"This looks wonderful. Where did you learn to cook like this?"

"My grandmother. She was an invalid in her later years and talked me through some recipes."

Remembering the twinkling eyes of his grandmother always did something to Dylan's heart. Though he'd lived with her for only eight years and had gone through hell before he'd gotten to her, those had been some of the best days of his life.

Jamie took a bite of roast and closed her eyes on a groan of appreciation. All thoughts of his grandmother disappeared as Dylan's entire mind went blank. One small groan from this woman could make him harder than steel. If she ever truly tried to attract him, he figured, he'd expire.

Determined to ignore the now throbbing arousal, he bent his head to his meal. Other than the clang of silverware and a couple more appreciative groans from Jamie, there was silence in the room. And if she groaned one more time, Dylan was going to have to either tell her to shut up or kiss her.

Before he could come up with a solution that wouldn't

hurt her or kill him, she said, "You lived with your grandmother? Where were your parents?"

If there was a question that could dispel any good or normal feelings inside him, Jamie had just nailed it. No way in hell was he going into detail about what happened in his childhood. That was only fodder for horror movies and nightmares.

Softening his answer never entered his head. "Dead."

Though she jerked a bit at the harsh one-word answer, it didn't deter her. "What happened?"

"It's not something I like to talk about."

"I'm sorry. It's painful, isn't it?"

Jamie would know about that kind of pain. Her own parents had been murdered. Her soft eyes were sympathetic and understanding.

Thing was . . . he couldn't call what he felt pain. It was sordid and dirty, and he did his damnedest to never think of it, but when he did, pain wasn't what he felt. Refusing to lie, but still not willing to go there, he shrugged. "I'm just not one who likes to dwell on the past."

"The past helps define us."

Dylan snorted. "That's bullshit."

"Excuse me?"

"What I said . . . bullshit."

"So you don't think what happens in your childhood affects you?"

"That's not what you said. You said it defines us. We make our own way in this life."

"I agree, but you have to admit that what happens to us, especially in early childhood, helps shape us. Psychologists will tell you that—"

Dylan's chair scraped against the hardwood floor as he pushed it back abruptly and stood. He went to the sink and began to rinse the dishes. How the hell had he gotten caught up in an argument about the past? Didn't matter that part of him agreed with her. Unfortunately, there was no way to end the conversation easily. Fuck it, he didn't care. He wasn't going to continue down that road. Turning, he snarled, "My past isn't up for discussion or analysis. Drop it."

Her eyes went wide, and he knew he'd shocked her with his behavior. She realized she'd gone too far. Good. Now she knew what was off-limits. He refused to feel any guilt over her hurt feelings.

Instead of apologizing for delving into an area she had no right to go into, instead of crying over hurt feelings, instead of getting up and storming out of the room, Jamie, predictably, did the unpredictable. Leaning back against her chair, she said softly, "So it's okay that you know every aspect of my life, but I can't know any of yours."

"This isn't a group therapy session. If you need more counseling, I'll get your therapist to come for a visit." He turned back to the sink, not wanting to see the damage his words inflicted.

The scraping of her chair against the hardwood floor told him she was leaving. Good. Now they could get back to the business at hand, and she had learned a valuable lesson to boot.

A soft touch on his arm was his first indication that with Jamie, he should never assume anything. Turning, he looked down at her and almost forgot every promise he'd made to himself not to kiss her. She was so damn beautiful, inside and out.

Her expression one of understanding and compassion, she said softly, "Sometimes it helps to talk to a friend about it. Someone who knows what it feels like."

"Friends? Is that what we are?"

Though her throat convulsed slightly as she swallowed, that was the only sign she gave that she was nervous. "I'd like to think so."

Dylan pulled away. There was no way he could stay close to her right now and not reveal that friendship was the last thing on his mind. "Think again. We're not friends. I'm your trainer; you're my student. That's it."

He had been pushing to get her to back off and finally succeeded. Though her eyes went bright as if tears might fall, she maintained the dignity that had impressed him so much when he'd first met her. "I'm sorry you feel that way."

She backed away and headed toward the door. Calling himself every vile name in the book, Dylan closed his eyes and told himself to let her go. He had nothing for her other than knowledge and skill for her training. That was it.

Instead of doing the smart thing, he heard the truth tear from his mouth: "My father killed my mother."

She stopped at the doorway and turned. The expression on her face wasn't shock or disgust . . . it was compassion. Hell, he'd rather have the disgust. It was easier to take.

"When? What happened?" she asked softly.

"When I was a kid." He shrugged. "He was a mean drunk. One day he went too far."

"Is that when you went to live with your grandmother?"

If only. "No."

"But how . . . ?"

The discussion had gone on long enough. Just because he'd revealed something only a handful of people even knew about him, that didn't mean he was going to spill the entire sordid story. "It's not important. I just . . ." Hell, he just what? He shrugged and said, "I'm sorry I was a jerk. Okay?"

Though he saw the questions shimmering in her eyes, he was glad she did nothing more than say, "Thank you for telling me."

Before he could say anything else, she turned to the door and walked out of the room. The breath rushed from Dylan with a giant, rasping wheeze. Holy hell, why had he shared that with her? He could have apologized without divulging part of his shitty life story.

Cursing his stupidity, Dylan proceeded to put the leftovers away and wash the few dishes they'd used. Normally Jamie would have offered, but he figured she wanted to get away from him, and he was glad. Having her around was a distraction he didn't need right now.

Besides the fact that sharing such intimate information wasn't his thing, letting her be aware of his past might have one valuable aspect. She now knew that he was the son of a cold-blooded killer. Hard not to be disgusted by that fact. Those glimpses of hero worship and attraction he'd seen in her eyes would now be completely gone.

At that thought, a deep pit opened up in his stomach and something kicked him hard and deep. Ignoring the pain, Dylan resumed what he'd been doing since he'd met her: burying his need beneath a mountain of denial.

eight

Reddington's island

Raphael stepped off the boat and onto dry land at last. Nerves and seasickness weren't a good combination. The first half of the trip, he'd had his head in a bucket. The last half, he'd been praying for death.

The nerves might not have been so bad if not for the intrusive, full-body patdown and then having his phone confiscated before he was even allowed inside the limousine. Now, two plane rides and two boat trips later, he was on solid ground, and it was his sincerest hope that the trip was at an end. No wonder no one could find Reddington. Here Raphael was at the man's home and he still had no real idea of where it was. Having been told to stay below while on the boats had crushed his chances of identifying his location.

In between bouts of sickness, he'd worked up the courage to ask one of Reddington's men where they were going and had gotten an abrupt answer: "Canary Islands."

Not terribly helpful, since that was a big freaking area. And since they'd taken his phone, Noah couldn't track him. So, for better or worse, he was on his own. Raphael straightened his shoulders. What better way to prove that he was capable and mature enough to be an LCR operative?

"Raphael, my boy, welcome to my home."

Stanford Reddington's booming voice jerked him out of his thoughts, reminding him that he had a role to play. Staying on Reddington's good side was imperative.

Holding out his hand, he firmly shook the older man's. "It's good to see you, sir. Thank you again for this opportunity."

The first time he had met Reddington, he'd been surprised. The man was no more than five foot seven, and though he looked like he'd put on some weight since Raphael had last seen him, he was still a small man. As if in apology for his unimpressive size, Mother Nature had gifted him with a thick head of silver hair—prematurely silver since the man was probably only in his forties. That, along with sharply piercing blue eyes and the most dramatic voice Raphael had ever heard, created an image of a powerful and successful man.

"Did you have a good trip?"

Raphael grimaced and shook his head. No use lying about it. Reddington's men had never made a derogatory comment to his face, but he'd seen their amusement. "Unfortunately, I suffered from some airsickness and seasickness, but I'm much better."

"Excellent. The trip is grueling, I admit, but it's necessary." Reddington's smile held more than a little condescension. "When one is a wealthy, powerful man, one collects enemies and has to take precautions. Protecting my family is of the utmost importance."

Yeah . . . right.

"But don't you think the trip was worth it?" At those words, Reddington spread his arms wide.

No way could Raphael deny the beauty of the setting. Just standing on the pier, he was able to see a pristine expanse of shoreline that looked miles long. Down the beach, another larger pier extended farther out into the water. Attached to one side of it was a pool house. Even from this distance, Raphael could see water glistening from a giant swimming pool. Up on a hill above the beach, surrounded by giant palms, fruit trees, and exotic flowers, was a massive Spanish-style villa.

"It's beautiful, sir."

"Let's not be so formal. Call me Stan."

Swallowing back the panic at what this man would do to him if he ever found out Raphael was here as a spy, he nodded his agreement. "Stan it is."

"Let's head up to the house and get you settled." Since Raphael stood a good five inches above Reddington, the older man wrapped a strong arm around his waist and pushed him forward. "After you refresh yourself, you can come down to lunch and meet the rest of the family."

"Lance is here?"

The mouth that had been smiling so pleasantly, now twisted with bitterness. "No, unfortunately, Lance is still away."

Raphael hadn't seen Lance since the night of Jamie Kendrick's rescue. He'd done what Noah had told him to do: unlock the back door and then stay the hell out of the way. To avoid suspicion, the police had arrested Raphael along with all the other men that night. Noah had retrieved him hours later.

Stanford Reddington and his son seemed to have little in common except, perhaps, morals. They looked nothing alike. Lance was tall and slender, with brown hair and light blue eyes. And where Stanford was always friendly and personable, Lance was belligerent and sarcastic. It had been a huge disappointment to Raphael when he'd heard that Lance and his father weren't going to prison.

"So Lance is still in Germany?"

"Yes, though I'm hopeful he'll be able to come home

for a visit soon." Putting the smile back in place, Stanford beamed up at Raphael. "Perhaps he'll make it home before you have to leave."

The nod Raphael gave was as noncommittal as he could manage. The invitation hadn't come with a timeline. How long Reddington intended for him to stay, he didn't know. But as long as he was here, he planned to make the best use of his time.

Smiling down at the man who seemed to like him a little too much, Raphael said, "That would be wonderful."

As Reddington led him up a long walkway, Raphael took in the grandeur. Had the man's legitimate businesses bought him his wealth or was slave trading responsible for all of this?

Stepping onto a tiled patio, Stanford threw his arms out again in an extravagant, grandiose way—something he seemed to do a lot. "Welcome home, Raphael."

Before Raphael could question Reddington's strange wording, he heard a sound behind him.

"Papa?"

The musical, feminine voice had both men turning their heads. All the breath left Raphael's body. The girl was beautiful: tall, slender, with long black hair and large, dark brown eyes. She wore a short yellow dress, revealing smooth golden skin and the longest, sleekest legs Raphael had ever seen.

"Giselle, my love. This is the young man I told you about. Come say hello."

Dry-mouthed and speechless, Raphael stood rooted to the ground as she came closer.

"Raphael, this is my oldest daughter, Giselle."

He knew he held out his hand, because he could feel her small, soft hand in his. Words were a different matter. The best he could do was offer her a nod.

Thankfully, she seemed fine with his nonverbal greeting. "It's nice to meet you, Raphael. Papa has talked of nothing but how pleased he is about your coming for a visit."

With a warm and friendly smile, she waited silently for him to respond. And Raphael would have loved to do just that; unfortunately, he couldn't get his mouth to work. He wasn't usually shy or awkward, but this beautiful girl left him speechless.

Apparently realizing that he wasn't going to speak, she turned to her father. "Mama told me to tell you we're having lunch on the second-floor terrace today."

"Excellent. Raphael and I will join you in a moment."

With one last smile, she glided away from them. There was no way he could make his eyes move away until she disappeared from sight. Even knowing that her father could see his expression, Raphael couldn't force himself to do the smart or wise thing.

"I see my Giselle has caught your eye."

Finally words returned to Raphael's brain. Clearing his throat, he turned to the older man and said, "She's lovely."

Instead of looking disturbed that Raphael had practically salivated over his daughter in front of him, Reddington's face brightened with the broadest, friendliest smile he'd ever seen from the man. "Exactly what I was hoping for."

With those enigmatic words, he pushed Raphael forward. "Let me show you to your room, and then you can meet the rest of the family."

Feeling as though the earth had just shifted on its axis, Raphael followed the man inside. What was the real reason Reddington had invited him here?

Last Chance Rescue headquarters
Paris

Raphael had disappeared. It'd been a long time since Noah had been this furious with himself. How the hell could he have agreed to let the young man do this? And now he had no idea where he was or what kind of trouble he was in.

After hearing about Reddington's invitation, Noah had banked on the man not being suspicious of Raphael. Hell, Reddington was the one who'd reinitiated contact. But the old slave trader had been around too long to take chances, even with people he supposedly trusted.

An LCR operative had been outside Raphael's apartment when a limo had arrived. According to the operative, Raphael's cellphone had been dumped into a waste can before they'd even let him inside. The operative had followed the limo to a small airstrip outside Madrid and had even managed to get hold of the flight plan the pilot had filed. They knew the plane had landed at another small airstrip, outside Lisbon, Portugal. They also knew that he'd gotten into another plane, but that's when contact had been lost. The second pilot hadn't filed a flight plan, and no amount of digging could turn up where the plane had landed.

Noah had to regroup. Finding Reddington had already been a needle-in-the-haystack, going-nowhere, piece-of-shit investigation. And now this.

"You know, if you continue pacing like that, you'll wear a hole in the carpet."

Lucas Kane's calm voice did nothing to ease Noah's anger at himself. "There's got to be a way to find this bastard."

"Do we know where the son is?" McKenna asked.

"Germany," Noah answered grimly. "And that's all we know."

McKenna jumped up and joined Noah in his pacing. "We've got to get to Reddington before Jamie finishes her training."

"Have you talked with her lately?" Noah asked.

"We talked last night."

"And she still thinks you're on board with her plan."

McKenna's lips trembled with emotion. "She knows we're all searching for Reddington. I told her that if we can get to him first, we will." Her desperate eyes took in Noah's and Lucas's. "We've got to find him before she tries to do this on her own."

"And she's given you no idea how she's planning on getting to him?"

"None. She just said she had an in that no one else would have."

"How's her training going?"

"I can't speak for Dylan, but she seemed pleased with her progress."

Noah sat down again and sprawled back in his chair. "She give you any idea of a timeline? I'm assuming that at some point she's going to say she's had enough training and just go for it."

"Two more months."

"Then our timeline is one month. Let's find the bastard before Jamie finishes her training and before Reddington gets any idea that Raphael isn't the puppet he seems."

nine

West Virginia mountains

Panting lightly, Jamie circled her opponent. The gleaming challenge in Dylan's eyes told her he was going to be more than ready for whatever she threw at him. Though a master at keeping his thoughts hidden, Dylan occasionally gave off some tells. After several weeks of training with him, she'd learned a few. For just an instant, his eyes flickered to her left hand. He thought she was going to jab with her left and then follow up with a kick. Satisfied that she'd read him correctly, Jamie threw a single kick toward his middle. The next second, she was on her butt looking up at the too handsome, slightly smirking man.

"You got too cocky."

She snorted and took the hand he held out to help her up. "This coming from the man who could have a PhD in cockiness."

"That was my goal, but I chose psychology and English instead."

Jamie showed no excitement and barely any interest in this rare nugget of information he'd just tossed her. She had discovered that if she seemed the least bit inquisitive, Dylan shut down. Not that she'd learned much anyway. She knew he'd grown up around Georgia and Florida, that he'd lived with his grandmother for several years before she'd died, and that his father had killed his mother. That wasn't a lot, but it was more than she'd known before. And despite the man's irritating grumpiness and gruffness, he still managed to fascinate her.

She grabbed a bottle of water she'd placed on the floor beside the mat and took a long swallow. Replacing the cap, she put the bottle down and said casually, "I went to a small college outside Baton Rouge, but my dream university was Tulane. Where'd you go?"

"University of Georgia for my undergrad and then Florida State for my master's."

"Master's in psychology?"

"Yeah."

Afraid that he'd shut down if she questioned him further, she threw him her best smirk and said, "Well, analyze this!" With those words, she shot out the quick left punch and kick she'd thought he'd expected before. The blow glanced off his chin and the kick barely pushed him backward, but, dammit, she'd made contact.

She stepped back a few feet and grinned.

"I think we've found your best weapon."

"What's that?"

"Say something to throw your opponent off, then take him down."

"Who knew being a smart-ass would come in handy?"

"Don't overuse it."

She cocked her head. "You're serious, aren't you?"

"Hell yeah, I'm serious. To survive, you use every weapon at your disposal, especially the unexpected ones."

"What? I don't look like a smart-ass?"

"No, you look like a—"

"I look like a what?"

"A fairy princess."

Jamie couldn't have been more shocked if he'd told her she looked like a Vegas showgirl. She knew she was attractive, but Dylan's words called to mind more than a pretty woman. He saw an innocence and purity in her. Jamie swallowed the lump in her throat. It had been so long since she'd felt innocent or pure . . . or even pretty.

"Thank you, Dylan."

He bent to grab a towel, but not before she saw a slight flush bloom over his face. Dylan . . . blushing? The day was full of surprises.

Without a hint of warning, Dylan dropped the towel, lunged toward her, and grabbed her in a choke hold. Instinctively, Jamie raised her right arm and poked him in the trachea. Dylan backed away slightly, and Jamie followed with a punch to his neck. When he bent over, she threw a kick to his stomach.

She'd learned during their first day of hand-to-hand training to pull back on her punches. Last week, Dylan had started wearing protective gear. He'd told her she needed to get used to the feel of a real hit. Still, when it came to certain unprotected areas of his body, like his throat, she held back.

Dylan nodded his approval. "You did good."

Praise from Dylan was rare, making the words even more special. Glowing from his approval, she asked, "What's next?"

"This." With that, he whirled her around and grabbed both of her arms. Jamie slammed her head back against his face and stomped on his foot. The instant Dylan's hands dropped, she whirled away. His hands were covering his face, so she delivered a quick kick to his upper torso and then backed away.

Dylan lowered his arms and said, "Okay, what'd you do wrong here?"

She grimaced. "I should've run when your hands were on your face."

"Remember, survival is the name of the game, not beating the hell out of him. Okay?"

She nodded, irritated that she'd needed the reminder.

"Let's take a break."

Jamie picked up her towel and wiped her face. Her adrenaline still in overdrive, she went back to the mat. "I think I'm going to practice a little more."

"Don't overdo it. If the weather cooperates tomorrow, we'll go out to the obstacle course."

She nodded and tried not to grimace. They'd moved on to the second course a week ago. Since Dylan could finish it in under a minute and it was still taking Jamie almost three minutes, she knew she needed the practice. Her speed was faster than when she'd first tackled the course, but not fast enough. If Dylan was a tough taskmaster on the self-defense training, he was a drill sergeant on the obstacle course. When she'd asked him why he was so much tougher, his explanation had been characteristically brief and blunt. With those green eyes almost flat and lifeless, he'd drawled, "Reddington finds out who you are, you damn well better be able to jump, climb, and crawl with extreme speed. If not, he'll kill you."

From then on, she had worked even harder at improving her time.

Aware that Dylan was leaning against the wall, watching her, Jamie went into her stance and then did her best to force him out of her mind.

Dylan took a long swallow of water as he kept an eye on Jamie's movements. What she lacked in strength, she made up for with grace and precision. She wasn't a natural, but that didn't concern him. He'd never seen anyone more determined. He had no worries that once she left here, she would know how to defend herself against any predator who came her way. That still couldn't include Reddington and his henchmen.

Even though she hadn't mentioned her purpose for training in a while, he knew she hadn't changed her mind. She still planned on going after the bastard.

Dylan's plans hadn't changed, either. He still had every intention of thwarting those plans.

When she'd first arrived, she'd told him her timeline was approximately three months. Time had moved quickly, and he now had just a little over a month left to convince her that she couldn't handle such a job, but he had to do so without destroying the confidence she'd gained. When he'd agreed to this, he'd known it wouldn't be easy. Being attracted to the person you were training was bound to hinder your concentration. Turned out, it hadn't. Oh, the attraction was still there—had grown even stronger. But Jamie's determination to learn had helped him focus on making sure she learned everything she could. Saving her life was his number one priority.

He had hoped that LCR would have found Reddington's hiding place by now. Giving her the news that she no longer needed to worry about the bastard would've been worth all of the sleepless nights.

She had no idea that she was driving him crazy. He'd made sure of that. Since being an asshole was as natural as breathing to him, he knew exactly how to act to keep her from guessing.

He'd never met anyone like Jamie. After all the things that had happened to her, she maintained a shining optimism. One that refused to be shattered by the deeds of evil men. She was like sunshine.

Mentally rolling his eyes at his thoughts, Dylan took the last swallow of water from his bottle and pitched it into a recycling bin. He'd already told her she looked like a fairy princess today. Now he was thinking of sunshine. Where this weird shit came from, he didn't know. Didn't want to know. He liked women. Hell, he'd been married to a stunningly beautiful woman and never had he considered spouting poetry or flowery words. Of course, the fact that Sheila had been an amoral bitch might've prevented that.

"I've got some things I need to do. Take a break for the rest of the day."

She completed the strike-kick combination and then stopped. "For the whole day?"

He almost smiled at her dismay. "Watch some training DVDs. Give your body a rest. I'd like to see you cut your time on the course in half tomorrow. If you're sore, that's not going to be possible."

Fighting the compulsion to kiss the little pout that curved her mouth, Dylan turned away and headed upstairs without waiting for a reply. Most days he could ignore that need, but lately, it had become a constant want.

What would she do if he kissed her? Held her against him and let her feel the arousal that never eased? Would she be surprised? Run away, afraid of him? Or would she respond?

Dylan slammed the door to his bedroom and dropped into a chair by the window. Snow still covered a large part of the grounds, but it had been raining the last couple of days, melting much of it into a sloppy mass of slush. The heavy snowfall this winter had been a hindrance for more than one reason. Being able to use the obstacle course only a few days each week had slowed down her training. He wanted Jamie to be able to defend herself, but he also wanted her to be able to escape from whatever situation she might find herself in someday.

That wasn't the only detriment, though. Being cooped up in the cabin with her had increased his awareness and desire. Sexual denial wasn't a new thing for him. While on an op, which could take weeks or months, either those kinds of needs got put on the back burner or he took things into his own hands. With Jamie, the desire was front and center, and easing his own arousal was about as appealing as eating dry toast.

Cursing his weakness, Dylan grabbed the phone on the bedside table. Time to check in with McCall.

His ear to the phone, Dylan barely heard half a ring before McCall picked up. "Still nothing."

Sighing at the news, he rubbed a finger against a throb between his eyes. "No word from Raphael?"

"Nothing other than that cryptic email."

Raphael had been with Reddington for almost a month now. Two weeks ago, he'd sent an email to Noah at a dummy address LCR had set up to intercept messages for undercover ops. The sender could put anything in the address, as long as it contained the correct combination and a certain sequence of letters and numbers, and the message would get to LCR. And McCall was right about cryptic. The email had been two lines: *Please suspend my subscription to* The Lark *magazine. Will renew upon my return.*

An obscure magazine in Spain called *The Lark* covered nightlife for Madrid and the surrounding areas, and according to reliable intel, Raphael did indeed have a subscription. However, he had sent the email to LCR; the message had been for Noah.

They'd spent days trying to decipher what Raphael had been trying to convey. Three conclusions were finally made: Raphael was alive; he was staying for an indefinite period of time; and—possibly the biggest stretch—he was trying to reveal his location. Samara, Noah's wife, had come up with the idea of the Canary Islands.

Raphael was untrained in LCR ways, but using a bird's name in his message seemed too coincidental not to consider. Each operative had to learn code words and phrases that said one thing and meant something else. If he was using Reddington's computer to send the message, he had to know the man would read the email.

Having a subscription to the magazine only helped it look like a credible message.

Problem was, the Canary Islands covered a damn big area. So until they received better intel or something more from Raphael, they continued to search for a man who seemed to have disappeared into thin air.

"We did get one bit of good news, though 'good' is a helluva description to use."

Dylan sat up in his chair. "What's that?"

"We think he's going to be resuming business soon."

"How do you know?"

"A few of our sources have heard that Reddington's infamous market day is coming back."

McCall was right: "good news" was a relative term here. If Reddington was headed back to his marketing-day sales, that meant he was back in the business of trading and selling humans.

"Any idea when?"

"Within the month."

Hell.

"How's the training?"

"Other than her speed, she's doing damn good. The weather has hindered the outside training."

"Yeah, we've been hit hard here, too. I'll keep you updated."

"Thanks." Dylan looked out at the melting snow again; an odd desperation filled him. He was running out of time.

Jamie stretched and worked to loosen her muscles. She hadn't run the course in days, but she felt more ready than she'd ever been before. During the last week, her strength and stamina had increased tremendously. Without a doubt, she would cut her time in half today.

With an expression even darker than usual, Dylan held his stopwatch in his hand and snapped, "Ready?"

Jamie concentrated her full focus on the course ahead of her, then shouted, "Ready!"

"Go!"

She took off. The very air seeming to give her an extra lift, she leaped over wooden hurdles, one after the other. Dropping to her hands and knees, she tunneled through a short tube and then sprang to her feet. Her concentration fierce, she ran to the sand trap, grabbed hold of the rope, and swung over the oblong area. With barely a pause to land, she leaped over two more hurdles, ran through tires, and then climbed over a short wall. Landing on the other side, her breath coming in controlled pants, she looked up in triumph at Dylan. She already knew she'd made great time.

"Ninety-eight seconds."

Delight filled her. "Really? That's even better than I thought it was."

"It's better. Still not good enough."

"Well, at least give me credit for almost cutting my time in half."

His gaze cutting like green glass, he snarled, "You think Reddington's going to say, 'Hey, Jamie, you impressed me so much with your speed, I won't kill you'?"

Her hands went to her hips. "Dammit, I thought my goal here was to improve my speed. The least you can do is say something positive before you get so hateful."

"I don't have time to be positive. You're here to get trained, not get gold stars." He looked down at his stopwatch. "Do it again."

Cursing softly at his stubbornness, Jamie bent over and put her hands on her knees. She needed her breath back before she tried it again. What Dylan's problem was, she couldn't begin to fathom. Yesterday, after she'd come back upstairs from practicing by herself, he hadn't been around. Last night, he'd said only a handful of words to her. This morning, he hadn't even bothered with that much. The last couple of weeks, he hadn't been verbose by any stretch of the imagination, but at least he'd been civil. Now he was back to acting the way he had when she'd first arrived.

"Any time now, Jamie."

The overexaggerated feigned patience putting her teeth on edge, Jamie went to the starting point and glared at him in challenge.

"Go!"

Fury giving her impetus, she flew over the hurdles and scampered through the tunnel like a four-legged creature. Triumphant at her improved speed and skill, she spared a glance at Dylan. The hollow look in his eyes startled her. What was his problem? She grabbed hold of the rope and swung across the sand trap. Rattled, her concentration off, she let go too soon and landed face-first on the sand.

Stunned, she felt panic seize her as her lungs worked to expel breath that wasn't there. She couldn't breathe. Hard, callused hands turned her over gently. She stared up at Dylan, unable to find the air to speak.

His deep voice soothing, he said, "Take it easy. You just got the wind knocked out of you. You'll be fine."

The roaring in her ears decreased; seconds later, her breath returned. Jamie focused on Dylan's dark green gaze as she pulled air back into her starved lungs. Feeling somewhat normal, but totally embarrassed, she put her elbows on the ground to lift herself up. Dylan's grasped her shoulders, holding her in place.

She frowned up at him. "Let me up."

"No, I need to check for broken bones."

"I'm fine."

"I'm checking. Stay still."

Since his tone brooked no argument, Jamie lay silent and unmoving while Dylan ran his hands up and down her body. Though his touch was impersonal, she was acutely aware that the hands belonged to a man she was both crazy about and wanted to smack on a daily basis. Other than their practice sessions, this was the first time he'd ever really touched her. The anger she'd felt before disappeared as desire unfurled and bloomed, heating her from the inside out.

It was all Dylan could do to keep his hands from shaking as he ran them up and down Jamie's soft, slender body. His heart had been in his throat when she'd fallen; now he was putting himself through more hell by touching her. Dammit, where was that iron control he used to pride himself on?

"Dylan?"

As Jamie's soft voice pulled him from his crazy, reckless thoughts, he moved his gaze to her face. And lost his battle. Her eyes were heated, filled with a want that echoed within him. With a groan of surrender, he lowered his head and took her mouth. He softly teased her lips, her taste sweeter than every fantasy he'd ever had. When he felt her hands on his shoulders, pulling him closer, he licked at her lips, seeking a sweeter, deeper taste. The opening of her mouth took his breath. There was no hesitancy in her actions. Her tongue met and dueled with his, drawing at him.

Lowering his body over hers, careful of his weight, he propped himself on his arms, allowing only his lips to touch her. Angling his mouth, he pressed deeper, withdrew, and plunged again. Thrusting and retreating, over and over, mimicking the motion for what another part of him ached to do.

Soft, insistent hands tugged at him, pulled him closer. Dylan lowered himself until he lay on top of her. Still mindful of his big body over her much smaller one, he tried to keep most of his weight off her. Jamie was having none of it. Pulling him harder, she spread her legs and allowed him to settle between them. Dylan nudged his erection against her mound. They groaned into each other's mouths at the delicious contact.

Warm, soft hands moved beneath his shirt. Needing the same contact, Dylan slid a hand under her sweatshirt and felt the soft, supple skin he'd dreamed about for months. Silky and firm, she was every man's fantasy . . . and Dylan's only dream.

A dream that couldn't come true.

What the hell was he doing? Pulling away from her abruptly, he looked down to see her soft eyes looking up at him with a desire he'd never imagined. Holy hell, what had he done?

"Dylan, what's wrong?"

"We can't do this."

She laughed softly. "I admit it's a little damp and chilly, but I—"

He pushed himself away from her and stood. "I can't do this."

Not moving, she lay there, so damn beautiful, so damned desirable, so damn out of his reach.

Self-control firmly back in place, he ignored his need along with the shock in her eyes, which was quickly turning to hurt, and glanced down at his watch. "Run the course one more time; then we'll call it a day."

"No."

"What?"

Scooting on the ground to get away from him, she stood. Fury and hurt intermingled in her eyes. "You heard me. I'm tired of your arrogance and your hatefulness."

"I warned you going in that this wasn't going to be fun time. You're the one—"

"Yes, I'm the one who wanted to learn how to defend herself." Burying her hurt beneath an avalanche of anger, Jamie let wrath take full control. Her body shaking with a myriad of bubbling emotions, she took a giant step toward him. "I'm the one who wants to go after the creep who's kidnapping people and selling them like they're meaningless property. I've done nothing wrong, and yet you've treated me as if I'm guilty of some kind of crime."

His face expressionless once more, Dylan shook his head. "Not for a second do I think you've done anything wrong. You've misinterpreted my intent."

Damn, he was good. "So it's my misinterpretation that's the problem here. Not you."

"I don't see that there is a problem. I'm your trainer; you're the student. If you don't like it, you're welcome to leave."

"And what just happened? Is that part of your training program—an approved LCR technique?"

Something flickered in his expression, so fleeting that she couldn't read it before it was replaced with an even colder mask. "That was a mistake."

What had been one of the most magnificent moments of her life had just been ground to dust with four simple words. Fury, hurt, and a thousand other emotions swirled together into a combustible firestorm she couldn't contain. Whirling around, she took off running.

"Jamie, dammit. Where the hell do you think you're going?"

"Away from you."

"Get in the truck. I'll take you back."

She spared him a contemptuous glance. "I'll walk back to Paris before I accept anything from you again."

She heard a softly worded "Shit."

With her fury leading the way, the fact that she didn't know where she was going didn't stop her. At some point she'd end up on a road somewhere. Walking back to Paris might not be possible, but she had told the truth. Dylan Savage had stomped on her feelings for the last time. She hadn't learned all that she needed to learn, which meant she would have to go to Plan B and find someone to finish up her training. If she never saw Dylan again, it'd be too soon for her.

Yes, she knew that the biggest part of her anger was her hurt at his reaction to their kiss. After months of wanting that stern, beautiful mouth on hers, needing him with a want she'd never imagined, he had finally given her what she wanted and then had taken it all back.

Anger receded, cooled by the frozen and slushy snow she trudged through. Galloping aimlessly through a frozen mass of yuck dressed only in long tights, a sweatshirt, and running shoes wasn't the brightest move she could have made. The temperature was rapidly falling, and the heat generated by her anger was fading away. Shivering, Jamie hugged herself for warmth.

"Jamie. Stop!"

Refusing to turn around, she increased her pace. Easy to do, since she was going downhill. When she reached a flat area, she sped up, almost running now. Though the mushy wet mess had now soaked her shoes, no way was she going back.

"Jamie, dammit. Look at me!"

She shouted, "Leave me alone!"

"You have to stop. Now! Don't move."

Something in his voice caught her attention. She stopped and turned. Dylan stood several yards away from her . . . his expression of alarm alerting her that something was very wrong.

"I want you to walk slowly toward me. Don't veer off. Take the same steps you took before."

Wary, no longer willing to give him her total trust, she asked, "Why?"

"Because this flat area holds the runoff of the snow. You're standing in the middle of a frozen pond. I don't know how solid it is."

Great, Jamie. The one time you stomp off in a huff, you end up needing to be rescued again.

She looked down at the footprints she'd made. Having no choice but to head back the way she came, Jamie stepped in the first print. Relieved that it seemed to have no impact, she took another, then another.

"You're doing good," Dylan shouted. "Just a few more—"

Something moved beneath her foot. Her head jerked up, she managed to scream, "Dylan!" before she plunged through the ice and was swallowed whole.

ten

Fear rocketing through him, Dylan whipped his head around, looking for a tree branch . . . anything he could use. Seeing absolutely nothing, he did the only thing he could. Running forward, he reached the spot where Jamie had disappeared.

Her head bobbed back up, her eyes wild with panic.

With time of the essence, he dropped his body to lie flat on the ice and demanded, "Give me your hand."

A slender, sodden arm came up, uncoordinated and almost lifeless. Dylan grabbed hold and pulled. The ice shifted beneath him. Dammit, it wasn't going to hold.

Adrenaline, fueled by panic, gave him a strength he never would have had on his own. With one long, hard jerk, he pulled her completely out of the water.

She landed beside him—soaked to the skin and freezing. Praying that his luck would hold, Dylan scooped her into his arms, and stood. Taking long, swift strides, he ran for safety. The cracking, shifting ice beneath his feet warned him that time had run out.

Pressing Jamie tight against his chest, he growled, "Hold on!" and leaped. Flying through the air, he shifted his body in mid-flight and landed with a hard thud on his side, with Jamie on top of him.

Fear running like a rampaging river through him, Dylan looked at the soaked, shivering woman in his arms. "Are you okay?"

Her eyes wide with pain and fear, she nodded. Shudders quaked through her body; her lips, blue from the cold, tried to form words and managed only a stuttered whisper: "C-c-cooold."

It was at least half a mile to his truck. Thick clouds now covered the sun, and the temperature had dropped dramatically . . . was probably in the lower twenties. He made a decision she might not like, but at this point, he didn't care. He went to his knees, pulled her beside him and with quick, efficient moves stripped off her clothes.

She never protested . . . never said anything. Her eyes were locked on his, motionless in her deathlike white face. There was no change of expression. Was she going into shock?

He whipped his sweatshirt off, wrapped it around her, lifted her in his arms, and took off again. He had to get her into some warm water and get some hot liquid inside her. If not, hypothermia could set in.

As he ran, he started a one-sided conversation, having no real idea what he was saying. Keeping her awake was imperative. Though she still didn't talk, her eyes never left his face.

The sight of his SUV was the most beautiful one he'd ever seen. He opened the passenger door and hauled himself inside, still holding Jamie tight in his arms. He pressed the start button and the engine rumbled to life. With a flip of the heat switch, air blasted on high—cold but it was still warmer than outside. Scooting sideways, he slammed his foot on the gas pedal and shot forward. He was five minutes from the cabin.

"Dylan?" she whispered.

He glanced down to see that her eyes were closed. "No. Open your eyes, Jamie. You can't go to sleep."

Her eyelids fluttered, and he knew she was doing her best to stay awake. Hoping to get a reaction from her, he said, "You're right. I'm an asshole."

Though her entire body shook as if she had palsy, her

lips twitched slightly as if she were trying to smile but it was too much effort. "You think I'm going to argue with you?"

Her voice was weak, but he heard the amusement in her tone. An emotion he didn't recognize caused a sting in his eyes and a lump in his throat. "It'd be the first time you haven't argued."

"It's because you're so easy."

Seeing her eyes flickering closed again, he said, "Keep those eyes open. We're almost there."

Heavy eyelids blinked up at him. "Sorry I stormed off like that. Not very mature."

Since his own behavior had been adolescent at best, he had no room to criticize her. "I'm sorry for what I said."

"Wow, I think the earth just shook. Dylan Savage apologizing."

He snorted. "Don't get used to it."

Jerking to a stop in front of the cabin, he shoved open the door. "Can you put your arms around my neck?"

She nodded slowly and complied. His arms tight around her, Dylan jumped out of the cab and stalked inside the cabin.

Jamie locked her jaw to keep her teeth from chattering. She was cold . . . so very cold. And so very tired. Beneath half-closed eyes, she watched Dylan. The grim set of his mouth wasn't unusual, but the stark fear in his eyes was new. She'd been under the water for only a few seconds, but it had felt like an eternity. Once again, Dylan had been her rescuer.

He pulled out the vanity chair beneath the counter of her bathroom, dropped her into it, and then handed her a towel. "Sit here while I run some water. Okay?"

Her limbs so heavy with cold and exhaustion they felt like lead, Jamie lowered her head and patted at her streaming hair. Weary from the effort, she leaned back against the chair and held the towel against her chest for warmth.

His movements swift and sure, Dylan plugged the tub and turned the water on. Jamie eyed him dreamily. A part of her knew that if she didn't feel so cold and tired, she'd still be angry or, at the very least, hurt by what happened earlier. Right now, she wasn't thinking about that. All she could concentrate on was watching a shirtless Dylan draw her a bath while she fantasized about sharing it with him.

Yes, she knew it was a stupid, hopeless fantasy. The kiss had been an anomaly. He'd been aroused, but what healthy, heterosexual man wouldn't get an erection when a woman practically threw herself at him. She'd been the one to pull him closer, the one to pull him down and grind herself against him, the one to make room between her legs for him. Heat, welcome and intense, flooded through her at the memory.

"Can you stand?"

She nodded and pulled herself to her feet. When she swayed slightly, Dylan caught her by the shoulders. As much as she wanted to lean into him, she couldn't. He had made it clear that what had happened before was a mistake. She wouldn't compound that mistake by offering herself to him again. Making a fool out of herself twice today was going to be her quota.

"Here, let's get you into the water."

Holding her with one arm, Dylan pulled the shirt still wrapped around her and dropped it on the floor. Before she could protest, he lifted her in his arms and lowered her slowly into the water.

"It shouldn't be too hot. Feel okay?"

A delicious warmth spread through her body. "Feels wonderful."

"Still feeling sleepy?"

"A little."

"Lean back against the tub."

Sliding deeper into the water, Jamie leaned against the back of the tub and sighed. She knew she should be feeling some kind of embarrassment. Though she'd never been particularly shy about her body, a rational part of her brain reminded her that this man had just rejected her advances.

"I'm fine," she assured him. "You don't have to stay."

Instead of leaving or telling her he wasn't going anywhere until he knew she was fine, Dylan did something completely unexpected. Picking up the bottle of lemon-scented shampoo on the side of the tub, he poured a small amount into his palm and said, "Sit up a little."

Jamie sat up and then closed her eyes on a sigh at the glorious feel of Dylan's firm, hard fingers and hands slowly massaging her scalp. The fragrance of lemons wafted through the air, and every argument she had just given herself evaporated. Heat bloomed everywhere, and a moan escaped.

"Feel good?"

The husky, thick tone in his voice was so unusual, Jamie opened startled eyes to look at him. Desire, hot and potent, like a thousand blazing candles, burned in his eyes.

Too afraid to take that look for what she thought it was, she whispered, "Dylan?"

"Lie back so I can rinse your hair."

Her eyes locked with his as she lowered herself into the water. Dylan held her head in one of his big hands and used the other to rinse the soap from her hair.

No way he didn't see the need and want on her face. Not only that, her breathing had become more labored and her nipples were peaked . . . the thought of having his mouth on them made them even harder.

He finished rinsing. "Sit up a little."

Mesmerized, her body throbbing with anticipation of what might come next, Jamie once again sat up.

Dylan pushed her gently back against the tub and took a washcloth from the shelf beside him. He soaked the cloth with water and then tenderly bathed her face.

Needing to speed things up, to appease the desire thrumming through her body, and answer the aching throb between her legs, she said, "Dylan . . . please."

"Shh, just relax."

Her heart pounding, Jamie kept her eyes glued to his—the desire and need she saw in them turning her on almost as much as his hands. With intense concentration, Dylan moved from her face to her throat and then her shoulders. Her breath held in suspension, she felt the cloth move lower, to her breasts. When the cloth rubbed against a taut nipple, aching for his mouth, she was unable to control her gasp.

"Feel good?"

Swallowing hard, she whispered, "Yes."

The cloth moved to her other breast, and he circled her nipple gently; then he moved slowly, deliberately down her torso, over her stomach, and veered to her right hip. Jamie couldn't prevent a moan of disappointment that he hadn't gone to the spot that needed him the most.

The gentle lapping of the water as it moved over her body and the increased breathing—hers and his—were the only sounds in the room. She continued to watch his face carefully. The taut line of his jaw indicated that he was striving for control. Her gaze went back to his eyes. She had to know . . . had to ask. If he stopped and pulled back . . . if he said it was a mistake again, she wouldn't be able to handle it. "Dylan, what are you doing?"

"Making you feel good."

Because of what happened earlier? Did he feel guilty

about it and this was his way of making it up to her? That wasn't what she wanted. "You don't have to—"

"I want this . . . need this . . . please, Jamie?"

Tightness filled her chest. Big, gruff, and grumpy Dylan Savage was saying please . . . asking for permission to touch her. Giving up her body completely to his ministrations, Jamie relaxed against the tub again and watched as the cloth in his hand moved back up her leg and then stopped at the inside of her thigh. "Part your legs for me, sweetheart."

Whether it was the words or the acknowledgment of his first endearment, she didn't know. But the instant he spoke, the aching need between her legs grew stronger and became an unrelenting throb. Opening them, Jamie gasped as he tenderly rubbed the cloth over her mound and then in between the folds of her sex. As if consumed by a raging wildfire, all cold dissipated, and heat zoomed throughout her body. The throbbing became an excruciating, pulsing need, begging for an end to the increasing, tormenting pleasure.

Her whisper of "Please" was answered in the best way possible. Dylan dropped the cloth into the water and Jamie watched, breathlessly, as his fingers disappeared inside her. Strokes, gentle but firm, played and strummed at the top of her sex. Of their own volition, her legs went wider, and Dylan met her invitation by pushing his fingers even deeper. She pushed upward to meet him, her body clenched and spasmed, and a burning, glowing ecstasy followed. Her eyes closed as the intensity of orgasm hit its peak, bright flashes of light appearing before her closed lids.

She heard moans, gasps, and then a husky, aroused voice that sounded so unlike Dylan's growled, "Look at me."

Feeling languid and needy at the same time, she

opened her eyes. Dylan's expression held fierceness and more emotion than she'd ever thought she'd see in him.

"Do you want more?"

Unable to verbalize just how much, she splashed water everywhere as she reached for him. Grabbing his shoulders, she pulled him down and answered him with an openmouthed invitation against his lips. With a growling groan, Dylan put his hands around her waist and picked her up. Suddenly, Jamie was out of the tub, wet and deliciously aroused, and clinging to Dylan's hard body.

Never letting go of Jamie's lips, Dylan snagged a towel and headed into her bedroom. When he dropped her on the edge of the bed and began to dry her hair, she surprised the hell out of him and took the towel from his hands. "I can do this." Her gaze dropped to his pants. "Your clothes are all wet. Why don't you get out of them?"

The confident, sultry tone in her voice almost undid him. A sexually assertive Jamie was a turn-on beyond his imaginings. Dylan stripped, and in seconds was on the bed with her.

Their arms closing around each other, hands caressed, lips met, parted, delved into each other, and passion, need, and burning desire shut out everything else. The war Dylan had waged for so long was lost . . . the battle over, as a lifetime of denial disintegrated beneath an onslaught of fierce, burning need.

A brief semblance of sanity put passion on pause; he lifted his mouth from hers. "I don't have any condoms."

"I do."

At some point, he'd be shocked by that news and want to know more. For right now, he was too damn grateful to do anything other than ask, "Where?"

"Bedside table."

Dylan rolled over, found the package, and ripped into

it. Sliding the rubber onto his erection, he turned back to her and had to stop. He hadn't taken the time to relish this moment as he should have. He'd been about to mount her as if she were just another woman to slake his lust with, instead of who she was: the most beautiful, precious thing in the whole world.

He could've lost her today. His stupidity and arrogance could have cost him the one woman he'd gladly give his life for. The fact that he had no future with her no longer mattered. If he did nothing else right for the rest of his life, he would give Jamie a night to savor and remember forever.

With that in mind, Dylan retained control of his emotions and lust, and bent down to give her the satisfaction she deserved.

Lying on his side next to her, he pressed his mouth softly, briefly to hers and then feathered kisses, one after another, on her sweet lips. Her breath hitched, and Dylan took it into his mouth, blending her gasps with his own. Moving his mouth lower, he followed the silken skin beneath her chin and then her neck. Stopping at the hollow of her throat, he bathed her skin with his tongue. When she groaned, "Oh yes, Dylan, more," he thought he would lose it. Desire pounded through him, and he closed his eyes for a moment to regain control. After dreaming about this every night for months, damned if he'd rush to the end. Not when the journey was so unbelievably delicious and worthwhile.

"Are you okay?"

He opened his eyes to see Jamie's concerned face. A small smile lifted his mouth. "Yeah. Just want to take my time . . . but it's getting harder and harder." And he meant that literally.

Her fingers trailed down his chest in a soft, teasing caress. "You don't have to go slow."

"Shh." His tongue swirled around a taut, beautifully

erect nipple. A little gasping sigh and the way she arched her body, as if offering him more, told him she was right there with him.

Gliding his tongue over to her other breast, he sucked gently. He loved her taste, the sexy, sweet moves of her body, the soft moans she gave with each new area he licked. Dylan was quickly realizing that no matter how slow or how fast he went, he was never going to get enough of her.

Jamie groaned again as Dylan moved from her breasts over to her abdomen, stopping at her navel for a quick swirl of his tongue. She was going insane. Never had she realized how torturous pleasure could be. Her body was so ready for him, she could feel the warmth of her arousal on her inner thighs.

She closed her eyes on a gasping sigh. How much longer could Dylan hold out? How long could she?

The answer came faster than she expected. Opening her eyes, she watched Dylan move to the end of the bed . . . with deliberation and utmost care, his hands parted her thighs and pushed her legs up. And then his tongue was there—in the exact spot she needed it the most. Her body came off the bed, and with a soft scream, pleasure flooded through her.

She came back to herself and realized that Dylan was gently licking, softly thrusting. She was still throbbing, the deliciousness of her release still zooming through her, and amazingly, she felt a new tension, another need. This time, she wanted him with her.

"Dylan, please . . . come inside me."

He raised his head, and Jamie lost what breath she'd been able to catch. His expression was a look of such need and want, she almost cried. Holding out her arms to him, she said softly, "Come here. Please."

With a guttural groan, Dylan lowered himself over her and, with one hard thrust, buried himself deep.

Jamie wrapped her legs around his hips and held him as his control shattered. As he plunged and retreated over and over, she held on, loving the hard body above her, the steely hard penis inside her. This was what she'd wanted for what seemed like forever. And then all thought and reason disappeared as climax was upon her again—sweeter, hotter, and even more wonderful than before. Jamie closed her eyes and let the magic happen once more.

As if he'd been waiting for her release, Dylan increased his thrusts, covered her mouth, and plunged his tongue with the same earth-shattering rhythm of his erection. And as he issued another deep growl, Jamie felt the throbbing inside her. Then his entire body stiffened and he came.

His breathing labored, Dylan moved off her and held her close. Jamie snuggled against his chest. She wanted to ask him what he was thinking. What did this mean to him? Had it been momentous and life-changing . . . as it had for her? Or was this just a life-affirming event after the scary experience in the water?

Too afraid to ask . . . to know the truth, Jamie closed her eyes and treasured these moments in his arms, because a growing dark dread within told her it might be the last chance she ever had.

Dylan looked down at the woman in his arms. Her face glowed softly, and a small, satisfied smile covered her beautiful mouth. She looked happy, content. But he had to ask . . . had to make sure. "No bad moments?"

Her eyes lit up and, if anything, her expression grew even more content. "Absolutely none at all."

Swallowing an unexpected lump in his throat, he tightened his arms around her and blew out a silent sigh of relief. He'd seen and felt no hesitancy, no fear. She'd gone into his arms willingly, passionately, eagerly. But until he'd heard those words, he hadn't been completely sure.

He didn't want to think about the monumental event that had just taken place. His body felt sated and at peace—a feeling he hadn't had in years. Hell, had he ever felt this way? The answer would be no. He'd had sex before. This had been on a whole different plane.

From the moment he'd rescued her, seen the tears shimmering in her eyes and that brave, determined chin lifted in defiance, he had loved her. For a man who'd never loved anyone other than the frail old woman who'd taken him in when the law finally caught up with his old man, to acknowledge that he loved Jamie was huge. Not that admitting it changed a damn thing. His life and her life had intersected because of one horrific incident. That was it. If things had been normal, she would have gone back to her former life and he would have gone on with his. That was still going to happen; it had just been delayed a while. With Reddington not getting the punishment he deserved and Jamie's need for retribution, matters had gotten complicated. Once Reddington was behind bars, life could go back to the way it was meant to be.

He'd fucked up a lot of things over the years, but this might be his biggest mistake yet. How the hell was he going to explain that what had just happened couldn't happen again . . . shouldn't have happened at all? He didn't want to hurt her . . . but, hell, was it possible not to?

"You know, all of that thinking can give you a headache."

Should've known he wouldn't be able to hide from her for long. Since telling her his thoughts would either hurt her or start an argument neither of them could win, he asked a question that pleasure had relegated to the back of his mind until now. "Why'd you bring a box of condoms with you?"

She was silent for several seconds and then said, "I like to blow them up and make little animals out of them."

Chuckling at the image, he tightened his arms around her and asked quietly, "Why, Jamie?"

She shrugged. "Because I hoped. That's why."

"Hoped what?"

Rising up on her elbow, she gazed down at him. Her hair looked like a dark gold waterfall around her slender shoulders, and Dylan clenched his fist to keep from grabbing a handful of it and rubbing it against his face to inhale the fresh scent. She looked like a mussed, rumpled, deliciously satisfied angel. Unable to keep from touching her, he brushed a damp strand of hair from her face. "What did you hope?"

"You can't be surprised that I was attracted to you."

No, he'd seen it in her eyes . . . one of the many reasons he'd been such an ass. Had thought that if she hated him, the hero worship would pass. Instead, she had taken his snarls and given them right back to him.

Apparently not expecting an answer, she said, "Can I ask you a question?"

He tried not to react, but despite his efforts, he found himself holding his breath. A lifetime of hiding behind a mask of indifference had already cracked wide open today. Sharing more was well beyond his limits. Nevertheless, he had to say, "Yeah. What?"

Though the room was dim, he had no trouble seeing the hesitancy in her expression or the glint of hurt in her eyes. Guilt stabbed him deep. After sharing her body in the most selfless way possible, she had every right to ask him anything she wanted.

"What will LCR do to Reddington if they can get the proof they need?"

It wasn't the question she wanted to ask . . . he knew that much. She had probably realized the pointlessness of asking anything personal. His chest tightened. Jamie was already recognizing the reality—she couldn't count on him. Though it was a necessary lesson, that didn't lessen the regret he felt for hurting her.

If he could give her nothing else, he could give her this assurance. "It's a question not of if, but when. We will find what we need. And when we do, we'll have enough evidence to prove, without a shadow of a doubt, what he's been doing. No amount of money or influence will protect him then. He'll go to prison forever, Jamie. I promise you that."

"And his son?"

"Since he was grooming the kid to take over for him, we'll do our best to nail him, too. Just depends on what evidence we can get on his involvement."

Nodding, she put her head back on his chest, and without any effort at all, Dylan closed his arms around her. Stupid, he knew. They needed to get up. Jamie was still damp from her soaking . . . her hair was still damp, and she needed a meal after all the energy she'd expended during the last few hours.

This was the first time in days she'd brought up Reddington. He should be asking her questions, trying to ease out any information she was keeping from them. Hell, he just needed to get away from her before he did something else stupid. Instead, he held her tighter and savored the warmth of her soft, delicate body.

Surprising him, she was the one to pull away. "I think I'll go start dinner."

Dylan lay still and watched her get dressed. "How are you feeling?"

In the middle of buttoning her shirt, she looked at him. "Hungry and kind of tired but not too bad . . . considering."

"I'm sorry I pushed you."

"You didn't push me to do anything. You acted like an ass. I had a choice of either giving it right back to you or running. I made the wrong choice."

He had to smile at her logic. Trust Jamie to give her own interpretation of the events. "I shouldn't have acted that way."

"And I shouldn't have let you get away with it. When I first arrived here, you told me I was too easy. You're right, I am too easy. In more ways than I want to even contemplate right now." And with that mysterious double entendre, she walked out the door.

eleven

Jamie closed the door behind her before she said something else she would probably regret. She had no right to be hurt. Getting Dylan to open up and talk to her just because they'd had sex was ridiculous. He was a handsome, virile man who probably had sex quite frequently. She was the only woman around for miles. Maybe it only made sense that he'd eventually want sex with her. Reading more into it than that would only invite more pain and heartache. Still, no matter the reason, she refused to regret that it had happened.

She stopped at the entrance to the kitchen and leaned against the doorjamb. Okay, so what if her throat had a giant lump she couldn't seem to swallow around. When the man you're quite sure you're in love with makes love to you like he has to have you or he'll die and then when it's over, treats you like you just shared a delicious meal and nothing more, what woman wouldn't be a tad hurt?

Dylan wasn't going to open up with her and tell her his secrets. She had known that when she'd gone into his arms. That hadn't mattered at the time, but now that the passion had subsided, it did matter. She wanted to know him, but if he wasn't willing to share himself after what had happened today, expecting him to open up at any other time was a lost cause. The man wanted to keep himself at a distance. That was an attitude she needed to take, too.

Straightening her shoulders, Jamie set to work making a meal. After running the obstacle course, taking an icy dunk in the pond, and making love, she was famished and more than a little weak in the knees.

She felt Dylan's warmth behind her before she heard him. Strong, muscular arms encircled her and pressed her back against him. "Easy? No, sweetheart, there's nothing easy about you."

The heart that only a few seconds ago was set to be hard and unyielding went mushy again. Turning in his arms, Jamie pulled his head down and let him devour her mouth once more. Sweetly, insistently, he plumbed the depths, drawing a new passion from her. This was the kiss they should have shared after they'd made love. This was what she'd wanted and needed.

He pulled away slightly. "Want to play a game for the rest of the day?"

Surprised at the almost teasing glint in his eyes, she looked at him warily. "What kind of a game?"

"We're just two people, alone in a snowbound cabin, enjoying each other's company. There're no bad guys out there. Nothing and no one exists but the two of us."

Dylan wanted to play make-believe? This last year, her life had been all about fear, recovery, or retribution. The thought of allowing herself to forget for a few hours that nothing existed beyond this cabin was too enticing to refuse. And that Dylan had come up with the suggestion made it even more appealing. No way would she say no.

"Sounds wonderful."

"Good. So, what are we making for dinner?"

"I was thinking something quick and easy, like spaghetti."

"I'll brown the meat, you boil the pasta."

And with that, he released her. Lighthearted for the first time in forever, Jamie set to work. Usually when one of them cooked, the other one stayed out of the kitchen. She'd rarely cooked with anyone before; the short time she'd been married, her husband had come into the kitchen only to see what she was making for him.

Dylan's presence was both comforting and exciting. Jamie watched him out of the corner of her eye, enjoying how at ease he appeared. Since he was single and in his early thirties, it made sense that he'd cooked more than a few meals for himself.

She put on the water to boil and then dug into the back of the cabinet to find the bottle of red wine she'd discovered weeks ago. "Do we have a corkscrew?"

Instead of rummaging around in a drawer, looking for one, he worked his hand into his pocket and produced something. "Give it here."

Jamie handed him the bottle and watched him uncork the wine in seconds. "Wow, that's a handy little tool."

He handed the open bottle back to her. "The only thing my former wife gave me that I kept."

Her stomach dipped and she felt as if a huge hole had appeared beneath her feet. Dylan had been married? Would he tell her more? They had agreed on no talk of past events, but Dylan was too deliberate to make that kind of mistake, wasn't he? Testing him, she said, "You've been married?"

"Yeah, a long time ago."

"What was her name?"

"Sheila."

"Does she live in the U.S.?"

"Not anymore. She's dead."

Gasping, she turned around. "What happened?"

He shrugged. "An old boyfriend."

"I'm sorry."

"The marriage wasn't a good one, but she didn't deserve what happened to her."

Wanting to get the grim look off his face again, she

handed him a glass of wine. "Sip on this while I get the pasta sauce. What do you think about brownies for dessert?"

He took a swallow of the wine and nodded. "With ice cream and chocolate sauce?"

"Sounds wonderful."

"Jamie, it doesn't bother me to talk about her. Okay?"

Disturbed that he'd read her so well, but relieved that talking about his ex-wife didn't bother him, she asked, "How long were you married?"

"Almost two years."

As she began to mix the batter for the brownies, she said, "My marriage lasted barely a year."

"Where's your ex now?"

She shook her head. "Probably sleeping off a hangover somewhere, or maybe in jail again. After the judge gave him another month in jail, I left. Figured if he didn't know where I was, it was better for both of us."

"Sounds like a sleaze. How'd you meet him?"

She shoved the brownie pan into the oven and turned. "My senior year of college, he was in one of my classes. He was a good-looking guy who said all the right things." She grimaced. "Well, at least until after we were married."

Dylan handed her a glass of wine. "How about we not talk about former spouses?"

She took a sip of the fruity merlot and smiled. "Deal."

While finishing the dinner preparations, they skirted any personal or intimate topics. She learned that Dylan lived in an apartment in Paris, had a flat-screen television, and was an avid Atlanta Braves fan. Jamie knew almost nothing about sports. She had played a little softball in high school and remembered how much her dad had loved his Monday night football. Watching Dylan's expression when he talked about his favorite sport made Jamie wish she knew more so she could carry on an intelligent conversation about something he obviously enjoyed.

Once the food was set on the table, they grew quiet as they dug in. Jamie had always had a healthy appetite; tonight she was famished. Several minutes into the meal she looked up from her plate to see Dylan staring at her with a hot, hungry expression—as if he'd rather be devouring her than his dinner. Though the look thrilled her, setting off all sorts of heat sensors throughout her body, it also made her self-conscious and nervous. And, as usual, when she was nervous, she blurted out her thoughts: "Sex makes me hungry." Blushing to the roots of her hair, she backtracked and added, "I mean, I used up a lot of energy today."

His mouth curved slightly, but his eyes grew a dark forest green as they settled on her mouth. "I know what you mean."

Her meal no longer important, she said, "Want to go sit by the fire?"

He had to recognize the invitation . . . one she thought he'd jump on. Instead, he leaned back in his chair and took a swallow of his wine. "Finish your spaghetti. You might need the nourishment."

She hadn't thought she could get any hotter. Refusing to let nerves get in the way of a fantasy come true, Jamie attacked her plate with delicate savagery. Tomorrow the world would intrude once again. She would come down from this cloud of make-believe and remember what she was here for and the challenges ahead. For right now, she wanted to hold on to the magic just a little longer.

Dylan tried to ignore the loud voice blasting inside him, asking him if he'd lost his freaking mind. He'd been skating on the edge since they'd begun their training. Today, he'd plummeted into an abyss, and he had no idea if there was a way to return. Kissing her had been crazy wrong; what had happened next was so off the charts he had no words to describe it. And just now, his words had been of unmistakable intent.

The smart thing to do would be to get up from the table, apologize for being such a prick, and walk out the door. Let someone else finish her training. He could concentrate on finding Reddington. Putting the man behind bars would give Jamie the peace she needed. Staying here, making love to her, being with her like this—as if they were a normal couple—was insane.

Still, as he saw the contentment on her glowing face, watched her mouth tilt up in that sweet smile with her eyes gleaming like a satisfied cat's, he couldn't make himself do the smart or wise thing.

A future for them wasn't possible, but the future was tomorrow, and that was hours away. Dylan was human enough to want to stretch out a fantasy as long as possible. Standing, he took her hand and pulled her up and into his arms. "Why don't you go sit by the fire. I'll take care of the few dishes here and then bring you dessert."

She gave him a sweetly teasing smile. "A handsome man bringing me my favorite dessert in front of a roaring fire? Sounds like one of my fantasies."

Unable to let her go without tasting her again, he whispered against her lips, "Let's see how many fantasies we can accomplish tonight." And then, giving in to one of his own, he let his mouth come over hers, devouring and savoring the sweetness.

Tonight was all about pushing reality away. With that in mind, Dylan lifted Jamie into his arms and carried her to the living room. His mouth still connected to hers, he lowered her to the rug, in front of the fireplace.

Lifting his mouth, he whispered, "Be right back."

When he would have let her go, her slender arms tightened around his shoulders. "Wait."

"What?"

"Thank you."

He jerked at the words. "For what?"

"For this. I've never been romanced before."

If there was anyone who deserved to be romanced, it was this woman. And the truth was, he'd never romanced anyone before—he was going on instinct alone. Pressing a quick kiss to her mouth, he got to his feet. About to ask if she wanted ice cream with her brownie, he swallowed his words. He'd never seen anyone more beautiful. Her hair, no longer damp, had dried in a mass of golden waves and was spread out on the rug like ripples in a pond. Eyes, usually a clear blue-gray, were gleaming pools of midnight blue, and the mouth he'd just tasted, glistened from their kiss.

He held himself still as desire pounded through him . . . it was all he could do not to forget about dessert and devour her instead. The only thing that stopped him was the knowledge that if he went back for another taste, he wouldn't get up before he had tasted all of her again. Her body had already been through too much today. Damned if he'd increase her discomfort by taking her on the floor.

"Be right back." Before she could say something to tempt him even more, he hurriedly stacked the dishes in the dishwasher and then prepared a decadent dessert of warm brownie, vanilla ice cream, and chocolate sauce. Dessert in one hand, the bottle of chocolate sauce in the other, Dylan returned to the living room. He halted in mid-step, immediately putting his plans on indefinite hold.

Jamie had succumbed to the exhaustion of the day. She lay the way he'd left her, her expression one of soft, sleeping innocence. How the hell was he going to let her go?

The dessert in his hands no longer appealing, he returned to the kitchen and dumped it into the garbage. Returning to the den, he scooped Jamie up and carried her to her room. Not wanting to wake her, he eased her onto the bed, slipped off her shoes, and covered her with a blanket. He was about to leave when she whispered, "Dylan? Stay with me?"

Unable to deny himself this, Dylan settled onto the bed beside her. Tomorrow was soon enough to face reality. Tonight was still theirs.

Jamie woke the next morning with a small throbbing in her head, an ache in every muscle, and a smile on her face. Even though she'd fallen asleep and missed out on the dessert, she'd slept all night in Dylan's arms. And just before dawn, he'd woken her with a kiss and they'd made love. Tenderly, sweetly, beautifully, Dylan had held himself back, giving her immense pleasure again and again.

The question he'd asked yesterday came back to her. He'd wanted to know if she'd had any dark moments. She had told the truth; there had been none. She trusted Dylan more than she'd ever trusted any man. Yes, he could infuriate her, and yes, he had the power to wound her emotionally, but physically, she knew he would never hurt her. They'd trained for weeks and not once, even during their fiercest bouts, had he caused one bruise. The man would deny it, but she had never known anyone as gentle.

So what now? She didn't know where Dylan stood. Yesterday, they'd avoided all things related to the past, but today that wouldn't be possible. She still had a goal she had to achieve. And if there was one thing she was absolutely certain about, it was that Dylan would never approve of her plan.

After they'd made love, he'd said something that gave her an idea of what today held. He'd kissed her forehead and said, "Back to reality in a few hours."

Did that mean they would pretend this had never happened? He'd given her no promises. Told her nothing of his feelings. She had no idea if he wanted a future with her or if this was what she'd feared, just a one-night fling.

Jamie had no ambivalence about her own feelings. From the moment he'd held her in his arms, she'd felt a connection with Dylan she'd never felt with anyone. Maybe in the beginning it had been hero worship, but no longer.

Once everything was over with and finished, was there a future for them? She wanted one . . . but what did Dylan want?

Jumping out of bed, she grabbed her sweats and pulled them on. There was only one way to find out what he wanted—she would ask him.

twelve

Dylan turned when Jamie stepped onto the porch. He'd been out here for over an hour, trying to come to terms with what he knew he had to do.

"Oh, wow, it's a beautiful day. Looks like spring is finally here."

Funny, he hadn't even noticed that the sun was out or that the temperature was probably already in the forties. Warmer weather meant more training time outdoors. It also meant that time was running out and the training was going to get even tougher. Was she ready for it?

"Let's have a light breakfast and head out to the obstacle course. You need to run it at least half a dozen times today."

Instead of arguing with him, challenging him, or giving him one of her smart-ass responses, she did something completely unexpected. She reached up and pressed a quick kiss to his mouth. "Sounds good. I'll go make us some oatmeal and toast."

He should have stopped her right there, told her that today couldn't be a repeat of yesterday. Instead, he stood mute as she turned and went back inside. Yesterday, she'd been beautiful. Today, she was something more. Not only was she glowing, she looked relaxed and confident . . . happy. How the hell could he take that away?

Once they were on the course and she had a successful day behind her, then he would talk with her. She needed to know that the next few weeks would be the toughest yet and that there was no way in hell they could continue as lovers. He refused to regret yesterday, but damned if he'd have cause to regret today.

The cellphone vibrated in his pocket. Checking to make sure she'd gone back inside, he looked at the display before he answered and was puzzled. McCall's normal check-in day was tomorrow. "What's up?"

"Just got the word. He's scheduled his first market day."

"When?"

"Three weeks from Tuesday."

"How do we know?"

"He put the word out to his contacts."

"You got a plan yet?"

"Yeah, I'll need you to come here for a briefing."

"When?"

"Next Tuesday."

"And then?"

"Then you're on the op."

Dylan closed his eyes. "So that gives me seven days."

"Seven days to find out what she's hiding. I can send Aidan to complete her training."

An unexpected and off-the-wall surge of jealousy went through Dylan. Aidan Thorne was as capable as any LCR operative, and Dylan trusted him with his life; but the thought of the man coming here to train Jamie slammed him hard. He'd heard more than one female LCR employee sigh over Thorne's golden-blond good looks and the charm that went with them.

In the next instant, he silently cursed himself. He had no hold on Jamie's life, and having her prepared for any threat in the future was his main concern. When the hell had he gotten so selfish?

"Thorne's a good trainer," Dylan said flatly.

McCall didn't even try to hide his amusement. "Or I could send Livingston instead."

At the thought of the no-holds-barred daredevil Jared Livingston having anything to do with Jamie's training, Dylan snapped out a "Hell no." The last thing he wanted was for Jamie to start believing she was invincible, which was apparently how Livingston saw himself.

"Send Thorne. She'll feel easier around him. Besides, she's almost ready . . . two, three weeks tops should round out her training."

"You think you can get what you need before you leave?"

His thoughts as bleak as the landscape before him, he watched a large clump of melting snow crash from a tree branch to the ground. Before yesterday, he'd been her trainer. Gathering any intel she might be keeping from them went with the territory. But that was before he'd slept with her, before she'd trusted him with her body. As lovers, they might share confidences that wouldn't ordinarily be given. If he used their new relationship to find out what she was hiding, he'd go a thousand miles past being a bastard. But if he didn't use any and all means to get the information and Jamie ended up getting killed? Hell, there was no choice. He'd take her hatred any day over having something happen to her.

His voice grim, he answered, "I'll get it."

"Think you'll be able to convince her not to try anything by herself?"

"Yeah, I can do that, too." Dylan closed his phone, the heaviness in his chest caused by something more than the impending dread of doing what he had to do to get the truth. Seven days from today, he'd be leaving Jamie for good.

Jamie stood at the starting line and stretched out her muscles. Energized and ready to go, she could barely wait till Dylan finished clearing the course. Her entire being felt wired, almost electrified. The difference between yesterday and now was amazing. Maybe she'd needed a fall through the ice to wake her up, but she knew that wasn't the cause for her change. That reason was in front of her, his expression once again grim and unwelcoming.

She hadn't asked him about the future. The moment she'd walked out and seen that forbidding look back on his face, she'd chickened out, but damned if she'd pretend that last night hadn't happened. It had been an amazing experience and one she wanted to repeat frequently. So instead, she'd changed tactics, and so far, it was working. She had thrown Dylan so completely off balance, he had no idea how to respond.

Kissing him this morning had been an irresistible impulse . . . the expression on his face had been priceless. The discovery was unbelievably exciting. Dylan might continue his gruff, austere front, but Jamie knew that's all it was—a façade. They would never go back to the way things were before . . . she wouldn't let them. From now on, every time he made a terse or aggravating comment, she would do what she'd done this morning. She would kiss that grim mouth and know a secret no one else knew.

"You ready?"

She nodded. At his "Go!" she shot off, leaping over hurdles, running through tires, swinging on the rope that had defeated her yesterday. Everything she did felt fabulous and new, as if she had a different body, a new spirit. Her focus total, she soared over the last hurdle, landed on the other side, and turned to Dylan, waiting for what she knew would be her best time yet.

"Eighty-nine seconds. You beat your record by nine seconds."

Shouting her glee, she ran toward Dylan, who had no choice but to open his arms as she flung herself at him.

As his arms closed around her, she hugged him hard. Once again she knew she'd thrown him for a loop, but keeping him off-kilter was even more exciting than beating her time. Suddenly she felt as if there was nothing she couldn't do.

Though he held her tight, he didn't return the hug. That was okay with her. This was something he would get used to. Pressing a quick kiss to his cheek, she dropped her arms, and Dylan dropped his quickly, too.

"Eighty-nine seconds isn't a record, you know."

She grinned. "For me it is. Didn't you say that's the only thing that counts? That I'm only in competition with myself?"

Clearly not appreciating her using his words against him, he scowled at her. "Do it again."

She nodded. "Gladly." And with that, she went back to the starting point and waited for his signal. If he thought he could put her in a bad mood or get her off her game, he was wrong. She'd show him.

At his shout of "Go!" she was off again.

Though he kept his focus on her form, Dylan couldn't help but move his gaze up from time to time and watch her face. He'd never seen her so focused or sure of herself. She was running the course like a pro. And dammit, if she threw herself at him or kissed him one more time, he was going to . . . Dylan sighed. He was going to kiss her back.

He should've talked to her this morning at breakfast. He was her trainer; she was his trainee. They couldn't have this kind of intimate relationship; it would throw everything out of balance. He ignored the little voice inside him that said she was performing much better than she had when they'd been snarling at each other. "Inappropriate" seemed an old-fashioned term, but it was the only one he could come up with. It was totally inappropriate for her to fling herself at him or tease him. He had to put a stop to it.

He clicked the watch as soon as she landed from her last jump. *Hell.* "One second faster than last time. What's gotten into you?"

Giving him a sultry, confident look, she walked slowly toward him. Dylan's heart pounded and his body tightened, going stone hard. She stopped inches from him and said softly, "What's gotten into me? I would think that's an obvious answer."

He wanted to respond with sexy banter, laugh at her obvious sexual innuendo. Hell, he wanted to pull her against him and feast upon that sweetly curving mouth. If he did that, he was done for. There was no going back. If they didn't return to their old, distant relationship, he'd never be able to do what had to be done. She was already going to hate him. Damned if he'd give her even more reasons.

"What the hell do you think is going on here?"

"What do you mean?"

"Jamie, yesterday can't happen again. You do understand that, don't you?"

There was only a small flicker of hurt in her eyes before that chin, delicate but oh so damned stubborn, rose. "Excuse me, but I don't believe I've stripped off my clothes and jumped on your sexy body, have I?"

"No, but—"

"But nothing. Dylan, if you can't handle a little harmless flirting, that's your problem. Not mine."

And with those words, she turned and walked to the truck. Not looking back, she said, "I'm going to get some water. Want some?"

Arousal pounded through him with every step she took. He should've known that Jamie's smart mouth and sass would see her through. She'd just turned the tables and made it all about him and his hang-ups. Problem was, he wasn't so sure she wasn't right.

His fists came at her hard and fast. Jamie blocked each one with her arms, whirled, and threw a sidekick, knocking Dylan in the chest. He scooted out of the way and came at her again.

With each successive move, he grew more aggressive, and though he got in a few hits, she was able to deflect the majority of them.

Their training had gotten tougher in the last couple of days. If he'd been grim-faced before, now he was granite hard. No amount of banter, teasing, or even the occasional unexpected kiss moved him. He didn't push her away . . . he just didn't respond.

No way could she deny the hurt. What she had hoped was something special to him had turned out to be what she'd feared—nothing but a crazy, impulsive act that he was determined not to repeat. When they weren't training, he kept himself separate from her. And though they still sat together at mealtimes, there was almost no talking. When she did ask a question or even tried to start an argument, she got grunts and the occasional one-word answer.

"Let's call it a day."

She jerked at the news. "It's only a little after five."

"We need to talk."

Were there ever any more chilling words than those? Every time someone said that, it was never "We need to talk because you just won the lottery" or "You just got a big raise." It was always, always bad news.

"What?"

"Let's go upstairs."

"No, if you have something to say, I'd just as soon you say it right now."

That damn brow arched again. "Come upstairs." And with that, he turned and headed to the stairway.

She was tempted to stay put just to spite him, but since she wanted to know what it was they needed to talk about, she had no choice. Which, of course, he knew.

Following him up the stairs, she watched him head to the living room and stand in front of the fireplace. Since it'd gotten much warmer outside, Dylan had stopped building a fire. Now the area looked cold and uninviting—much like the demeanor of the dark, brooding man who stood in front of it.

Perched on the edge of a chair, she looked expectantly up at him, waiting for him to deliver what she already knew was going to be disturbing news.

"Reddington's resuming business."

This was his news? Of all the things he could have told her, this was the least surprising. She had known that Reddington would get back to business at some point. This news didn't change her plans at all. Yes, she hated that hapless victims were being bartered like cattle, but her focus was on the endgame: putting the man behind bars forever.

She shrugged. "We knew it was coming."

"I thought you'd be more upset."

"If there was something I could do about it right now, I would. There's not."

"But you do still intend to try to do something, don't you?"

"Yes."

His eyes narrowed, as if to pierce through her resistance. "You told Noah that you'd reveal your plans once you went through training. He's kept his end of the bargain. Don't you think it's time you did, too?"

"Is my training over?"

"Almost."

"Almost is not the same as over."

"And you promise you'll go to Noah and tell him everything?"

"I'm not a liar, Dylan. I'll keep my end of the bargain."

"Have you ever thought that if you'd told him, he would've been able to get to Reddington sooner?"

"There's no information I could give you that would've helped LCR get to him any faster, so don't try to put me on a guilt trip."

His gaze grew even harder and more determined; Jamie stifled a shiver, in equal parts unbelievably aroused and totally intimidated.

"Whatever your plan is, you're going to fail."

"No, I won't."

"It takes months, sometimes a year, to perfect an undercover disguise. You're not only naïve, you're going to end up getting yourself killed. Just what the hell is that going to do to McKenna? Don't you know it would destroy her to lose you again?"

Oh yeah, he was using the big guns now. No more "You're not ready" or "Don't you feel guilty?" pesky little shots that dented but didn't penetrate her armor. Thinking about McKenna in pain was a surefire way to weaken her defenses.

"If there's anyone who understands and supports me, it's McKenna."

"Just because she understands doesn't mean she wants you to put yourself in danger."

"Noah's already used the McKenna card on me. It didn't work."

"You'll never be prepared to do what needs to be done."

"You're repeating yourself. Besides, you don't even know what my plan is, so don't tell me I can't do it." She gave him her own hard stare. "What's this really about?"

He was silent for so long, she didn't think he was ever going to answer. Finally, he said, "I wanted you to know about Reddington." He shrugged. "I thought it would upset you more than it did."

"I hate that he's back in business, but it's no surprise."

"We're going after him, Jamie. You do realize that, don't you? And we will get what we need to bring him down."

"Good. I'm all for it. Whatever it takes, I'm for doing it."

Shit. Dylan didn't know who he was angrier with, Jamie or himself. He'd wasted five damn days without doing what was expected of him: getting the information she was hiding and convincing her that she wasn't qualified to carry out whatever harebrained scheme she had concocted. Instead, he'd trained her as if he wasn't leaving soon, as if they had all the time in the world. To make matters worse, he'd been a jerk for those five days—an attitude that wasn't exactly conducive to encouraging her to share her secrets.

Dylan knew he had many flaws, but until now, procrastination had never been one of them. That had to stop; he could no longer put off the inevitable. What he was about to do was something he'd never forgive himself for and would most certainly make Jamie hate him, but she'd given him no choice.

He drew a silent breath and stood. "Why don't you take a hot shower? We worked a little harder today than usual, so your muscles might be sore. I'm going to start dinner."

"That's it? That was your 'We need to talk' conversation?"

He shrugged. "That's it."

Dylan saw confusion mixed with relief as she turned and disappeared into her bedroom. She'd thought he was going to tell her something devastating. After all she'd been through in her life, getting crushing news was probably something she expected far more than getting good news. And, dammit, that was one of the biggest reasons he wanted to protect her. She'd been through so much. Why was she putting herself at risk when she didn't have to?

His mind resolute, Dylan headed to the kitchen. If nothing else, he would make tonight as good for her as possible. She'd hate him afterward, but he could damn well make certain that until the hatred came, she would know nothing but pleasure.

thirteen

Jamie took her time showering and dressing, her thoughts on the disturbing conversation. After months of knowing her course, her decision about Reddington certain and unyielding, Dylan's disapproval and dire warnings made her question herself again—something she was sure he'd be pleased to know.

While in that dank, dark room of Reddington's, she had overheard many discussions. Not everything she'd heard had concerned his business dealings. Much of it had been of a personal nature, especially the conversations with his wife. Those discussions had seemed mundane and uninteresting, but she had listened to as many as she could. And she was so glad she had, because one very detailed conversation with his wife had given her exactly what she had needed.

After her rescue, she had been confident that Reddington would be put away and had pursued every legal avenue to ensure that this happened. Had talked to the prosecutor's office until she was hoarse and limp with exhaustion, detailing her experience. Nothing had worked. Reddington had come away looking like an aggrieved do-gooder, and she'd seemed like an ungrateful bitch and a raving lunatic.

She'd been depleted and on the verge of just giving up when a specific conversation he'd had with his wife had popped into her head. And the idea had been born. She had the qualifications and she had the knowledge; all she needed was a plan.

In Paris, when she'd been recovering and getting to know her sister again, things had coalesced in her mind. McKenna hadn't known it, but she'd given Jamie the information she'd been lacking.

Once it was confirmed that no charges would stick, Jamie had put that plan into place. And as soon as she finished her training, it would be time to put that plan into action.

Standing in front of the mirror, she took in her appearance. Her favorite lavender shirt deepened the blue of her eyes and her jeans hugged her body emphasizing her curves. She'd also taken special care with her hair, washing it with her lemon-scented shampoo and then blowing it dry until it looked like a bright, gleaming waterfall. Putting on a lot of makeup would have been too obvious, but she did add some subtle color to her lips and darken her lashes with mascara.

She took a step back and nodded her satisfaction. For the last few days, Dylan had treated her as if she were an asexual entity he could barely tolerate. Raising her chin to its customary defiant level and veiling the hurt of his rejection, Jamie turned to go out the door. She'd just see about that.

She stopped in the middle of the living room, startled to find a cozy fire blazing in the fireplace, a bottle of Shiraz and two wineglasses placed on the coffee table, along with a tray of cheese, crackers, and black olives.

"Since we don't have a lot of fresh food, putting together appetizers was a little difficult."

Dylan leaned against the doorjamb at the entrance to the kitchen. He had apparently been very busy. Not only had he showered and changed into a pair of jeans and a charcoal-gray shirt; the fragrances emanating from the kitchen told her he had a delicious dinner well under way.

She gestured at the wine and the cheese tray. "This looks wonderful."

He came toward her and then stopped to pick up the wine bottle. He poured two glasses and handed her one. Taking the other glass, he clinked it against hers and then took a long swallow.

Eyeing him from beneath her lashes, Jamie sipped the wine, savoring the variety of flavors on her tongue. She had set out to seduce Dylan, and he'd turned the tables on her.

"Why the change of heart?" she asked.

"What do you mean?"

She gestured at the cozy scene. "You're obviously expecting more tonight than just a discussion of successful martial arts moves or how to spot a predator."

He took another swallow of wine and set his glass down. "Just tired of the tension between us. This is my less than subtle way of hoping we can put an end to it."

"And that's it?"

He moved close, within inches of her, and said softly, "Do you want something more?"

Jamie almost groaned; the heat in his eyes was melting her insides. Before she could answer, Dylan covered her mouth with his, swallowing the "yes" she was about to give.

The mouth she'd dreamed of nightly covered hers in a hot, devouring kiss that poured heat throughout her body. With a groan of surrender, she raised up on her toes and sank deeper into him.

Releasing her, Dylan took the glass she still held and set it down. Then, with a deliberateness that stole her breath, he unbuttoned his shirt and dropped it to the floor. Jamie reached out a hand and pressed her fingers to his chest, the heat of his body almost singeing her skin. When she would have moved in to taste him, he put his hands on her shoulders to stop her.

"What?"

"Raise your arms."

Her entire body now a mass of quivering, aroused nerves, Jamie lifted her arms and Dylan whipped her shirt over her head. Then, with speedy efficiency, he unhooked the front clasp of her bra.

His voice thick, he growled, "Take off your shoes."

Feeling hypnotized by the hot green eyes holding her gaze, Jamie slipped her shoes from her feet. Quickly, he took her jeans, along with her panties, and shoved them down her legs.

"Step out of them."

Once again, Jamie complied. Breathing was becoming increasingly difficult. Dylan was giving her no time to think, to do anything other than follow his gruff commands.

The knowledge that she was completely nude and he was still partially dressed penetrated her haze of lust. She had never felt vulnerable with him, and though the heat inside her could almost make her forget, she couldn't help but feel a little uncertain.

As if he could read her thoughts, Dylan used the same quick efficiency on himself and in seconds was stripped bare. Jamie let her eyes feast on him: the rock-hard chest, copper-colored nipples, and light sprinkling of springy black hair that trailed down the unbelievably hard abdomen. Her eyes went lower, and her entire body clenched at his penis jutting out toward her. The other night, the room had been dark, and though she'd felt his erection inside her, she hadn't touched him the way she'd wanted to. Tonight, she wanted to know Dylan in every way possible.

Her hand went tentatively toward him, and Dylan caught it before it could reach him.

"What's wrong?"

He tugged at her arm. "Let's lie down in front of the fire. We didn't get to do this the other night. I want to make up for it."

Following him, she asked, "Do what?"

He pulled her down onto the rug and lowered himself beside her. "Explore." And with those words, Dylan pushed her gently onto her back and began a heated and thorough exploration she wasn't sure she would survive. Starting at her neck, he tenderly bathed her with his tongue, then nibbled his way down to her breasts, where he spent torturous, bone-melting moments sucking and licking. Before he could continue farther, Jamie stopped him with her hands on his shoulders. "Wait."

"What's wrong?"

"When do I get to do the same thing to you?"

For an instant, before he quickly masked it, something like astonishment flared in his expression. "I want to make you feel good."

She almost laughed. "Touching you will make me feel good."

Pressing a quick, hard kiss to her mouth, he moved to lie back on the rug. "Then have at it, sweetheart."

Feeling as though she'd been given the keys to fantasyland, Jamie placed her hands on his chest and began to live out what she had only dreamed.

At the first touch of her soft, delicate hands on him, Dylan knew he was in trouble. Control during sex had never been a real issue with him. Giving pleasure to a woman was one of nature's greatest wonders, and he'd enjoyed the hell out of it more times than he wanted to count. The other night, though he'd come close to losing it a couple of times, she had allowed him to give her pleasure without the need to caress him. Tonight, she wanted to play, and while he couldn't deny that it felt better than damn good, losing control wasn't a comfortable place for him. Locked inside him were fierce emotions that were rarely unleashed. He didn't lose his temper, rarely said things he didn't mean, and almost never veered from a set course. Trust Jamie to tempt him like no one else.

Her hands glided down his chest and stopped on his stomach. Dylan ground his teeth as she slowly caressed him, her hand going lower and lower, until she stopped at his throbbing cock. A cool, soft hand closed around him, and he bucked up, hissing his pleasure. He hadn't come prematurely since puberty, but damned if he didn't think that was about to happen.

"You're like hard steel encased in satin."

He'd been watching her hands, but at the wonderment in her voice, he moved his gaze to her eyes. She looked so enthralled, almost enchanted. He'd never seen that look on a lover's face before. Jamie was truly enjoying touching him.

At that realization, Dylan knew he'd hang on. Tonight would be the last time they'd be together. The memories would have to sustain him for a lifetime; he'd be damned if he'd shorten her pleasure or his by coming too soon.

The first lick of her tongue almost had him changing his mind. Gritting his teeth, he endured the delicious feeling of her hot, tight mouth sucking on him and then taking him deep, almost to her throat. He endured until it was no longer humanly possible.

With a gentle touch to her face to get her attention, he pulled out of her mouth. "Don't think I don't love this, but . . ." Unable to speak with any coherence, Dylan grabbed a condom he'd hidden beneath the rug. After easing it over his erection, he rolled, taking Jamie with him. Above her now, he set out to make sure she was fully with him. Kissing her deeply, he sucked on her tongue, loving her moans, her fingers digging into his back. He lifted his mouth and trailed kisses down the length of her body, stopping at the juncture of her legs; then he lowered his head and delved deep with his tongue. She was wet and so hot he almost lost control again as he imagined what it was going to feel like to slide inside her.

Unable to wait, he shifted between her legs, raised them up, and pressed into her. His gaze locked with hers, and her eyes widened as he went deeper, and then deeper still. Finally buried to the hilt, Dylan lost all hope of maintaining any kind of control. Setting up a hard, driving thrust and retreat, he rode her until explosion loomed. Determined to make sure she was with him, he put his thumb on her clitoris and pinched. She gave a soft little scream and spasmed around him. Finally giving in, he groaned her name as he came.

Sated and so relaxed she could barely move, Jamie rubbed her face against Dylan's chest. The experience had been beyond her comprehension. The other night, Dylan had been passionate but so controlled. Tonight that control had broken. He had groaned her name several times, and while the pleasure he'd given her had been phenomenal, his obvious pleasure had increased her enjoyment even more.

As if in deep thought, Dylan absently caressed her hip. She wanted to ask him what he was thinking, but she feared the answer. Would he go back to treating her as if she barely existed? No, she wouldn't allow that.

His voice grumbled under her ear. "Dinner is probably ruined."

She wanted to say that it was okay, she wasn't hungry. Unfortunately, her stomach, at the word "dinner," gave a loud, rumbling reminder that it was empty.

Another rumble sounded under her ear, this time husky laughter. The sexy, masculine sound sent heat running through her veins again. "I guess that means I need to get up and find us something to eat."

"We never did eat the cheese and crackers."

Dylan rolled her over, pressed a quick, hard kiss to her mouth, and got to his feet. Grabbing the tray of cheese and crackers, he set them in front of her. "Munch on these. Be right back."

Enthralled, Jamie watched a very naked Dylan pull on his jeans and pad into the kitchen. When she could no longer see him, she picked up a piece of cheese to nibble. She was tempted to offer to help, but he seemed so intent on doing everything himself, and Jamie couldn't deny her delight at the thought of Dylan wanting to please her.

She had barely swallowed her second piece of cheese when he appeared at the kitchen doorway and announced, "It's salvageable."

Before she could ask what that meant, Dylan headed toward her with two steaming plates. She looked around and quickly cleared off a place on the coffee table.

As he set the plates down, Jamie was suddenly very aware that she was nude. Though he'd seen, tasted, and touched every part of her body, the thought of eating a meal naked was a little too extreme.

"Here."

She turned to catch the shirt Dylan tossed her—his shirt. Standing, she shrugged it on and stood still as he buttoned it for her.

"Though I'd much rather take your clothes off than put them on you, I figured you'd be more comfortable." Leaning down, he gave her a quick whisper of a kiss. "Besides, I'll look forward to taking it off you after dinner."

Jamie was tempted to tell him to forget about dinner. Before she could open her mouth, he turned away. A ragged sigh escaped her. The man was too potent.

Dropping a plump pillow on the floor next to the table, he held out his hand. "Come eat."

Jamie sat down and breathed in the fragrance. "Smells delicious."

"My grandmother's lasagna is hard to mess up."

Jamie took a bite; flavors exploded in her mouth. "Oh wow, this is good."

"I made it yesterday while you were working out and kept it in the fridge overnight. That was one of her secrets . . . she said it brought out the flavors."

"Your grandmother must've been a wonderful cook."

Without looking up from his plate, he nodded. Jamie mentally shrugged. Dylan wasn't the type to be forced into anything. When and if he ever told her anything more about his past, it would be because he wanted to, not because she'd coerced the information from him.

From talking with McKenna, she knew that many LCR operatives had come from horrific backgrounds or circumstances. It hurt her to know that Dylan's childhood had scarred him so deeply. The one clue that he'd given her—that his father had killed his mother—was certainly enough to damage any person for life. But Jamie had a feeling that there was even more behind his inability to share. She sensed a deep, never healed wound. Would he ever let her get close enough to soothe those hurts?

Feeling his eyes on her, she raised her head and swallowed a startled gasp. There was a look on Dylan's face she'd never seen before—a dark, hard, almost ruthless expression. In the next instant, it was gone, replaced by a wry grimace. "Wish we had some of those brownies you made the other day."

Suddenly nervous and not sure why, she turned her mouth up in a tense smile. "I could whip some up for you."

"That's okay. There's something I'd rather have anyway."

"What's that?"

"You."

It was an odd feeling to shiver with excitement and blush at the same time. Though they'd made love less than an hour ago, the memory of Dylan's kisses, of his mouth on her breasts and between her legs, of his hard body driving into her caused a reaction in every erogenous zone she possessed.

"Are you finished?"

Had his voice gotten thicker? Heat flooding through her, she nodded. Thinking to help him clear the dishes, she stood and picked up her plate. Before she could move, he took the plate from her and set it back on the table.

"I'll clean up later." Surprising her, he scooped her into his arms and strode toward her bedroom.

Something had changed Dylan's mind tonight. At some point, they'd have to talk about what and why, but that could come later. For now, she wanted to revel and delight in the knowledge that this brave, gorgeous man wanted her. Everything else could wait.

His jaw tight, Dylan dropped Jamie onto the bed and followed her down. He'd started the night with the clear intent of finding out Jamie's secrets. Instead, he'd gotten completely off track, detoured by the sheer need to kiss her, hold her, and be inside her.

That couldn't happen again. He might hate himself for what he had to do, but he'd hate himself a lot more if Jamie went through with her cockamamie plan and ended up dead. Seducing a woman to get information from her wasn't his forte. Dylan knew he didn't have the charm it took. However, never had he been more determined to seduce a woman in his life.

Unbuttoning his shirt, which she was still wearing, he

slowly uncovered her beautiful breasts—round with dark pink nipples that were peaked and hard, as if begging for his mouth. He knew their taste, how they would redden even more once he'd suckled on them, and knew the moans she would make deep in her throat.

Moving the shirt over, he shifted his gaze to her flat stomach and her delicate little belly button. His eyes went farther, taking in her sleekly toned legs and narrow, feminine feet. Her body quivered, and he was startled to see her arch upward toward him. Unable to resist, he trailed his fingers over her torso, bypassing the dark gold curls at her mound, and traveled down one leg and then came up the other leg.

"Dylan, stop torturing me."

The husky, aroused voice almost did him in . . . almost made him forget his goal once again. Desire pounded through him; he wanted nothing more than to mount her and reignite the fire they could create within each other.

His eyes roamed up and down her body, devouring her. He was ready to kiss, caress, and love her until she was so insensate with need, so desperate for release, she would hold nothing back from him. She would give him everything in return for the intense pleasure only he could offer.

He raised his gaze to her eyes—a fatal mistake. Desire shimmered within their depths, but he also saw the innocence and the trust. She had given him her body so sweetly. Trusted him not to hurt her, not to take advantage of that gift. And now, what was he about to do? He was about to breach that trust. Holy hell, was he any better than the bastards who'd hurt her before?

Cursing violently, Dylan shot off the bed.

Jamie gasped and sat up. "What's wrong?"

"I can't do this."

"Do what? I don't understand."

She looked at him as if he were crazy. Damned if he could argue with the assessment. He knew what he looked like. Standing in front of the bed, half naked, wild-eyed with lust and an erection so hard he could hammer nails with it. Hell, she was probably wondering why she'd wanted him in the first place.

Reason and anger were all he had left. He opted for reason first. "You need to tell me what you know about Reddington."

Her eyes went wide with astonishment. "I don't understand. . . . Why are you bringing this up now?"

"Because time is running out. The bastard's returning to business as usual. If you're holding back information that could get us inside his organization, it's not only damn irresponsible, it's fucking selfish."

She flinched, but he refused to feel guilty about his bad language. If the F-word bothered her, she was in for a hell of a wake-up call.

"I've already told you that—"

"Yeah, I know. You'll tell McCall when your training is over. That's not soon enough. I need to know now."

"Why?"

"Because I'm leaving."

Her entire body jerked as if he'd slapped her. "Where are you going?"

"I've got a new op."

"But what about—"

"Aidan Thorne's going to finish up your training."

"But why?"

"Because I've got a new job."

As if just realizing that she was naked she jerked the shirt over her body. Her hands were shaking, and he knew that no matter what he said or did, there was no way she wasn't going to be hurt. Might as well get to it and get it over with.

"You're not trained, Jamie. You'll never be trained for

this kind of operation. You're a schoolteacher. A young woman who something bad happened to. It's only natural that you want revenge, but—"

Like Venus rising from the sea, she rose slowly from the bed and got to her feet. "Don't you dare tell me what I am. I know what I am, Dylan Savage. And I know who I am." Her voice was shaking badly, and at first Dylan thought it was because she was about to cry. When he saw her eyes, he realized that the tremble in her voice came from fury, not tears.

"You think this is all about revenge, you go right ahead. I know my reasons." She turned and opened a dresser drawer.

"What are you doing?"

"Packing."

"Jamie, stop it."

"No. My training is over as far as I'm concerned."

"Dammit!" Grabbing her shoulder, he pulled her around to face him. He should have remembered that he'd trained her for this kind of attack. She whirled and punched his face. Dylan jerked back, but she still got in a stinging blow to his jaw.

Refusing to let that deter him, he wrapped both of his arms around her and pulled her off her feet. Throwing her onto the bed, he pinned her down and growled, "Dammit, settle down and listen to me."

Furious breaths heaved through her body as she glared up at him. "Let. Me. Go."

"As soon as you calm down."

She bucked up and tried to throw him off. He had more than a hundreds pounds on her and a hell of a lot more training. He didn't budge.

"Let me up."

"Damn you, Jamie. You can't even handle me. How the hell do you think you're going to not only survive in a snake pit with Reddington and his minions but steal information from him?" He lowered his head and growled into her ear: "Tell me what I want to know and I'll let you up."

As if they both realized that this was the final act— that whatever came next would be the end, one way or the other—they froze in place, neither of them breathing. Seconds passed. Then finally, inevitably, Dylan felt Jamie's surrender. The breath whooshed from her lungs as she wilted like a scorched flower. "I know where he gets his domestic help."

"What?"

"The company he uses in Madrid to get his domestics is called Superior Services. I thought if I could apply as a maid, I could get into his home and steal his files."

At the thought of her actually going to Reddington's hideaway, Dylan's blood froze. "Dammit, Jamie. We have credible intel that the bastard sold several of his domestics when he tired of them."

"That's why I wanted the training. To get what I need and then get away from him."

He was torn between shouting at her for being such a naïve fool and kissing her for wanting to be so brave and creative. He did neither. With the knowledge that no matter if she stayed for further training or left now, whatever they had between them was over, Dylan pulled away from her and stood.

Jamie didn't move. Just continued to lie there as if she had no life left in her.

Regret like bitter bile in his mouth, Dylan fought the intense need to comfort her. Instead, he nodded grimly and said, "I'll call McCall and let him know."

In a voice lifeless and dull, she asked, "Was that what tonight was all about?"

There was no point in keeping the truth from her. "I couldn't think of any other way."

She didn't respond to that, just rolled over in bed, her back to him.

"I think it would be good for you to stay and let Aidan finish up your training. He's—"

"What I do or don't do regarding my training is no longer your concern."

"Promise me you won't try this harebrained thing. That you'll let LCR handle this."

"Fine. I won't do it."

"You promise?"

"I said I won't. If that's not enough for you . . ."

"Okay, fine. Good. We'll get him, Jamie. I promise. Why don't you go and spend some time with McKenna? I'm sure she—"

"Get out of my room, Dylan."

With the ache in his gut intensifying, he could only say, "I'm sorry it had to end this way. I didn't want to hurt you."

Again there was no answer.

Dylan left, closing the door softly behind him. She hated him now, and though he told himself he'd only done it for her own good, the bitter taste in his mouth told him differently. Tonight, before dinner, he'd lost control. That hadn't been about seducing information from her; it had been about making love to the woman he loved.

Dylan knew to his soul that he would never make love to another woman ever again. Oh, he'd probably have sex again, at some point, but the part of himself he'd always held back had been revealed with Jamie tonight. Now that part was wrapped up tight, never to be revealed again.

At dawn, Jamie rose from her bed, got dressed, and started packing. She'd lain awake all night, dry-eyed, torn between an agonizing hurt that went straight through bone and a fury that fueled a determination that no one, not even Dylan Savage, could squelch. Now, hours later, she just felt empty.

She opened drawers and threw clothes into her suitcase without regard to wrinkles or care. Silence wasn't a concern, either. Dylan had excellent hearing, so even if she tried to be quiet, he'd be able to hear her. What was the point? He knew she was leaving. And there was no reason to stay. They had used each other to get what they'd needed. Dylan had gotten the information he wanted, and she had gotten the training she needed. Neither of them were happy with the outcome.

Marching into the bathroom, Jamie dumped her cosmetics into a small bag. She glanced up at the mirror and almost gasped at the stranger looking back at her. Her face was drained of all color and her eyes looked dead—as empty as she felt inside.

The knowledge that she'd allowed this to happen only intensified her anger. She had known that Dylan wanted whatever information he'd thought she was hiding. He'd made no secret of that. And instead of questioning his motives for his little seduction scene last night, she'd eagerly gone into his arms like a love-starved teenager going out with the high school jock. She'd never been an easy mark, but Dylan hadn't even had to sweet-talk her. She'd been so damn thrilled that he'd had a change of heart. Never had she felt more disgusted with herself.

She slammed the drawer closed and turned back to her bedroom. Grabbing her bags, she went into the living room and dropped them on the floor. They thudded loudly. She returned to the bedroom, grabbed the last suitcase, and dropped it beside the others. Without her permission, her gaze went to the closed bedroom door. There was no way he hadn't heard her . . . no way he didn't know she was about to walk out the door.

She took a shaky breath. Her bags were packed; she

was dressed. There was nothing keeping her here, no reason not to leave. Still, she paused. Her eyes on the door, she waited. The clock above the mantel sounded unusually loud in the dead silence. No sounds came from the bedroom.

With her chin tilted at a defiant angle, she bit her lip to control the slight tremble of her mouth and picked up all three bags. Without a backward glance, she carried them to the door, opened it wide, and stomped out onto the porch. She then turned and pulled the door shut, very quietly.

She trudged down the steps and headed to the back of the cabin, where her SUV was parked in the detached garage. Practically throwing the bags inside, she got into the vehicle, started it up, and drove away. Once again, not bothering with a backward glance.

Dylan had almost managed to do something that her past experiences hadn't been able to accomplish. He'd almost broken her. There was a burning in her chest and a flood of tears just waiting to break behind her eyes. But Jamie knew she was made of sterner stuff. Damned if he would ever know how much he'd hurt her . . . damned if he would know how much she had loved him.

And damned if he would know that she hadn't told him the truth.

fourteen

"Aren't you coming for a swim with me this morning?"

Looking up from his plate, Raphael almost choked on his breakfast. Giselle stood before him dressed in an almost nonexistent bikini. Her lithe, golden body already slicked down with sunscreen, she was the epitome of a bright and oh-so-beautiful young woman.

Since normal breath was almost impossible right now, he swallowed the food in his mouth to clear his air passage. In Giselle's presence, he was either breathless and enchanted or infuriated and impatient. And always, all the time, he was aroused.

He'd been on Reddington's island for months. During this time, he'd learned innumerable things, including three absolutes. One was that Stanford Reddington was a brilliant businessman. Second, he'd discovered, to his dismay, that Reddington's family had no idea of the man's illegal activities. Third and most disturbing of all: Raphael was in love with Giselle Reddington, the daughter of a human trafficker and slave trader.

When Reddington had invited him for a visit, Raphael had known it was an open-ended invitation. He just hadn't realized that Reddington would be the one to decide when it was time for Raphael to leave. So far, there'd been no indication that the man was ready to allow that to happen.

Each day after breakfast, except on Sundays, Raphael spent the morning with Reddington. He had to give the guy credit: he was doing what he'd promised and showing Raphael the ropes of running a multibillion euros enterprise. And Reddington had been right—Raphael was learning much more here than he probably ever would in a university. Problem was, he wasn't getting what he'd come to the island to learn. Everything Reddington shared with him dealt with only the man's legitimate businesses.

Equally alarming, but in a different way, was the fact that Reddington had made it clear that he highly approved of a relationship between Raphael and Giselle. Under ordinary circumstances, Raphael would have been thrilled. To be in love with a beautiful woman and have her adoration, as well as her father's approval, would be any man's dream. Unfortunately, nothing about this was ordinary. If and when he got the chance, he planned to find the information LCR needed. Even though her father was a slimy criminal, Raphael knew Giselle would never forgive him.

A small, gurgling laugh reminded him that he'd yet to answer Giselle's question. "Raphael, you look like you're in a trance. Are you okay?"

He grinned. "Just enjoying the view."

Laughing softly, she whirled around. "It just arrived yesterday. You like?"

"Like" was too mild a word for his thoughts. Hard to believe that a seventeen-year-old girl could be so unaware of her own beauty. He had no doubt that Giselle knew of her appeal, but she didn't use her looks as a weapon, as did many young attractive girls he'd been around. She had a sweet personality and a self-deprecating humor he found delightful. Problem was, he could do nothing but admire her from afar.

"It's beautiful, as are you."

Her smile went even brighter, and she dropped into a chair across from him. "Thank you, Raphael. You always say kind things. Will you go swimming with me this morning?"

He shook his head. "I'm afraid not. Your father gave me several projects to work on, and I'm eager to get started on them."

Her full lips came out in a little pretend pout, and Raphael groaned under his breath. If she ever realized what she did to him, the "let's just be friends" discussion he'd had with her would be meaningless.

"Sundays are supposed to be spent with those you care about." Her dark eyes gleaming with a sweetly teasing wickedness, she added, "Does that mean you don't care about me?"

"You know better. I just want to make a good impression on your father."

She got to her feet. "How about sailing with me this afternoon? The weather's supposed to be perfect."

Unable to resist, Raphael nodded. "I'll meet you on the boat at one o'clock. Okay?"

"Perfect. I'll pack a picnic for us." Blowing him a kiss, she turned and disappeared down the stairs that led to the beach.

Raphael waited for several minutes to make sure she didn't come back. Sunday was the one day the entire family did their own thing. Reddington rarely came down for breakfast on Sundays, preferring to spend the morning in his suite with his wife. And Giselle was correct—Sundays were generally work-free on the island . . . at least for everyone but the servants.

Work wasn't exactly what Raphael had planned, either. At least not anything Reddington would approve of. Last week, he'd noticed that the large portrait of Reddington's father that hung in the man's study was crooked. Not an odd occurrence by normal standards, but Reddington was anything but normal. He was meticulous and incredibly anal about everything.

After months of subtle searching of the entire island, Raphael had come up with nothing to show for it. According to LCR sources, Reddington kept all of his private files and records at his home. Raphael had almost despaired of finding anything until he'd seen the crooked frame. Could Reddington be so cheesy and old-fashioned as to have a safe or secret hiding place behind the framed picture of his father?

Raphael set his napkin beside his plate and stood. Even though Sundays were relaxed and informal on the island, he was rarely alone. If he wasn't with Reddington, then either Giselle was around or Reddington's younger daughter, Amelia, was regaling him with questions about his travels.

He had been on the island for a couple of weeks when he'd realized something not only disturbing but downright cruel: the family never left the island. Though they seemed content, Raphael wondered if they had ever asked Reddington why he kept them prisoner.

Taking care to appear as if he was indeed going to work, Raphael grabbed the files he'd brought down with him. He didn't want to get caught in the man's private office. Most of the time, they conducted business in a larger office on the third floor of the mansion.

Reddington's private office was on the first floor of the mansion and much smaller. Raphael had been allowed in it only a few times. If he did get caught, he had the credible excuse of needing a computer to compile some spreadsheets. After a lengthy and exhaustive search, he'd realized that this was the only computer on the island. Incredible as it seemed, the man was determined that no unapproved information reach his family. The Internet was filled with the scandal of Jamie Kendrick's accusations.

Keeping his island insulated from the world was a full-time job, and Reddington employed several people who appeared to have only one priority: keeping his family in the dark.

With the files under his arm, Raphael made a beeline to the man's office. If he acted as if he had every right to be there, no one should give it a second thought.

The tasteful but obvious wealth of the mansion no longer awed him. When he'd first arrived, he'd figured he'd looked like a kid making his first visit to an amusement park. The opulence had been overwhelming. After he'd gotten over his initial shock, he'd reminded himself where Reddington's money had come from—the wealth was nothing more than a façade to cover evil.

Looking neither left nor right, he entered the private office. This was the first time he'd gone in alone. The office was about half the size of Reddington's other office. There was a large desk on one side, with a computer the only thing on it; two sofas situated together in one area; a conference table and six chairs across the room; and, in a discreet corner, a fully stocked bar.

Raphael headed immediately to the computer. If someone came in, he needed to be able to show what he was working on. Opening the folders he'd brought with him, he spent half an hour developing a spreadsheet and inputting numbers. Then, satisfied with the ruse, he stood and went to the painting. He noted that it had been straightened and figured the minute Reddington had seen the tilt, he'd immediately set it to rights.

The condescending image of Reddington's father stared down at Raphael as he eased the picture aside. He was so intent on his task, he didn't hear the door open until it was too late.

"Raphael, what are you doing?"

Last Chance Rescue headquarters

Noah flipped through his thick file of notes on Reddington. He'd been through them so many times he knew them by heart, but still he searched. What information they had on the man was a whole lot of nothing. They knew his family had moved to Madrid from Newark, New Jersey, when Stanford was still a child. Horace Reddington had held strong Mafia ties, but things had gone wrong, and he'd fled in disgrace.

Horace died when Stanford was in his early twenties. From all accounts, the elder Reddington had had several legitimate businesses and did slave trading only on the side. After Horace's death, Stanford maintained those legitimate businesses, but he used them as cover for the less savory but much more lucrative business of human trafficking and slavery.

Each bit of information they had on Reddington should have added up to something—at the very least, the location of his hideout. But no records could be found to tie him to any locations other than the homes Noah and the rest of the world knew about. And none of these places was where Reddington was hidden away.

At the sound of a soft sigh from the other end of the conference table, he looked up from the file. McKenna and Lucas sat together, reading their copies of the information. Jared Livingston sat across from Noah. The gloomy, dour expressions of the three LCR operatives reflected his own thoughts.

Lucas closed the file in front of him. "What about Raphael? Anything else from him?"

Noah shrugged. "Nothing but those two damnably vague emails. The one about canceling his subscription to *The Lark* magazine. And then the one about a month after he arrived at Reddington's." He held up the sheet of paper with the printed email, though he had memorized the short, uninformative message by heart: "*Dude, forgot all about our lunch plans. Sorry about that. Will call you in a few months when I get back.*"

McKenna sighed her frustration. "He's already been there almost four months. Just how much longer is he supposed to stay?"

A familiar tension swept through Noah. He should have figured out a way to prepare Raphael better. Should have given him an untraceable device instead of the cellphone Reddington's men had made him discard. Hell, he should have found a way to keep the kid from going. Now, not only did they not know where Raphael was, they had no way to find out if he had been caught snooping. Noah refused to consider that Reddington might have disposed of him. Just what the hell did the bastard want with the kid?

Aware that McKenna was waiting for some kind of response to her rhetorical question, Noah said, "Dylan will get him."

"What's Savage's status?" Lucas asked.

"He's in Madrid. Embedded. Using the name John Wheeler. He's already attended two auctions. Reddington wasn't at either of them. The bastard's second-in-command, Armando, has taken a liking to him. When we arranged for Dylan to bring him two attractive candidates for their auction, that sealed the deal."

"How'd that happen?" For the first time since he'd walked into the conference room, Livingston spoke.

"The women are LCR operatives. They took down the purchasers and handed them over to the authorities."

"I wish the information Jamie gave us had panned out," McKenna said. "Going in as a domestic would've been a good setup."

"If and when he ever hires another domestic, we're ready to go. Our people confirmed that he does use Superior Services. Problem is, he doesn't use them that often. Hasn't hired a new employee from them in over a year." He shot her a searching look. "Any word from Jamie?"

"Not for a couple of weeks. She's teaching this summer, so I know she's busy."

Everyone had been relieved when Jamie had announced that she was returning to teaching. What no one, especially McKenna, had expected was that she'd return to the States to work.

Noah had seen Jamie right before she'd headed back to the United States. Though she had thanked him for arranging the training and told him she hoped Reddington could be caught soon, he'd seen a toughness and grimness that hadn't been there before. Had she gotten that way from her training or from the obvious anger she had at Dylan? At the mere mention of his name, an expression had come into her eyes that warned him not to go further.

Dylan had been even more closemouthed. He'd returned to Paris, gotten his assignment, and stormed out the door. Noah hadn't asked about what had happened. He had known going in that he was assigning his operative the toughest job he'd ever been given. Dylan had been doing his best to deny his feelings. Being that close to Jamie had to have been tough, especially since he'd been delving for information, too.

And now Dylan was doing everything he could to work his way inside Reddington's organization and then his home. If he could do that, he could rescue Raphael and get the information they needed. And the revenge Jamie had wanted.

"Maybe getting into a normal routine is what she needs," Noah said.

McKenna nodded. "That's what she told me. I just wish she'd wanted to do that here."

"We're waiting for her next break, and then we're going for a visit," Lucas said.

Though McKenna smiled at her husband, Noah could see the shadows. He had deliberately kept her out of the loop regarding Jamie's training. Details of missions were shared on a need-to-know basis. Having McKenna know that one of Dylan's priorities had been to retrieve information from Jamie would not only have been none of her business but would have put a division between the sisters.

McKenna spoke again: "Knowing that she can take care of herself in any situation is a relief, though. And she told me she's going to continue training."

Noah nodded. Things might not have ended happily for Dylan, but the man had to be relieved that Jamie could defend herself if she ever found herself at risk again.

"So what's our strategy now?" Jared asked.

"Dylan's the only operative we've been able to plant. Reddington's still being extra cautious. We anticipate that Armando's endorsement will get Savage into his inner fold soon."

"So we just continue to wait?" Lucas asked.

Noah stood and went to the giant map of the Canary Islands he'd put up after he'd heard from Raphael the first time. "It makes sense that his home is here. There are dozens of small, uninhabited islands. Reddington has the money and clout to own one and hide under mountains of dummy corporations. Angela's been digging into the records, but there's still no indication, at least on paper, that he's there."

Noah sighed, then continued: "LCR doesn't have the resources to check every individual island. Our best bet is to wait until Dylan notifies us with a location." He turned back to the group and said, "So yeah, as much as I don't like it . . . we wait."

"What is the largest city you've ever visited?"

Raphael raised his head from the book he was reading and looked over at Giselle. After getting caught peering behind her grandfather's portrait, he'd had little choice but to distract her as quickly as possible. Explaining that he was straightening the crooked frame, he'd grabbed her arm and told her how glad he was that she'd come into the office. That it was too beautiful of a day to stay cooped up inside. Within seconds, he'd shut down the computer, grabbed his files, and herded her out the door.

That'd been a close call, but it'd been worth it for the most useful piece of information he'd gotten since arriving. There was indeed a wall safe behind the picture. When he was a teenager and living on the streets, he'd learned some questionable skills, including how to break into and hot-wire cars. Too bad he had absolutely no experience opening safes.

Aware that Giselle was eagerly waiting for a reply, he answered, "Probably Mexico City."

Giselle sighed. "You've been to so many places, seen so many things."

Raphael couldn't help but feel sorry for her. Yes, she had every luxury, but she was like a beautiful caged bird. And though he'd been warned by Reddington to discourage talk of the world outside her island home, he couldn't help but ask, "Will your father ever allow you to leave?"

Her mouth wobbled slightly before curving up into her inevitable bright smile. "I love my home."

"I'm sure you do, but there's a whole world out there to explore."

She gazed toward the distant horizon with such longing on her lovely face, Raphael instantly regretted bringing up the topic. Though Reddington appeared to be a loving father, putting Giselle in a position to question the man wasn't smart. If cornered, Reddington would lash out, and Giselle could very well get hurt in the process.

Criticizing Reddington could be dangerous for him, too. If Giselle mentioned their conversation, he could be booted from the island, or worse. Didn't Noah say they believed Reddington did away with people who didn't please him?

Quickly changing the subject, he asked, "Where's Amelia today?"

"Mrs. Jennings, her new teacher, arrived yesterday. They're going over some lesson plans with Mama."

Amelia was Giselle's eight-year-old sister and often their shadow. The news of the arrival of a new teacher wasn't a surprise. One thing he had to give Reddington credit for—whatever his family seemed to need, the man provided. Giselle had confided that Amelia's former teacher hadn't taken the job as seriously as the Reddingtons had hoped. She had been gone when Raphael arrived, and he couldn't help but wonder if she'd left the island alive. If Reddington wanted to make sure no one could find him, how did he ensure that when someone left the island they'd keep quiet? A hollow feeling developed in his stomach. Another reason he needed to stay on Reddington's good side.

"Mama says she's young but very serious. She recently lost her husband in a car accident and wanted solitude."

She would definitely get that here. Other than the

Reddington family and a dozen or so servants, there was no one else on the island. Did she know that she was likely here for the rest of her life?

"Raphael, will you kiss me?"

Giselle could change subjects with lightning speed. This was one subject he'd been avoiding. Even though Reddington had made it apparent that a match between them would be welcomed, Raphael knew he dare not cross that line. Her heart would be broken when her father went to jail; finding out that her boyfriend had been instrumental in seeing that take place would devastate her further.

He gave her a fond, teasing smile. "You're too young."

She snorted delicately. "I'm seventeen. You're only four years older."

He felt many years older, not only in experience but in knowledge of the world. Giselle had never even had a boyfriend.

"When you're eighteen, we'll kiss."

"But that's months away." Her pretty lips puckered into a sexy pout, and it was all he could do not to lean over and give her what she wanted.

He affectionately tapped her nose with his finger. "It'll give me something to look forward to." Glancing at the water, he turned back to her. "Now, are we going sailing or not?"

"I guess."

Raphael stood and pulled her up to stand beside him. It took every bit of his willpower not to pull her into his arms. Needing to get both their minds off what they couldn't have, he threw her a grin. "Race you to the dock."

A delighted smile erased her forlorn expression, and she took off running. Relieved to see her usual exuberance return, Raphael grabbed their towels and loped after her. He hoped that someday he and Giselle would meet under better circumstances, but he had grave doubts that it would ever be possible. The best he could do would be to protect her when her father's kingdom came tumbling down.

Karen Jennings held back a sympathetic smile at the sullen expression on her new student's face. Miss Amelia Reddington was not a happy camper. Not only was she apparently missing out on some fun on the beach with her sister and her boyfriend, but having to listen as her mother and new teacher discussed lesson plans and teaching theories was about to put the child into a coma.

She couldn't blame the girl. More than once, she had suggested to Sarah Reddington that the discussion could wait until tomorrow or could be done without Amelia's presence. Unfortunately, the woman seemed to be on a roll and had barely acknowledged the suggestion. But Karen had known before coming here that, where her children were concerned, Sarah Reddington had very definite ideas about their education. Having that knowledge had helped secure her the job.

Mrs. Reddington was a beautiful woman with ink-black hair, an olive complexion, and coal-black eyes. Since Karen hadn't known what to expect, it had been a surprise that the woman was not only lovely but also incredibly young-looking. The Reddingtons had a twenty-one-year-old son, but Sarah Reddington didn't look like she could be older than her mid- to late thirties.

The older woman's warm, caring demeanor was disarming, and she had conducted the interview with poise and grace, asking pointed, intelligent questions like a seasoned professional. If Karen hadn't known what she did about the family, she would have been very impressed.

The interview had taken place on the island. She'd

been told to come prepared to stay; if, during the course of the interview, it was decided that she wasn't right for the job, she would be returned home. Thankfully, she and Amelia's mother had hit it off, and she'd spent her first night on the island last night.

The island was a marvel. She'd been told almost nothing about where she would be living. She'd thought her explanation of needing to know what clothes to bring might have given her some idea. Instead, the answer had been to bring what she liked. If she needed different clothes, they could be provided. She'd also had to sign a contract saying that she would remain on the island for as long as they deemed she was needed. She'd had no problem making that commitment.

From what she could tell, the Reddingtons had created a tropical paradise that was independent from the surrounding islands—and the rest of the world, for that matter. Before she'd made the commitment for her extended stay, she'd been told that on the island, television was limited to only certain channels, computers were nonexistent and telephones were scarce. She'd asked a few questions to waylay suspicion, but she hadn't probed deeply. None of those things had mattered.

Though she'd been listening to Mrs. Reddington's one-woman crusade about the importance of a good education, she interjected a comment when the woman paused for a breath: "I've brought several tests with me. I think it'll give me a more detailed account of where Amelia is in her studies. Would you like to see them?"

"Absolutely."

Having a good relationship with Mrs. Reddington was important to her employment, but developing a good rapport with her new student was vital. If Amelia resented her new teacher, it would do neither of them any good. With that thought, she said, "Why don't I go get them and you and I can review them and chat. And then, tomorrow morning, Amelia and I can get to know each other better."

Out the corner of her eye, she saw a glint of appreciation sparkle in Amelia's. The little girl turned to her mother. "Can I leave now? Please?"

Sarah Reddington laughed as she looked down at her excited daughter. "Oh, all right. Just don't get in Giselle and Raphael's way."

The cup Karen was holding trembled in her hand. She quickly placed it on the table and stood. "I'll just go get the tests. Be right back."

She and Amelia walked out of the room together. Stopping in the hallway, she winked at the dark-haired, sweet-faced child. "See you tomorrow morning."

Surprising her, Amelia winked back. "Thanks for breaking me out of there. See you tomorrow."

Karen swallowed a laugh and kept a smile on her face all the way down two hallways, until she reached her room. Once inside, she closed the door, leaned against it, and released a long, shaky breath. Raphael was here? On the island? But why?

Would he recognize her? They'd never met, but she was sure he'd seen photographs of her.

Going to the full-length mirror across the room, she carefully examined her image. Shoulder-length, dark brown hair framed a round, slightly chubby face that went with her chunky body. Thick, black-rimmed glasses slightly obscured her light brown eyes. A mouth, thinned by a skillful application of lipstick, covered slightly protruding teeth. With all of this, along with the careful makeup she applied each morning to make her look older and the mouthpiece she'd had made to subtly change the shape of her face, even she barely recognized herself. No way could someone who'd seen her only in a photograph know her. And Reddington, who'd attended the beginning of her interview, hadn't recognized her. Although, since he'd barely glanced at her, maybe she shouldn't be patting herself on the back for that yet.

She took a step away and gave herself an all-over searching look. No, there was no way anyone would recognize her. She was safe.

Satisfied, she pulled out several tests she'd prepared in advance and headed for the door. If she barely recognized herself, how could anyone else know that Jamie Kendrick had finally arrived to fulfill her mission?

fifteen

Madrid

Dylan stood beneath the hot scald of the shower. Even though he knew it wouldn't help alleviate the filth, it was the only method he had to feel even the slightest amount of cleanliness.

After weeks of living in refuse with sewer rats as his only companions, he was beginning to wonder if, even when the job was over, he'd ever feel clean again. Hell of it was, this wasn't the worse job he'd ever been on. He'd been working undercover ops for years. Been exposed to the dregs of society. Reddington's people were scum, but no more so than many others he'd dealt with.

No, the reason he felt the sliminess so deeply this time was personal. These were the men who'd held Jamie. Who'd treated her as if she were some kind of livestock they could buy or sell at a whim.

When the water turned cold, he turned it off and opened the shower curtain. Stepping out, he grabbed a towel and rubbed himself down. Seemed stupid to clean up, considering tonight was going to be shitty. Dylan figured he'd come back to the apartment and shower again after it was over.

For the first time, Armando had asked him to go hunting. When the bastard had posed the question, Dylan had known exactly what he meant. They were going to hunt down and abduct people.

He pulled on jeans and a black T-shirt. As he combed his damp hair, he avoided looking at his eyes, since he knew what he'd see: an emptiness that went straight through his soul.

Turning away from the mirror, he glanced around the dismal, utilitarian apartment. Reddington's men would probably be back again tonight for another search. Even though he'd been working with them for weeks, they were taking no chances. Though they were careful in their searches, he knew exactly how many times they'd broken in and rifled through everything he owned.

He had nothing to hide and was actually more than happy to have them search as much as they liked. He'd even stacked the odds in his favor with a few porno magazines and a couple of low-budget skin flicks. Anyone looking through his stuff would assume he was as sick and twisted as the rest of the organization.

Tonight's hunt was new territory for him. Dylan hoped it represented a graduation of sorts. The more Armando trusted him, the more likely he'd be to spill his guts. What Dylan wanted was an invitation to Reddington's hideaway. Even though it was probably too soon for that intimate a gesture, he planned to make sure that when Armando spoke of him to Reddington, it would be in the most glowing of terms.

Dylan had yet to meet or even get a glimpse of the big man himself. Armando had explained that his boss was taking a lengthy sabbatical but was aware of all business transactions. Unable to ask questions without showing his interest in the man, he'd shrugged and grunted through Armando's explanation of Reddington's absence—as if it made no difference to him if he ever met the boss, instead of the truth, which was that meeting the bastard meant more to Dylan than he could ever express.

His only ease in this entire mess was the fact that

Jamie was completely out of it. Even though he'd hurt her deeply and damaged any future relationship, friendship or otherwise, knowing she was safe made all the difference. With her safe and thousands of miles from danger, he could do this job, concentrate fully on bringing the pervert down.

When McKenna had told him that Jamie had returned to the States and had found a teaching job, his initial reaction had been a deep stab of guilt. He had hurt her even more than he'd thought. And while he'd known it was inevitable, that hadn't eased the ache.

He'd heard her leave the cabin that morning. Had actually been on the other side of the door with his hand on the knob, alternately cursing and lecturing himself on his weakness. Even though he'd had no other choice, letting her go had deadened something inside him. Since then, he'd been acting on autopilot. Being with Jamie had brought life and light into his world, and the instant she'd left, it had grown dark and still again.

Bringing Reddington to justice wouldn't garner her forgiveness. That wasn't what he was expecting. Jamie deserved to have her pound of flesh for what the man had done to her . . . and his son, too. She hadn't told him specifically what had happened while she was in captivity, but he knew she'd suffered from the experience. She had said her need to bring Reddington to justice wasn't out of revenge. Dylan couldn't say the same. Yeah, the man needed to be stopped for what he'd been doing for years . . . that went without saying. But the minute he'd rescued Jamie, bringing Reddington down had become his own personal mission. Jamie might not want revenge, but Dylan wanted it for her. And he intended to see that she got it, one way or the other.

Pulling away from his dark thoughts, he grabbed his car keys and leather jacket. Moping about wouldn't get the job done. With his mind back in auto mode again, he stalked out the door, ready to deal with the devil's minions in hopes that someday very soon, he'd be dealing with the devil himself.

Dylan took another small swallow of his watered-down beer. The smoke-filled room burned his eyes and seared his lungs as if he held a cigarette in his mouth. How were they supposed to find whatever the hell they were looking for when he could barely make out anyone's features?

Armando was acting strange, too. The tall, thick man sat beside him at the bar, nursing his beer and barely looking up. This had been the agreed-upon meeting place. Maybe they were going somewhere else.

"I thought we were supposed to be hunting. I can't see a damn thing in here."

"Yeah . . . in a minute."

Armando's gruff voice always sounded like he had gravel stuck in his throat. Dylan knew the man could speak fluent English, but when they were alone, he always spoke in his native tongue—an odd dialect that, with his raspy voice, made many of his words come out garbled and unintelligible. Armando's poor speaking ability was just one of his many unattractive traits. Informants had told them that Reddington insisted that those close to him speak only English in his presence. Dylan figured Armando's penchant for speaking only Spanish was his small rebellion against his employer's edict.

Always aware of his surroundings, Dylan felt a strange chill zip up his spine. He took another glance around the room, careful not to settle on anyone in particular. In a shithole like this, if you made eye contact, you were in trouble. His quick scan gave him an update: eight men and three women in the room with him and Armando. Most of them were doing their own thing—a couple playing pool, one man throwing darts. One man in the corner was getting a not so discreet blow job from a woman, while another man leaned against the wall and watched, probably waiting his turn.

Dylan turned away. Yeah, he'd definitely been in classier joints.

Still, that feeling of being watched, being considered, lingered. There were eyes on him. He shot another glance at Armando, who dropped his gaze quickly, almost guiltily. *What the hell?*

They came at him from both sides. Two men, about Dylan's height but muscle-bound and thick-necked— men who could be used as cautionary tales against steroids. Neither of them rushed him; they just came toward him slow and menacing. Their blank, soulless eyes left no doubt of their intent.

Dylan didn't bother to look at Armando for help. The man had set this up for some reason. Had his cover been blown or was this a test? At this point, nothing mattered other than surviving the next few minutes.

As if taking a leisurely swallow of his beer, Dylan lifted his glass and, in a flash, slammed the heavy mug into the face of the man on his right. Knowing that'd take him out of the fight for only a few seconds, Dylan immediately whirled around to the other man. With his right arm, he blocked the meaty fist headed toward his head and followed with a left hook to the guy's jaw, a hard kick to his chest, and then a punch to his groin. The guy staggered, giving Dylan time to handle the man he'd tapped with his beer mug. Twisting halfway, he side-kicked the guy's already bloodied nose and then slammed a controlled fist into the man's throat. A harder hit would have killed him . . . a kill wasn't his intent. That'd bring attention no one wanted, especially an undercover LCR operative.

With one man down, he turned to deal with the other

one, but not before a thud to the side of his head almost brought him to his knees. Ignoring the pain, Dylan made use of his bent knees, grabbed the stool in front of him, and whirled. He saw the guy's eyes widen in terror a split second before the stool slammed across his face. Blood spurted and the man fell to his knees, grabbing his face and neck where the wooden legs had slashed deep crevices. The creep hadn't been pretty before and was even less so now.

With his breath settling down, Dylan became aware of the dead silence in the smoke-filled room. All eyes were on him, and even through the fog, he could see the grudging respect in the patrons' expressions. If nothing else, at least these vermin wouldn't try to challenge him, too.

Turning back to Armando, Dylan wasn't surprised to see the wide grin on the man's face. Apparently this had been a test, and judging by the man's pleased expression, Dylan had passed.

Raising a brow, he asked, "So, are we going hunting now or you got something else to throw at me?"

Guttural laughter exploded from Armando. Slapping Dylan on the back, he called out, "A round of drinks in honor of my very good and talented friend."

More shouts of laughter and a few "hear hears", and then, as if nothing unusual had occurred, each person went back to what they'd been doing before. Dylan noted that the man who'd been waiting for his blow job was now being serviced. The two men he'd knocked out were silently pulled out the door. And life, in all its disgusting wonder, went on.

Armando gave Dylan another hardy slap on his back and pulled out a stool for him. "I knew you were going to be able to handle yourself, but, man, you did better than I ever expected."

Taking a swallow of his beer, Dylan shrugged. "You want to tell me what that was about?"

"You graduated, my friend. That's what it was all about."

"Meaning?"

"I told the boss man about you." Armando thudded a fist against his own chest. "He values my opinion above all others. This was your final exam before I introduce you to him." He grinned again, revealing small, slightly yellowed teeth that reminded Dylan of a piranha's. "Soon you will meet him."

Though showing no emotion was Dylan's normal expression, it was more of a struggle than usual not to react with elation at the news. Yes, dammit, yes! He was going to get close to the son of a bitch.

With a jerk of his head, Dylan nodded. "Good."

"Ready to go hunting?"

"No."

The gleam left Armando's eyes. "Why not?"

Dylan knew he was taking a risk here, but he believed it was the right move to make. Being a pushover and a follower didn't impress anyone, even scumbag human traffickers. "I kicked the shit out of those two pieces of vermin. A couple of weeks ago, I brought you two prime pieces of ass that sold at a damn fine price. I sat through auctions that made my dick so hard I could crush a rock with it and didn't take a fucking thing for myself. That's enough. If your boss wants me to work for him, then it's time to move forward. If not, I've got plenty of other options."

A flash of anger came into Armando's eyes but was quickly doused. He had wanted an underling—a buddy to pal around with and play his sick games with him. Instead, he had gotten an equal. He nodded. "I'll call the boss. See when he might be available."

Unable to sit beside the creep any longer or suffer the

stench of bad cigarettes and body odor, Dylan stood. "Call me." With those words, he took his time walking through the bar. He could feel eyes on him, but he had no concern that he'd be confronted again. He'd earned his place at the bar; more importantly, he'd earned his place with Reddington.

Armando would be getting in touch with him in a few days, and then, hopefully, he'd be meeting the head slimeball himself. For now, Dylan wanted to go back to his crappy apartment, take another shower, and think about sunshine.

sixteen

Reddington's island

A gurgle of laughter brought a smile to Jamie's face. How could she have forgotten how much she loved teaching? Even though there was another purpose for being here, having an opportunity to teach Amelia Reddington was still a delight.

She tried not to think about what this precious child was going to suffer once her father went to prison. Dwelling on that would do no good. The man had to be stopped.

Though she'd been on the island for only a week, from what she could tell, Reddington's family knew nothing about his illegal endeavors. Which really shouldn't be a surprise, since they were cloistered and isolated from the rest of the world. How did they stand the remoteness? Jamie had never considered herself a world traveler, but at least she had a choice. Reddington's family was well taken care of and given every luxury. But the beauty of their surroundings didn't negate the fact that they were prisoners.

Giselle, Reddington's seventeen-year-old daughter, was as delightful as her sister. Seemingly content with her life, the young woman acted as if there was nothing odd in not being allowed to leave the island, even for a day of shopping.

In talking to the teen, she learned that she and her

mother perused catalogs and magazines; whatever they wanted was purchased. Deliveries were made once a week, and she had been encouraged to order whatever she wanted, too.

Jamie had nodded and made appreciative comments, knowing that if she said the wrong thing, she'd be in a world of trouble.

None of this was really her business. She was here to find the information she needed to bring this man down, not bring the twenty-first century to the island. Technology wasn't necessarily a good thing, and the children probably were better read for not having the distraction of computer games and cellphones. At some point, though, they would have to join the world. What kind of future would they face when they'd had no exposure to prepare them?

She glanced over at Amelia. The child was deep into a Junie B. Jones adventure. That series had been one of Jamie's favorites as a kid. After Amelia finished, they had plans to walk on the beach and discuss the story.

So far, she'd been consumed with her job and had done nothing to advance her agenda on obtaining what she'd come here to get. She and Reddington had seen each other twice. Once when she'd first arrived; and the second time had been two nights ago. She had taken a walk on the beach and entered the house from a side patio. He'd been walking down the hallway and had looked directly at her. It had been all Jamie could do not to freeze up, terrified that he would somehow recognize her. Instead, she had smiled and said a soft good night. Reddington had grunted and kept on going.

Soon she would face the real test. Jamie usually ate dinner in her room, but Mrs. Reddington had stopped by the classroom this morning and invited her to have dinner with the family on Friday night. She would not only be within a few feet of Reddington; she would have to carry on a conversation with him.

Added to that worry was Raphael. So far, Jamie had seen only glimpses of him, but he was sure to be at the dinner. Would either of the men recognize her? Why was Raphael even here? Was he working for LCR, working on his own, or had Reddington managed to turn a decent kid into a fiend like him?

No, from what Noah had told her, Raphael had been dealt more than his share of hard breaks. Not only that, he had assisted in her rescue. There was no way he'd turned to the dark side.

But from what she remembered, Noah had strongly encouraged him to stay out of LCR business. So he was doing this on his own?

Jamie was struck with indecision. She'd been so focused on being the lone person to find the information, she wasn't sure what to do now. Should she continue to keep her identity to herself or should she try to get Raphael alone and see if they could work together?

At that thought, she immediately pulled back. Revealing herself could open up a chasm she wouldn't be able to close. Even worse, she could wind up putting the young man in danger. She had come prepared for the risk; the last thing she wanted was to involve someone else.

What more did LCR know about Reddington's location? McKenna had told her that LCR would never give up. Pain squeezed her chest when she thought about what she was keeping from her sister. Would McKenna ever forgive her?

After leaving the cabin that spring morning, Jamie had set her plan into motion. It had taken her three hours to get to the airport in Charlottesville. She'd spent much of that time on the phone, getting in touch with people she'd put off contacting. Okay, admittedly, the first half hour had been spent crying and cursing Dylan.

But by the time she was at a lower elevation, she had recovered. She had survived worse than a broken heart. When she'd pulled into the airport parking lot, most of her plans had been in place.

The toughest part of all was visiting McKenna in Paris and telling her that she was no longer intent on going after Reddington and, instead, wanted to return to the States and find a job. The dead silence after she dropped that bombshell had her almost spilling everything. But she couldn't do that. If she revealed her plans to McKenna, not only would her sister be horrified, but she'd tell Noah and Dylan, and then everything Jamie had done would have been for nothing.

Once this was over, once she had accomplished her goals, she would apologize and ask for forgiveness.

"Are you all right?"

Jamie jerked her head up to see a sympathetic and worried Amelia standing in front of her.

Stretching her mouth into her best fake smile, she said, "I'm fine. Did you finish your book?"

"Did someone hurt your feelings?"

Jamie jerked at the question. "Why would you think that?"

"Because you were crying."

Touching her face, Jamie felt the tears she hadn't known were falling from her eyes. Great, just what she didn't need—questions about her stability.

She took a breath. Well, she had a cover, and it was time to put it to good use. "I guess I was just thinking about my husband."

Looking wiser than her eight years, Amelia nodded. "Mama told me your husband went to heaven."

Tears blurred her eyes again. How ridiculous—now she was about to start sobbing over her fake husband? Thankful for the box of tissues on her desk, she quickly dried her eyes and blew her nose. Then she smiled again, this time for real. "He's in a much better place, so I shouldn't be sad about that." She gestured at the book in the girl's hand. "Did you enjoy your book?"

In a flash, the wise look was replaced with an impish eight-year-old sassiness. "I wish I could get away with some of the things Junie gets away with."

Jamie laughed. "I think your mother might have some issues with that." Standing, she looked down at her watch. "Why don't you change into your play clothes and meet me on the east patio in about twenty minutes. We'll walk on the beach and talk about the problems Junie could avoid if she wasn't so mischievous."

With an enthusiastic nod of agreement, Amelia turned and, feet flying, ran out the door.

Jamie leaned against the edge of the desk and bit her lip. She hadn't planned on liking Reddington's family, but other than the man himself, his family was hard not to love. Sarah Reddington was obviously devoted to her children, and though she had a no-nonsense approach to Amelia's education, she also had a gentle humor and a quiet dignity Jamie couldn't help but admire.

Giselle was lovely and kind, Amelia was a delight, and the other child, a little boy named Eric, was a chubby, happy three-year-old.

To an outsider, the Reddingtons looked like the ideal family. And if it wasn't for the vile side business Jamie was all too aware of, Stanford Reddington would appear to be the epitome of a devoted husband and father. His ideas about keeping his family isolated and co-cooned from the world might seem to be merely the whims of an overprotective and eccentric millionaire.

But Jamie did know the truth. Reddington had isolated his family on this island for one reason only: to keep the truth from them. As much as she'd hate to see their disillusionment and hurt when that reality was revealed, Jamie knew she had no choice. Even now, the man was abducting and selling people who'd done nothing wrong other than be in the wrong place at the wrong time.

Her course was set. She would do everything she could to minimize the family's pain, but she refused to back down. Stanford Reddington would pay and, hopefully, so would his vile, disgusting son.

With her chin back up in the air and her determination reestablished, Jamie headed to her room to change. After their walk, it would be naptime for Amelia. Which meant it would be the perfect time to begin her search.

Madrid

Engulfed in his sumptuous leather recliner, Stanford puffed on his treasured cigar and waited for the sale to begin. How he had missed this aspect of his business. Now, after months of lying low and keeping a diligent eye out for any possible infiltrators into his private affairs, it was time to resume life as usual.

Though the auctions had started up again last month, Stanford had kept himself away. That had been a test. Were anyone watching and waiting, they would have pounced at that time. Instead, the sales had gone through without any problems or concerns.

The danger had passed. Now it was time to make up for lost revenue.

After the sale, Armando wanted to introduce him to a young man named John Wheeler he claimed he was mentoring. When Stanford had heard about him, his radar had gone on high alert. What better way for the LCR organization to get to him than to sneak one of their own into his organization?

Armando had fiercely denied the possibility. The young man had proven himself over and over. Had brought excellent merchandise to the market. Seemed to have a flair for determining quality and price. The other night, he had passed a test Armando always insisted on giving, and from the sound of it, Wheeler had been able to handle himself quite well. Having Armando's respect wasn't an easy accomplishment. However, the most important thing, at least from Stanford's perspective, was that the young man understood the flesh market.

The endorsement of his trusted employee meant a lot. Armando had been with him for years and had shown his loyalty time and again. However, taking a new man into his organization was too important to leave to chance. Stanford had hired his most trusted investigator and, yesterday, had received a detailed report. When Stanford had read about Wheeler's impressive background, he'd had to admit that this man might well be a solid addition to his staff.

Cautious to a fault, Stanford would reserve final judgment until he met the young man in person. He would see it in the man's eyes, his demeanor. If Wheeler lived up to the hype, Stanford would offer him permanent employment, along with a substantial salary.

A slight noise below pulled him back to the present. His anticipation zoomed once more. Though he sampled the merchandise only occasionally, he always felt rejuvenated after a successful auction. Sarah had often been the recipient of his fired up libido. By the time he made it home to her, he would be almost overwhelmed with need. Stanford smiled. Even his wife benefited from his business.

The first piece of merchandise appeared. Dressed in plain white cotton underwear and nothing more, she wore an expression of abject terror. Stanford ignored that. Her emotions weren't his concern. Eyeing her up and down, he accessed in a few short seconds what she could bring and which of his business associates would be most interested.

With a slight hand gesture, Stanford indicated that she should be led off the stage. After jotting detailed notes in his journal, he took another puff from his cigar and waited for the next item to appear. Yes, it was definitely good to be back at work.

Dylan stood back, away from the sad line of terrified humans waiting their turn. The stomach-churning scene was beyond nightmarish. There were twenty of them, mostly women of varying ages, and all petrified.

Even though this was the third of Reddington's auction he'd attended, the inhumane and sheer vulgarity of the event wasn't something he could just take in stride. Besides, the big man himself was in the audience today, which apparently meant a bigger production.

Instead of parading a line of people through a small room as before, Armando had set this auction up like an audition. A small staging area was used to prepare each person; then, one by one, the "merchandise," as Dylan had heard them referred to so many times, was told to walk out onto a platform.

Reddington was apparently in the darkened area below, invisible to everyone, but the stench of his cigar wafted through the air.

Dylan wanted to jump down into that area and get it over with. Never had he wanted to kill anyone so much. Even as much as he'd hated his father, he'd never felt this way about another human being.

This was the man Jamie had wanted to go after. The sheer gutsiness of the woman would forever amaze him. He was just damn glad she'd seen the ridiculousness of her plan. While he had deep regrets and enormous guilt for all that had transpired, at least she was safe.

"Stop it! Don't touch me, you bastard!"

His entire body clenched with the effort to maintain his cover as he watched a woman, probably in her early twenties and obviously terrified, fight back as one of the men shoved her forward.

No visible bruises were allowed. Armando had informed him that Reddington reviled damaged flesh. If discipline or punishment was required, it had to be done without leaving marks. As Dylan watched, the man who'd pushed her forward grabbed a wad of her hair and pulled hard as he spoke into her ear. Whether it was from the pain or from the man's words, Dylan didn't know, but the woman's face went paper white. Nodding her head in quick, jerky motions, she turned awkwardly and walked out onto the platform.

Watching her, the man grinned his satisfaction.

Unable to do anything but stand by as this took place was, by far, the toughest part of Dylan's assignment. He could save these people right now. Doubting his abilities didn't even come into question. As usual, when he entered a room, he immediately looked for weapons. Today had been no different. Not far away was a two-by-four piece of wood. Within a minute, maybe less, the three men back here with him would be incapacitated or dead and the hell these people faced would never be realized.

Gripping the post he was leaning on, Dylan held himself back. Rescuing these people would feel good in the short term, but what about all the others that had been sold over the years? The ones that only Reddington's records could reveal?

No, they'd come too far to end this here. But soon Reddington, Armando, and the whole band of perverts would know exactly how their victims had felt. Then, and only then, could justice be served.

"You ready to meet the man?"

With his game face back on, Dylan turned to a grinning Armando. Hell, the guy looked like a proud papa about to parade his son in front of his boss. His nod cool, his expression arrogant, Dylan followed the older man down the stairs to where Reddington sat. The sounds of sobbing and human suffering grew dimmer with each step. The goods had been assessed and priced. A more formal auction of the best "merchandise" would be held tomorrow. The rest of the group would go to various people to be sold again or used in any way their new owners wanted. Just another day in the busy and lucrative life of a human trafficker.

Reddington sat in the darkness. Even as Dylan and Armando approached, the man did nothing to reveal himself. He was a dim shadow, and other than his head full of silver hair, which caught any available light, he was almost invisible.

"Sit down." The man had an impressively deep and cultured voice, almost as if he were theatrically trained. Dylan dropped into a chair and waited.

"Armando seems to think a lot of you."

Until he was asked a direct question, Dylan preferred to maintain his silence. Talking without being asked a direct question could show a lack of control or an eagerness to please. Still, he'd have to walk a fine line . . . an appearance of arrogance could well backfire and get him killed.

There was a long pause, most likely to test his control. Dylan waited.

"You have an impressive résumé."

Since Dylan hadn't supplied Reddington with one, he could only assume the investigation Reddington had done on him had checked out. Score one for LCR cover stories.

When Dylan didn't reply again, Armando shifted restlessly beside him. The man was probably getting nervous, but Dylan had seen too many controlling bastards to let Reddington fluster him.

Reddington finally asked a question: "Why do you want to work for me?"

"Money," Dylan replied.

"That's the only thing that drives you?"

"I have skills suited to the business. I'm good at what I do."

"Such as . . . ?"

"I know quality and value when I see it. And I know how to obtain it without getting caught."

The silver head bobbled with a nod. "Important skills, to be sure."

Again Dylan maintained his silence.

"Why do you want to work for me?"

Dylan shrugged. "You're the best."

"Have you worked for anyone else?"

"No."

"Elaborate," Reddington snapped.

"I've worked for myself for the last few years. Grabbing a tasty piece here and there, making a nice profit. I had several regular customers with specific needs. They would come only to me because they knew I could provide what they wanted."

"What changed?"

"I was getting some heat back in the States. Thought a change of scenery would be best. One good sale can last me a few months, but I like the idea of a steady income."

"Armando indicated that you refused to go hunting the other day. You do understand that this is a requirement of your employment. Correct?"

Dylan didn't bother to offer an explanation of why he had refused Armando. "I've got no problem with that."

"What kind of cut do you want?"

"Fifty percent on what I bring you. Ten percent of the total day's earnings."

"Armando doesn't even make that." There was amusement in the man's voice.

"Maybe he should."

Armando gasped beside him, and Dylan almost smiled. Would Reddington think Armando had put him up to complaining about his pay? It'd be nice if Reddington got rid of Armando before Dylan had to.

"Armando," Reddington asked silkily, "are you unhappy with your wages?"

"Absolutely not. I don't know why—"

Reddington cut him off. "Very well, Mr. Wheeler. Fifty percent of what you supply and ten percent of the day's earnings."

Careful to reveal no triumph over the man's concession to his terms, Dylan nodded his acknowledgment. But still, he waited. Reddington wasn't going to be this easy to win over.

"Has Armando mentioned that I have special clients?"

Surprised but not about to show it, Dylan just shook his head. Armando had shared a lot but hadn't mentioned specific clients.

"I have a request from one of these clients. They're very generous, so I do all I can to provide for their needs." A piece of paper was thrust out of the dark, in front of Dylan. "My client's order. Fulfill it by the end of the week and there will be a bonus."

Shit. The client was ordering a specific kind of female, the way a normal person might order a meal. Dylan didn't glance at the list. That would give the impression that he had doubts that he could deliver everything Reddington wanted. He slid the paper into his pants pocket.

Reddington was once again silent. The interview was

over, but Dylan knew the man was still testing and accessing.

"I'm giving a little dinner party at my home on the eighteenth. Why don't you join us?"

Another test? Or was this invitation because he'd passed the test? Was Reddington on to him and wanted to get him alone? No, that made no sense. The man would have no problem blowing his brains out right here. This was the opportunity they'd wanted.

Determined not to show any emotion or eagerness at the invitation, Dylan shook his head. "Thanks, I already have plans."

"Break them."

Dylan allowed a small flare of anger to show, but only briefly. After several seconds, he nodded again.

"Excellent. We'll get to know each other in a much less formal setting. I'm assuming Armando has filled you in about my family?"

Yeah, that had been one of the first things he'd learned and probably the first thing that had surprised him. "Yes. They don't get involved in your business."

"Exactly. No business, ever, is to be discussed around them. Understand?"

Sensing that this meant more to Reddington than just about anything, Dylan nodded. "I understand."

"Good." The silver head turned to Armando. "You have done well, my friend."

Beaming like a proud father, Armando said, "Thank you, sir."

Armando stood, and Dylan took his cue and got to his feet. Surprisingly, Reddington stood as well. He held out his hand and shook Dylan's in a hard, firm shake. "I look forward to doing business with you."

"And I you."

With those words, Dylan turned and walked away. He was more than aware that both men stared at him until he was out of the building. Knowing that eyes could be anywhere, at any time, he maintained his demeanor even as he jumped onto a city bus. He didn't know where it was headed, and he didn't care. The most important thing was to get away from that place.

Late afternoon meant a bus full of people heading home from work, their minds on what to have for dinner, how their kids' or spouse's day had gone, or maybe a television show they were looking forward to watching. Normal people going about their everyday lives and most never realizing that garbage such as Stanford Reddington lived within their midst. He was a well-known and widely respected businessman here in Madrid, envied and admired by many. Little did the city's residents know that beneath the polish and the sophisticated façade lurked a soul-deep filth.

Crammed into a tight space, Dylan paid little attention to the chattering voices around him as he reviewed every sentence and undertone from the meeting. His undercover story of sleaze and corruption had held up. LCR had some of the best cover-building people in the business. Within hours, any operative could be anyone. Still, with Reddington being on higher alert than most, Dylan had wondered if there would be trouble.

The only hiccup had been the specific request. That was new information. Would Reddington have these clients' names written down? Dylan cursed silently. They were banking so damn much on Reddington's records. With Noah's intel that the man was anal about record keeping and the information Jamie had gleaned, getting to those accounts was their best bet for nailing the bastard.

The prosecutor's hands were tied without proof, and though the information would be obtained outside the norm, with those records in hand, they'd have a good chance of not only shutting the bastard down and putting him behind bars but finding all of the people he'd sold through the years.

Wheels squealed as the bus made a stop, and almost half the bus unloaded. Dylan got to his feet and followed other riders out. He needed to get back to his apartment and make the appropriate contacts. First, he needed McCall to find him a female operative with the specifications this client had requested. And he needed to update his boss about the invitation.

The plan would have to be fluid until he arrived at Reddington's home and figured out what he faced. Getting there didn't mean the records were going to be easy to find.

Another job, and equally important, would be finding Raphael and getting him the hell out of there. Dylan just hoped to hell the kid hadn't gotten caught trying to find the information on his own.

Hailing a taxi in the middle of workday traffic would be pointless. Dylan started down the narrow streets, dodging harried pedestrians, bicyclists, and the occasional streetwalker. Always aware of his surroundings, he knew no one had followed him from the meeting or from the bus. Still, he wasn't surprised to see a shadowy figure hovering at the corner of his apartment building nor to glimpse a man inside his apartment, passing by the window. How many times was he going to be searched before they realized there was nothing to find?

The goon on the corner was one he recognized from the bar where Armando had set up his test. Figuring the guy knew what could happen to a pissed-off Dylan, he strode toward the creep. "Hey, asshole, you got a reason for being in front of my place . . . like wanting to get your face flattened?"

It was apparent the guy didn't speak English, and Dylan didn't bother to translate. The closer he got, the wider the man's eyes grew. When Dylan was within ten steps of him, the man whispered, *"Lo siento. Dirección equivocada"* and took off running.

Wrong address, my ass. Shrugging, Dylan headed inside. The lookout would have been the weakest one. The man in his apartment would be tougher. The meeting with Reddington had left him disgusted and angry. Nice that he now had an outlet for his pent-up rage.

Inside the dingy foyer, which always held an interesting fragrance combination of urine and cinnamon, Dylan stooped down and withdrew his Glock from his ankle holster. He preferred hand-to-hand combat, but going into a room without a weapon drawn was asking for trouble. He didn't want trouble . . . he wanted to kick ass.

Easing up the stairway, he stepped lightly around the areas he'd memorized his first day here. Knowing which part of a stairway creaked made a surprise entry so much more fun.

On the fourth-floor landing, Dylan stopped for a listen. Other than a crying baby, a couple of cats screeching outside, and a too-loud television, he heard nothing. His room was at the end of the hallway. Taking the same care he'd used coming up the stairs, he made his way down to within a few feet from his door.

He glanced down at the large crack under the door. One advantage to living in a shitty residence was that there was plenty of space to see beneath the door. The lights were off, but he sensed the man's presence inside the room.

His hand on the doorknob, Dylan twisted, and was pleased the man had left it unlocked. With his gun at the ready, he exploded into the room, then came to a screeching halt. The man sitting in the lone chair beside the window wasn't a threat, even though he'd pissed Dylan off on occasion.

Lowering his gun, Dylan flipped a light switch near

the door and frowned at the dark countenance of LCR operative Jared Livingston. "What the hell are you doing here?"

Broad shoulders shrugged. "Thought it best to get out of town for a while."

No other explanation was needed. Livingston walked on thin ice with McCall on a weekly, if not daily, basis.

Dylan holstered his gun and headed to the kitchen. Pulling two beers from the fridge, he returned to the living room and threw a bottle toward the other man. Catching it with one hand, Jared twisted the cap off, took a long drink and sighed. "Thanks. I wanted one but hated to take it without asking."

Almost choking on his mouthful of beer at the outrageous lie, Dylan swallowed quickly and said, "How very polite of you."

Livingston took another swallow, then gestured at the window with his bottle. "You take care of the giant outside?"

"Yeah. Barely said boo before he ran. I figured he'd brought a friend who would be here, waiting for me."

"Wished he had."

Dylan couldn't argue, since he'd been looking forward to letting off a little steam. "There's a boxing gym a block from here."

"Good."

Staying in shape on an op wasn't a huge issue for most operatives. A person could do plenty of physically challenging exercises without special equipment. But releasing pent-up energy wasn't as easy. Since he'd been looking forward to kicking ass, Dylan was grateful to have a worthy sparring partner.

"We'll go after I finish my beer." Dylan stood to begin his nightly search for planted bugs.

"I've already checked."

Nodding his appreciation, he headed to his bedroom

to change. Doing a sweep for bugs was as natural to him as taking in air. One slip and an entire op could come crashing down on him, getting him and others killed.

As he emptied his pockets, he came across the piece of paper Reddington had given him. For the first time, he glanced down at the requirements and was surprised by not only the detailed specificity of the physical features but also the experience and education sought. Hell, the guy wanted the woman to be able to speak English fluently, have at least a four-year degree and the kind of social skills to host parties. These weren't the usual kinds of sex-slave requirements. This man was looking for a companion—long-term or just for the night? Whoever he was, there was no doubt the man had major money to spend.

The reasons behind the detailed needs heavy on his mind, he almost missed the bug. A tiny microchip attached to the edge of his right sleeve. Shit, when had that happened? When he'd shaken hands with Reddington or when Armando had bumped up against him earlier that day?

The men were taking no chances, but neither was he. Leaving the bug in place, he changed quickly and walked back into the living room. He held the shirt up and nodded at it, knowing Livingston would catch on. "Got a job. You interested?"

His slate-gray eyes gleaming with knowledge and challenge, the LCR operative asked, "What's the cut?"

"Twenty percent of my take."

"Fifty."

"Thirty."

"Deal."

Dylan handed him the paper with the specific requirements. "Got any ideas where we can find one like this?"

Livingston's eyes widened slightly, revealing the same surprise Dylan had felt. They both knew that not only were specifics like this rare, but the man who wanted this kind of female wasn't worried about getting caught. This type of woman would have a family, friends . . . a job. Unlike a homeless person or a prostitute, this person would be missed.

"I can think of a couple of places to hunt."

Grabbing his keys, Dylan headed to the door. "Let's talk on the way to the gym."

Livingston stood and followed Dylan out the door. The gym was the perfect place to take the discussion. Renaldo, a friend to LCR ever since his niece had been rescued by one of their operatives, owned and operated the gym and could vouch for every person who came through the doors. He also had an office in the back with a secure phone line and computer, the two things Dylan didn't have in his apartment.

For the first time since he'd gotten the invitation, Dylan allowed himself to feel satisfaction. Very soon, Reddington would be behind bars for the rest of his life, and Jamie could finally find the peace she deserved.

seventeen

Reddington's island

Tonight was the dinner she'd been alternately dreading and anticipating for days. Dreading, because she wasn't totally sure of her disguise—though sitting at a dinner table with Reddington should answer that question. The anticipation stemmed from the relief she'd feel if she pulled this off.

Instead of taking her usual walk on the beach with Amelia, she headed to her room as soon as she dismissed class. Now, hours later, she stood in front of the mirror and tried to see Jamie Kendrick behind the dark-haired, brown-eyed woman wearing thick glasses and a slightly outdated dress. The padding she wore beneath her clothing added about twenty pounds to her frame, and the soft rubberized mouthpiece she'd had made to place above her gums, along with skillfully applied makeup, made her face seem not only older but fuller and less angular.

Raphael would be at the dinner, too. She'd seen little of the young man, who seemed to spend much of his time with Giselle. The glimpse she'd gotten of them today had made her heart hurt. Even though she'd been standing a distance away from them, she'd heard youthful laughter and had seen a spontaneous hug. It was apparent that they were fond of each other. What would happen when Reddington's empire crumbled?

Jamie shook her head. There was nothing she could do about broken hearts. She had more than enough on her plate—mainly, how to find the records and then get off the island.

In between teaching the precocious Amelia and dreading tonight's dinner party, she'd spent hours roaming the island. Though she wanted to find the records and believed Reddington's office would be the best place to start her search, it had occurred to her that if she needed to get off the island immediately, she'd better have a plan. Her findings weren't encouraging: a remote island with the beauty of paradise and no visible way to leave it.

Since there was little she could do about that right now, Jamie refocused on her appearance and flashed a smile at her reflection. Did she have the distinctive kind that people would remember? She snorted softly . . . how incredibly foolish. Reddington sure as hell had never seen her smile.

The dinner chimes she'd only recently gotten used to hearing sounded. Giving herself one last nod of encouragement, Jamie turned and left the room. Time to see if her disguise held up and time to test her mettle.

Raphael took a long swallow of his tropical-fruit drink and waited for Giselle to come down to dinner. His nerves felt as though they were jumping out of his skin tonight. He had to get off the island before he either went crazy or did something even crazier, like kiss Giselle. Falling in love with Reddington's daughter was an insane thing to do, but so far, he was the only one who knew. If he stayed much longer, he wouldn't be able to keep his feelings a secret.

He was now ready to admit that he'd been stupid to come here. He'd had no training, formal or otherwise, to do what needed to be done. Each visit he'd made to

Reddington's private office had been pointless. The first time, he'd gotten caught by Giselle. On his second visit, he'd managed to get a good look at the wall safe. Not that it'd done much good—he had no idea how to crack open a safe. It was locked by a combination of a key and a series of numbers. A couple of years ago, he'd seen a movie where a guy tried to break into such a safe and alarms blared throughout the house. The risk was too great for something he knew he couldn't crack in the first place.

Since then, he'd been concentrating on the files on the computer. And those results had been about as useless as his efforts with the wall safe.

Noah had tried to warn him that he'd be getting in over his head. And while he respected the LCR leader more than he could express, he hadn't believed him. Helping in Jamie Kendrick's rescue had given him a false confidence. And now not only was he behind enemy lines, he was in love with the enemy's daughter.

"You look handsome but very worried. Is something wrong?"

He turned to face Giselle and swallowed hard. Why did she have to be beautiful not only on the outside but on the inside, too? If she had just been a pretty shell, he could have admired her beauty without losing his heart.

"Not worried. Just thinking about a conversation I need to have with your father."

"I'm afraid it will have to wait. Mama said he sent a message that something came up and he won't be back until next weekend."

Another week would make little difference except for the damage to his sanity. Since that was already gone, there was nothing he could do but wait till next weekend. Maybe by then, he would've come up with a reason Reddington would accept for his need to get off the island.

Giselle took his arm and pulled him toward the door. "Dinner is ready. Mrs. Jennings, Amelia's new teacher, is joining us."

Resigned to one more week of torture, he followed Giselle. After only catching glimpses of the teacher since she'd been here, he was eager to meet the newest resident of Reddington's desolate island. Did she know what she'd gotten herself into? Did she know that she was now a virtual prisoner? He hated to think that another person had fallen victim to the man.

The family was already seated when they arrived. Mrs. Reddington sat at one end of the table. To her left was Amelia, and to her right was the dark-haired woman he'd seen only from a distance.

"Sorry we're late, Mama."

With a solemn nod of her head, Mrs. Reddington acknowledged the apology. There were strict rules in the household, and being even a few minutes late for dinner was met with disapproval. Raphael had found that out a couple of days after he'd arrived. Reddington had barely talked to him during the meal and, once it was over, had pulled him aside and explained that tardiness would not be tolerated.

When Reddington wasn't around, the entire household seemed to breathe more easily; still, being late was a habit no one wanted to get into.

Raphael pulled out a chair for Giselle, then sat across from her. The minute he was seated, Sarah Reddington made the introduction. "Raphael, this is Amelia's new teacher, Karen Jennings."

Flashing her a smile, he said, "I've heard good things about you from Amelia."

Meeting his smile with a polite one of her own, she said, "And I you. Amelia told me you live in Madrid."

Raphael nodded. "Mr. Reddington was kind enough to invite me to stay here for a few months."

He detected a question in her eyes, but she just nodded and smiled, then moved on to a comment for Amelia.

As Raphael ate his excellent meal, he fielded questions from Giselle, made Amelia giggle with his comments, and watched Karen Jennings. Giselle had told him she was a widow who'd lost her husband only a few months ago, in a car accident. She had no children and no real family. There was an air of sadness and isolation about her. Though she joined in the conversation, and smiled on occasion, she seemed to hold herself back with a reserved kind of dignity.

She looked to be about thirty, maybe a little older. And though she was slightly plump, she ate only small amounts of her dinner. Was she nervous about having dinner with the family? If so, it was probably best that Reddington wasn't here for her first time. The man had the kind of presence that sucked up all available space and energy. It'd taken Raphael over a week before he'd been able to eat a full meal with the man around. Reddington inspired nervousness.

Amelia said something, and Karen responded with a laugh. Raphael jerked at the familiar sound. Where had he heard someone laugh like that? It had a husky, slightly sensuous sound and seemed completely incongruent with her appearance.

"Something about you seems so familiar. Have we met before?"

Since the conversation had been about a book Amelia was reading, everyone turned to look at him. Mrs. Reddington, Giselle, and Amelia all appeared surprised by his question, but Karen had an oddly different reaction. Had he seen a flash of fear in her expression before she covered it with a small smile?

Jamie was sure everyone at the table could hear the sudden pounding of her thundering heart. She had thought she was doing so well, with no gaffes or mis-steps, and now Raphael had recognized her?

She mentally shook herself out of her terror. After months of preparation, she damn well better not mess this up. With her composure back in place, she shook her head. "I can't think where that would have been."

The young man's eyes flickered strangely, but all he said was "Your laugh reminded me of someone. Can't place it, though."

McKenna. How stupid not to think about that. She and McKenna had almost identical laughs. Even Lucas had commented on the similarities. Disguising her laugh would have been so easy. Knowing there was nothing else she could do, Jamie relied upon her cover. With a sad smile, she said, "My husband once called it infectious. A student of mine happened to be standing close by at the time and asked me what disease I had."

Everyone laughed politely. Okay, so it was a lame joke, but at least it took the attention off Raphael's comment.

"What was your husband's name?" Giselle asked.

Grateful that the conversation had shifted, Jamie said, "Sam."

"How long has he been gone?"

The warm sympathy in Giselle's question almost made Jamie smile. She really was a kind and lovely person.

"I lost him less than a year ago. We were childhood sweethearts. I thought we would grow old together, but we were married less than six years."

The silence that followed was the awkward kind that often came after someone said something that made people uncomfortable. For Jamie, it was a welcome re-lief. Even Raphael looked ill at ease.

Letting out a steadying breath, she took another bite of her tasteless meal. Any other time she would have enjoyed the grilled prawns, but nerves and appetite weren't a good combination.

Thankfully, Mrs. Reddington moved on to another topic of conversation, and the awkwardness passed. For the rest of the meal, Jamie made a point of not laughing. She was almost sure Raphael hadn't made the connection, but she wasn't going to chance it.

When she'd learned that Reddington wasn't going to attend the dinner, she'd been enormously relieved, thinking she'd been granted a temporary reprieve. Since she and Raphael had never met, she'd convinced herself that he would pose no problem. Thanks to her overconfidence, she'd almost blown it.

At last, dessert arrived, and Jamie relaxed. Now her only concern was to survive this last course, get back to her room, and come to grips with her nerves. The lemon pie that appeared in front of her changed all of that. The instant she saw it, Dylan immediately came to her mind. Lemon pie was his favorite dessert. Tears sprang to her eyes, and a lump developed in her throat. Great, why couldn't she have conjured these tears when she was talking about her poor dead husband? Getting all emotional over lemon pie was going to look damn stupid.

Thankfully, everyone seemed immersed in devouring the dessert, leaving her to be sappy over the pie all by herself. Able to take only one bite before her throat closed up on her, she carefully returned her fork to the table.

"Did you not like the pie, Mrs. Jennings?" Amelia asked.

Hoping her eyes didn't show any remaining tears, she lifted her gaze to the little girl. "Oh yes, it was wonderful. I'm just full from the delicious meal."

"I'm sorry Stanford couldn't be here tonight," said Mrs. Reddington. "He relishes our family dinners."

"I look forward to seeing him next week."

Jamie stood and addressed the table without meeting anyone's eyes. "Will you excuse me, please? I feel a slight headache coming on." A mild understatement as she suddenly became aware of the vicious pounding at her right temple . . . no doubt caused by tension and nerves.

"Of course," Sarah Reddington said. "I hope you feel better soon."

"I'm sure a good night's sleep will work wonders." After pressing an affectionate hand to Amelia's shoulder, Jamie turned around and, as sedately and calmly as she could, fled.

She made it back to her room in record time. Of all the freaking times to get emotional about Dylan, this was probably the worst. For months she had worked on her cover, perfecting and refining it. She had continued her training and had even added to it with the contacts she'd made. The hurt Dylan had dealt her had been firmly squashed. And now, because of a stupid dessert, all of those feelings had reappeared.

Locking her bedroom door, Jamie tore off her clothes, stripped off the padded bodysuit and underwear, pulled out her mouthpiece, and headed to the shower. A deep ache in her chest told her she needed immediate privacy. The shower was the only place she knew she could go.

She turned the water to full blast, stepped inside, and let go. Sobs, guttural and soul-deep, exploded. Her forehead pressed against the shower wall, Jamie cried for so many things: Dylan's betrayal, her stupidity in falling in love with him after he'd made it clear he wanted information from her, the knowledge that she'd given her heart and body to a man she really didn't know. After her rescue, she'd made the decision to get control of her life, to stop being a victim, which was one of the many reasons she had been determined to do this job. Instead, she'd found herself right back in victim mode. And it made her damn mad.

Straightening her shoulders, Jamie inhaled a steamy, bracing breath. The tearfest was over, and her emotions were on lockdown once more. Even though her head continued to pound, her body felt lighter, freer. Maybe this was what she'd needed: a good, girly cry to get it over and done with.

She quickly washed the makeup from her face and turned the water off. Then, grabbing a towel, she wrapped it around herself and headed back to her bedroom. She had a lot of things to think of and plans to make. One more week before Reddington arrived. Could she find what she needed before then? And when she did, how was she going to get off the island?

With her mind back on her purpose, she dressed in loose, dark clothing and slicked her wet hair up, pinning the mass into a bun. If anyone saw her, the loose clothing should hide the fact that she wasn't wearing her padding. Now all she needed to do was wait until the household was sound asleep; then she would begin. On her first day here, she'd been given a tour of the mansion, and she knew exactly where she planned to start her search: Reddington's private office.

Raphael paced back and forth in his room. He had to make one last effort on Reddington's computer before he left the island. So what that each time he clicked on the computer it was one more failed attempt; he had to keep trying.

He knew much more about computers than he did about wall safes. Unfortunately, not as much as he needed to, though he had managed to open a couple of files that had revealed some assets he was sure Reddington had hidden from the government. Illegal, yes, but not the illegal activity he'd hope to find.

A couple of days ago, he'd found several password-protected files he'd been unable to figure out. The other ones had been relatively easy to access, but these files were totally different. Not only did they have several security decoys, they were held by a password system that only allowed two tries. Typing in the wrong password twice would produce a total lockout of the entire system.

He often asked himself what Noah would do in this kind of situation, and each time he came up with the same answer: he would do whatever he had to do to get the job done. So that's what he was going to do. Whatever it took.

He opened his door and looked out into the hallway. Even though he could easily get away with saying he was working on a project that he needed the computer for, he preferred not to see anyone at all. If a family member were to mention to Reddington how late in the night his protégé was working, the man would be sure to grow suspicious. He'd left Raphael with some minor projects, but nothing that would require late nights spent at the computer.

The household was quiet. The only sounds were the large grandfather clock in the foyer chiming 3:00 A.M. and the distant surf hitting the shore. Keeping his steps light and silent, he slipped down the stairway to the first floor and headed to the back of the mansion, toward Reddington's office.

At the doorway, he stopped. Was that a noise inside the office or just his thudding heart? He pressed his ear to the door and heard nothing. Turning the knob, he eased the door open, then stopped abruptly. A woman dressed in black was bent over, trying to open a drawer in the credenza against the wall.

Frozen in place, Raphael was torn between saying something or just leaving. She had yet to hear him. And though he hadn't seen her face, he already knew who it was: Karen Jennings, Amelia's teacher. But why was—

The memory of her laughter echoed in his head, and then it hit him. Now he remembered where he'd heard that laughter before. In shocked disbelief, Raphael whispered harshly, "McKenna?"

eighteen

Jamie whirled around and almost lost her balance. Holy hell, her first time snooping and she'd already been caught. Then the name Raphael whispered caught up with her frozen brain. He thought she was McKenna.

She knew she could try bluffing, pretending that she didn't know who or what he was talking about. But that would require her to come up with a reason why she was trying to break into Reddington's file drawers. Besides, if he knew the truth, they could join forces and work together.

"Close the door," she whispered.

Raphael quickly complied, then moved toward her. "You are McKenna. Right?"

Jamie shook her head. "I'm her sister . . . Jamie."

If she had told him she was Santa Claus, she didn't think he could look more shocked.

"What the hell are you doing here?"

"The same thing you are, I imagine. I'm trying to find the information to nail the son of a bitch."

He shook his head slowly as though he still couldn't believe her. "After all he put you through? Why would you do that?"

"Because he needs to be stopped."

"But LCR's working on that."

Yes, she was more than aware that most everyone, including Dylan, thought she was an absolute idiot for wanting to put herself at risk again. Having Raphael reiterate that point wasn't a surprise.

"They weren't getting anywhere. I found a way in and decided to use it."

"Does Noah know?"

"No. No one does."

"Not even your sister?"

Jamie didn't flinch as she shook her head. She knew full well that when she saw her sister again, she was going to have to make major amends. Worrying about that now would do no good.

"Why do—"

"Look, we can stand here all night and argue about whether I should be here or not. I'm here, and that's that. Do you want to help me or not?"

He grimaced. "Yeah, but I don't know how much help I can be. I've been in those cabinets you're about to go through. There's nothing incriminating. Mostly tax papers and things to do with his legitimate businesses."

"Well, at least I know where not to waste my time. Where else have you searched?"

"The computer is our best bet." He pointed at the wall beyond her. "There's a safe behind that picture, but it needs a key and a combination. I couldn't figure out how to open it."

Safecracking hadn't been on her training agenda, either. Stupid not to have thought of that. She gave a mental headshake. Seems like she'd been saying that to herself a lot lately.

"What about the computer? Have you been able to get into any of his files?"

"A few, but nothing that mentions anything about slave trading or human trafficking. Just some offshore investments."

Jamie headed to the desk and sat down. Flipping the switch, she waited for the computer to boot up. When

Raphael came to stand beside her, she looked up at him. "How did you get here, and how long have you been here?"

"Reddington contacted me and offered to tutor me in business. I thought it was too good an opportunity to pass up. I've been here about four months."

Jamie gasped, unable to hide her dismay. And she'd thought she could find something in just a few weeks here. "And you haven't found anything?"

"No, but Reddington just left a couple of weeks ago. While he was here, I didn't get much of a chance to look."

That made her feel better, but only slightly. Raphael was obviously an intelligent young man with a sincere desire to help put Reddington away. If he hadn't been able to uncover any information, then what could she do?

"Does LCR know you're here?"

He nodded. "I contacted Noah before I left. He didn't want me to come, but it was an opportunity no one else would get. He gave me a phone to bring with me, but they made me throw it away. As far as I know, LCR still doesn't know where I am. I've managed a couple of vague emails just to let him know I'm okay."

Noah was probably worried sick about Raphael, and with good reason. She refused to consider that she was pretty much in the same boat as he was. No one knew she was here, either.

"There are several files on his computer I haven't been able to access," Raphael said. "They're password-protected. Two wrong tries and then it locks down the system. I found that out the first time I tried." He pulled a piece of paper from his pants pocket and handed it to her. "Since then, I've tried one different password each night and wrote them down so I wouldn't use them again."

Jamie glanced at the paper. Raphael had used the names of Reddington's children and his wife. And one birth date. She looked up at him. "This birthday . . . is it Giselle's?"

A tender expression flickered on his handsome face. "She volunteered that information."

Jamie's heart hurt for him. It was obvious that he was in love with the girl. At this time, Giselle probably felt the same way, but how would she feel if she learned Raphael was here to try to put her father behind bars?

The computer screen flickered, bringing Jamie's focus back to their search. Several icons appeared on the screen, but the one that caught her attention was for a spreadsheet program. She pointed to it. "Is this the one you've tried?"

"Yes. Each file's name is a date . . . some going back several years. I checked the calendar. Most of the dates were on a Tuesday."

A cold chill swept through Jamie. Every other Tuesday was Reddington's market day. This had to be it—irrefutable proof that the man was in the human-trafficking and slave-trading business. One of the many things she'd heard about while Reddington was talking with his son was his obsessive need to document each purchase, including the location where each person was obtained, their name, and a description. He had explained that with documentation, he could trace each person's origin for the buyer. He'd said his own father had been a sloppy record keeper, but that he'd changed that when he'd taken over.

"He told his son that he jots down everything in a journal and then each time he comes home, he scans the information into his computer."

Raphael stooped down beside her. "Do you have anything to copy it to? I was just going to try to remember as much as I could, in hopes that we can track some of the people he's sold."

She nodded. "Even though my stuff was searched before I got on the plane, I managed to hide a couple of flash drives in my cosmetics bag." She'd actually hidden them in a tampon box and had almost smiled when the big, burly man who'd pawed through her stuff had looked panicked and embarrassed when he'd come across the feminine hygiene package.

"I don't suppose you overheard any passwords when Reddington was talking to Lance?"

"No." If only she had, this would be a snap. Now they were limited to one try per night, and the password could be anything.

She glanced down at the paper again at the words Raphael had tried. "What about a middle name? Does Reddington have one?"

"He might, but I don't know what it is."

"Okay, what about Giselle's middle name? Do you know it?"

"Marie."

She shrugged. "It's worth a shot." She clicked on a file and when the password question came up, she typed in "Marie" and hit enter. *Invalid password.* With each successive file, she tried the same name and came up empty each time. If she tried another name or word and it wasn't the correct one, the entire system would shut down for twenty-four hours. Though she doubted anyone on the island other than Reddington used the computer, she couldn't take the chance of anyone realizing someone had been trying to access the files.

"This could take years." Blowing out a sigh, she shook her head. "We need to figure out how to get into Reddington's mind."

"He'll be here next weekend. I can try—"

A slight shuffling sound hit her ears. Jamie held up her

hand to warn Raphael. With her heart in her throat, she held her breath. The light switch was beside the door, across the room. There was no way either of them could get to it in time to turn it off.

"Get under the desk," Raphael whispered. "I have an explanation for being here, but you don't."

Sliding from the chair, Jamie sank to the floor. The sound had stopped abruptly, almost as if whoever had made it had realized they'd been heard. Her eyes stayed on Raphael, knowing he'd alert her if he saw anyone.

One minute became two, and still no more sounds. Raphael pressed a finger to his mouth and disappeared from sight. Jamie heard a whoosh as the door opened; she could only assume he was looking out into the hallway. Seconds later he came back and said, "There's no one out there now."

She got to her feet, not surprised to find that her knees were shaking. Having Mrs. Reddington walk in on them would be the end of everything.

"We'd better call it quits for tonight." Raphael shrugged. "Just in case."

She agreed. The tension from tonight's dinner, her meltdown, and now this had exhausted her. "We'll give it another try tomorrow."

Raphael clicked off the computer. "Go on ahead. I'll wait a few minutes."

She headed to the door, then turned around. "I never got a chance to thank you in person . . . for what you did. You saved my life."

A smile brightened his handsome face. "It was my pleasure."

"See you tomorrow." Jamie turned and went through the door. With her mind on how to proceed the next day, she never saw the shadow attached to the wall.

nineteen

The Atlantic Ocean, near the Canary Islands

Sprawled on the leather sofa of his new boss's yacht, Dylan was the embodiment of "I don't give a damn" machismo. Reddington had brought several of his men along—two bodyguards, the faithful Armando, and a man named Bruno, who, with his thick neck and dead eyes, looked like a cross between a wrestler and a hit man. So far, they'd all kept Dylan at a respectful distance. Having earned the reputation of being able to kick anyone's ass and deliver whatever Reddington wanted had elevated him to a stature few had attained.

Even Armando seemed to be in awe of him now. Armando's initial attitude toward Dylan as a prospective employee had turned into an uncomfortable hero worship. The man turned to him for approval almost as much as he did to Reddington. Nice to know he could still fit in with the cesspool of humanity. And he'd thought his old man's training had been good for nothing but nightmares.

Dylan was more than ready for this mission to be finished. Reddington had been fucking the world for too long. When it was all said and done, he'd love the opportunity to visit the bastard in prison and tell him that Jamie Kendrick had been the reason for his downfall. Jamie had given them much of the intel they'd needed. He wouldn't do that, though. Even behind bars, Reddington might still have influence. The last thing Dylan wanted was to put Jamie back on the man's radar.

He did want to see Jamie again, just once more . . . just to see the knowledge in her eyes that she had achieved the revenge she'd so desperately wanted. Would that give her the peace she sought?

Dylan knew he'd screwed up badly. He never should have agreed to the assignment. He had known how attracted he was to her. Being cooped up in a cabin for months . . . Shit, he should have realized he'd let his guard down eventually. And what had happened? He'd slept with her. Had done his best to make sure she realized how weak she was, and had almost seduced her to get information. Hell, he was lucky he hadn't taught her how to shoot. He'd hurt her so damn bad.

His only solace was that Jamie was somewhere safe and out of harm's way, and soon Reddington would be in a place where he could no longer hurt anyone. Would she be surprised that her happiness was of the utmost importance to Dylan?

He shook himself out of his introspection. Being the hard-assed, cold-blooded criminal didn't exactly go with being a brooding, lovesick idiot. Two days ago, the mystique Dylan had been building had solidified and his reputation for finding and delivering the juiciest pieces of flesh had become awe-inspiring.

LCR operative Sabrina Fox had arrived in Madrid for her new assignment only hours before he was to deliver her to Reddington. Though Dylan knew she'd come fully prepared and completely familiar with her mission, he had briefed her again. Putting anyone in Reddington's clutches, no matter how well trained, didn't sit right with him. Just under six feet tall, with flaming auburn hair, creamy skin, and a body that would make most any man drool, Sabrina had the exact specifications Reddington's client had requested.

After that briefing, Dylan had delivered her to Reddington. And Sabrina, hands bound together, wearing only her underwear, acted appropriately terrified and submissive. Reddington's eyes swept over her, his gaze coldly calculating. Then he turned to Dylan. "Damn, you do know your flesh. That's about as fine a specimen as I've ever seen." His eyes went cold again. "You didn't sample her, did you?"

His expression coolly bored, Dylan shook his head. "I don't play with the merchandise."

Approval and something like admiration flickered on the older man's face. "How did you find one so fine and so fast?"

Dylan shrugged. "Picked her up at a bar in Barcelona."

"And she meets all the criteria?"

"I wouldn't have brought her here otherwise."

His eyes still focused on Sabrina, Reddington said, "I need a name and location for my records."

Dylan handed him a slip of paper with the specifics. Reddington glanced at the paper briefly; then his eyes returned to Sabrina, but his words were for Dylan. "Take her out the back door. There's a limo waiting in the alley. Put her in the back and collect the payment. Don't open the envelope. Bring it back to me."

Dylan nodded, grabbed Sabrina's upper arm, and pushed her forward. This was the hardest part for him. At least with Reddington, he was by her side if something went wrong. Delivering her to an unknown man brought out all of his protective instincts.

Being Sabrina, she sensed his reluctance and whispered, "Don't worry. I'm looking forward to this."

Even now, days later, he thought about that reassurance and could almost smile. Sabrina had been with LCR for only about a year, but had developed a reputa-

tion for thoroughly enjoying certain aspects of the job—
taking down perverted assholes was one of them.

And she'd been right. A few hours after Dylan had
pushed her into the car and taken the payment a long,
bony hand had held for him, he'd heard from Jared Livingston. Sabrina was fine, and Portuguese businessman
Darius Azedo had been quietly taken into custody. Reddington was none the wiser.

A slimy sleaze was in jail, and Dylan's status had been
elevated in Reddington's eyes. All in all, a successful part
of the mission. Now on to the finale: bringing the bastard down for good.

Stanford sat at his desk, the smooth glide of water
beneath the yacht a soothing and joyful reminder of his
destination. Going home after being away for a few
weeks always made him happy. Knowing he had a loving, adoring family waiting for him made all the difference.

Life was finally getting back to normal. His moles had
dug up nothing new on Last Chance Rescue and their
efforts to infiltrate his organization. He had figured his
legitimate businesses would be seen as a soft target; an
operative would weasel their way into the ranks, then
work from the ground up. That concern had caused him
to enforce a hiring freeze. He had blamed the economy,
but his number one concern was protecting himself. His
personnel managers had told him there'd been numerous job applicants. It delighted him to think that some
of those were LCR people. Outsmarting them was one
of this year's highlights.

Another highlight was his interesting new employee,
John Wheeler. Stanford had been in the game for a long
time and could spot a natural in an instant. The man
knew his flesh. And damned if Wheeler didn't have a

talent for getting the most succulent pieces he'd seen in years.

The information he had on Wheeler was reassuring and interesting. The man had a reason for knowing the flesh trade. He had a reputation in North America that even Stanford envied. But he'd been on the verge of getting caught and had left the country. Probably lost a lot of money, but Wheeler's loss was his gain. With this man's know-how, Stanford anticipated making double what he ordinarily would. A good thing, since his profits had decreased considerably this year.

Life was not only returning to normal, it was getting even better. Raphael was clearly enamored with Giselle. And though his daughter's happiness was important, his main goal was to bring a man into the family business who could take over when the time was right. He'd seen Raphael's potential and ambition early on. As his son-in-law, the young man would feel a loyalty to him and the Reddington empire. And Raphael would get a beautiful wife in the bargain. A win-win for everyone.

Stanford leaned back in his chair with a sigh. In just a few hours, he'd be back with his family. And little did his dear wife know, but he had a special gift being delivered to her just in time for her birthday. At last, his entire family would be together again.

Reddington's island

Raphael sat on his favorite lookout point on the island. The rocky point jutted toward the water as if reaching out its hand, searching. He kind of knew how it felt. After months on the island, he found himself wondering if he'd ever see civilization again.

His only bright spot had been the time he'd spent with Giselle. He knew he was young to be making a major decision about wanting to spend the rest of his life with a woman, but what he lacked in age, he more than made up for in experience. Having been on his own since he was thirteen years old, he'd been around long enough to know what he wanted. Giselle was it for him.

An ache grew in his chest—a permanent affliction, he feared. Even if her father hadn't been a low-life human trafficker, her brother a first-rate creep, and Raphael himself working to destroy part of her family, what future could he offer? He had no money. Giselle had grown up on her own island, and though she'd been deprived of many advantages, material things hadn't been one of them.

Besides that, he was probably the first guy she'd been around. Aside from her family, the only other people on the island were servants, and the youngest man was at least fifty. Was it any wonder she'd fallen for Raphael?

He had a sick suspicion that Reddington had brought him here specifically for Giselle. The question was, why? A test of Raphael's willpower and loyalty? Or was it something even more sinister? Had he been brought here as a match for Giselle? Was her father choosing him as her future husband? Under ordinary circumstances, he'd say no man would do something like that, but there wasn't anything ordinary about Reddington. He was so used to manipulating people and controlling his family, choosing his daughter's future husband probably seemed normal.

Reddington would be arriving tomorrow, and time was running out for all of them. Not only had he and Jamie come up empty in their search, Raphael had a feeling that the man would be asking questions about his daughter Raphael didn't want to answer. Would Reddington come out and ask him point-blank to marry Giselle? What if he said no? Would the man let him leave? Alive?

The crunch of rocks barely gave him a warning before a soft, slender hand touched his shoulder. "What are you doing out here all alone?"

He turned and smiled. "You were so immersed in your book, I didn't want to disturb you."

"Books can always wait." She sat down beside him and laid her head against his shoulder. "You know I always have time for you."

Shifting slightly away so he could look at her, he asked, "What do you want out of life, Giselle?"

Her eyes flickered briefly away from him before she returned her gaze to his and gave him her sweet smile. "That's a very weighty question for such a beautiful day."

"What do you dream of? Do you ever think about going to college? Having a career? Doing something besides living here and reading about the world? Don't you want to see it, explore it?"

Tears pooled in her eyes. "I used to dream of that every day, but no more."

"Why?"

"Because there's no point. My father has made it clear that this is my life. I must accept and enjoy it. I have no other option."

This was the first time she'd confided that to him. "Did he say why?"

She shook her head and looked away, her eyes on the horizon. Even in her profile, he could see the longing. "I learned very early in life not to question my father. I know that he loves me and believes he is doing what he thinks is best."

She turned back to him. "That's why he brought you here."

His heart pounded harder. Even though he'd figured that out, albeit too late, hearing her actually confirm his thoughts stunned him. "What do you mean?"

"Papa married Mama when she was very young. When Papa told me you were coming, I knew his reasons. I was so worried about what you would be like. If you would be mean and nasty. But you were even more than I could have hoped for."

Raphael surged to his feet. "I'm not a pet, Giselle. I came here with the intent to learn your father's business, not find a wife."

She got to her feet. "So you feel nothing for me?"

"I didn't say that, but I damn well like to make my own decisions. Being led around by my dick is not my idea of a good time."

She flinched at his crude language. Any other time, he'd be appalled that he'd dare to speak to her like this, but her confession had blown him to bits. Hell, she was as manipulative as her father, and he'd never even seen it.

"Tell your father to find you another man." He turned and started down the path, back to the house. "I'm not for sale."

"Raphael . . . wait! Please! I'm sorry!"

Fury, humiliation, and a deep crushing hurt forced his body forward. There was nothing she could say that would make this any better. The best thing he could do was find a way off the island. Now, if only—

Giselle screamed and then was silent.

Raphael turned around. She was no longer there. Where had she . . . God. No! With his heart thundering for a new reason, he rushed to where she'd been standing and looked down. She was about fifteen feet below, on a rocky ledge. Facedown, she wasn't moving.

Scrambling down, he reached her in seconds. There was barely enough room for one person on the ledge; squeezing in a second was almost impossible. Standing on the edge, he whispered, "Giselle?"

"Raphael," she whispered back, "I'm hurt."

The relief he felt as he heard her speak almost made him tip over. He'd thought she was dead. Still unable to see her face, he asked, "Where does it hurt?"

"Everywhere, but mostly my right leg."

"Stay still. I'm going to see if you have any broken bones." Running his hands up and down her slender body, he felt no protrusions until he reached her right leg. It was broken in at least two places.

He looked up from where she'd fallen. The distance seemed insurmountable, yet he had no choice but to carry her up. "I'm going to turn you onto your back and then put you on my shoulder. It's going to hurt, but it's the only way I can get you up."

"Okay."

The trusting tone in that one word almost made him cry. He'd caused all of this by his cruelty. Easing her over, he noted that she had two bloody scratches on her face and her arm was bleeding. She hissed in pain, and his heart wrenched. He would soon be causing her even more pain.

"I'm sorry. I'll try my best not to hurt you."

Though tears glinted in her eyes, she gave him a shaky smile, and it was all Raphael could do not to kiss her. Lifting her gently, he put her over his shoulder. "Okay?"

"Yes. It's fine."

"Okay, here we go, *querida*. Nice and easy."

She whimpered just twice as he climbed his way up the craggy rock. He knew she was probably being quiet for his benefit, but he almost wished she were screaming and spitting mad at him. Instead she was suffering in silence.

Finally on level ground, he eased her off his shoulder, sat her on a rock, and squatted down to look up at her. "How are you?"

Biting her lip, she shook her head in reply. Tears streamed down her face, which was almost ghost white . . . she could very well go into shock if he didn't get help soon. Standing, Raphael lifted her into his arms and started running toward the mansion.

Jamie was on the patio with Amelia when she heard Raphael shout for help. She jumped up and peered over the shrubbery. The instant she saw him with Giselle in his arms, she looked down at Amelia. "Sweetie, would you run upstairs and see if your mother can come down for a minute? And then why don't you read a few chapters in your new book."

Her eyes wide, Amelia nodded and took off. The instant she disappeared, Jamie ran down the steps of the patio toward Raphael. Reaching them in seconds, she asked, "What happened?"

"She fell. Her leg's broken."

The pain on Giselle's face was reflected in Raphael's. Since she couldn't help him carry her, she ran beside them, whispering encouragement to Giselle.

They reached the patio just as Sarah Reddington came through the door. "Giselle!"

Raphael placed the girl on a lounge chair. His breathing labored, he said, "We need to get her to a hospital."

Sarah was on her knees beside her daughter. When she heard Raphael's words, she looked up at him, panic on her face. "But she can't leave."

Touching the woman's arm gently, Jamie said, "She has to, Sarah. She needs medical attention."

"I'll get Joseph. He has first aid training. I'm sure—"

Horrified but knowing that showing it wouldn't help the situation, she took the older woman's hand. "First aid training isn't going to be enough. She might need surgery. She has to go to a hospital."

Visibly collecting herself, Sarah nodded and stood. "You're right. I just . . ." Another panicked look and then: "There's a boat, beneath the pool house floor. Stanford said for emergencies only."

Jamie nodded. "This definitely qualifies."

With the decision made, Sarah went into action. "I'll get Joseph to help you carry her, Raphael." She disappeared into the house, and within minutes she returned with Joseph. His cold eyes questioning, he examined Giselle's leg. Then standing, his face even harder, he nodded. "Let's go."

While Joseph and Raphael carried Giselle to the pool house, Jamie ran upstairs to pack a small overnight bag for her, assuming that Sarah Reddington would be packing her own bag.

Unsurprised that she couldn't find a suitcase in the girl's room, Jamie ran to her own bedroom and grabbed one of her small duffel bags. Shoving Giselle's clothes, shoes, and toiletries inside, she zipped it up and raced down the stairs.

When she got to the pier, Giselle was lying on a wooden bench, her head in her mother's lap. Jamie dropped the bag beside them and then, as nonchalantly as possible, walked over and peeked into the pool house. Her heart thudded in excitement as she watched Joseph produce a shiny black speedboat from beneath the floor. The instant he started it up, Jamie stepped away.

Seconds later, the boat appeared beside the pier. Raphael stepped down into it and spoke with Joseph, their voices low and serious.

Jamie stooped down beside Giselle, who was white-faced from the pain. She gave the girl an encouraging smile and then looked up at Sarah Reddington. "I'll make sure Amelia and Eric are fine. I—"

Sarah shook her head. "I'm not going."

Hiding her surprise was impossible. "But you'll need to give permission if she needs surgery. I can take care of the children until—"

The woman shook her head emphatically. "No, I can't leave. Raphael has my permission to tell them he's her husband. He can sign for anything that needs to be done."

Though stunned at the woman's decision, Jamie would say no more. As Joseph gently lifted Giselle into his arms and placed her on the cushioned bench on the boat, Jamie turned to catch Raphael's attention and gave him a telling look. She hoped to heaven he understood what the look meant. She wanted him to get away and stay away. Joseph could handle Giselle's return to the island; this might be Raphael's only chance to escape. He had to take it.

As the boat moved away from the dock, Jamie stood with Sarah and watched it pick up speed and move away.

"The closest island is La Rosa, about thirty miles away," Sarah said. "They have a hospital there. Amelia had to have her tonsils removed when she was four. Stanford said they took good care of her . . . they'll take good care of Giselle."

The admission that Sarah hadn't been at her four-year-old daughter's side when she'd had her tonsils removed was probably unintentional. Still, Jamie was unable to keep her mouth shut. "Why didn't you go with her?"

Her mouth trembling, tears sparkling in her eyes, Sarah shook her head. "I just can't." Turning, she began a slow walk toward the house, moving like an elderly woman; her usually energetic and quick steps were now sluggish and halting.

Jamie's eyes stayed on Sarah Reddington until the woman disappeared from view. How had she missed the unhappiness and misery of Reddington's wife? She had thought the woman content with her seclusion and isolation. It had been hard to look at the agony in the older woman's eyes and not offer some kind of comfort.

When Jamie had arrived here, she'd thought she would be the only person on the island hiding behind a façade. Now, seeing Sarah Reddington's pain, she began to wonder how many more secrets the Reddingtons were keeping.

twenty

Twenty hours after they started their journey, Reddington's yacht docked at his private island. Dylan stood on the deck and watched their destination come closer. LCR's theory had been right: Reddington's hideaway was in the Canary Islands. He hadn't been sure until a couple of hours ago. Hell, they'd been on a plane, a speedboat, and a yacht. Much of his travel time, he'd been inside. Fortunately, he'd managed to walk outside at the right time and had recognized an island he knew all too well. A few years back, he'd had a harrowing mission in Tenerife. Seeing that familiar terrain in the distance, Dylan had felt a small measure of relief that he at least knew their approximate location.

Now that they had arrived, he realized their travel time had been extended considerably and much of the route had been a diversionary tactic. One of the many ways Reddington made sure he was never followed. And though Dylan didn't know for sure, he could almost bet that the man changed his routes every so often to ensure his location could never be pinpointed. *Wily bastard.*

Reddington had made himself scarce on the trip, apparently spending most of his time in his suite. About an hour before arrival, he'd asked to see Dylan. After offering him a drink, which Dylan declined, the man gave him a final warning about his family and some interesting news: "I keep my personal life and my business life separate. On my island, my family is protected from the world and all its evil. I intend to keep it that way."

Dylan issued his usual nod and blank stare. The fact that Reddington wanted to protect his family from evil when the man himself personified the concept was laughable. And unless the Reddingtons lived without computers, television, or any kind of news medium, they had to know what he'd been accused of last year. Of course, he'd been able to buy his way out of trouble, so convincing his loving family that he was innocent should have been no problem.

Reddington continued: "My wife's birthday is in a few days, and tomorrow a special gift is being delivered to her. My son has been away for several months, but he's flying in just for her party. While he's here, I'd like you to spend some time with him."

Oh, hell yeah, he wanted to spend some time with the bastard. Dylan raised his brow in inquiry. "And the reason?"

"You have natural talent. My father didn't train me as well as he could have because he relied only on his own expertise. Because of that, it took me years to learn the business. I don't intend to make the same mistake. I want you to tutor Lance, teaching him what you know."

That comment, probably more than any others Reddington had made, surprised Dylan. The man's ego seemed too large to admit this. On the other hand, making a profit at business was important to him. Apparently that trumped ego.

"I'm assuming I get some sort of tutoring fee?"

"Twenty-five thousand and a small additional bonus."

"Such as?"

"At our next auction, you may have your choice of merchandise."

"Fifty thousand and two pieces of merchandise."

"Two?"

Dylan nodded.

"Fine. Two it is."

That had ended the conversation, and Dylan had been allowed to leave. Now, as he leaned against the railing and waited for the yacht to dock, he watched a handful of people gather on the pier. He saw a dark-haired woman standing with two young children and assumed they were Reddington's family.

Other than the illegal and sleazy side, LCR knew little about the Reddington's life. His marriage license and his children's birth records, normal documentation, had been covered and buried so well, the man could have dozens of children and they'd never know. Lance Reddington was the only one they were sure about.

The woman holding a small child waved, and the other child, a little girl, jumped up and down excitedly. A nice homecoming for any man, and one this man definitely didn't deserve.

As soon as the walkway was lowered, Reddington stepped onto the pier and wrapped his arms around his wife. Then he turned and picked up the little girl and swung her around. She squealed with glee, just like any young child delighted to see her father. Poor kid was soon going to have her whole world torn apart.

Stepping out onto the dock, Dylan stood at a respectful distance. Though he couldn't hear the words, Reddington and his wife were whispering furiously with each other. In an abrupt move, Reddington grabbed his wife's arm and pulled her down the pier, toward the large mansion on the hillside.

The crestfallen expression on the little girl's face made Dylan want to say something to her. He couldn't, of course. He watched her chin quiver, and then she turned and followed slowly behind her parents.

Dylan's gaze moved back toward the couple, who were almost running toward the mansion now. Reddington's hand was still wrapped around his wife's arm, and the child she held, a little boy of about three, was sobbing. Whatever had set Reddington off must've been major. He'd never seen the man behave so erratically.

"We'd better lie low for a while. Looks like there's trouble."

Dylan kept his eyes on the Reddingtons until they disappeared from view, then glanced down at Armando, who stood beside him. "He looked pissed."

"Yeah. Best to stay out of his way till he cools down."

"I'm assuming it's okay if I explore the island?"

"Just stay away from the mansion and don't talk to anyone."

Dylan nodded and took off. While exploring, he would look for an escape. Getting the records and going back with Reddington would have been the easier method. He couldn't do that, though. Raphael would be leaving with him, which meant they'd need a boat. If the yacht was their only mode of transportation, he'd take it, but he'd prefer something smaller and a hell of a lot faster.

Where was Raphael? The fact that he hadn't been on the pier to greet Reddington was disturbing. Since Reddington's wife and kids had been the only ones to greet him, maybe he'd been told to stay away. Wherever he was, Dylan wanted to find him as soon as possible. The kid would have a good knowledge of the island by now. And hell, maybe he'd been able to get to Reddington's files.

Tonight, if Raphael didn't have what they needed, Dylan would explore the mansion, find Reddington's office, and get the files. This was what they'd been waiting on for months. By tomorrow, if there were no glitches, he'd have what he'd come for, and then he and Raphael would be on their way back to Madrid. By the time Reddington woke up and realized what'd happened, it would be too late.

That is, if there were no glitches.

Her hands gripping the railing, Jamie stood on her bedroom's balcony and looked at the yacht. She had known Reddington was arriving. The dread of his arrival had been softened by the knowledge that at least Raphael was safe. Joseph had returned with the boat last night. He had reported that Giselle's broken leg had required surgery, but everything had gone fine and she should be released from the hospital in a couple of days.

When Reddington learned that Giselle and his protégé had left the island, what would he do? From the panicked look on Mrs. Reddington's face yesterday, Jamie feared the worst. Would he go to the hospital and try to retrieve his daughter immediately? If he did, would Raphael be able to stay out of the way? Jamie had seen how much he cared for the girl. Would he be able to let her go back with her father, knowing he might never see her again?

They still had nothing on Reddington. Each morning at three, while the household slept, she and Raphael had sat at Reddington's computer and punched in password after password, in the vain hope that they'd get lucky. Yesterday morning, after another failed attempt, they'd both agreed that Reddington's arrival was a good thing after all. Getting inside his head would be the only way to determine what passwords were needed.

That was up to her now. With Raphael out of the picture, she would need to talk with the man. Easier said than done. With Reddington's obviously low opinion of women, having him sit down for a conversation with her might well be impossible. Nevertheless, she had to try.

Her attention returned to the pier, and she watched

the Reddingtons greet each other. If she'd known nothing about the family, she would have assumed that this
was a loving, happy reunion. At first, Reddington honestly seemed exuberant. Jamie could tell the exact moment he learned of Giselle's accident. Even from this
distance, she could see his entire body stiffen. His jerky
movements as he spoke to his wife indicated fury. Seconds later, he grabbed his wife's arm and pushed her
forward, toward the house. Poor Amelia watched them
leave, and then, dejection in every step, followed behind
them.

Knowing that the little girl could use some cheering
up, Jamie was about to turn around and go to her student. A movement on the pier stopped her. A tall, muscular man with dark hair and a slow, deliberate stride
came into her view. In an instant, her world turned upside down.

Dylan.

Excitement zoomed through her, and her body sang
with joy. Her foolish heart didn't care that he'd stomped
and crushed it. For the first time in months, she felt
alive. Yes, she was still angry and hurt, but for right
now, none of that mattered. Jamie wanted to run down
and fling herself into his arms.

Of course, she could do nothing of the kind. Dylan
was undercover, and so was she. Both covers had to be
maintained if they were going to stay alive and succeed.
But she did need to let him know she was here. He was
going to be furious, but he'd just have to get over that.
They could work together to get what they needed.

For now, she had a job to do. Without apparent care,
Reddington had just crushed his daughter's feelings. The
child needed solace and a distraction. Her responsibility
as Amelia's teacher was to find and console the little girl.

Amelia took a siesta every afternoon at two. Since
Jamie usually spent that time exploring the island, no

one would think twice if the new schoolteacher just happened upon the handsome stranger and started talking to him.

With that plan, Jamie left her room and went in search of her student.

The dinner chime sounded, and Jamie scurried out of her room. Being late for dinner tonight of all nights could not happen. Calling extra attention to herself wasn't something she wanted.

She'd spent additional time on her appearance tonight, which had caused her to run late. Making sure Reddington didn't recognize her was important. Equally important was ensuring that Dylan didn't recognize her, either—at least not yet. Would her disguise stand up to his intense scrutiny?

Her plan to happen upon him during her daily walk had been scrapped by an afternoon thunderstorm. By the time it was over, Amelia was up from her nap, and they had two more hours of lessons before the day ended.

Skidding to a stop at the entrance to the dining room, she took in the people already seating themselves at the long, narrow dinner table. Reddington was at one end, Sarah at the other. Amelia sat close to her mother. Two men she'd never seen sat on either side of Reddington. Dylan sat in the middle. The only empty seat was across from him.

The one saving grace was that the giant chandelier above the table had been dimmed and the candles on the table were the main lights in the room. Everyone's face was in the shadows.

As she seated herself, Jamie took a small breath to calm her nerves. Tonight was like any other night. She was Karen Jennings, an elementary school teacher, widowed, and slightly awkward in social settings. Her disguise was good, her cover impenetrable. She had nothing to worry about.

Glad that she'd set herself up as being shy, she didn't feel the need to do anything but eat and offer the occasional smile. She had felt Dylan's eyes on her several times but hadn't yet had to meet his gaze. They were on the main course when all eyes turned to her.

"Stanford," Mrs. Reddington said, her voice unusually husky, "just in the short time Mrs. Jennings has been here, Amelia has read a dozen books."

Though Sarah was no doubt trying to get him to give some attention to his daughter, Reddington looked at Jamie instead. "And how is your new student behaving?"

Jamie replied truthfully: "Amelia is an intelligent young lady with a vivid imagination." She smiled at the young girl. "And we're getting along just fine."

Reddington shot a look at Amelia, then turned his attention back to Jamie. "She's going to grow up to be as beautiful as her mother and sister."

Replying with a snarky comeback was not in her best interest, but Reddington's comment gave her good insight into what he thought was most important, at least for the women in his family. Though taking the words at face value was her best bet, she refused to outright agree with him. "You have a beautiful family, Mr. Reddington."

His mouth twisted slightly, as if he realized she didn't totally appreciate his statement. Jamie knew she needed to be more careful, but intimating that Amelia's looks were more important than her intelligence or talent went against everything she believed in as a teacher.

"And you like your new permanent residence?"

Again, the way he phrased his words bothered her. Was this a common occurrence with this man—speaking with hidden meaning? Refusing to give any indication of her unease, she said, "The island is lovely."

Apparently satisfied that he'd paid enough attention to the new employee, Reddington turned his attention to the brutish-looking men beside him. They spoke in low voices, excluding everyone else from the conversation.

Thankful to have the focus of the table off her, Jamie kept her eyes lowered and concentrated on her meal. Unfortunately, the butterflies in her stomach she'd started the evening with had coalesced into one gargantuan creature. Swallowing anything else was impossible, unless she wanted to call more attention to herself by throwing up. How silly to think she could carry on a civil conversation with a man who'd bought her like a farm animal. Who was she kidding? She wasn't cut out for this undercover stealth.

"Playing with your food never makes it disappear."

Breath caught in her throat. The slightly amused masculine voice had come from the handsome man across from her. She'd dared look at him only once, but now, she couldn't ignore him. Jamie raised her eyes and lost all breath. How could she have forgotten how beautiful Dylan was or what he could do to her blood pressure with just one glance from those gorgeous green eyes?

With her heart chugging like a locomotive, she gave him a small, twisted smile. "I guess it would look strange to ask for a doggie bag."

His mouth twitched with a slight humor. "Especially if you don't have a dog."

Two things occurred to her simultaneously: Dylan was trying to ease her obvious discomfort with gentle, humorous banter. And he had absolutely no idea who she was. Jamie didn't know which one amazed her more. When they'd been together, everything he'd said or done had seemed to be designed to either piss her off or turn her on. This compassionate side startled her. And she couldn't deny the little tingle of satisfaction that he didn't recognize her. How many times had he told her she wouldn't be able to pull this off? And now he had no idea that the woman he'd made love to only a few months back, with such focused need and heat, sat across the table from him, inside the enemy's camp.

The triumphant feeling lasted until she reminded herself that, so far, she'd found out nothing useful in this self-assigned undercover mission. And when he learned her identity, the shit would hit the proverbial fan with a giant, snarling splat.

Since there was nothing she could do about his upcoming fury, she made herself concentrate on the here and now. Keeping the conversation light, she said, "No dog, but I have adopted a line of ants on my balcony."

He cocked his head in curiosity, and Jamie figured the jig was up. Instead, he said, "You don't have a distinctive accent, but occasionally I hear a midwestern twang. Where are you from?"

Her ability to disguise her voice was something she'd practiced long and hard to perfect. *Thank you, Aunt Mavis, for making me take speech and diction lessons.*

"You have a good ear, Mr. Wheeler. I spent most of my childhood in Illinois, around the Champaign area. I moved to Chicago to go to school and never left."

"Until now."

"Yes."

Reddington said something to get Dylan's attention, and he looked away from her. Finally she allowed herself to breathe again. And though she was glad he hadn't recognized her, she was suddenly deflated. She and Dylan had just had a conversation like any man and woman who'd just met might have. And, if she wasn't mistaken, she'd seen a spark of attraction in his eyes. So now, not only was she sad because this had been one of the most pleasant conversations she'd ever had with him, she was having jealously pangs—about herself. Could this night get any weirder?

Dylan answered Reddington's question about deep-sea fishing, aware that it had been asked to turn his attention away from Karen Jennings. Did Reddington not like his hired hands to socialize or was there another reason he wanted to discourage their conversation? Was the woman more to him than just his daughter's teacher?

The woman didn't seem Reddington's type. She was attractive, but in an understated, bland kind of way, almost as if she wanted to blend into the background. Compared to Reddington's wife, who was exotic and stunningly beautiful, the Jennings woman was like a small, brown sparrow.

Something about the woman drew Dylan to her, though. He liked the intelligence in her voice and her obvious affection for her student. The disquiet she'd felt at Reddington's comments about his daughter's potential beauty had been obvious. He saw backbone there. In an odd way, she reminded him of Jamie. Not so much in looks—Jamie was much prettier—but in the way she held herself, turned her head. And the one small smile she'd offered him had reminded him of Jamie's.

Dylan pulled his thoughts away from Karen Jennings. She wasn't his concern. He was here to do a job, and the best he could hope for regarding the teacher was that she would have no trouble finding new employment, because soon, her employment here would end.

The exploration of the island this afternoon had been interesting but frustrating. The island was small, maybe about three-quarters of a mile long, and totally secluded. He'd spotted a larger island in the distance, but getting there would require a boat. And that was what he'd found the most frustrating. Finding the files might be a piece of cake compared to the difficulty of getting off the island. So far, his only viable option was hijacking the yacht. As a rule, yachts weren't the best mode of transportation for a speedy getaway.

Knowing he could do nothing about that until the time came for escape, his mind turned to another worry, this time a major one. Raphael was nowhere to be found. After exploring the island, he'd taken a quick look around the mansion. He'd even located what he thought was probably Reddington's private office. What he hadn't found was the kid. Where the hell was he?

And the hell of it was, he couldn't ask anyone. He wasn't even supposed to know that Raphael existed. His last hope that the young man was just in another part of the mansion disappeared at dinner. If he was still on the island, he would have attended the dinner.

The thought of something having happened to the intelligent young man who'd been so eager to work for LCR that he'd put his life on the line twice tore at Dylan. The only thing saving Reddington from a severe beating until he came up with Raphael's location was Dylan's need to stay undercover. However, before he left here, he would find out about the kid. If Reddington had hurt him, he'd pay.

Her knees weak with relief, Jamie pushed open her bedroom door. Never had she been happier for an evening to end. She had anticipated being uncomfortable. Seeing Reddington up close and personal was something she'd been dreading. Sitting across from Dylan and being someone else had been an additional stress she hadn't anticipated. And then, before she'd left the table, she had realized a new worry: she had attracted more than one admirer tonight. The thick-necked giant sitting to one side of Reddington had given her a few covert glances during the meal, but when she'd stood to leave the table, the subtlety had disappeared. The look had all but stripped her clothes off and told her exactly what he wanted to do to her. What little food she'd been able to swallow had surged up her throat. She'd whispered a hasty good night and zoomed back to the safety of her room.

A tension headache hammered. Taking off her disguise, swallowing some aspirin, and covering her aching head till morning held great appeal. She couldn't. Even though Reddington's presence increased the danger of getting caught, she had to continue to try to get into those files. It was the reason she was here.

Removing her clothes and extra padding, Jamie wiped off her makeup and dressed in her dark sweats. As was her usual routine, she set her alarm for two-fifty A.M. and lay down on the bed. If she was lucky, she'd get in about three hours of sleep before she had to get up. She closed her eyes, wondering groggily if, when this job was over, she'd ever be able to go back to sleeping a full night.

The nightmare attacked without warning.

The house was silent. Had night fallen again? With shutters over the small lone window, she had no idea if the sun blazed outside or if the stars were twinkling. Her whole world had become this room.

She had no idea where she was or what had happened to her. She knew she hurt everywhere and she had a vague sense of violence, but that was all.

How long had she been here? Days? Weeks? She knew she'd been unconscious at some point. Knew that a doctor or some medical professional had examined her, put bandages on cuts, probed her ribs, and said something about bruising. And she'd felt the bruises between her upper thighs. She had a vague sense of who'd caused her pain, but her mind veered away from thinking.

Voices outside the door caught her attention. She twisted her head on the pillow and tried to move her body. For some odd reason, she couldn't. Why? Forcing her fogged brain to think, she told her arm to move. She wasn't paralyzed—there was feeling there—but something impeded her movement. Her arm tugged, and she heard a clank against the wood frame of the bed. Restrained. She was handcuffed to a bed.

Her heart thundered; her breathing turned to panting. The pain in her ribs exploded, but she could concentrate on only one thing. She was handcuffed—a prisoner. Who? Why?

The doorknob rattled and light from an open door flooded the dark room. She twisted her head. Two men stood in the doorway. She couldn't make out their faces. Did she know them? Bright light flashed as someone flipped a switch. Despite the need to see her captors, she closed her eyes against the intense brightness.

"Damn, she's ugly. Why'd your dad buy you such an ugly bitch?"

"She's supposed to be good-looking. My dad got her at a bargain since she's messed up. The doctor said in a week or two, she'll start looking better."

"Hell, I hope so."

"Look at this."

Jamie had yet to open her eyes, but when a cool breeze hit her body, they popped open. She looked up at two young men, probably about twenty. They were gazing down at her with the slimiest, most evil expressions she'd ever seen on anyone's face.

"Damn, you're right. Once those bruises go away, we're going to have some fun."

A hand came out and touched her breast, and for the first time, Jamie realized why she was cold. The sheet that had been covering her had been taken off. She looked down at the hand on her naked breast. Horrified, her eyes went farther. She was completely nude, covered with bruises, and handcuffed to a bed.

She looked up at the two strangers and screamed.

Jamie shot up from the bed and flew across the room to the door. Her hand was on the doorknob before she realized it had been a nightmare. Vivid and all too real, but only a nightmare.

Her breath coming in gasps, she leaned against the wall. Months without even a hint of a nightmare and now, though it had been a mild one, she knew exactly where it had been headed. She checked the clock. Only one-thirty, but she couldn't lie down again. No way in hell was she inviting more of the same. Other than her therapist, no one knew what had happened during those long, dark days and nights. Damned if she'd give the memories permission to return and wreak their havoc.

Settling into a chair by the window, Jamie concentrated on everything other than the nightmare. And as usual, Dylan came to mind. She'd had a lot of time to think about her time with him. Falling in love with him had been no surprise. She'd been halfway in love with him from the moment she'd met him. She had left the cabin that morning heartbroken and angry, but in retrospect, she'd had no real justification for her anger. Dylan had made it no secret that he intended to get the truth from her. The seduction scene he'd set up the night before she left had infuriated her, until she'd remembered her thoughts before walking into the living room. She'd had seduction plans of her own. Maybe not to get information, but did the reason even matter? She'd been no innocent lamb being taken advantage of by the big bad wolf. Jamie had gone into that room under her own steam, with every intention of having sex with Dylan. To pretend otherwise would be a lie.

When all of this was over, could they start again? He didn't love her, but the attraction was more than obvious. She smiled at the thought of them going on a real date and behaving like a normal couple. After all that had happened to her in the last couple of years, that sounded so tame, ordinary . . . and absolutely wonderful.

The alarm beside her bed beeped, letting her know it was time to go and try once again to break into Reddington's computer. She opened her bedroom door, listened intently, and then peeked out. All clear.

As she made her way down the wide staircase, her steps soft and silent, the uselessness of this act hit her. Sneaking inside and trying yet another password that wasn't going to work made her want to turn around and head back upstairs. How on earth could she hope to come up with the right one out of trillions of possibilities?

Quietly opening the door to Reddington's office, Jamie stepped inside, then shut it behind her. Pointless and useless though it was, right now this was all she could do. Hopefully when she and Dylan talked, he'd have a better plan.

"You're earlier tonight."

Jamie froze. Horrified, she watched as the chair whirled around and Sarah Reddington rose to her feet behind her husband's desk.

twenty-one

In a matter of seconds, myriad excuses flitted through Jamie's mind: I was looking for a book to read. I wanted to use the computer to send an email to a friend. The light is better in here. *What, Jamie, what? Say something!*

"Mrs. Reddington, I—"

The older woman held up her hand to stop her. Since Jamie still had no idea what she intended to say, stopping was easy.

"I know you and Raphael come in here every night at three. And even though he's not here, I assumed you would continue your search."

Still Jamie had no words. The woman knew she was searching for something. Did she know what?

"I've decided to help you."

Of all the things Jamie expected this woman to say, this would have been the last one. Finally, she managed her first word: "Why?"

"Because it's past time for it to stop."

"It?"

"I don't really know all of what he's done, though I have my ideas. I only know that living like this is no life at all."

What had Reddington done to change her mind? Though Sarah looked lovely with her shoulder-length midnight hair pulled back into a severe knot, emphasizing her beautiful bone structure and classic features, Jamie noted that her mouth was slightly swollen and her eyes were red-rimmed and gleamed brightly. She had been crying. The dimmed lights at dinner now made sense. What had the bastard done to hurt her?

"I see the questions on your face," Sarah Reddington said. "I won't answer them."

"I understand." And she did. Having her own share of painful secrets, she respected the woman's right to keep hers to herself.

Jamie shot a glance at the desktop computer. "I've been trying to open the files. I believe there's incriminating evidence on them. Evidence that your husband would probably kill to keep hidden."

A small, sad smile fractured Sarah's soft mouth. "My children's safety is all I care about. Dying no longer frightens me as it once did."

For weeks, Jamie had thought Sarah Reddington was totally clueless about her husband and that she was very much in love with him. When Giselle had been hurt, she had realized that all was not as it seemed. Now the stark pain on the older woman's face told of something even more ominous and chilling.

The need to comfort the woman was strong, but having no idea what to say, Jamie turned to the reason she was here. "Do you have any idea what password he might be using to protect his files?"

A small breath shuddered through the other woman. "Guinevere."

"Why Guinevere?"

"Because that's my real name."

There was a major story behind that explosive statement, but Mrs. Reddington had made it clear she wasn't willing to talk about her reasons for helping.

While respecting the woman's privacy, Jamie felt excitement bloom in her at the thought that this could be the key to everything. Crossing over to the desk, she sat down and clicked on the computer. As she waited for it to start up, she glanced up at the woman who stood behind her and was surprised to see a look of wonder on her face.

"What's wrong?"

Sarah shook her head. "I've never seen it turned on before."

The thought that in this day and time, anyone other than someone in a third world country had never seen a live computer screen amazed her. It shouldn't have, though. If the woman had lived here for years, secluded from the world, it only made sense that she'd had no exposure to such things.

When the icons appeared, Jamie took a deep breath. She told herself not to get her hopes up. Guinevere was one name in millions. The chances of it being the right one were beyond remote. Still, her fingers shook as she brought up the list of files and clicked on the first one. After typing in "Guinevere," she hit Enter and held her breath.

A screen filled with names, dates, and prices appeared. Jamie felt as if she'd won the lottery, Publishers Clearing House, and a game show grand prize all at once.

"Is that what you're looking for?"

With excitement numbing her mouth, unable to articulate a sound, Jamie nodded.

"These are names of people he sold, aren't they?"

Recognizing the pain in Mrs. Reddington's voice, Jamie twisted her head to look up at her. "I'm sorry."

"Don't be." She opened a drawer and said, "Do you need paper to write them down?"

Jamie shook her head and withdrew the flash drives from her pocket. She inserted one into a port. "I'll copy them onto this."

Her eyes wide with amazement again, Sarah said, "All of that can go into something that small?"

"Yes." Quickly saving the information to the drive, Jamie clicked on another file. She dared not hope it was the same password, but she had to give it a try. And once again, the file opened.

For half an hour, Jamie opened file after file and copied the information. Mrs. Reddington stood behind her, unmoving. What had this woman gone through in her lifetime? At one time, Jamie had worried what would happen to Sarah and the children once Reddington was behind bars. Now she knew that whatever happened, not only would be it better than what she had to deal with now, but that Sarah Reddington was apparently ready to meet those challenges.

When the last file had been copied, Jamie carefully closed it, shut down the computer, and stood. She turned to Mrs. Reddington, unsure of what she should say. The risk this woman had taken awed her. If her husband ever found out . . . Jamie mentally shook her head. He would never find out; she would make sure of that.

"Thank you for this."

"Did he hurt you, too?"

The sad words gave Jamie even more insight into the older woman's life. "Yes, he did. He . . ." What could she say? The woman knew that her husband was a corrupt, evil man. Did she know that her son was a perverted sex fiend? Hadn't she been through enough? Problem was, if these files incriminated her son too, Mrs. Reddington would certainly know soon. Wouldn't it be kinder to go ahead and tell her?

She started: "Mrs. Reddington, your son . . . he . . ." Good Lord, she couldn't do it. How do you tell a mother that her son is a sadistic pervert?

The expression on Sarah's face made it unnecessary.

She might not know the details, but she knew. Her sad words "He's like his father in many ways" confirmed it.

"I'm very sorry."

Sarah shook her head. "I'm sorry he hurt you."

Coming right after the nightmare she'd had earlier, these words almost made Jamie cry. Never had she thought to hear an apology, especially from the mother of her abuser.

"I'm fine now." She pocketed the flash drive. The later it got, the more the risk of getting caught increased. "I'd better go."

"When will you leave?"

"Tomorrow, maybe." She couldn't tell her about Dylan. The less the woman knew, the better her chances of being able to hide everything from her husband.

Mrs. Reddington nodded. "I'll stay in here for a few minutes. It would be best if no one sees us together."

"You and the children can come with me. You don't have to stay here."

"Yes, I do."

"Why?"

Instead of giving a direct answer, Sarah shook her head. "I'll wait out the storm here."

Jamie went to the door and opened it softly. Then she turned, unable to leave without asking one last question. "Why did you stay all these years?"

With stark desolation in her eyes, Sarah whispered, "There are thousands of excuses and reasons I could give you. Funny, but none of them seem valid any longer. I only know I can't live this way anymore."

Dylan woke the next morning, rock hard and angry—never a good combination. During the little sleep he'd managed, he'd been plagued with odd, erotic dreams.

Since he'd met Jamie, sex dreams had become a frequent occurrence. Now a new twist had been added, because the woman he'd met last night, Karen Jennings, had been in a few of them. He told himself that being attracted to another woman meant he was moving on and accepting that there was no future with Jamie. While that might have been true, he couldn't deny the guilt, almost as if he had been unfaithful.

That wasn't the reason he was angry. Last night had been a total waste of time. He'd waited until the household had settled down. Three-fifteen in the morning should have been prime searching time. He had believed that until he'd gotten to Reddington's office and had heard voices. The door and walls were too thick to hear what they were saying, but he'd heard at least two distinctive, if muffled, voices.

Since he couldn't just hang out in the hallway, hoping they'd leave, he'd returned to his room and waited. Half an hour later, he'd gone back and found the office empty. Not that it'd done any good. He'd found a safe that most assuredly had an alarm attached to it and a computer with the most sophisticated password-protection device he'd seen. Going undercover with Reddington was going to be a breeze compared to breaking into his files.

After nothing but invalid password messages to show for his time, he'd given up. He'd just have to figure out a way to get Reddington's passwords. Some of the desk drawers had been locked. Maybe the man had written them down somewhere. Tonight he'd concentrate on the drawers, along with the ones in the credenza.

Today he faced an interesting challenge: meeting Lancelot Reddington and, instead of beating the shit out of him, actually teaching him how to determine the dollar value of human flesh.

With a snort of disgust, Dylan pulled himself out of bed. At least he had good accommodations. The view from his balcony looked out over the ocean. Would be nice if he could sit out there and drink coffee. Unfortunately, Reddington expected him for a breakfast meeting in—Dylan checked his watch—twenty minutes.

After a quick shower, he pulled on a pair of faded jeans, a T-shirt, and his oldest pair of running shoes. Dylan had never seen Reddington in anything other than a suit. Even Armando and his other goons dressed like they were businessmen. Maybe it was the man's attempt at feeling less like a sleaze. It amused Dylan to dress in the complete opposite style. Pissing Reddington off this way was a petty indulgence, but he'd take what he could get.

He arrived at the south patio to find Reddington, Armando, and Bruno just sitting down to eat. Apparently this was going to be a working breakfast, which suited him fine. Having Reddington's wife and daughter around, not to mention the schoolteacher, would only be a distraction.

A slight tick in Reddington's jaw told Dylan that the man was still pissed about something. The obvious argument he'd had with his wife seconds after they'd arrived must've been something else. Last night, the anger had been seething but toned down. Today, he didn't bother to hide his displeasure.

And when Reddington described the reason for his anger, Dylan's day got considerably brighter.

"My daughter had an accident a couple of days ago and hurt her leg. Instead of handling the injury here on the island, she and her boyfriend chose to defy my orders to never leave the island. She's in a hospital on La Rosa."

He turned to Armando. "Since you're going to collect Lance this afternoon, I want you to go earlier and pick up Giselle and Raphael as well." He expression hardened. "They must come home immediately."

As Armando gave his reassurance, Dylan's mind tried to get into Raphael's head. Would the kid take the chance he'd been given and get the hell away? Raphael was a smart kid, but just how did he feel about Reddington's daughter? Reddington had referred to him as his daughter's boyfriend.

The optimism Dylan had felt at learning that Raphael had gotten away disappeared. Armando would have no qualms about using force. The kid was untrained, unable to defend himself.

"Want me to help Armando?" he asked. "Might give Lance and me a chance to get to know each other."

Armando shook his head emphatically. "I can handle the job." The glare he shot Dylan was telling. Apparently, the admiration the man had for Dylan had morphed into jealousy. Great, just what he needed: a jealous psycho.

Reddington nodded. "I have full faith that Armando will return with Giselle, Raphael, and Lance."

Dylan shrugged as if he didn't care. Arguing would only create suspicion. The best he could hope for was that Raphael's good sense and instincts had told him to run while he could. "What do you want me to do today?"

"You and Bruno can both take the day off. Lie on the beach. Enjoy the beauty of my home."

Wouldn't hurt to take another look around. Unless Armando was using the yacht to retrieve Reddington's kids and Raphael, there was another way to get off the island. Maybe things were looking up after all.

"I think I'll pay that pretty teacher a visit."

Dylan's head jerked up at Bruno's statement. *What the hell?*

Reddington chuckled. "I thought I saw interest in your eyes last night. Be warned, though. She's newly widowed and may not be interested."

Bruno smiled. "I can be very persuasive."

"No." The word was out of Dylan's mouth before he could consider the consequences, but damned if he'd regret it. The image of this hulking giant getting close enough to touch Karen Jennings caused Dylan's breakfast to surge up his throat.

"So you have an interest in the little teacher, too," Reddington said. "Interesting."

"I called her first," Bruno grumbled.

Dylan swallowed a comeback that would only rile the bastard. Defending a lady's honor wasn't something John Wheeler would do. Men like Wheeler and Bruno wanted women for only one thing.

Turning to Reddington, he said, "You told me I could have my pick of two women at the next auction. Instead of taking two then, I'll go ahead and take this woman as my bonus."

Bruno opened his mouth to speak, but Reddington raised his hand to stop him. A glint in his eyes told Dylan he wasn't going to like what the man was about to say.

"It's true, you did ask for two women as a bonus. But Bruno asked for this woman first. I think the best way to solve the problem is to have a competition."

"What kind of competition?" Bruno asked.

Reddington eyed Dylan up and down and then turned back to Bruno. "Wheeler here doesn't have as much bulk as you do, but I've heard he's quite talented. And I've seen you in action. Let's see who's the toughest. Winner gets to court the teacher."

Cursing under his breath, Dylan kept his face impassive. Even though Bruno had about fifty pounds on him, Dylan didn't doubt his own abilities. He'd end up with some bruises and a cracked rib or two, but he'd had worse.

"I'm game," Dylan said.

A slow smile spread across Bruno face. Apparently, he was just as sure of his abilities.

"Excellent," Reddington said. "We'll have it tonight, after the party."

With a jerk of his head in agreement, Dylan stood. If he had the day to himself, spending any more time in the company of sleaze was a waste of good air. "Until tonight."

Turning, he walked back inside, away from the men, his mind on a new concern—one he hadn't anticipated. Winning this fight wasn't an issue. Bruno probably had little formal training. Brute force had likely won him his share of fights. Dylan did have formal training, along with down-and-dirty street-fighting experience. He knew he could bring the giant down. His concern was what would happen after he left. Did Karen Jennings realize she was in a pit of vipers?

The best he could do would be to warn her about what she'd gotten herself into. Once he got the files, he'd talk with her and give her the option of staying or coming with him.

About to run upstairs to start searching for her, Dylan saw a small, dark blur running down the steps outside. Amelia Reddington was headed toward the beach. Behind her, going at a slightly slower pace, was Karen Jennings.

He shot a glance back at Reddington and Bruno. Glad to see they were deep in a discussion, he veered around and headed out a side door. Reddington wouldn't appreciate the young teacher being given unsavory information about her employer, but he'd be damned if he wouldn't at least warn her.

Running down the steps, he saw Amelia dart off down the beach. Karen Jennings called out, "Don't get too far ahead," and then she laughed.

Dylan jerked to a stop. That laugh. *Holy shit!*

twenty-two

Jamie laughed as an energetic and exuberant Amelia ran ahead of her. The little girl's feelings had been hurt yesterday, but this morning, she was acting as happy as always. One of the things Jamie loved the most about working with children was their incredible resilience. Thank God Amelia had that, since her life would most likely become even more difficult when her father was put away.

Today was a day for action. Last night she had achieved her goal. Her astonishment at who had helped her achieve that goal hadn't diminished. Sarah Reddington had always looked so serene and happy. Had she adopted that attitude to deal with difficult circumstances or was it for the benefit of her children? The stark pain in the woman's eyes told a story of a torturous life.

As much as she wanted to help her, Jamie knew that the best thing she could do was get the information to the proper authorities and let them deal with Reddington. Having her husband behind bars might not repair the damage that'd been done to Sarah, but hopefully it would give her some peace of mind.

Jamie understood that the next step in her plan might well be her most difficult. She had to get Dylan alone and—

A hand grabbed her arm and spun her around.

Instinct and training kicked in; Jamie swung a right

jab toward her assailant's face. The man blocked her easily and pulled her hard against him.

"What the fuck are you doing here?"

She had never seen him so angry. Even during their worst arguments, he'd been coolly controlled. Jamie took a breath to still her pounding heart and quell the flush of need that was already zooming through her body. She raised her chin. "You know exactly why I'm here."

His hands tightened on her arms, and his eyes went that dark forest green. For just an instant, he lowered his head, and Jamie knew he was about to kiss her. The hard masculinity pressing against her stomach was a clear indicator that desire had trumped anger. Swallowing a groan of anticipation, Jamie stood on her toes to meet his mouth.

In the next instant, he pushed her away. His eyes on full glare now, he snarled, "You have got to be the most stubborn, idiotic fool this side of the equator."

"I may be stubborn, but I'm not a fool. I told you I had a surefire cover. You chose not to believe me."

"You also told your sister that you were working as a teacher in Louisiana."

"The location might be different from what I said, but I am working as a teacher."

"Do you know what you've gotten yourself into?"

"I knew exactly what I was doing."

"And do you know that you've got a goon fighting me for your attentions?"

"What are you talking about?"

"What's wrong?" piped a small voice.

Crap, they'd been so involved in each other, neither had heard Amelia. Jamie smiled down at the little girl. "Nothing's wrong. We're just having a minor disagreement."

"Like Mama and Papa do?"

Hell, she hoped not. Jamie shook her head. "It's nothing . . . really." She gave Dylan a telling look. Upsetting Amelia would serve no purpose. "Mr. Wheeler, Amelia and I need to start our school day. Perhaps we can talk about this at another time?"

Dylan gave her a stiff nod, then glanced down at Amelia and winked. "Guess I just woke up on the wrong side of the bed this morning."

Taking the little girl's hand, Jamie started back to the mansion. "I'll talk with you later, Mr. Wheeler."

"I look forward to continuing our discussion, Mrs. Jennings."

Jamie moved as fast as her feet would carry her. Fortunately, this speed was normal for Amelia and the child had no problem keeping up with her. Her mind was whirling as quickly as her feet. The reunion with Dylan hadn't exactly gone as she'd hoped. She had expected he'd be furious . . . she just hadn't known how furious. Nor had she known that the instant she realized who'd touched her, she had immediately started wanting him. She was used to her silly heart longing for him, but did her body have to be equally as silly?

"Do you have a crush on Mr. Wheeler?"

So much for hiding her thoughts. Jamie shrugged. "He's kind of handsome, isn't he?"

Amelia gave an emphatic nod. "Almost as handsome as Raphael and my papa."

Jamie swallowed a laugh. She didn't know who would be the most insulted, Dylan, Raphael, or Reddington.

"How about we check that math homework I gave you and then see what Junie B. Jones is up to today."

Another emphatic nod and the girl took off running. Jamie followed her at a slower pace, her mind on the upcoming confrontation she and Dylan were going to have. She hadn't even had the chance to tell him she had the files.

At that thought, she smiled to herself. She may not have gone about it the way he would have liked, but she had accomplished what she'd set out to do. Dylan would have to admit that.

She stood in the middle of her bedroom, stiff and still. She knew he was there. Dylan had learned early that Jamie had good instincts.

He wanted to shake her until her teeth rattled, and at the same time he wanted to kiss her until neither of them had any breath left. How the hell had he missed it last night? He had sat across from her, talked with her. Hell, he'd even flirted with her—sort of.

And she'd sat there, smiling and chatting as if they'd never met. As if he hadn't ever kissed her breathless, licked every part of her body, or been so deep inside her that her heartbeat had felt like his own.

Dylan swallowed back a groan. He'd walked around the island at a punishing speed and was still pissed. Didn't help that the moment he'd walked into the bedroom and smelled lemons, he'd gotten hard again.

How long had she been on the island? What the hell had she hoped to accomplish? Yeah, he knew she thought she was so damn smart to have fooled Reddington. And she'd probably gotten a good chuckle over fooling Dylan. But just what did she think she could really do here? The files weren't just lying out in the open for her to grab. And even if she'd been able to accomplish stealing the files, how did she plan to get off the island?

Halfway around the island, he'd realized something. He was as angry at himself as he was with her. He'd been stupid to take her at her word. He dealt in lies and deceit daily, but when it'd come to Jamie, he had believed her . . . trusted her. Even knowing how determined she was and how angry she'd been when she had left the cabin. He had called her an idiot, but that was the pot calling the kettle black.

Now he had to figure out how to get her off the island before she got hurt. He'd come here expecting to rescue Raphael, so this really didn't change his plans that much. Well, with the exception that he was going to have to fight Bruno for her.

Without turning to look at him, she said, "Are you going to say anything?"

"What's there to say?"

She turned around, and Dylan felt the gut punch he always felt in Jamie's presence. Hell, no wonder he'd been attracted to Karen Jennings. Looking at her now, he saw Jamie, not Karen. Though her hair and eyes were brown, she wore glasses, and she'd done something with the shape of her face to make it look different, he could now see Jamie clearly.

"I know you're still angry, but when you—"

Dylan raised a hand to cut her off. "You still don't get it. You not only put yourself in unnecessary danger, you've put me in a position of protecting you. I don't need the hassle."

"I don't know what you're talking about. No one has any idea of my identity. I don't need your protection."

"Really? Well, tell me why I'm fighting Bruno over you tonight."

A wrinkle developed on her smooth brow. "Who's Bruno?"

"Reddington's man. The one who looks like a gorilla on steroids. He's interested in you."

Her nose scrunched in a grimace. "I saw him looking at me last night. But why are you fighting him?"

"Reddington's idea. Bruno said he wanted you . . . I took exception to that. Tonight, we're going to decide who gets to court you."

Her hands went to her hips, indignation and temper

heightening the color in her face. "I'm not a pork chop for two dogs to fight over." She turned to the door. "I'll go set Reddington straight right now."

Dylan was on her before she could move another step. Bringing her body flush against his, he said, "You'll do nothing of the sort. If he knows I told you, he'll get pissed. I need to stay on his good side until I can get what I came for and we can leave."

Jamie closed her eyes at the sensation of being pressed against Dylan's hard body. How was it with that one touch, he could make her forget everything? The anger from seconds ago had just been doused by a major case of want and need.

"Okay." She winced at how breathy she sounded. Why couldn't she at least act a little sophisticated? With Dylan, her body knew nothing about denial or playing hard to get. It wanted what it wanted.

Apparently, Dylan also felt that need. Pulling her closer, he wrapped his arms around her and growled in her ear, "I'd forgotten how damn good you feel." He paused, then added, "Have you put on some weight?"

Jamie snorted out a laugh. "That's one question you should never ask a woman."

He turned her slowly around, and it was all she could do not to wrap her arms around him. She couldn't do that. Even though his body was giving every indication that he'd welcome the advance, throwing herself at him again would be stupid.

Dylan surprised her by pressing a kiss to her forehead and then leaning his forehead against hers. "We need to come up with a plan to keep you safe until I get what I need."

"I have what you need."

A groan came from deep in his chest. "Yeah, but that'll have to wait until I get this job done."

Exasperated, Jamie pushed away from him. "That's not what I was talking about. I have the files."

Dropping his arms, he backed away from her. "You have them? How? Where?"

"I copied them onto a flash drive. It's in my cosmetics case."

"How did you get them?"

"Mrs. Reddington."

His face went dark in suspicion. "Why would she help you?"

Jamie explained how she and Raphael had been trying to get into Reddington's files using a different word each night for a possible password and how she'd gone by herself last night only to find Mrs. Reddington waiting for her. "I think something he did yesterday must have tipped the scales for her. She looked hurt and sad but very determined."

Dylan nodded. "She and Reddington had some harsh words as soon as he got off the yacht."

"Probably because of Raphael."

"That's what I figured. I hope to hell the kid's thousands of miles away by now."

Jamie shook her head. "I don't know. He and Giselle are crazy about each other. I'm not sure he'd leave her."

"He'd better. Armando is going to the hospital today. Reddington told him to bring both of them back."

"Then I hope he's far away, too. Giselle is safe here; Raphael's not."

"There's someone else Armando's bringing back."

She didn't have to ask . . . she could see it on his face. "Lance."

"Yeah. It's Reddington's birthday present to his wife."

She was once again back in that room, hearing his voice, seeing the evil in his eyes. Revulsion churned her stomach, threatening to bring up everything she'd eaten today.

"Jamie, look at me."

She jerked back to the present. Dylan was standing only a foot away from her, his eyes dark with concern.

"You can plead illness. You don't have to see him."

Her heart picked up an optimistic beat. "Neither of us do. We have what we need. We can leave."

"We can't . . . at least not yet. Armando took the boat, and from what I can tell, it's our only mode of escape. Also, if I don't show up for the fight, they'll start looking for us immediately. Our best bet is to leave after everyone has gone to bed. We can be gone hours before they notice. I'll come to your room about three."

She nodded. Even though she hated that he'd have to fight the brute, Jamie knew he was right.

"I'd better get out of here before I get caught."

"I'll see you at dinner."

"Jamie, you don't have to come."

"I know, but facing my demons is the only way I'm going to get past this." It was the first time she'd given any indication that Lance Reddington had done something to her. She hoped Dylan didn't ask her any questions. Just making that statement had been a breakthrough. Revealing the truth was going to take more time.

"I'll be there if you need me."

Unable to stop herself, Jamie leaped into his arms. As they closed around her, she held him tight. "Thank you, Dylan."

He pressed his lips briefly against her hair, then dropped his arms and walked out the door.

Stanford stood by the wide window of the ballroom, separated from the rest of the party. It was, by necessity, a low-key affair. Sarah didn't have friends. But with a family like theirs, friends weren't necessary.

Giselle had returned home. Armando had picked her up from the hospital. The doctors hadn't wanted to let her go, but Armando could be very persuasive. Raphael had been nowhere around. When Armando had asked about the young man's whereabouts, his daughter had reportedly burst into tears and claimed he'd left her, without explanation.

Had Raphael not been as enamored of the girl as he'd thought? Giselle's face was pale, her eyes red-rimmed, and for the first time ever, Stanford thought she looked plain and unattractive. Did he need to have a talk with her about keeping herself presentable? Was that why Raphael had left? Had she let herself go and the young man had lost interest?

When he'd arrived yesterday and discovered Raphael and Giselle's absence, he'd been livid. Though Sarah had insisted that there had been no other option, Stanford had questioned the veracity of her word. Had there been a flicker of secrecy in her eyes?

He'd spoken with Joseph, who had assured him that Giselle's injury was indeed serious. And though reassured that a hospital had been a necessity, he'd chosen to chastise Sarah anyway. The punishment had been quick but effective. She'd cried and whimpered throughout the process, as usual. Sarah had known about these rules for over two decades, and it had been years since she'd broken them. A reinforcement of his mandates was just an added insurance that they could never be broken without dire consequences.

But now, things were back to the way they should be. Once again, she was happy and content. The joy on her face when she'd seen Giselle had been worth the trouble.

Lance was in his room. Soon he would make a grand entrance and her birthday present would be complete. Nothing made his dear wife happier than to have all of her babies in her nest.

He glanced over at the other guests. Armando was having an intense-looking discussion with Bruno, which was interesting. The two men didn't normally acknowledge each other, much less carry on a conversation.

John Wheeler stood apart from the party. The man wasn't the social kind, but what he lacked in those skills he more than made up for with his knowledge of the business. Stanford anticipated that Lance would learn much from his new tutor.

The teacher, Karen Jennings, sat beside Giselle and seemed to be trying to comfort the girl. That was good. Maybe she could encourage his daughter to improve her appearance. Not that the Jennings woman was much of a looker, but she had a certain attractiveness that would appeal to some men. Wheeler and Bruno certainly thought so.

After the party ended, the real entertainment would begin. Watching the two men fight over a woman appealed to Stanford's romantic nature. Of course, once it was clear who'd won the contest, he'd take them aside and explain the rules of the island. Taking a woman by force was sometimes a necessity, but in this case, he wouldn't allow it. Amelia seemed to like her teacher. And the woman got on well with Giselle and Sarah. Having her damaged would upset the serenity of the island.

He didn't anticipate any problems. The woman was widowed and would probably welcome a man's attention. Once the party was over, he looked forward to confiding to her that two men were fighting over her. Any woman would be flattered with such attention. He hoped blood didn't bother her, since he anticipated an entertainingly brutal event.

He checked his watch . . . finally time for the grand entrance. Stanford moved toward his wife, and held out his hand. "Sarah, it's time for your final present of the evening."

Smiling up at him with the same grace and beauty that had captured his attention when they were both still teenagers, she stood beside him. "I'm sure it will be wonderful."

"Turn around and look at the door."

Still smiling, Sarah twisted around and gasped. Lancelot stood at the entrance. With a smile as cocky and self-assured as ever, he held his arms outstretched for his mother to walk into them.

Instead of running to him, Sarah took a startled step back. Stanford frowned down at her. "Go to him. He's your gift, my dear."

With her face pale but composed, she stretched her lips into a smile and rushed toward Lance. "Darling, how wonderful to see you again."

In the middle of taking a sip of her drink, Jamie froze. She knew he was at the door. Somehow one just knows when evil arrives. Her hand wasn't as steady as she'd like, so she put her drink down. Spilling it would call attention to her, and if there was one thing she didn't want right now, it was to have anyone looking at her.

Of course, that didn't include Dylan. He'd stood separate from everyone else, but the instant Lance appeared, he moved closer to Jamie. One of the many things she loved about Dylan—he didn't have to know details to be protective. It was as instinctive in him as evil was to Reddington and his low-life son.

Both Giselle and Amelia seemed pleased to see their brother, but he barely spared them a glance. He hugged his mother, and then Reddington grabbed his arm and immediately brought him over to Dylan.

Jamie couldn't look at Lance. She kept her eyes on

Dylan, concentrating on his rock-solid steadiness, the strength of character in his face. And somehow, without him even looking directly at her, she knew he was aware of her and was giving her comfort.

Emotion swamped her. She loved him. God in heaven, how she loved this man. Everything he had done, even when he was bullying her, frustrating her, and growling at her, he'd done because he cared. Maybe he didn't love her, but she owed him so much. And other than thanking him for rescuing her, she'd done nothing to repay him.

"Karen, are you all right?"

Taking her eyes off Dylan, she turned to Giselle. "I'm fine. It's been a long day, and I guess I'm more tired than I thought."

Giselle offered her a sympathetic smile, and once again, Jamie felt guilty. The poor girl looked as though she'd been crying for days. Her leg, encased in a cast halfway up her thigh, had to be causing her discomfort, but Jamie got the feeling that it was Raphael's desertion that was hurting her the most. When she'd asked about him, Giselle's lips had trembled and her eyes had filled with tears. "He said he had to leave, but we would see each other again."

Jamie had responded with what she was sure was the truth: "Then if he said you'll see him again, you will."

Giselle had seemed to take comfort in that, and though Jamie felt sad for her, she was glad that Raphael had gotten away. Had he gone back to Madrid or was he with Noah in Paris? Either way, as long as he was far away from Reddington, he was safe.

Reddington's voice boomed out, startling Jamie: "Come, everyone. Let's go to dinner and celebrate the birth of the most beautiful woman in the world."

As she headed to the dining room with the rest of the

group, Jamie was aware of Dylan's presence behind her. Just knowing he was there gave her comfort, along with the courage to sit down to dinner with the monster who starred in all of her nightmares.

Dylan had never come closer to blowing a mission in his life. As he stood talking with Lance Reddington, acting as if he were interested in what the creep had to say, he could feel Jamie's pain as clearly as if it were his own. Whatever Lance had done to her, she still suffered. And Dylan wanted to make him pay.

He could do nothing other than stay as close to her as possible and let her know that she wasn't alone. Taking his revenge would do nothing more than get one piece of scum removed from the world.

The best revenge for everyone was to stop Reddington and rescue as many of the people he'd sold over the years as possible. That would destroy the man and, ultimately, his son.

He ate a light dinner. In an hour or so, he was going to fight. The thought of puking his guts up all over Bruno was enticing, but he intended to beat the hell out of the guy, not gross him out.

Though he was aware of everyone at the table, his senses homed in on Jamie, who sat across from him and to his left. Thankfully Reddington and his son were at the other end of the table. Dylan noted that Jamie picked at her food, and he was sure she was counting the minutes until she could get away.

If all went as planned, they'd both be gone in a few hours. Dylan had been standing out of sight, not far from the pool house, when Armando arrived this afternoon with Lance and Giselle. He'd crept closer and watched through the window as the man placed the keys underneath the seat and then closed the fake floor that covered the boat.

Once he finished with Bruno, he'd grab his stuff, get Jamie, and be off.

Dylan didn't bother to question if he was making it all seem too easy. Easy or hard, they were getting out of here tonight.

twenty-three

Jamie stood at the entrance to the gym. Large and spacious, it held a nice assortment of equipment and free weights. She figured the giant red-and-black cage across the room, where several men stood, would be the fight location. Apparently, this kind of entertainment wasn't unusual on the island.

Reddington had stopped her on her way out the door after dinner and told her she was invited to attend "tonight's entertainment." She'd smiled politely, as if she didn't know what he was talking about—as if some concert were being held, as opposed to what she knew it to be: two men beating each other up for a chance to court her. She was in equal parts infuriated and horrified. Reddington's opinion of women was no surprise. Maybe what surprised her most was how he had gazed down at her as if he thought she would be pleased. Only a sick, twisted pervert would think a woman would be happy to be fought over like she was a piece of meat.

She was dressed and ready for their escape as soon as Dylan gave the word. Taking anything other than the flash drives and her fake identification would be pointless. There was nothing else she wanted to keep. She had changed from the dress she'd worn at dinner to a comfortable pair of loose black pants and a matching long cotton shirt. Beneath her shirt, she'd tucked her identification and the flash drives into a small pouch attached to her belt. Once they were safely away, she looked forward to ditching the extra padding she had to wear.

A smiling Reddington appeared in front of her, his eyes glinting with excitement. "Welcome, Karen. I think you'll enjoy tonight's show."

At a loss for an appropriate comeback, Jamie returned his smile and remained silent. She wanted to ask him exactly what part of tonight's entertainment she was supposed to enjoy: the sweat, the blood, or the possibility of broken bones?

Yes, she knew many people enjoyed watching fights. Fighting for money, to defend someone, or, hell, even for the fun of it wasn't the issue here. This fight was essentially for ownership of a person—namely, Jamie.

Reddington led her to a row of chairs beside the cage. "Have a seat. We'll get started in a few minutes."

Since she wasn't supposed to know what this was about, Jamie glanced around the gym and then up at Reddington. "But where are Mrs. Reddington and the rest of the guests?"

"She's squeamish when it comes to this kind of entertainment. This is a men-only event, but I invited you because you're the main attraction."

"Excuse me?" There was no way she could fake her response or appear anything less than insulted.

Reddington chuckled, apparently not disturbed by her reaction. "You don't have to do anything but sit and watch, my dear. As soon as our contestants arrive, I'll explain everything."

A sound behind the man caused him to turn. Peering around him, Jamie caught her breath, and a new, larger worry surfaced. She'd been selfishly focused on the insult to her without considering what Dylan was going to have to go through. She knew he was strong and well trained, knew he could move with amazing speed. But now, as she stared at the hulk that had just arrived, she felt major doubts.

Bruno wasn't as tall as Dylan, but what he lacked in height, he made up for in bulk. She'd seen him dressed in suits that had probably been tailored for him and had hidden some of that massiveness. Now, wearing only a pair of tight, spandex shorts, he flexed his bulging muscles. Nausea roiled in her stomach at the thought of what kind of damage this man could do.

Seconds later, Dylan appeared. Dressed in a pair of ragged-looking army-issue khakis, he looked muscled and toned. With eight-pack abs, broad shoulders, and muscled arms and chest, he exuded masculinity and strength. But would that strength and training hold up against sheer brute force?

With her eyes and her worry focused on Dylan, Jamie didn't notice that anyone else was close until someone sat beside her. She turned her head and, in an instant, felt as if the floor had opened beneath her.

Flashing a charming smile, the young man held out his hand and noted, "We didn't get to officially meet earlier. I'm Lance Reddington."

She made herself lift her hand and place it in his, heard herself mumble something. Whatever she said, it must have been appropriate enough because he let go of her hand and said, "This must be very exciting for you."

Bile came into her mouth. Not only was her worst nightmare sitting beside her, he was expecting her to carry on a conversation about the upcoming event—to be excited and happy. She couldn't answer; there were just no words anywhere in her frozen mind that would sound even moderately sane.

Numbly, she heard voices and looked up. Dylan and Reddington seemed to be having an argument. Finally Reddington nodded and turned to the small group of people that were sitting in the row of chairs with Jamie.

She recognized many of the male staff on the island. They had arrived without her even being aware of them . . . her total concentration had been on the demon sitting beside her.

With Bruno on one side of him and Dylan on the other, Reddington addressed the audience: "It's been a while since we've enjoyed this kind of entertainment on the island. Tonight, we have two gentlemen who are vying for the affections of our newest resident, Karen Jennings. Each man has indicated an interest in courting her, so to settle this dispute, we're having a battle of sorts. As I informed the men earlier, there's only one rule." Reddington paused for effect and then grinned as he continued: "Nobody dies."

Dylan murmured something; Reddington nodded and added, "Mr. Wheeler and Bruno will have a brief moment with Mrs. Jennings before the proceedings begin." He grinned again. "A precursor to romance, if you will."

Reddington came toward her and said, "Mrs. Jennings, come with me."

Getting away from Lance Reddington was such a welcome relief, she gladly took the older man's hand. He led her to an isolated corner. "Bruno will go first. He'll have one minute to charm you. Then Mr. Wheeler will have his turn."

Bracing herself against the wall, she watched Bruno clomp toward her. Oddly enough, he looked completely sincere and serious. Jamie had no idea what to expect when he stopped in front of her.

"It gets lonely on the island." His large throat worked as he swallowed hard and added, "I didn't know I'd be expected to say anything to you."

With each passing moment, the evening grew more bizarre. Unable to find anything remotely encouraging or fitting to say, she murmured the first thing that came into her head: "A good book can be a lot of company."

She didn't know which of them was more astonished by her inane statement. His expression one of confusion, he nodded and backed away. The instant he left, she regretted not saying something that would make her the last person he could be attracted to.

Dylan came toward her, and Jamie forgot everything but the need to throw herself into his arms and tell him how sorry she was that he was having to do this.

As usual, Dylan didn't waste time on niceties. "If this thing turns to shit, don't wait until three to leave. Find a way to get to the boat and get the hell out of here."

Afraid that someone might read her expression, she kept her face as blank as Dylan's. "I'm not leaving without you."

"Listen to me," he whispered furiously. "Just because no one's going to die, doesn't mean there won't be injuries. If I'm unconscious or incapacitated, you have to go on your own. Head to the closest island, buy a disposable cellphone, and call McCall. Then lie low till he comes for you. Understand? My cover is still tight. I'll leave here when Reddington does."

What he said made sense, but the thought of leaving Dylan behind was like a punch to her chest. Breathing became difficult.

"Look at me."

She jerked her head up, unaware that she'd been staring into space.

His eyes pierced hers. "We'll get through this . . . trust me."

There were few absolute certainties in her life anymore, but this was one she could unequivocally state: "I do."

With a final nod, he turned away and headed to the

center of the ring, where Reddington and Bruno were waiting.

Strangely calm, Jamie went back to where the rest of the audience was sitting. Hoping no one noticed the slight, she chose another chair, as far from Lance Reddington as possible. With her eyes on the ridiculous debacle in front of her, Jamie waited for the fight to begin. And she prayed.

Dylan wanted to get this over and done with as soon as possible. Jamie's white, strained face said she'd reached her limit of stress. And he'd personally reached his limit of machismo bullshit.

As Reddington issued final instructions and preened like he was some sort of fight master, Dylan planned his strategy. Bruno was beefy, thick, and had probably cut his teeth on beating the shit out of people on the toughest streets in Spain. No way did he underestimate the man's strength or skill.

Speed was going to be Dylan's secret weapon. Everything he did, every move he made and every word he spoke, indicated a slow-talking, laid-back man. What he'd learned as a child to keep from calling attention to himself and irritating his old man had paid off many times for him as an adult. By the time most people realized that they'd underestimated him, it was too late.

Bruno had something more planned than what Reddington expected. Dylan had been around too long not to see that coming. Three times today, he'd spotted Armando and Bruno with their heads together. An unfortunate by-product of needing to get in Reddington's good graces quickly had been to diminish Armando's influence on his boss. No doubt the man was pissed and had asked Bruno to step up for him.

Death wasn't on either man's mind. They wouldn't want to anger their boss by killing Dylan. Especially since he was soon to be Lance Reddington's tutor. But Dylan had a feeling that Bruno planned to get as rough as he could without crossing the fine line into murder.

Reddington went out the cage door and shut it, then jumped from the platform. Dylan and Bruno nodded once at each other and began circling, looking for that first movement or any vulnerability. Dylan liked his opponent to go first, so he waited patiently, knowing the man would eventually give up and go for it.

Surprisingly, Bruno was more patient than most. After the third full circle, Dylan did the one thing that always worked—he smiled. Worked like a charm. Bruno frowned, let out a low growl, and charged forward. Dylan swooped left, and Bruno ran past him and bounced against the cage wall.

An unfortunate consequence of that move was the surprised laughter that always came from the onlookers and the subsequent rage of his opponent. With a roar, Bruno came after Dylan again. This time, Dylan leaned forward and ducked, causing the man to fall over him and land on his back. Recovering quickly, he came at Dylan again, slamming a brawny fist into Dylan's face and then following it with a quick jab to his ribs. Blood spewed across the floor.

Shaking off the sting, Dylan growled, "First blood. Feel good about it, asshole."

Bruno frowned as if a little disconcerted by his words, but Dylan didn't give him time to wonder. With a series of punches, whirls, and kicks, he pummeled the man's face, chest, and abdomen. Bruno grunted, stumbled, and dodged. Every time he missed one of Dylan's hits, he caught another. After a succession of blows, Bruno was bleeding from his nose and mouth, and his eyes were looking decidedly glassy.

The shouts from the men outside the cage were becoming louder and more boisterous. Knowing the audience wouldn't be satisfied with such a brief performance, Dylan delivered another series of blows with his fists. Bruno's only defense now was to hold his arms in front of himself and try to block the swift, stinging punches.

Dazed, with blood flooding from his nose and drizzling out his mouth, Bruno wobbled. He was close to toppling over, but sheer stupidity kept him on his feet. *To hell with it.* He wasn't going to incapacitate the man just to please a group of bloodthirsty assholes. Going for the knockout blow, with a quick twist, he kicked high, aiming for Bruno's big head. Dylan saw the knife too late.

The blade sliced across his torso and then dropped lower, catching his thigh. The pain would come later; for now, he took advantage of the extra adrenaline from the surge of anger at himself. Dammit, should've seen that coming.

Dylan swung into the man's gut, again and again, each successive strike harder and more measured. Though Bruno still held the knife, he did nothing with it other than grip it in his hand as he tried to protect himself from the punishing blows.

And then it was time—Dylan went for excruciating agony. Kicking hard and quick, he jammed his foot deep into Bruno's groin. The squeal the man released could probably be heard all over the island. Bruno finally dropped the knife and grabbed his balls with both hands. Dylan took advantage and landed the knockout blow to his head. Bruno flew across the cage; his back slammed into the padded wall. His eyes rolling back, he slid halfway down and then dropped face-first onto the floor.

With his breath rasping against his lungs, Dylan leaned against the other side of the cage and accessed his injuries. Bruises, a sore but not broken nose, a gash on his side, and an insignificant cut on his leg. He glanced down and was pleased to see that the slice on his side wasn't as deep as he'd feared.

A towel landed at his feet. Dylan looked up to see Reddington standing inside the cage, admiration and awe on his face. "Knives were strictly forbidden. He got in a couple of good slices and you still beat him."

Since the man's approval was no longer necessary to his plan, Dylan ignored him as he grabbed the towel and pressed it against his torso wound. He needed to see how Jamie had fared.

She was still in her chair. Her hands were gripped together so tight, even from this distance he could see the whites of her knuckles. What struck him the most was the calmness of her expression. And though her face was as pale as milk, he was damn proud of her composure.

"Don't just look," Reddington urged. "Go to her. You won her fair and square."

The man's permission to talk to Jamie meant only one thing to Dylan. She could leave the gym with him and no one would follow.

Holding the towel at his bleeding side, Dylan went through the cage doors. He dropped down to the floor and made his way over to Jamie, who'd yet to move.

"Let's go."

"Are you okay?"

"Yeah . . . fine. I've got some bandages in my room."

She stood and, to his surprise, put her arm around him. "Lean on me."

A burst of laughter exploded behind him. *Reddington.* Apparently the man believed he was a real-life matchmaker.

"Let's go before we have unwanted company."

Since it was after midnight, they made it inside the mansion and to his room without anyone stopping them. They were inside the room, the door closed behind them, when he realized Jamie's face was wet, as silent tears fell from her eyes.

"What's wrong?"

"This is all my fault."

Dylan shook his head. "If it wasn't you, it'd be someone else. Reddington wanted his fight. Any woman on the island would be vulnerable to something like this."

She sniffed delicately and wiped her sleeve against her face. "I can't wait to leave here."

"Just a few more hours."

Pulling gauze, antibacterial spray, and bandages from a small bag he got from the closet, Dylan dropped them onto the bed. Tending his wounds by himself was something he was used to doing, so when Jamie disappeared into the bathroom, he thought little of it. Dabbing the wound on his side with the gauze, he was about to douse it with the antibacterial spray when a soft, warm cloth appeared; Dylan held his breath as Jamie gently cleaned his wound. His heart thudded against his chest . . . he had the thought that his pulse hadn't pounded this fast even when he was fighting Bruno. Jamie was the only one who could create this kind of reaction.

In silence, he stood still while she finished cleaning the cut, gritted his teeth as she applied the icy-cool, antibacterial spray, and then held his breath when she used butterfly bandages to close his wound.

She finished, then stepped back with a small, slightly self-conscious smile. "It's not as bad as I thought it would be."

"I have a cut on my thigh." His hands went to his zipper, and then, feeling almost awkward, he said, "I need to take my pants off."

Instead of sharing his awkwardness or stepping away from him, Jamie surprised the hell out of him again. "Let me help you."

Sex should be the last thing on his mind. Hell, he

ached all over, was bone tired, and in a couple of hours, he was going to have to steal a boat and escape from a madman and his goons. The hardening flesh between his legs couldn't care less about those kinds of details. Anytime Jamie was close, it behaved this way.

Hoping the sight of his erection wouldn't scare her off, Dylan unbuttoned his pants and eased the zipper down over his erection. His best bet was to get the antibacterial spray on his cut as soon as possible. If pain didn't diminish his arousal, nothing would. Well, one thing would, but that was something he definitely couldn't do.

As if treating men with gashes in their legs and sporting massive erections was an everyday occurrence, Jamie helped Dylan lower his pants to the floor. So what if he was aroused. That didn't mean anything. The adrenaline rush from the fight had probably caused it. She'd read somewhere that some men became sexually aroused after a fight or a near-death experience.

"Step out of them and lie down." Her cheeks heated at what sounded like an invitation. "I'll go get another wet cloth." She turned away before she could be caught salivating. Of all the times to fantasize about the sexy, almost naked man lying on the bed waiting for her, now wasn't one of them.

She returned to see Dylan dabbing at the wound with the gauze. "Is it still bleeding?"

"No. It stopped." He took the washcloth from her hand and put it over the cut.

Jamie went to her knees beside the bed. Using another cloth she'd dampened, she dabbed gently at his nose. When he flinched, she pulled back slightly. "Does it hurt?"

"Not really. Just a little sore."

Taking that as a sign that she could proceed, she wiped the blood from his face. He had a gash at the bridge of his nose, but she didn't think it was broken. He closed his eyes as if what she was doing gave him pleasure. Jamie folded the cloth to find a clean area and then bathed his entire face.

His eyes opened, the green depths swirling with some kind of emotion she couldn't place. Her gaze locked with his, Jamie held her breath, wanting, needing, but so afraid she'd make a mistake.

A soft sound outside the door caught their attention. Jamie went to her feet, alarmed.

Dylan stood, and though she knew his leg must be hurting, she barely saw him limp as he went to the door. With a sudden wrench of the knob, he jerked the door open.

Mrs. Reddington stood at the entrance, apparently getting ready to knock. "I'm sorry to disturb you," she whispered. "May I come in?"

Dylan nodded and closed the door behind her. Apparently realizing he was standing almost nude in front of a woman he barely knew, he grabbed a pair pants from the bureau and slid into them.

Mrs. Reddington didn't seem to notice anyone's discomfort. She turned to Jamie. "Is he . . ." She swallowed and made a gesture toward Dylan. "Is he with you?"

Jamie shot a glance at Dylan, waiting for his approval. When he nodded, she looked back at the woman and said, "Yes."

"You're leaving tonight, aren't you?"

"Yes, we are."

"I thought you might, since you have what you came for." She withdrew a piece of paper from the pocket of her skirt and held it out to Jamie. "I know you can't take his physical files without him knowing they're gone, but when you can take them, you'll need the combination to his safe. It's a twelve-number sequence; then you turn the key, once to the left, twice to the right. He keeps the key on his key chain. You have to be careful, though. If you make a mistake and enter the numbers the wrong way or in the wrong sequence, a built-in system will destroy the contents."

Jamie knew Dylan still had his doubts, so she asked, "How do you know this?"

A small, wry smile broke the solemn sadness of her face. "I've lived with Stanford for more than half my life. I've gotten good at being invisible. Following him around for years, watching him, is finally paying off."

Jamie smiled her gratitude. "This will be very helpful."

"Also, about the boat. I wanted to warn you that it will have only enough petrol to get you to La Rosa. That's Stanford's safeguard if anyone tries to leave here. That's the only place anyone can reach with that amount of fuel. He has friends on the island and can alert them immediately."

Before Jamie could thank her again, Dylan spoke: "Why are you telling us this?"

Instead of answering him, she turned back to Jamie. "You asked me why I stayed. When he first brought me here, I tried to escape, several times." Her mouth twisted. "As you can see, I wasn't successful. I'm the reason he keeps the boat only partially fueled. When I became pregnant, I stayed for a different reason. Stanford knew I wouldn't put my children in jeopardy."

"What's changed?" Jamie asked softly.

"You came."

"What do you mean?"

"I don't know what he did to you, but instead of accepting it, you came after him. You reminded me that I once had that kind of courage."

A lump in her throat kept Jamie from responding, so she nodded her head in appreciation and smiled.

"You and your children can come with us."

Jamie whirled around to stare at Dylan in wonder. Offering to take Reddington's family upped the risk quotient dramatically. He had nothing to gain by doing this, other than to be the man he was—a hero and a rescuer.

Mrs. Reddington smiled with appreciation. "Thank you, but no. We'll stay here and ride out the storm."

She turned to go toward the door, but Jamie called to her, stopping her. "Tell Amelia that she's a bright, talented girl and is going to have wonderful adventures one day."

"I will." She turned back to the door, and Dylan opened it for her. He looked out into the hallway and then back at the older woman. "All clear."

With the dignity and regal bearing that Jamie had been impressed with at their first meeting, Mrs. Reddington went through the doorway.

Dylan closed the door behind her and looked at Jamie. "Let's get my leg bandaged and get the hell out of here."

twenty-four

Their steps were so silent on the walkway that Dylan checked behind just to be sure Jamie was still there. She was so quiet, he couldn't even hear her breathe. Outfitted in black pants, shirt, and sneakers, she'd also pulled a black skullcap over her head; the only color she presented was her pale, still face. He expected her to look frightened, maybe even excited. Instead, she had that chin cocked at an angle he knew all too well. Determination.

He wanted to tell her he was proud of her for what she had accomplished; he wanted to yell at her for being so damn stubborn as to risk her life. He wanted to— holy hell, he wanted to kiss her deep, hard, and forever.

"You okay?" His voice was barely a shadow of a whisper.

She nodded and gave him a thumbs-up sign.

Dylan turned around and moved down the path that led to the pool house. Jamie had explained how it worked. When Giselle had been taken to the hospital, she had been there and watched. She said that Joseph had opened a small compartment in the wall of the building, pressed a button, and the floor had opened, revealing the speedboat. When he'd pressed another button, the boat had been lifted and then he'd pushed it into the water.

Sounded damn easy. He only hoped there weren't any hidden alarms attached to alert Reddington that the boat was being taken out. They'd waited until four A.M. to leave. With the men getting into bed later than normal because of the fight, Dylan had wanted to make sure they'd be deeply asleep.

The pool house was bathed in darkness, like the rest of the buildings on the island. Reddington wasted no energy on unnecessary lights since no one was supposed to be about this time of night.

If all went as planned, they'd be miles from the island before anyone noticed they were missing. It was frustrating, but he was damn glad to know about the shortage of gas in the boat. Mrs. Reddington had been of monumental assistance in helping bring her husband to justice. He just hoped to hell the man never found out, at least until he was behind bars. Dylan hated to think what he would do to her.

Bringing her and the children along with them would have slowed them down and increased their risks, but he'd had to make the offer. Leaving vulnerable people behind didn't sit right with him. He hoped she had made the right decision.

A whisper of a sound caught his attention. Dylan stopped abruptly, and Jamie, only a couple of feet behind him, stopped, too. Neither of them breathed as he listened intently. Yes, there it was—a shuffling of some sort. A small animal rooting around for food? Or something more ominous?

Dylan took Jamie's arm and pulled her down to the ground with him. With his mouth over her ear, he whispered, "You hear it?"

Her skullcap rubbed against his mouth as she nodded.

"Can you tell where it's coming from?"

She shook her head.

Dylan pulled away and tried to do a 360-degree search around them. Clouds obscured the moon, and the only lights were a spattering of sparkling stars in the northeast corner of the sky. The entire island was in inky darkness. If anyone was wandering around, wouldn't they, at the very least, have a flashlight?

Since time was running out and he saw nothing, Dylan made the decision to move on. They had to get out of here before the sun started brightening the sky.

Putting his hand on Jamie's arm, he brought her up with him. Flush against her body, he spoke into her ear again: "I don't see anyone . . . probably a small animal foraging for food. I want you plastered to my ass, just in case. Understand?"

She nodded.

Dylan turned and started down the steps again, feeling Jamie's softness pressed up against him. With his ears alert for any more suspicious sounds, he speeded up his steps. A few feet from the pool house, he stopped and turned. "Stay close to me. As soon as I pull the boat up, you jump in and I'll follow."

Dylan strode toward the doorway. Wrapping his hand around the doorknob, he twisted, pleased that it turned easily. Having to pick a lock wouldn't have delayed them for that long, but every second counted. He eased the door open and then heard a sound that didn't belong to either of them. He jerked to a stop, and Jamie bumped into him.

"Going somewhere?" Armando's slurred voice growled from the shadows.

Shit, just what he didn't need—a jealous psycho who was also, apparently, drunk.

Pulling Jamie behind him, Dylan turned to see the hulking dark shadow swaying in front of him. "Thought I'd take my new lady friend for a boat ride and a swim."

"Cold to be swimming."

"We were planning on keeping each other warm, if you know what I mean."

"You fucked up my life."

"Hate to tell you, but your life was fucked up long before you met me. Now, if you'll excuse me, we—"

Armando growled and moved closer. The moon made a quick appearance as a cloud moved past, revealing a glint in Armando's right hand. *Shit, a gun.*

The moonlight disappeared, shrouding everything in darkness again. Dylan could feel Jamie beside him. Knowing Armando couldn't see them any better than they could see him, Dylan grabbed Jamie's arm behind him and pushed her into the pool house.

He heard her almost soundless whispered "No" but ignored it. Getting the man closer so he could disarm him was a must. Dylan's gun had been taken away from him the instant he'd stepped onto the plane with Reddington. The man had assured him that the procedure was routine and that all weapons were taken from everyone. *Yeah, right.*

Dylan moved forward, his hands at his sides. He knew he was quick enough to kick the gun out of Armando's hand. Problem was, he couldn't see shit.

"What's your beef with me, Armando? I thought we were friends."

"Beef?" The man sounded confused. "I don't know what a beef is . . . I only know that you owe me for bringing you to Stanford's attention, and what do I get in return? A fucking demotion. He wants to make you his right-hand man, instead of me."

"You can have the job. I was only doing it for the money."

"The only way for me to get back into his good graces is for you not to be around."

"Fine, I'll quit. Whatever. I just want to spend some time alone with the lady. Get my meaning?"

"No, he won't let you quit. The only way is for you to disappear."

Dylan refrained from telling the idiot that disappearing was exactly what he was trying to do.

"I'll have to make sure they won't find your body."

Shit.

Dylan was tired of trying to reason with the man. They had to get out of here or they were going to have to scrap their plans and wait for another day. Damned if this creep would delay them any longer. He glanced up at the sky. The clouds were moving again, and the moon would soon make another brief appearance. He had to be ready.

Just as the darkness began to lighten, an instant before Dylan lunged, he saw a movement barely a foot away from Armando. Everything within him went still. *Jamie.*

She had gone through the pool house and come out another door. If Armando turned around and saw her, he'd shoot her at point-blank range and she could be dead in an instant.

Dylan was on his toes, ready to spring forward and take the man down, when Jamie did something totally unexpected. She stooped behind the man and grabbed his leg.

Startled, Armando looked behind him, which gave Dylan the opportunity he needed. He leaped, knocking the gun out of the man's hand. Armando fell backward, and, as if she had been doing this all her life, Jamie dropped to her knees and bowed her head. Armando fell over her and landed on the other side.

Dylan was on the prostrate man in a flash. Though he looked close to passing out already, Dylan couldn't take the chance that he'd make it back to the mansion and warn the others. He slammed his fist into Armando's jaw. The drunken man huffed out a gasp of pain and closed his eyes into unconsciousness.

Getting to his feet, Dylan glanced around for the

gun and found Jamie standing behind him, holding it in her hand. The moonlight bright on her face, her eyes gleamed with excitement as she said, "We make a good team."

Once again, he fought the urge to shake her and kiss her at the same time. Refusing to get into an argument about following orders, he looked back down at Armando. "We need to find something to tie him up with, to keep him out of the way for a few hours."

She nodded and ran back to the pool house. "There's some rope on the wall."

Dylan grabbed Armando's feet and pulled him through the door. While he secured the man, Jamie opened the panel she'd described and pressed a button. The floor beside him shifted. He finished his task and stood, watching as the floor divided and a black speedboat appeared.

With Armando's bound feet in his hands, he dragged him inside a small storage room and shut the door. Once it was discovered he was missing, the search would be on. Armando's yelling would bring him rescue as soon as he was heard.

He turned to see Jamie stepping down into the boat. Dylan untied the line and pushed the boat backward, into the water. The instant the boat was floating, he jumped in, landing beside her.

Though they needed to get away as soon as possible, he was leery of starting the engine so close to land. Reddington's men might not be able to chase them in the yacht, but bullets would have no problem reaching them.

He grabbed emergency oars, handed one to Jamie, and they began to paddle from the shore. It would take longer than he'd like, but if anyone heard the motor, shots would be fired before questions were asked. When, at last, they'd gotten a couple of hundred yards from the island, deeming the distance safe enough, Dylan cranked the engine and putted farther out. A full ten minutes later, he gunned the engine and they were off.

Anger burned through him like a furnace. Glaring down at a barely conscious Armando, Stanford didn't know if he'd ever been this furious in his life. The urge to alleviate his anger by splitting the weasel's neck and severing his head from his body was great. If it would make the situation any better, he wouldn't hesitate.

He'd risen at dawn; anticipation strumming through him had kept him from his sleep. A new project always affected him like this. The eagerness to get started pumping excitement through his blood would keep him going for hours without needing rest.

He had just taken in his first mouthful of coffee for the day when Joseph had pounded on his door, startling him so much that he'd spewed coffee everywhere. Sarah was standing behind him at the time, and if he didn't know her better, he could have sworn she snickered. Before answering the knock, he'd glanced at her, but she'd looked serene and lovely as always.

The news that Armando had been found tied up and barely conscious in the pool house had been shocking; learning that Wheeler and the Jennings bitch had stolen his boat and left the island had trumped everything. Why the hell had they done it?

"I'm sure they'll be back," Armando mumbled. "He said he just wanted to take her for a little ride . . . be alone with her."

He ignored the man. The stench of alcohol permeated the air around him. Whatever Armando said meant nothing. Bottom line: Wheeler and the woman were gone. Armando knew that there were no excuses for allowing such an event and that punishment would be forthcoming.

Stanford stood on the pier, looked out into the vast ocean, and tried to comprehend why Wheeler would risk his fury. Had he fallen so hard for the teacher that they'd decided to run away together? A romantic at heart, Stanford knew that this was possible. Hadn't he fallen for Sarah that quickly? The moment he'd seen her, he had known she had to be his. But no, that didn't happen often, and John Wheeler didn't have that type of personality.

Which meant they'd left the island with no intention of returning. But why? In the back of his mind, he had a niggling suspicion, but he refused to give it credence. There was no way these people had hoodwinked him. No way Wheeler could have infiltrated his tight-knit organization. And it was laughable to even consider that the dowdy Karen Jennings had come to the island for any other reason than to teach his daughter.

Whatever their reasons, they would be captured soon. For years, he'd had an agreement with several of the employees at the La Rosa marinas. Unless notified beforehand, by either him or Joseph, that someone was coming to La Rosa, the men were to take immediate action if his boat was spotted.

Wheeler and the Jennings woman would be bloody when they returned to the island, but that was fine with him. Once he got an explanation for their departure, he'd give the bitch two options: continue to teach his daughter or die. It made no difference to him.

He'd spare Wheeler's life for as long as the man fulfilled the promise he had made. He'd gone to a lot of bother for Lance to come here for training. He refused to be denied.

Armando said they'd left just before dawn. Any minute now, his two wayward employees would be receiving an unexpected greeting from his friends on La Rosa.

* * *

Jamie sat on the bench seat of the boat, behind Dylan. Arms crossed over her body, she clenched her teeth to keep them from rattling. Though the night was chilly and the wind cut through her clothing, the cold wasn't making her shake. Adrenaline from their escape had overloaded her bloodstream.

She inhaled slowly, evenly, hoping to calm her breathing and the surge of nervous energy rushing through her body. It was over. Thank you, God, it was over. Now all they had to do was get on dry land and call Noah. With the information they had, Stanford Reddington might be in jail by this weekend.

And then what? She had been working toward this goal for so long, she honestly couldn't answer that question. A quiet, calm vacation in the West Virginia mountains sounded like heaven. Autumn would be coming soon, and the leaves in that area of the country were said to be spectacular. Going alone would be calming but so very lonely.

An ache developed in her chest as she gazed longingly at the man in the driver's seat of the boat. There was only one person she wanted to be with, but she didn't know if that would ever be possible.

Their speed slowed abruptly; Jamie got to her feet and went to stand beside Dylan. "What's wrong?"

"We're approaching La Rosa. And Mrs. Reddington was right. The boat's almost out of gas."

"What's the plan?"

He gave her a grave, thoughtful glance. "Can you swim?"

"Yes. Why?"

"I don't want to risk attracting attention by pulling into a marina. I doubt that Reddington's aware of our absence yet, but just in case, I think it'll be safer if we head to the opposite side of the island away from the marinas, abandon the boat, and then swim the rest of the way."

"What about the flash drives? They can't get wet."

He held out his hand. "Give them here. I've got some plastic ziplock bags. I'll double-bag them, wrap them in clothing, and put them in my backpack. They'll be fine."

Jamie withdrew the drives from the pouch around her waist and dropped them into Dylan's hand.

"Hold the wheel steady while I get these ready. We'll need to be prepared to jump within the next couple of minutes."

Jamie stood at the wheel and watched the island come closer. Was anyone waiting for them to arrive, hoping to catch them for Reddington? They'd come this far; she refused to let anyone or anything stop them now.

The engine stuttered. "Dylan?"

He was beside her in an instant and shut off the engine. "Okay. Looks like this is it." He glanced down at her, the darkness of his expression telling her he was worried. "I checked. The bastard has no life preservers on the boat."

"I'll be okay."

"Take your shoes off and tie the laces together."

While she did this, Dylan pulled his off and did the same thing.

"I'm going to tie a ski rope around your waist and loop it to my belt. The current shouldn't be too strong right now, but I'm not going to take any chances. Okay?"

She nodded and then, unable to stop the impulse, leaned up and kissed his mouth. "We're going to be fine."

Instead of deepening the kiss, he pulled her into his arms and held her tight against his chest. Treasuring the moment, Jamie relaxed into him; she inhaled musky masculine sweat and the scent of the ocean. Of all the moments they'd shared, this was one of the most special.

Dropping his arms, he said, "Okay, sweetheart, let's get out of here."

She followed him to the edge, and while he tied the rope around her waist, she looked out toward the land. Was that someone walking on the beach? She stiffened as she saw two more people, each coming from a different direction.

"Dylan. Look."

At the sound of urgency in Jamie's voice, Dylan's head jerked up. Unzipping his backpack, he pulled out a small pair of binoculars and focused on the beach. Hellfire. Three men armed with what looked like AK-47s stood on the shore, waiting for them.

Replacing the binoculars in the pack, Dylan quickly untied the rope around Jamie's waist.

"What are you doing?"

Draping the backpack over her shoulders, he took one arm at a time and fastened the snaps at her chest. Then, working with amazing speed, he took the shoes she held, and looped and tied them around one strap of the backpack.

"Dylan?"

"I'll draw their fire. You head in the other direction." He nodded toward a small copse of trees farther down the beach. "Hide there. I'll come for you as soon as I lose them."

"Like hell, Dylan. I'm not going to let you—"

His grabbed the backpack's straps and jerked her close. "We don't have time to argue. I can swim underwater and escape them."

"But I—"

"Please, Jamie. For once, don't argue with me. Okay?"

The tilt of her chin didn't bode well for her obedience, but Dylan had to trust that she'd follow his orders on this. He'd trained for this kind of escape scenario; she hadn't.

Her eyes searched his and then, finally, thankfully, she nodded. "I'll see you soon."

Using his body to block hers from the view of the men on the beach, he watched as she sat on the edge of the boat, slid down into the water, and began to swim toward the beach.

Dylan waited for a couple of minutes, until she was a good distance from the boat. Then, making as big a spectacle as possible, he went to the other side of the boat. Standing on the edge, he looked out at the men who stood on the beach waiting, apparently thinking he was going to swim right to them.

Taking a deep breath, he made a smooth, clean dive into the cool, crisp water and swam deep. It wasn't until he leveled out that he saw the bullets zinging and scattering about him. Damn, these men meant business.

With the hope of getting out of their shooting range, Dylan swam away from the land, but his biggest concern was Jamie. Had she gotten away without them seeing her? Or were they shooting at her, too?

twenty-five

She heard the guns long before she reached land. Her strokes strong and steady, she gritted her teeth against the cool bite of the churning water and concentrated on her target: the white stretch of sand and trees in front of her. She wanted to turn around to see if she could spot Dylan. She wouldn't. Of all the times she'd argued and disagreed with him, Jamie had recognized that this was one time when she needed to keep her mouth shut and do what she'd been told.

That didn't mean she liked it or that she wouldn't try to help him once she reached her destination. Dylan was so damn heroic, he'd stand in front of a firing squad and demand they shoot him before he allowed anyone else to be hurt. She loved him too much to let that happen.

The water wasn't as choppy as she drew closer to the shore, but a strong current began to pull at her. She ground her teeth together and persevered. She and McKenna used to compete with each other when they were kids. McKenna was the faster swimmer, but Jamie was the stronger. She thanked God for that strength today.

Raising her head, she treaded water to check her distance. About forty yards and closing. Out of the corner of her eye, she saw movement. The gunmen were running down the beach, away from her. They were chasing Dylan.

With a renewed surge of energy and strength, Jamie

took off again. Once she reached shore, she needed to figure out a way to distract the men so Dylan could get onto the beach. He couldn't stay beneath the water much longer. She refused to acknowledge that he'd already had to surface. And that when he had, bullets might have hit him. She couldn't let herself think that.

Her foot hit something, and relief mingled with exhaustion. The water was shallow enough that she could touch the bottom. Lowering her legs, she waded toward the shore. Though every muscle in her body ached and her breath rasped painfully through her lungs, she couldn't allow herself to rest. She had to figure out a way to help Dylan.

Her legs, shaky and weak, stumbled to find footing. She was grateful for the shoes tied around the backpack. Running barefoot would've been tough.

Now ankle-deep in the water, she felt her legs give out, and she fell to her knees. Crawling the last few feet, she collapsed onto the sand. Though she was exhausted and dizzy, she refused to give herself any time for recovery. Dylan's life was in danger.

Rolling over onto her back, she sat up and pulled at the backpack. Her arms were so rubbery, it took three tries. At last able to pull the pack off, she untied her shoes. Her socks were soggy, but she couldn't take the time to find dry ones in Dylan's bag, if he even had any. She had to get going.

With her shoes on, Jamie stood and tested her legs. Yes, they were shaky, but they would work.

Making a note of the area where she'd last seen the men, Jamie headed straight ahead into the tree-covered area. Once inside, she veered right. As she ran, maneuvering around trees and bushes, her mind came up with and then threw away every scenario she could think of. Confronting a group of armed men was out . . . they'd just shoot her. Finding the police and getting help would take too long. Waiting until she knew what she faced before she made a decision was her only option.

She reached the edge of the treed area. Peeking around a tall, thin palm, she spotted the three men easily. They were the only ones on the beach, and they held wicked-looking weapons. She could hear them talking as they gestured with their guns toward the water, but she couldn't make out their words. Their voices sounded angry. She hoped that meant good things for Dylan.

A small sand dune behind the men had concrete steps; a sign beside them indicated that they led to a parking lot. Jamie turned back into the treed area and ran up the hill toward the parking lot. She stopped at the top and looked down into the almost empty lot. Two black SUVs were parked side by side. With her heart in her throat, her feet kicking up sand, she ran down the hill. Stopping at one of the SUVs, she tugged on the driver's door . . . locked. She turned to the other and found the same. Hell, these men had submachine guns and they were afraid someone would steal their cars?

Frozen in indecision, Jamie looked around for something, anything. Rapid gunfire shocked her into action. She looked down, picked up the nearest and biggest rock she could find, and smashed the side windows of both vehicles. In an almost answering rhythm, alarms blared.

With the hope that she'd bought Dylan a little time, Jamie darted under one of the vehicles and prayed with all her might that no one would look underneath. She saw big, booted feet run toward her. The men yelled and snapped at one another, gesturing with their guns as they discussed who'd broken their windows. Finally, two of the men headed back to the beach. Another man stood guard in front of the vehicles. Could she handle one man? *Yes.*

Sliding out on the other side of the SUV from the man,

Jamie came at him from behind. She kicked him hard in the back. When he stumbled forward, she took advantage of his loss of balance, jumped onto his back, and wrapped an arm around his neck. He dropped his gun; his fingers and hands tore at her arms as he whirled around and around, trying to shake her off. Gritting her teeth, ignoring the scratches and gouges from his nails on her tender skin, she determinedly hung on as she pressed her forearm hard into his throat. At last she felt him weakening; his leg buckled beneath him and he fell forward.

Letting go, she jumped to her feet and grabbed the gun. The man lay unmoving, unconscious or dead; she didn't know which. If he was dead, there wasn't anything she could do. If he was unconscious, that was what she wanted.

Jamie examined the giant gun. She had never seen anything like it before. However, she knew which end to point, and, if she had to, she could damn well press a trigger and shoot. Pulling in a deep breath, she ran across the parking lot, toward the two men over the hill. She never saw the body flying toward her until it tackled her and took her to the ground. The gun skidded across the pavement.

Doing his best to lessen the impact, Dylan twisted and took the brunt of the fall. He didn't know what he would have done if she'd managed to reach the two men. She'd been holding the AK-47 in the most awkward way he'd ever seen anyone hold a gun. He hadn't known any way to get her attention before they saw her, other than to tackle her.

Showing him that she wasn't going to give up without a fight, she squirmed and bucked beneath him. "Let me go, you bastard."

"Jamie, it's me."

She froze. "Dylan?"

"Yeah."

With both of them gasping so hard he could barely hear anything else, Dylan loosened his hold on her and got to his knees. "Are you hurt?"

She rolled onto her back. "No, I'm fine."

"Let's get the hell out of here before they come back to check on their man."

"How?"

"Let's see if the big lug you took out has keys. If not, I'll hot-wire it. We'll be out in a flash."

She got to her knees and then her feet. Once up, she swayed slightly.

"You okay?"

"Yeah, just a little tired."

The need to hug her and tell her how damn proud he was of her was strong. He made do with a grin as he held out his hand. "Come on. Let's find a place to hide, and then we'll get some rest."

Wrapping an arm around her, he led her back to where the man lay on the pavement.

"Is he dead?"

The tentative tone in her voice told him she didn't really want to know. Determined to lie to her if the man was dead, Dylan bent down and pressed a finger to his neck. He was thankful to be able to reply truthfully, "No."

A check of the man's pockets gave him what he needed: a set of keys. He stood and pressed the unlock switch on the car key to see which vehicle it belonged to. Then he held out his hand to Jamie. "Let's go."

Ushering Jamie into the passenger seat, he quietly pressed the door closed. Even though time was of the essence, he took a few moments to open the hood of the other SUV and rip out the plug wires. Satisfied that this would delay any kind of chase, he ran to the driver's side of the other vehicle and cranked up the motor, thankful that it was the quiet, purring kind. Backing out of the parking lot, he glanced over at Jamie and grinned. "I'm hungry. How about you?"

Though her laughter held the hint of a shaky sob, she nodded and said, "Anything but fish. I think I swallowed two during my swim."

"Steak it is."

Several thoughts hit Dylan as he headed down a narrow, two-lane road. Reddington probably had men all over the city looking for them. Every part of his body ached like a sore tooth. To make matters worse, he was lost and had no idea where he was going. One thing he knew for certain, though, was that there was absolutely no one he'd rather have at his side than the gutsiest woman he'd ever known: Jamie Kendrick.

Last Chance Rescue headquarters

Noah grabbed the phone on the first ring. He'd been on edge for a couple of days, ever since Raphael had called him. "McCall."

"It's me."

The gruff, raspy voice barely sounded human, much less like Savage. "You and Jamie okay?"

"Yeah, we're fine. Since you know about Jamie, I'm assuming you heard from Raphael?"

"Yes. He's in Paris and he's safe."

"Good. And we've got some intel you'll be interested in."

Noah blew out a ragged sigh. Hell no, the mission hadn't gone down like a normal op. Still, knowing not only that everyone was okay but that they had the intel to put Reddington away improved his mood vastly.

"Where are you?"

"La Rosa."

"Can you get out of there?"

"Not without attracting attention."

"Give me a number. I'll call as soon as I have an extraction plan."

"Sounds good." Dylan rattled off a number and then disconnected.

Pressing the End button, Noah then used speed dial for the one person who was even more on edge than he was.

McKenna answered, as he had, on the first ring. "Noah?" The fear in her voice was apparent.

"She's safe . . . they're both safe. I'm planning on an extraction tomorrow."

She blew out a shaky, relieved breath. "I'm going, too."

He didn't bother to argue with her. "I'll call you with the details as soon as I have them."

"And she's really okay?"

"Yes. I heard it directly from Dylan."

"Thank you, Noah. I'll talk to you soon."

Noah closed his phone and set to work. Reddington might well have friends in the city, but LCR had something he didn't have: the best people in the world. And when it came to LCR operatives rescuing their own, no one else came close.

Dylan dismantled the disposable phone and dropped the pieces in the garbage can. Before they'd checked into the hotel, he'd purchased two. Noah would call on the other one once he had plans in place.

He glanced over at Jamie, who was curled up in a ball on the bed, fast asleep. They'd driven outside the city, into a smaller community. The people of La Rosa weren't wealthy, but they were friendly and helpful—at least the ones not carrying guns. He'd stopped and asked for directions to a place to stay and had been directed to a small hotel. The manager had been only too happy to take his euros and arrange for a meal to be sent up.

Jamie had been at his side the entire time. Yeah, they'd both looked like bedraggled sea demons. Salt had dried on their hair, making it stiff and wild, and their wrinkled clothing smelled like dead seaweed. He didn't want to attract attention, but he wouldn't leave her alone again.

Knowing she was in the ocean by herself, battling choppy waves and possibly attracting the attention of the gunmen, had been torturous. Of course, when he'd watched her take down a man holding an AK-47, a man twice her size, the word "fear" had taken on a new meaning. Dylan was running toward her when it went down. He hadn't been close enough to help and couldn't shout at her. Seeing her leap onto the man's back and choke him into unconsciousness was a memory he'd never get out of his head.

Never, in his entire life, had he known anyone like Jamie. Even when the odds were against her, even when she wasn't qualified or trained to do something . . . or hell, even when someone else could get the job done, she didn't stop.

A small muttering sound caught his attention. She was dreaming, maybe even having a nightmare. After what she'd been through, not having nightmares would have been strange.

As soon as they'd gotten to their room, she'd gone into the bathroom. Five minutes later, she'd emerged with one towel around her body, another wrapping her hair. She'd grimaced. "Had to take a shower."

He'd been about to ask her how she felt when he saw her arms. They were covered in scratches and cuts. "What happened to your arms?"

She shrugged. "That man I jumped."

He'd wanted to growl at her for being so foolish and hug her for being so damn brave. And he'd wanted to know where she'd gotten that kind of training. He hadn't taught her how to choke a man into unconsciousness. But the whiteness of her face and the tension around her mouth had stopped all questions. She needed rest . . . the talking could come later.

She moved restlessly and then blinked her sleepy eyes open. "Aren't you tired?"

Her voice was raspy and rough, as was his. Swallowing and choking on copious amounts of seawater will do that to a throat.

"Yeah, a little. I called McCall."

"Did you tell him what we have?"

"Yeah. He'll call back tomorrow with a plan to get us out of here."

"Did he say anything about McKenna?"

He almost smiled at the timidity in her voice. She could take down a man twice her size without blinking an eye, but facing her sister's wrath was something she was obviously dreading.

"No, but I'm sure he called and told her you were fine."

She rolled over onto her back and sighed. "She's going to be so pissed."

There was no denying that. McKenna had been under the impression that Jamie was teaching school in Louisiana. Instead, she'd been halfway across the world, in the middle of the enemy's camp, single-handedly performing her very own sting operation.

They still hadn't talked about exactly how all of this had taken place. "How long were you working on the island?" he asked now.

"Only a few weeks."

"How'd you do it?"

She released a ragged sigh. "When I was locked up in Reddington's room, as you know, I overheard a lot of things. Once, during his daily conversation with his wife, they discussed the need for a new teacher for their young daughter, Amelia. I only heard Reddington's side of the conversation, but from the sound of it, Mrs. Reddington wasn't pleased with the teaching methods of her current teacher. Mrs. Reddington had specific requirements she wanted in Amelia's new teacher. And Reddington agreed that by June of next year, she could start interviewing for a new one."

"How did you know how to go about being interviewed?"

"He mentioned the agency he would use." Her shoulders lifted in a shrug. "It didn't really strike a chord with me at the time. I still thought that when I got out of there, Reddington could be prosecuted like an ordinary criminal. When I realized that wasn't going to happen, the conversation took on more meaning."

"That took fake IDs, a fake résumé, references. A hell of a lot of planning. How'd you pull that off?"

She sat up, propped a couple of pillows behind herself, and leaned against them. "After my rescue, during that month McKenna and I spent in Paris getting to know each other again, she told me about the men in Memphis who'd helped her with fake IDs. Settling things with my ex-husband took less time than I thought it would, so I flew to Memphis and made contact with them."

By choice and habit, Dylan wasn't a man who talked much. Now, for the first time he could remember, he was speechless. They'd shared that plane trip to the States. As he had sat beside her, thinking how vulnerable and fragile she was, she'd been planning this job.

Apparently not realizing that she had shocked him, she continued: "After my training with you was over, I was going to present everything to Noah. I knew that having LCR's backing would help."

She didn't need to explain why that plan hadn't panned out. He'd been instrumental in destroying it.

"I visited McKenna briefly after I left the cabin. I told her I was going to work in the States. That's when I went back to Memphis. My fake stuff was waiting for me, but I still needed more training. So, I sent my résumé, which listed the specific things Mrs. Reddington wanted, to the agency Reddington planned to use, and while I waited, I trained more."

"Who?"

"A couple of former military men had opened a gym in Memphis. McKenna told me she'd gotten a lot of her training in a similar way with a group of guys in Maryland. I figured these guys could teach me the same kind of stuff. When I showed them what I could do, what you had already taught me, they agreed to take me on as a special project."

At some point, he knew, he was going to be immune to shock, but he wasn't there yet.

"How could you be sure Reddington would hire you?"

"I wasn't. But I heard enough to know what they were looking for in a teacher to stack the odds in my favor. Reddington wanted her to be single, with little or no family, and American. Mrs. Reddington wanted a woman in her early thirties, with master's in both English literature and mathematics.

"With such specific requirements, I knew that the list of qualified candidates would be short. So I weighted my résumé with what I knew they wanted and then waited for them to contact me."

"Did you know that he probably wouldn't have let you leave the island alive?"

"I had to take the chance."

"Why, dammit? Why the hell would you put yourself at risk like that when someone else could have—"

Fiery eyes turned to him. "No, don't say it. Don't you dare say that someone else more qualified could have done the job just as well. I got myself trained. I set it up. I was the one who got the files."

"I'm not denying what you've accomplished, but you didn't have to do those things. You could have been teaching school, having a normal life, without any threats. Why would you put yourself through that?"

"I had to."

He recognized the mutinous expression. Determined to get the truth from her, he went in another direction with his questions: "You do realize that what we have on Reddington probably won't put his son behind bars, don't you?"

Her expression became even more closed, and in a way, he had an answer to his most burning question. Even though he had suspected it all along, it was now confirmed. "What did Lance do to you, Jamie?"

She was silent for so long, he wasn't sure she'd give him any kind of answer at all. When she spoke, as usual, it wasn't what he expected.

"Does it seem strange to you that there's very little you don't know about me and very little I know about you?"

"What?"

"You know everything, Dylan. My parents' murder, my crummy marriage, what happened with Damon Hughes, and most everything that happened in Reddington's house. Here's what I know about you." She held up a slender hand and ticked off each item as she spoke: "One: I know you grew up in the States. By the way, there are fifty of those now, so that's a damn large generalization. Two: I know you were once married. Three: I know you have a degree in psychology. And four: I know your father killed your mother." She glared accusingly at him. "Four things compared to my entire life seems damn uneven to me."

"What do you want to know?"

If she weren't so tired and dispirited, Jamie would've thrown a pillow at him. The instant she'd made that statement, his face had closed down. Why she'd thought confronting him point-blank would do any good, she didn't know. But the wariness of his tone told her he was back in that defensive mode again. Asking him questions when he clearly didn't want to tell her anything wasn't what she wanted. She wanted him to share with her . . . not turn their conversation into an inquisition.

Rolling over on the pillow, away from him, she said, "Never mind. I'm going back to sleep."

He was so silent, she couldn't hear him breathing, but she felt his eyes on her. Was he wondering why she suddenly didn't want to know about him? Did he get it? She knew the answer to that. Dylan wasn't stupid. He knew what she wanted from him. And the painful truth was, he didn't want to give it to her.

Closing her eyes against the tears that threatened, she forced her thoughts away from another bruise on her heart and thought about tomorrow—something she hadn't done in what seemed like forever.

She had to find a way to make it up to McKenna. Before she had left for Reddington's island, she had talked to her sister once a week. And each week, she had skirted the truth. Yes, she was pursuing a teaching job. Yes, she was beginning a new job. Yes, she was getting on with her life. And though, other than her location, she had never lied outright, she had misled her sister.

When she had decided on this plan, she had known the cost. She just hadn't considered what would happen once she had accomplished her goal. Could McKenna forgive her or had she driven a wedge between them that couldn't be healed?

Wrapping her arms around herself, Jamie let the tears she'd held back flow freely down her face, until sleep finally claimed her.

Sometime later, she woke in Dylan's arms. His shallow, even breaths told her he was deeply asleep. Rolling over to face him, she murmured her content and burrowed into his chest. The fantasy of having his arms around her forever lulled her back to sleep and into the most restful slumber she'd had in months.

Hours later, she opened her eyes to find Dylan gazing down at her. The early morning sun cloaked the room in a gray tinge, giving her just enough light to see his face but not his expression.

"Everything okay?" she asked softly.

"Yeah. Just like looking at you."

She'd gone to bed with her hair wet and figured she probably looked like some sort of woolly mammoth, so she was glad for the dimness of the room. Still, his words, unexpected and sweet, turned her heart over.

"Are you hungry? All we had yesterday was lunch, and we slept through dinner."

Actually, she felt as though she had a crater in her stomach, she was so famished. But lying in Dylan's arms, listening to his deep, still raspy voice, feeling his hard, warm body encircling hers? There was no food in the universe that could replace this wonderful sensation.

It seemed as natural as breathing to pull his head down and kiss him. Dylan's lips were deliciously soft, wonderfully male, as he kept the kiss light, allowing her to lead, to show him what she wanted. Jamie wanted it all. She licked at his lips and then opened her mouth, inviting him in.

The instant she opened her mouth to him, Dylan took control. Waking with Jamie in his arms had felt like a dream, one he hadn't wanted to wake from. He'd been lying here for a while, just watching her sleep. And now, right or wrong, he'd never wanted anything more than he wanted her at this moment.

The kiss went hot and deep, and suddenly, their hands were all over each other. Dylan was wearing only a pair of shorts; Jamie had on his T-shirt and nothing else. Gasping into each other's mouths, their hands frantic with need, they stripped each other bare.

And then, as if in mutual agreement, everything slowed. Dylan's mouth moved down the tender line of her jaw and stopped for a moment to pay special tribute to the chin that jutted out with determination whenever they argued. Needing to taste all of her silky flesh, he kissed down her slender neck and stopped at her breasts. He could stay here for hours, sipping, licking, and sucking. He licked a nipple, loving the way it tightened, hardened against his tongue. Covering it with his mouth, he suckled deep. Jamie's hands on his head, holding him against her, along with her breathy moans, told him she loved it, too.

His mind blurred with passion, it took him a few seconds to realize she'd said something. Raising his head, he said, "What, sweetheart?"

In a panic, Jamie shook her head and pulled him down to her again. He hadn't heard her. The words had slipped out, but to say them now, when he was looking down at her, asking . . . No, she could do a lot of things, but repeating "I love you" to Dylan wasn't one of them.

The bristly stubble on his face rubbed against her abdomen as his mouth traveled down. When his tongue swirled around her navel, Jamie arched up, needing and wanting his tongue somewhere else. She was burning from the inside out, turning into a molten pool of need, with every hot sensation coalescing between her legs. The thought of his tongue probing there put her at the very edge of climax. And then, oh yes, he was there, licking, thrusting, sucking. Arching her body upward, Jamie cried out his name as she spiraled into ecstasy.

Sanity returned slowly and, with it, renewed desire. Dylan lapped at her, licking with soft, sure strokes . . . the tenderness of his touch bringing tears to her eyes. Desire strumming once more, she whispered, "Dylan?"

This time he heard her. Raising his head, he said, "What, sweetheart?"

"I need you inside me."

As he leaned over the side of the bed, she heard a rustle. It wasn't until she saw the packet he was ripping open with his teeth that she realized he had pulled a condom from his backpack. Laughter bubbled through her. He had produced everything from bandages and gauze to a protein bar he'd given her on the boat, and then chewing gum when she'd needed to get the taste of the ocean out of her mouth. And now condoms. "What else do you have in that bag?"

"I'll let you explore later."

Taking the packet from his hand, she whispered, "Deal" and slid the condom over him. Dylan groaned and surged into her hand. Unable to let go, she held his erection in her hands, caressing the hard length.

"Enough," he growled. Suddenly, her world turned upside down as he dove into the bed and pulled her on top of him. Straddling him, she took him into her hands again and slowly eased him into her. A hissing sound brought her eyes up to his. "Okay?"

Hard, callused hands grabbed her hips, but with infinite gentleness and ease, he pressed into her until he was buried deep inside her, and then he answered with a husky "Perfect."

She couldn't have agreed more. Every worry, every problem disappeared from her mind. What today held for them, what worries she had about the future vanished. This was the man she had loved for so very long, and if this was the last time she'd be in his arms like this, then she wanted to have the memory untainted, with nothing other than pleasure and fulfillment in her mind.

Lowering her entire body over him, she covered his mouth with hers, tangling and dueling with his tongue, licking at his lips. Her body rode him, up and down, until waves of pleasure zoomed through her again.

Shudders of fulfillment went through her as she collapsed onto his chest, and then she held him tight and close as Dylan ground into her and found his release. Jamie took a deep breath, inhaling his scent into her memory. Her entire being felt like warm, melted wax. With Dylan's strong arms around her, his scent on her, and a part of his body still inside her, she drifted into a delicious and satiated euphoria.

twenty-six

The sun was high in the sky when Dylan woke again. The empty pit that was his stomach growled, reminding him that it'd been almost twenty-four hours since they'd eaten. They had to get some fuel inside them before an LCR team arrived. If there was going to be trouble, he'd sure as hell need to have the strength to fight.

Rolling over onto his side, he checked on Jamie. She was still sleeping, but he had a feeling that the moment she smelled food, she'd be wide awake.

He eased out of bed and picked up the hotel phone. Keeping his voice low, he asked for the most American-ized meal they had—steak sandwiches and fries. Sounded damn good to him.

Assured that the meal would arrive within fifteen minutes, he grabbed a quick shower and threw on a pair of pants. After their meal, he'd need to find some clothes for them. As beautiful as Jamie looked in his T-shirt, she couldn't wear it outside the room.

The instant he walked out of the bathroom, a knock sounded at the door. Checking the peephole, he saw a woman with a tray. He opened the door just enough to take the tray and hand her several bills for payment. She smiled and turned away.

Dylan took the tray of food and set it on the small dining table. And as he'd figured, Jamie began to stir.

She yawned widely and said, "Mmm. Is that food or am I dreaming?"

"Definitely food. Want me to bring it to you?"

"I need to run to the bathroom." She grimaced and pulled at her hair. "Think I'll take a quick shower."

"Don't take too long. I'm not responsible if your sandwich is still in front of me when I finish mine."

She jumped out of bed and scurried to the bathroom. "Be right back."

Since he'd ordered four sandwiches, he wolfed down the first. Before he could get started on another, Jamie emerged from the shower. With her hair once again damp, her face naked of makeup, and in the same T-shirt she'd worn to bed, she looked fresh, lovely, and so damn vulnerable. Beneath that façade of vulnerability lay a steely backbone.

Sitting across from him, she uncovered her meal and began to devour it in that feminine, delicate way that always made him want to smile.

With her sandwich half gone, she finally paused long enough to look at him. "This is delicious."

"There's another if you want it."

She shook her head. "This one will do it for me. You go ahead, though."

Taking her at her word, Dylan bit into his third sandwich. Halfway through it, he finally began to feel human again.

As Jamie worked on her meal, Dylan went to his backpack and repacked the few things he'd taken out. He'd checked the flash drives earlier and reassured himself that the water hadn't penetrated the plastic.

He was so intent on his tasks, Jamie's quietness didn't strike him as strange until he heard her expel a long, ragged sigh. He turned to find her gaze fixed on the wall in front of her; the desolate, tortured look in her eyes told him that her mind was in another time, another place.

Her voice low and husky, she began to talk: "My first

week with Reddington, I went in and out of conscious-
ness. There was a doctor there who treated me. He was
the only one I remember from those first few days. Then,
as I began to recover and become more aware of things,
I would see this man come into the room, several times
a day. At first, he just stood there and stared. It was dark
in the room . . . but I knew he was there. I could hear
him breathing. I tried to talk to him." She swallowed
thickly. "I begged him to let me go. He never said anything . . . just stood there.

"Then one day, I woke up and there were two of
them. They'd turned the lights on so they could see me.
One of them was Lance Reddington. I knew he was the
one who'd been coming into the room." She shook her
head. "I don't know who the other one was. He was
young too, about Lance's age."

Dylan wanted to go to her and hold her, but he
wouldn't. This ordeal had been weighing on her mind
for months, the memories torturing her. The expression
on her face, haunted but resolute, made him stay frozen
in place and listen.

"They critiqued my body. Talked about what they
were going to do to me once I wasn't so ugly." She swallowed a sobbing laugh. "Amazing that I was actually
glad of all the bruises. No one wanted to touch me because I was so disfigured and ugly.

"As I got progressively better, his visits became more
frequent and his words more vile and profane. I knew he
was getting turned on. He would rub himself through
his clothing as he talked." She swallowed hard again.
"One day, he unzipped his pants and masturbated in
front of me. He did that every day . . . several times a
day. And once, he brought his friend back and they both
jacked off. I closed my eyes, but I could hear them grunting . . . hear their filthy language. My hands were cuffed
to the bed . . . I couldn't cover my ears.

"I made myself laugh at them. Called them perverts, pigs, sleazebags. Every insulting name I could come up with."

She turned her head to look at him, and Dylan felt her hurt so deep, he wanted to cry. The stark pain in her eyes pierced straight through his soul. He couldn't stop himself. Maybe she didn't need to be held—she was so damn strong and brave—but he sure as hell needed to hold her. Striding over to where she sat, he plucked her into his arms, carried her over to a chair, and sat down with her. Holding her close against him, he waited.

"One day, he came by himself and did his usual performance, but he told me that the next day, he was going to make good on all those things he'd been promising me he was going to do. That he and his friends were tired of waiting."

She stopped talking, and Dylan wasn't sure he could handle what would come next. She had told him before that the bastard hadn't raped her, but what he had done was a rape of the mind, of her spirit.

Unable to not know the rest, Dylan rasped out, "What happened?"

"You."

He jerked at her one-word answer. "What do you mean?"

"You came that night and rescued me."

A burning sensation started behind his eyes. Pressing his face against the top of her head, Dylan said a prayer—his first one in a very long time—of thankfulness that he and LCR had been there to save her from further hell.

As a shaky breath whooshed through her body, she straightened in his arms and looked up. "I knew that going after Reddington might do nothing to hurt Lance, other than take away his opportunity to carry on the family business. But if bringing Reddington down saves one woman from being sold or going through what I went through, then the risk was worth it."

He was once again reminded that he'd never known anyone like Jamie Kendrick, and hidden deep, where he didn't want to consider the consequences of the truth, his chest ached with the certain knowledge that he never would again.

The cellphone buzzed, giving him a welcome relief from that painful truth. Since it was on the bureau across the room, Dylan had no choice but to move.

Feeling the awkwardness that's often the aftermath of baring your soul, Jamie rose from Dylan's lap. For just an instant, she'd felt a closeness with him that had exceeded even the physical intimacy they'd shared. Almost as if something within him had touched her heart. But now reality had reared its ugly head. The fact that she'd shared everything really meant nothing. Once again, he knew everything about her . . . and she still knew almost nothing of his past.

She returned to the table, where the remains of her meal lay, suddenly unappetizing and unappealing. Covering the food with a napkin, she turned and listened to Dylan's side of the conversation with Noah.

"No, tomorrow is fine. Yeah, I understand." His gaze locked with hers, he said something she'd never thought she'd hear from him: "I'm not worried about her. She's proven she can handle anything."

The knowledge that she'd earned Dylan's respect and endorsement went a long way in soothing her jagged and fragile emotions.

Dylan finished the call with "Will do" and closed the phone. His eyes still on her, he said, "They'll be here early tomorrow morning, about an hour before dawn. LCR had no contacts here on La Rosa, so McCall had to send for some operatives. They arrived last night and have the hotel under surveillance. They've spotted three men who are trying to keep a low profile—probably our friends from yesterday."

"So if they know we're here, why haven't they tried to get to us?"

A broad shoulder lifted in a shrug. "Could be Reddington told them to just keep an eye on us. Those men were close enough yesterday for some of their bullets to hit me, but they didn't. I don't think Reddington wants us dead . . . I think he just wants us. With us staying in the hotel and not coming out, he might think we really did just run off together for some hot and sexy alone time. I think they're going to wait us out, until we make some kind of move."

"So, what's the plan?"

"Since we still don't want Reddington to know we're anything more than two horny lovers, LCR's going to have to stay low-profile. An army of operatives descending on the building will tell him there's more to our game."

He grabbed a yellow notepad from the desk and a pen. As he began to draw, Jamie stood beside him and watched a surprisingly detailed sketch of the hotel emerge on the page.

Once he'd finished, he pointed at the three entrances to the hotel. "There's one guy here, at the main entrance. One is at the back, in the parking lot. And there's one at the service entrance, where only employees can enter.

"One operative will cover each entrance. I'm going to take the man at the main entrance. While I deal with him, you're going to jump into a car; as soon as I'm done, there will be another car waiting. We'll meet at the airport and be on our way."

It sounded easy, but anything could happen. Volunteering to take out one of the men herself would be foolish—no matter how much training she'd had, the LCR operatives were much better qualified. More importantly, someone had to protect the flash drives. They'd risked their lives for them. If the drives were taken or damaged, everything they'd gone through would have been for nothing.

"What about clothes?" She glanced down at the large T-shirt she'd borrowed from Dylan. "Not exactly dressed for a getaway."

"I'll call down to the lobby and see if anyone's willing to bring us some clothes." He tore a piece of paper from the notepad and handed it to her with the pen. "Write down your clothing and shoe sizes."

While she did this, Dylan called the front desk. She was amazed at the difference in his tone when he spoke. Masculine charm oozed, and she knew that if she were the one being asked the favor, she'd do just about anything to please the owner of such a sexy, persuasive voice.

In minutes, there was a knock on the door. After checking the peephole, Dylan opened the door only slightly for the woman who had agreed to buy them clothing. Handing her the page listing their sizes and several twenty-euro notes, he thanked her in a silky, sexy tone and then closed the door.

When he turned to face her, the tough-edged, hard-assed LCR operative was firmly back in place.

"Wow, you can turn the charm on and off in a flash, can't you?"

He answered her with the raising of that arrogant brow—the one that used to infuriate her. And now her silly, foolish heart thudded against her chest in excitement.

He held his hand out in invitation. "You want charming?"

With her body heat increasing by the second, Jamie moved toward him, loving this playful side of Dylan. When she reached him, he grabbed her hand and pulled her against him. Stopping his mouth a hairsbreadth from hers, he growled, "Just how charming do you want me to be?"

Since he could charm her with a raised brow and a growl, she sincerely didn't know if her heart could handle anything more. The man was beyond lethal already. Still, being a risk taker, she whispered, "Show me what you've got."

His green eyes flared with something hot and potently wild, and then his mouth was on hers. Plunging, devouring, his tongue slashed and licked against hers. Lifting her in his arms, he carried her to the bed and followed her down. Jamie closed her eyes and allowed Dylan to charm her with his body, taking her to the idyllic place where nothing else existed but heart-pounding, body-clenching pleasure.

Sated and so relaxed he could barely move, Dylan held Jamie's silken body close in his arms. How was he going to let her go? And yet what choice did he have? She deserved a normal life. And she deserved a good man to share that normal life with—one who didn't risk his life on a daily basis and one who was worthy of her love.

She deserved the very best of everything, and that meant she needed to learn why he wasn't that man. Her accusation yesterday that he knew everything about her and she knew almost nothing about him had slashed deep. The courage it had taken her to share the most painful moments of her past humbled him. He had done nothing of the kind for her . . . and it was way past time for her to know.

Opening his mouth, Dylan began to share a story he hadn't told in almost two decades: "My mother and father were both drunks. From what I remember, my mom wasn't a bad person . . . she just had an addiction she couldn't control. She'd get drunk, cry about her lot in life, apologize for not being strong enough, and then pass out. My old man was a whole different kind of creature. He was a monster."

She stiffened in his arms, so he knew she was listening intently. Dylan forged on, determined to get it all out in the open. "He wasn't evil just when he was drunk, he was evil all the time. And when my parents were drunk together, which was often, what happened was violent, sickening, and wrong. I don't know how many times he beat and raped her in front of me."

"How old were you?"

"Hard to say how old I was the first time I witnessed it. The first time I remember vividly was when I was five years old."

"Oh God, Dylan." Her voice was thick with tears.

"I remember that one time so well because I tried to stop him and he knocked me out. I woke up in my mother's arms. She was crying and apologizing." He shook his head in amazement. "She had bruises all over her and a bloody, swollen lip and she was apologizing to me."

He paused for a few seconds, needing the time to confess the worst sin he had ever committed. "And then one day it all stopped, because he killed her.

"I saw him do it. They were in the kitchen—he'd been slapping her around. She grabbed a knife off the counter and went after him. I'd never seen her try to defend herself before. I don't know if she just got tired of him hurting her or she wasn't as drunk as usual. Anyway, she got one good stab at his arm. Before she could pull back and get him again, he grabbed the knife, twisted her arm, and broke it. She was holding her arm, crying, when he took a heavy cutting board from the counter and slammed it over her head. She didn't get up."

Jamie didn't know when she'd started crying. Maybe

it wasn't even the words as much as the hollow pain in his voice. She had suspected that he'd had a rough childhood, had known that his father had killed his mother. Never had she imagined how horrific his life had been. And she had a feeling the worst part hadn't come yet.

"How old were you then?"

"Seven . . . I think. After she died, time sort of stopped. I lost count of birthdays."

"What happened after that?"

"He dumped her body in a large garbage can and put her in his truck. He drove a semi for a living, so on his next load—which happened to be the next day—he made an extra stop to unload her corpse."

A ragged sigh went through his big body. "Only problem was, when he went to dump her, she wasn't dead. I heard her whimpering. I screamed at him and tried to get to her. He threw me down . . . God, I don't know how many times. Finally, I couldn't get up anymore. I lay on the ground, watched him lift the can and roll it into this giant hole. It was a well . . . though I didn't know what it was at the time. I heard the thud when it hit the bottom, and then nothing else.

"He said if I ever told anyone about what I'd seen, he'd kill me. I knew he was telling the truth, so I didn't."

Seven years old. Jamie's heart shattered for that terrified, traumatized little boy.

"From then on, my old man made sure I stayed close to him. He took me on the road with him. Hid me when anyone came around. Fed me when he remembered and beat me when he was drunk."

"But what about school? Didn't social services come looking for you?"

"We lived in a Podunk little community in Ohio. I hadn't even started school, so if anyone knew I existed, they forgot about me."

"What happened next?"

"A whole lot of nothing. He continued to work, I traveled with him. That lasted for years." He paused for a second and then, his voice holding a warm affection, he added, "And then I got lucky."

"What happened?"

"We were at a rest stop. The old man always parked as far away from all the other trucks as possible. Which was a good thing, since that meant he'd let me walk around outside. That night, as I was walking around, stretching my legs, I heard something whimpering in the weeds. My dad was on the other side of the truck, so he didn't hear. I went into the weeds and found a small puppy. Apparently someone had just dumped her there. She was skinny, terrified, and starving. I had some peanut butter crackers in my pocket I was saving for later. She ate them up like they were ambrosia.

"I knew it was dangerous to take her with me, but I couldn't leave her there. So I hid her under my coat and snuck her into the truck."

Jamie could see Dylan as a little boy, finally finding his first real friend—one that had so much in common with him.

"I managed to keep her a secret for almost a week. Most times, I stayed quiet and out of the way to keep from irritating my dad. So, since he rarely looked at me, my only real concern was keeping Lucky quiet."

A smile lifted her mouth at his name for the dog. That's what he'd meant—"I got Lucky."

"Then, one night, he got drunk and started hitting on me. Lucky and all her three pounds of fur didn't like that. She went after my dad."

He paused. Jamie held her breath, the pain in her chest almost unbearable. The bastard had killed Dylan's mother in front of him. There was no telling what he would do to an innocent puppy.

"He was furious, of course. He grabbed her and threw her out of the truck. I was surprised he didn't choke her, but he had other things on his mind—namely beating the shit out of me. I passed out, and when I woke up, we were at another truck stop.

"He was sleeping off his drunk, snoring so loud I knew he wouldn't wake up for a while. That was when I realized I had to do something. I'd never had the courage before, but Lucky was the best thing that had ever happened to me." He shrugged and said again, "I had to do something.

"So, I grabbed the cash from my dad's wallet and took his truck keys. Then I got out of the truck and went looking for Lucky."

"Did you find her?"

"Yeah, took me all night, but I guess you could say I got lucky again. We were only about fifteen miles from where he'd thrown her out. It took me all night and most of the day, but I found the rest stop and Lucky was still there, almost like she knew I'd be coming back for her."

"Was she okay?"

"She had a broken leg and a gash on her head, but the instant she saw me, her tail went to wagging. I don't think anyone's ever been that happy to see me."

Jamie didn't say it, but she knew exactly how Lucky had felt. That was the way she'd felt when Dylan had rescued her.

"Since I'd taken my dad's keys, I felt safe in walking down the main highway. Finally, a state trooper saw me and stopped."

He fell silent again. Jamie was terrified to ask, but she had to know. "He didn't take you back to your father, did he?"

"No, he took me to the police station, gave me something to eat, gave Lucky some water, and asked me what had happened. I guess with all the bruises on my face, he knew it was something bad. I told him everything. Within hours, I was in a foster home while they tried to hunt down my dad . . . and then my next of kin.

"I didn't know it at the time, but my grandmother, my mother's mother, was still around. My mom had lost touch with her years ago. So, in a week's time, I moved to Georgia to live with her and my dad went to jail."

"Did you tell the cops about your mother?"

Again he was silent for so long, she knew that what was coming was hard for him.

"Yeah. Took them over a month to find her, since I couldn't remember the exact place. Turns out, to avoid the death penalty, my dad cut a deal with the prosecutor and told them where she was." His voice grew thick. "I overheard my grandmother on the phone when they found her body. There were claw marks on the walls of the well." He swallowed hard. "She had tried to climb out of the well."

Her eyes closed against her tears, but that didn't stop them from escaping. The guilt he'd felt for not saving his mother had been compounded with the knowledge that the fall hadn't killed her.

"You were seven years old, Dylan. There's no way you could have helped her."

"Part of me agrees with you, but there's another part that tells me I should have found a way. I should have escaped and told someone."

"He would have killed you."

He shrugged. "I still should've tried."

"What happened to him?"

"He died in prison about five years into his life sentence."

"What happened to Lucky?"

"She came with me. Fortunately, my grandmother lived on a farm and loved animals. Lucky was with me until my second year of college."

"How old were you when you went to live with your grandmother?"

"Twelve."

For five years, that little boy had endured hell with his abusive son-of-a-bitch father.

"Of course, it wasn't the easiest transition. I loved living with my grandmother, but since I'd never gone to school—hell, I could barely spell my name—I had to do a whole lot of catching up."

And he'd gone on to earn a degree in English and a master's in psychology. Jamie didn't know if she'd ever been so awed by anyone in her entire life.

"Is your grandmother still alive?"

"No, she died a year after I graduated from college. She gave me every advantage. She was a great grandmother."

"Is your mother the reason you started working with LCR?"

"One of the reasons . . . the biggest reason."

"Something else happened?"

Dylan dropped his arms and rolled away from her. He hadn't talked for this long in years. Every muscle in his body felt locked tight. He needed to get up and move around. Jamie sat up in bed, and though her questioning eyes followed him, she didn't speak.

Grabbing a bottle of water from a tray by the window, he guzzled half of it down. "Remember I told you I was once married?"

"Yes. You said an old boyfriend killed her."

He nodded. "Turns out, she had several boyfriends, even after we were married. When I found out, I told her to leave. She started crying . . . said that one of her ex-boyfriends was a psycho and had threatened to kill her. I didn't believe her. I filed for divorce the next day. Two weeks later, I found out she'd told me the truth. Her body was found in his trunk . . . he'd strangled her to death."

"That wasn't your fault, Dylan."

His eyes on the parking lot three floors beneath them, Dylan shrugged. "Maybe not, but having one more person's death on my conscience was more than I could handle. I'd heard about Last Chance Rescue. I called McCall and asked him for an interview. A couple of days later, he hired me."

"What did you do before you went to work for LCR?"

Almost embarrassed not to have told her this before, he said, "I was a high school English teacher in Dublin, Georgia."

The delighted smile she gave him made him wish even more that he'd told her earlier. Then she sat up straighter and said, "Do you know how grateful I am that you decided to work for LCR?"

"Someone else would have rescued you, Jamie. I just happened to be the one who opened the door."

"Maybe so, but I'm glad it was you."

He set the water bottle down. "I'm going to take a shower. If Adela comes to the door with our clothes, don't open it. Come get me. Okay?"

The instant he had her agreement, Dylan went inside the bathroom and closed the door. He'd almost rather take a beating than talk about his past. The nightmares would hit him tonight. Whenever he thought about his mother and her whimpering cries of pain, they always came. The demons in his mind would wait until he was deeply asleep and then they would attack, much the way his father had when he was a kid.

Standing under a hot, scalding shower, Dylan refused

to regret telling Jamie the truth. She deserved to know it all. How screwed up his childhood had been and, consequently, the garbage that still permeated his being. He told himself it was better this way . . . but for the life of him, he couldn't think why.

twenty-seven

Dressed in navy cotton pants and a light blue button-down shirt, Jamie watched Dylan, grim-faced, stand at the window, his eyes searching the parking lot. Ten minutes left before they were due to leave and he'd said maybe ten words to her. Looked like things were back to normal.

After last night, she'd naïvely thought that was behind them. That they'd made a connection nothing could sever. So much for optimism. If anything, he looked even more forbidding than usual, which she'd thought was impossible.

She wanted to confront him . . . ask him why he was acting like this again. Now wasn't the time, though. Personal issues were going to have to wait until this was over. Once they were safe and Reddington's files were in the right hands, she was determined to talk this out with him. Even if he didn't love her, he felt something for her. She refused to let him deny that.

"You comfortable with the plan?"

Jamie nodded. "You'll go first . . . the man watching us out front is outside and to the right, behind the large bush with the red flowers." Jared Livingston, one of the LCR operatives who'd arrived yesterday, had called with this information. Jared would be taking out the man at the back of the hotel. LCR operative Aidan Thorne would be handling the man at the service entrance.

"Count to thirty," Dylan said, "then come behind me. Be aware of your surroundings, but look neither left nor right. You zero in on that front entrance and get the hell out the door. The vehicle will be on your left—a dark gray Suburban. The back door will be open. All you need to do is dive in and they'll take off."

"And you'll be right behind me. Right?"

He nodded. "Once Reddington's goons are taken care of, Livingston, Thorne, and I will be right behind you."

Standing beside him, she looked out at the still-dark sky and then back at him. "This is going to work, isn't it?"

His expression briefly softened. "Yes. Everything will be fine."

Before she could say anything else, he glanced at his watch and said, "Let's get the backpack on you. It's almost time."

Jamie turned, and when he placed the pack on her back, she slipped her arms through the straps. Dylan came around to her front and secured it across her chest. Feeling the need to see him look less serious, if only for a moment, she quipped, "After escaping Armando and a barrage of bullets, this should be a cakewalk."

Instead of the amusement she was looking for, Dylan gripped the straps of the backpack, pulled her against him, and crushed her mouth with his. Before she could gather her wits to respond, he pulled away and growled, "Let's go."

Opening the door a crack, he peered out and then disappeared, closing the door behind him. The instant the door shut, Jamie started counting. When she got to twenty-five, she put her hand on the door. At thirty, she turned the knob and took off down the hallway.

Dylan had told her to use the elevator. He'd said for a small, older hotel, it was in surprisingly good shape. If she used the stairwell, she might get caught by one of Reddington's men. Her pace quick but steady, she jumped into the elevator and pressed the button for the first floor. So far, so good.

Jamie entered the small lobby. As early as it was, she wasn't surprised that no one was around. Her eyes focused on the door, fifteen feet in front of her. When she heard the footsteps behind her, she sped up. At the entrance, a hard hand grabbed her shoulder and an unfamiliar voice snapped, "Stop!"

Twisting around, Jamie aimed her fist at the man's face and connected hard with his nose.

She pivoted quickly and took off running. When she got out to the portico, she spotted the gray Suburban Dylan had described—the back door was open. She heard the gunshot just as she flew into its back. Landing on the seat, Jamie jumped up to her knees and looked out the rear window. Dylan and another man were fighting. Then she saw Dylan fall. Jamie screamed and put her hand on the door. For the first time, she realized the vehicle was moving, zipping through the parking lot, leaving the hotel . . . leaving Dylan behind.

She shouted over her shoulder at the driver, "Stop! Dylan's down. We have to go back."

The driver didn't acknowledge her, but the person sitting on the seat beside her did. A person she hadn't even noticed because she'd been so intent on watching Dylan. A soft hand touched her arm and a woman's voice said, "He'll be fine, Jamie. Don't worry."

Jamie turned to see McKenna beside her. The joy of seeing her sister was put on hold by the sheer terror of having watched Dylan fall to the ground. "We have to go back, Kenna. They're hurting him."

"Thorne and Livingston are there with him. They'll take care of him." The crisp British voice came from the driver—her brother-in-law, Lucas.

"But I—"

"He'll be fine," McKenna said again. "I promise."

Jamie glanced helplessly at the hotel, which was quickly disappearing from her view. Then, unable to do anything else, she did the only thing that made sense in the midst of all the craziness—she threw herself into her sister's arms.

"Ah, shit," Dylan mumbled.

"You know a man's going to live when he wakes up cursing."

Aidan Thorne's toothpaste-ad grin was almost too bright for Dylan's blinding headache. He tried to move and groaned at the agony. Hell, how much did his head weigh? And where the hell was he? Why was . . . ?

Jamie! Dylan bolted upright and then severely regretted the movement. His stomach roiled and bile shot up his throat. Rolling over, he threw up.

"Better go get the doctor."

With his nausea temporarily abated, Dylan rolled back over and squinted up again, recognizing the expressionless voice of Jared Livingston.

"Jamie? Where is she?"

"She's safe. McKenna and Lucas picked her up and took her to the airport. Since you needed immediate medical care, they went ahead and flew to Paris."

A rush of relieved breath went through Dylan, causing the nausea and dizziness to return. Gritting his teeth against the pain, he asked, "What the hell happened?"

"We didn't count on the front desk guy being one of Reddington's men. Turned out, he actually wasn't, but he didn't mind getting his hands dirty for some cash on the side."

"And he didn't touch Jamie?"

"Well, yeah, he did, but he immediately wished he hadn't. That woman's got a damn nice right hook."

If he'd been able to muster the energy, he would have smiled. Jamie continually surprised people.

A tall, thin, gray-haired man stood at the door of his room. "So our patient is finally awake. How are you feeling?"

"Like somebody hit me with a two-by-four."

"You have a slight concussion. I recommend at least twenty-four hours of bed rest."

About to argue that he wasn't about to stay in the hospital a second longer than it would take to get his clothes on, Dylan was preempted by Aidan Thorne, who said, "Might as well, man. The plane won't be back until the day after tomorrow."

Hell, Thorne was right. There was no point in going anywhere else. Staying here would keep him out of Reddington's sight. There was, however, one thing he had to do before he closed his eyes again.

"Give me a phone."

He ignored Thorne's overloud sigh and the knowing grin on his face. When the man punched in a number and then handed him the phone, Dylan grunted his thanks. Since the agony in his head made it difficult for him to focus, he'd put up with Thorne's perpetual ribbing.

Lucas Kane answered, "Kane."

"How's Jamie?"

"Worried sick about you."

"Let me talk to her."

Seconds later, Jamie's shaky voice said, "Dylan, are you okay?"

"I'm fine. You're not hurt? That man . . . he didn't—"

"No, he didn't touch me."

"Good. Give McCall the files . . . he'll know what to do."

"When will you—"

"Gotta go." Dylan swallowed hard and added, "You

did good, Jamie . . . real good." He hit the End button
and handed the phone to Thorne.

For once his trademark grin absent, Thorne growled,
"You're a real prick, Savage, you know that?"

Dylan closed his eyes. No use arguing with the truth.

Stanford stood over Armando's body and said goodbye to his friend and once faithful servant. The man had
known what was coming. With the disappearance of
John Wheeler and Karen Jennings, there had been no
one to punish . . . to answer for their sins. Armando had
paid. He should have stopped them from leaving. If he
hadn't been drunk, they never would have escaped.

Since the man had been with him for years, Stanford
hadn't prolonged his suffering. A bullet to his temple,
and that was the end. He nodded at Joseph, who started
the boat's engine and took off. Joseph would go a few
miles from the island and dump the body deep in the
ocean. His friend would never be seen again.

Even now, Armando's family was receiving the devastating news that he had suffered an apparent seizure and
fallen overboard while he and Stanford were out deep-
sea fishing. And, of course, Stanford had risked his life,
done everything he could, to save his good friend, to no
avail.

As he turned back to his home, his mind returned to
Wheeler. The Jennings woman didn't matter. Her reasons for leaving no longer interested him. Wheeler was
another issue. What would have caused him to just leave
like that? Had he been angry because of the arranged
fight? That didn't track with what he knew of the man.
And hadn't Wheeler won? No, that couldn't be the
reason.

Lance had returned to Germany. There was no need
to keep him on the island any longer. For some reason,
his mother wasn't as happy to see him as he'd thought

she would be. And, if he was honest with himself, Lancelot's arrogance and shallowness were wearing thin.

Nothing was turning out the way he'd thought it would, and for the first time in his memory, Stanford was depressed. Blowing out a sigh at the unfairness of life, he didn't hear the whirring until it was almost over him.

Looking up, his eyes wide with shock, he watched as the large blue-and-white helicopter hovered and then landed on a flat, grassy area beside the mansion. What the hell was going on?

A half dozen men jumped from the still whirring bird. Dressed in police uniforms, their guns pulled, they dispersed, running in different directions as they swarmed his island.

A large, rather bulky man, holding a legal-looking document in his hand, started toward Stanford. Why was this happening? How had they found his island? Wheeler? The Jennings woman? Raphael? He would find out; whoever it was, they would pay dearly. All of that legal nastiness was supposed to have been in the past. They still had nothing on him. Just how much more was this going to cost him in lawyers' fees?

As the man approached, Stanford caught a glimpse of another man stepping out of the helicopter. Tall, with black hair and broad shoulders—for an instant, he thought it was Wheeler. Then the man took off his dark sunglasses and Stanford realized he'd never seen him before. The puzzling part was the knowing, almost smirking smile on the man's face. As if he was in on something Stanford wasn't.

A sound behind him made him whirl around. Sarah stood at the doorway. "Go back inside," Stanford snapped. "This has nothing to do with you."

Her face almost glowed in the sunlight, and a smile of such loveliness lifted her mouth that he was awestruck by her beauty. He'd never seen her smile like that before. Overwhelmed by her magnificence, it took him several seconds to digest her words: "You're wrong, Stan. This has everything to do with me."

His heart thundered in his chest as realization slammed into him like a wrecking ball. Sarah, his beloved wife, the mother of his children, his soul mate, had betrayed him.

twenty-eight

Three weeks later
West Virginia mountains

Wrapped in a throw she'd snagged from the couch, Jamie sat in a rocker on the porch and listened to the leaves rustling beneath the tiny feet of squirrels as they foraged through the forest. Winter was coming on early this year, and they were already storing up food, getting ready for the long haul.

She had arrived yesterday afternoon. Noah hadn't asked her why she wanted to come back here. She was quite sure he knew her reasons. The man was as discerning as they came. He recognized a brokenhearted woman when he saw one.

She had thought about going after Dylan and confronting him. Had even jumped into a taxi and ridden to his apartment. Of course, the instant the cab had stopped, she had known she wouldn't be able to do it. He didn't want to see her—she'd been in Paris for several days. He knew exactly where she was—he just hadn't bothered.

There were a lot of things to be happy about, and she tried to focus on them. Reddington was now in jail, awaiting trial. After all the danger and excitement of her and Dylan's escape, the arrests had gone down in an extraordinarily calm fashion.

Noah had presented the flash drives to the prosecutor.

Using the descriptions, dates, and locations from Reddington's files, they had matched the listings to known missing persons. With the very first match, they'd had enough grounds to arrest the man.

And thanks to the safe combination that Sarah Reddington had given them, they now had paper files to go with the computer records. Reddington's meticulous record keeping had been a blessing. So far, seventeen people had been identified. Many more identifications were expected.

Noah had been invited to go along for the arrest, as long as he promised not to participate or interfere. On his return, he had called Jamie into his office and described the scene.

A helicopter had swooped down and landed on the island close to the mansion. Reddington happened to be standing outside at the time, and had stood frozen, mouth ajar, while police officers had dispersed and combed the island.

According to Noah, even in handcuffs, the man had been indignant and belligerent all the way to the police boat that had arrived to take him away. No doubt he had thought he'd be able to buy his way out once again. As soon as he'd learned that they had physical documents as evidence, he'd begun to argue that his rights had been violated because the files had been stolen from his property. And when he'd been told that his wife was the one who'd given the files up, he had screamed that she had framed him and was mentally unstable. How Jamie would have loved to have seen his face when he'd realized no one was going to believe him this time.

Not everything was perfect. Lance Reddington could not be tied to any of his father's abductions or auctions. And, of course, the younger Reddington had claimed shock and outrage when he'd heard that there was irrefutable proof. Rumor was that he was back in Germany, working hard to overcome his father's betrayal and the tarnish on his family's good name.

Jamie had accepted that Lance would never be punished for what he'd done. And she was at peace with the outcome. Someday, he would meet with the justice he deserved. Maybe, she thought, his father's woes would make him think twice before he hurt or sexually molested another woman again. Though she had serious doubts that he had learned any valuable lessons, she hoped for the best.

Perhaps the saddest and least surprising information that came from Reddington's files was the name of his first victim. LCR had known that Reddington's father had been involved with slave trading, passing the business to his son, who'd taken it to new levels. They just hadn't known that Sarah Reddington, once known as Guinevere Mangas, a fourteen-year-old child from Athens, Greece, had been purchased for a nineteen-year-old Stanford. Jamie's heart hurt for the woman who'd spent most of her life as the prisoner of a monster.

Sarah, Giselle, Amelia, and Eric were still on the island—this time by choice, not imprisonment. Raphael was there with them, too. She knew nothing more than that, but Jamie sincerely hoped that everyone, with the exception of Lance, would find the happiness they deserved.

Something Jamie was exceedingly grateful for was that her relationship with McKenna hadn't been irreparably damaged. A lump developed in her throat when she thought about her sister's first words once they were finally on the plane and headed to Paris. With tears glistening in her eyes, she'd said, "I don't think I've ever been angrier at or more proud of anyone in all of my life."

Then she'd hugged Jamie and whispered fiercely in her ear, "Jamie Kendrick, if you ever do anything like this again without telling me, I swear I'll channel Aunt Mavis's ghost."

Laughter had replaced the tears. The threat of a ghostly Aunt Mavis returning from the hereafter to give Jamie one of her stern lectures had been a humorous but appropriate threat. Her aunt would have had much to say about Jamie's behavior.

Even Noah, who'd told her that he wasn't any happier with her than McKenna had been, had admitted that he was impressed with her accomplishments and had actually offered her a job with LCR. She had turned him down.

The short amount of time she'd spent on Reddington's island teaching Amelia had reminded her of why she'd chosen teaching in the first place. She loved to see the light of discovery in a child's eyes. Helping children reach their potential and stretch their wings toward independence had to be one of the most rewarding careers in the world. She wanted to do it again.

But first, she had needed some time to herself. To think about Dylan. She loved him with an absolute certainty that would never fail or diminish. She wanted to spend her life with him. How did he feel? She had no clue. There was desire, admiration, and maybe affection—but was there more?

She knew he had returned to Paris. The concussion hadn't incapacitated him for long, which had been no surprise—the man had the hardest head of anyone she'd ever known. But she hadn't seen him or talked to him. Had no idea if he ever planned to see her again.

So she had come back to the place where she had fallen completely in love with him—to remember and, maybe, to reconcile herself to the idea that those few weeks were all they would ever have.

At some point, the hope would fade. When that day

came, she would go on, much lonelier and sadder, with an ache in her heart that would never leave.

Düsseldorf, Germany

Thick, gray clouds hid the late afternoon sun, darkening the interior of the parking structure. A cool wind blew through the open-air deck, causing Lance to walk with brisk steps to his Bentley. Tugging his cashmere jacket closer around his neck, he lowered his head and hunched his shoulders. The burning resentment of having to drive his own car gave him an extra amount of warmth against the crisp autumn air.

If his father had not been so stupid as to have gotten caught, his life would be perfect. Instead, much of the family's wealth was going toward legal fees. There was even the possibility that Lance might have to get a job to support himself. The appalling idea was too horrific to contemplate. As long as he had credit, he'd damn well have the life he enjoyed.

At some point, he would reinstate his father's business. The man would be in prison, but his legacy could still live on. Just in his few weeks of training, Lance had learned much about the flesh trade. He could reestablish the ties and connections his father had spent years developing. So what that Stanford Reddington was in jail. Business could continue, and as much as he hated managing menial day-to-day tasks, Lance knew he was going to have to overcome his revulsion if he was going to live in the style he deserved.

He was so intent on his plans for the future that he didn't see the man leaning against his car until he was a few feet from it. Lance jerked to a stop and yelled, "Hey, what are you doing? Get away from my car."

The dimness of the parking lot obscured the stranger's

face, but Lance could tell the man was tall, powerful-looking. Adrenaline rushed through him. Did this have something to do with his father? Or maybe it was about that prostitute he'd beaten up last month or that bitch he'd screwed last week who'd claimed he'd gotten too rough?

His hands trembling, Lance reached for his cellphone. "I'm going to call the police. You'd better leave."

The man never spoke, never moved. He just stood there, in a slouched, relaxed pose, with his arms crossed. Lance had never seen anyone so still and quiet . . . or so lethal-looking.

He squinted into the darkness, trying to see the man's features. And that was when his heart went into overdrive. The man was wearing a ski mask.

Panic blooming, his eyes scanned the dim parking lot. It was filled with cars, but there was no one around to help him. Was this man going to kill him? But why?

Perhaps he just wanted money. Withdrawing his wallet from his pocket, he threw it toward the man. "Here, there are a couple of thousand euros in there. Take it and leave."

The wallet landed about a foot from the man's boots, but he didn't acknowledge the wallet with even a glance. Just continued that penetrating, unblinking stare.

The guy was big . . . he shouldn't be able to move as quickly as Lance. He'd run for it. Get to the nearest exit and scream for help. Keeping his eyes on the man, watching for any quick movements, he took several steps back, slowly, carefully. Then, pivoting, he took off running. The nearest exit was to his right . . . he could make it; he *had* to make it. He was at the door before he saw the man standing there, blocking his exit. No, it couldn't be the same one. Though he, too, wore a ski mask and was about the same size, the ski mask was darker and this man was smiling. Lance could see his white teeth gleaming.

Now in full panic mode, his breath rasping from his lungs, Lance backed away again. There was another exit, on the other side of the lot. Could he make it without being attacked? He had to try. Turning, he zoomed across the lot, the only sounds his pounding feet and the hard thumping of his heart. He was running faster than he ever had in his life; he was going to make it. With his eyes on his target, he was a few yards from the exit when another large, masked man appeared, again blocking the exit. Who were these people? What did they want?

Backing up quickly, he ran into the middle of the parking lot and whirled around in a circle. "Help! Someone help me!"

Hot breath rushed down his neck. He froze. One of the men was right behind him. What could he do? He was a defenseless man, at the mercy of three monsters. This was so unfair!

"Turn around."

The voice spoke in German; the tone was guttural, without emotion or pity.

Tears sprang to Lance's eyes. His body trembling, he turned around and pleaded, "Please, if you want more money, I can get it for you. Anything. Just don't hurt me."

Big hands gripped the lapels of his jacket and pulled hard. Lance's legs dangled as he found himself suspended in air, held within the man's firm grasp.

"How does it feel to be alone and vulnerable, you little maggot? Are you scared?"

"Y-yes . . ." Lanced stuttered. "Please, I'm begging you . . . don't hurt me."

The man pulled him so close, Lance could feel the warmth of his breath on his face. "Listen well, because this is the only warning you'll ever get. If you ever touch a woman who doesn't want to be touched, say anything inappropriate, or do anything to hurt a woman ever again, I will rip your balls off and stuff them down your fucking throat. Do you understand me?"

Lance nodded quickly. He would do anything, agree to everything the man wanted.

"People are watching you, night and day, twenty-four/seven. They know where you go, what you do, when you scratch your worthless balls, even when you take a shit. One wrong step and that piece of meat between your legs will be chopped off and you'll be pissing through a straw for the rest of your very short life."

Lance kept nodding. Anything . . . he would do anything.

The blow was unexpected, busting his nose. Lance heard the pop, felt excruciating pain. Then another blow slammed into his stomach, then his groin. Falling to his knees, with blood pouring around him, Lance sobbed. Hard hands slammed him forward onto the pavement, and a big body came on top of him. Lance heard roaring in his ears . . . the man was going to kill him after all.

Knees dug deep into Lance's back as the man leaned forward and growled in his ear, "Remember this pain. It's nothing to what you will feel if you stray one inch."

Barely conscious, Lance managed one slow nod. Another blow slammed into his head, and blessed unconsciousness took him.

The assailant stood for several seconds over the piece of garbage lying on the ground. He had wanted to do more . . . but this would have to be enough.

He walked toward the men waiting for him. Tugging off his mask, he dropped it into the garbage can next to the exit. The other two did the same. Nodding his thanks for their assistance, he disappeared through the door.

Last Chance Rescue headquarters
Paris

Dylan entered McCall's office with the kind of urgency he hadn't felt in years. His boss hadn't called him to come in, but Dylan was going to give it a shot. He dropped his leather jacket on the chair in front of McCall's desk but didn't bother to sit. "I want an assignment."

McCall frowned. "I don't have anything for you right now. Besides, you deserve some downtime. Maybe next week I'll—"

"There's got to be an operation somewhere I can get involved with."

"We've got plenty of operations going on, but they're all assigned out. Take a few days and—"

"What about training? Any new operatives coming on?"

The implacable expression McCall was famous for never shifted as he slouched back in his chair. "I might have one for you." He nodded at the chair. "Have a seat."

Relieved, Dylan dropped into the chair and waited to hear about his new assignment.

"Tell me about Jamie," McCall said.

Dylan's insides jerked, and his heart slammed against his chest. "Why, has something happened?"

"No, as far as I know, she's fine. Last I heard she had decided to go back to teaching and is in the States."

Yeah, that's what McKenna had told him, after he'd gotten an earful for being such a jerk to her sister. He hadn't defended himself . . . how could he? She was right; he was a jerk. And he hadn't bothered to explain that Jamie was much better off without him. She could finally get her life back on track and push all of the bad things of her past away.

"Then what do you want me to tell you about Jamie?"

"I want to know why, if you love her, you wouldn't want her to know it."

There was no point in denying McCall's words. "She's better off without me."

"Why?"

Talking about feelings and emotions, especially with another man, was on Dylan's list of least favorite things, right behind root canals and getting kicked in the balls. Using the glare he saved for his most pissed-off looks and adding an arched brow, he stared at his boss.

A smile spread across the other man's face, telling Dylan that the look had no power over him.

Silence filled the office while they each tried to stare down the other. Seconds later, Dylan blew out a long sigh. Aw hell, what was the point? Shifting his gaze, unwilling to meet his boss's eyes as he spoke, he gave the man the truth: "I'm not good enough for her."

Instead of disagreeing, McCall sputtered with laughter. "You think I don't feel that way with Samara? There's not a day that goes by that I don't ask myself how the hell I got so lucky. Samara is the very best part of me . . . she's a much better person than I am. And she makes me a better man by loving me."

Moved and somewhat embarrassed by Noah's confession, Dylan swallowed hard. Stoicism and protecting himself from further hurt by not giving in to deep emotions had been his trademark his entire life. Until Jamie, he'd never known that so many emotions existed. Experiencing such a range of feelings because of one woman was exhausting.

McCall and his wife had a good marriage. And though there was nothing soft about Dylan's boss, he wasn't the cold, hard man he'd been before he married Samara. There was a contentment in him that hadn't been there before. Maybe McCall was right—having his wife's love did make him a better man.

But Dylan wasn't McCall, and Jamie deserved the very best kind of man—Dylan wasn't it.

He repeated the words he'd been saying to himself for days: "Jamie's better off without me." With the need to get the conversation back on a comfortable, even keel, Dylan said, "Tell me about this training project. Is this a new operative?"

McCall considered him for several long seconds, as if weighing his words. Then he gave a brief nod. "She's new. I was going to talk to Aidan, but if you think you're up to it, I'd rather you train her."

Dylan got to his feet, eager to start on his new assignment. "Where?"

"She lives in the southeastern U.S., so West Virginia will be the best location for her."

Dylan refused to flinch from the thought of going back to the cabin so soon. It was a great training location, and since the snow wouldn't have started yet, the weather would be perfect.

He pulled on his leather jacket. "I'll head out there tomorrow."

"What happened to your hand?"

Dylan's gaze went to the swollen, raw knuckles of his right hand. "It's nothing." He headed toward the door.

"I heard Lance Reddington met with some bad luck a few days ago in Germany," Noah said. "Seems he was beaten by what he called three giants. Spent a day or two in the hospital."

Dylan turned at the door, his eyes meeting McCall's. "It's a dangerous world."

"Yes, it is." Picking up the phone, Noah said, "I'll have an LCR plane ready for you in the morning."

About to walk out, Dylan stopped abruptly and

turned. "What's the name of this new person I'm train-ing?"

McCall's mouth twitched with a small smile, as if the name of his new employee amused him. "Her name is Bliss."

twenty-nine

West Virginia mountains

As Dylan steered his truck up the long drive, he fruit-lessly fought the memories bombarding him. He remembered sitting on the front porch waiting for Jamie to arrive, dreading the job he'd agreed to do, even while the thought of seeing her again had his heart thudding with anticipation.

Even though he'd already acknowledged that he had feelings for her, he had never foreseen how deep they would go. Jamie had surprised, enchanted, and enthralled him just by being exactly who she was.

What he'd told McCall was true. Jamie was too good for him. The garbage that had sired Dylan was in his blood. Adages like "The apple doesn't fall far from the tree" and "Blood will out" hadn't been created or repeated through the centuries without good reason.

He'd spent his life regretting not saving his mother. Then, when Sheila had come to him for help, his anger and pride had kept him from believing that she was in danger. If he had believed her, he could have saved her.

And Jamie meant everything to him. Would there come a day when the blood running through his veins overruled his love for her? He couldn't take the chance.

McKenna had said that Jamie had decided to teach again and was back in the States. He hadn't asked what state. Knowing would have been too much of a temptation. As Jamie had once told him, the U.S. has fifty states, and that's a damn big territory.

As he pulled to the top of the drive, he noticed that lights were on inside the cabin. Apparently, Bliss had already arrived. He'd been wondering about the name—was that her real one or a name LCR had provided? Many operatives, especially those who wanted to escape a dark past, changed their names. Dylan hadn't seen the need. His last name seemed damn appropriate.

He opened the car door and stretched, glad that the trip was over. Hopefully, Bliss wouldn't mind if he didn't stay up and talk. They could get to know each other at breakfast, when his mind was clearer and images of Jamie weren't clouding his every thought.

With his duffel bag in one hand, Dylan turned the doorknob and the door swung open. The cozy scene that greeted him slammed at him hard. A fire blazed in the fireplace, the fragrance of something delicious wafted from the kitchen, and soft music came from the built-in speakers. It took everything he had not to turn around and leave. Maybe the memories were going to be too much after all.

A small gasp came from the kitchen door. Dylan swung his head around; both the bag in his hand and his heart raced to the floor with a thud. A beautiful, golden-haired temptress stood in the doorway, looking as startled as he felt.

"What the hell are you doing here?" Dylan snarled.

A slight flinch and then the inevitable chin lift. "That was going to be my question."

"I came to train an LCR operative." Panic rushed through his veins. "Shit, did McCall take you on as an operative?"

"He offered me the job. I said no."

The relief that she wouldn't be making a career of

putting her life on the line was almost enough to overcome the shock of seeing her again.

"Then why are you here?"

White teeth chewed on her lower lips. Ah hell, did she
realize what that did to him?

"I just needed some thinking time. Noah said the
cabin was free."

McCall. Dammit, his boss's interference was not appreciated. What did the man think Dylan was going to
do—forget who he was and what he'd come from?

"I'll leave tomorrow."

Her words made him realize he'd been standing at the
door, most likely glaring at her.

"No, don't leave. I came here to do a job, and since
the job doesn't exist, I'll leave." He blew out a sigh and
added, "Tomorrow, if that's okay."

Her mouth trembled as if she wanted to say something else, but instead she just nodded her head and
turned back to the kitchen.

Dylan blew out a ragged sigh. *Hell.*

Jamie went back to the vegetables she'd been chopping for her vegetable soup. After all her aching and
pining for Dylan over the past few weeks, his less than
enthusiastic reaction to seeing her again was like a
punch into a gaping wound.

She hadn't known he was coming. Noah was trying to
play matchmaker. While she appreciated his efforts on
their behalf, Dylan's response had shown her there was
no hope.

The vegetables blurred in front of her. Knowing she
was going to lose it very soon, she made do with what
she'd already cut, dropped them into the boiling broth,
reduced the heat, and closed the lid. She had to get
someplace by herself before she fell apart and Dylan
realized the truth.

"Something smells good."

Damn. Damn. Damn. With her head turned away from him, she said, "Vegetable beef soup and home-made bread. Should be ready in a half hour or so." Skirting past him, she kept her back to him as she put the cutting board and knife in the sink. "I'm going to take a bath. Be back in a few minutes."

"Jamie."

Shivers of arousal struck her unexpectedly. The growling, husky tone in his voice reminded her of when they were making love. Late at night, when she couldn't sleep, she imagined hearing that voice, whispering in her ear, as he moved inside her.

But that was in the past, and she couldn't let him see what he was doing to her. The last thing she wanted was his pity. Still avoiding looking at him, she headed toward the door.

"Jamie, wait."

She jerked to a stop. Now there was regret and sadness in his voice. *Oh God, he knows.* Her fingers gripped the door frame tightly. "Let it go, Dylan. Please."

"I wish I could be what you need."

Unable to let this incredibly odd statement go without addressing it, she whirled around. "What exactly do you think I need?"

For the first time ever, Dylan looked at a loss for words. She watched his throat work as he swallowed, as if he were searching for the right thing to say. He also looked wonderfully dear and almost vulnerable. Jamie's hands clenched at her sides to keep from reaching out and touching him.

"I think you need someone as good as you are."

Now she was the one at a loss for words. She shook her head slowly, confused and almost insulted. "Are you insinuating that I'm too good for you?"

"You are."

Of all the reasons she could think of why Dylan didn't

love her or want to be with her, this was the last one she would have come up with. "What exactly makes me better than you?"

He shook his head and gave an exasperated grunt. "You know about me. I thought by telling you about my past, you'd understand."

"Understand what? That you had a shitty childhood?"

"I had alcoholic parents and a father who had nothing but evil inside of him."

"And you think you're evil, too?"

"No, but I . . ."

Temper flared, hot and bright—a welcome relief from her earlier, churning emotions. "Give me another reason, Dylan." She stalked toward him, stopping with her face inches from his. "Tell me you don't love me. That I'm not your type. Hell, tell me I'm not pretty enough for you. But don't you dare tell me you're not good enough for me. That's pure bullshit. If you're too afraid to take a chance with me, then at least have the guts to admit it instead of using lame-assed excuses."

"Jamie . . . I—"

"You told me once that we make our own way in life . . . that our past doesn't define us. So, either you were lying then or you're lying now. Which one is it?"

A war raged in his eyes. Jamie stared into them, willing him to change his mind, praying that he would fight for them. She could see the struggle—what he wanted versus what he feared. Seconds passed, the only sounds in the room the clock over the mantel and Dylan's slightly elevated breathing. Jamie held her breath, waiting for a miracle.

The miracle didn't happen. He turned away and headed out of the room. "I'm not hungry after all. See you in the morning."

Seconds later, his bedroom door clicked shut and any hope that he would change his mind was demolished.

Jamie rolled over in bed. The sun streaming through the window blinds told her it was late morning. Her mind felt foggy and dull . . . sadness pervaded her entire being. How could he be so damn stubborn? Did he really think that what his father had done meant he would do the same thing?

She had seen deep inside Dylan . . . she knew what he was made of. Was he perfect? Absolutely not. He was stubborn, growly, and grumpy, and had a tendency to think his way was the only way to do something. He was also the bravest, strongest, and most gentle man she'd ever known. So no, he wasn't perfect. But he was perfect for her.

She had hoped that after a good night's sleep, he would be willing to talk about it. But that wasn't going to happen. Just after dawn, she'd heard him leave. Just like that. Without so much as a "Goodbye" or "Have a nice life," he'd walked out the door.

Jamie had cried herself back to sleep. Now, hours later, with her determination back in full force, she needed a massive amount of coffee so she could figure out how she was going to get Dylan to come to his senses. She refused to give up on them.

Pulling herself out of bed, she dressed and brushed her teeth and hair, all with the intent of making herself feel better. Next came coffee, and then she would plan her attack.

She headed to the kitchen, studiously avoiding looking at Dylan's closed bedroom door. He wasn't in there, and she refused to do the pitiful thing and enter the bedroom just so she could feel close to him. That screamed of desperation, and she would not accept defeat.

She was sitting in the living room, sipping her second

cup of coffee, when she heard a vehicle drive up outside. Wondering if perhaps the operative Dylan had thought he was supposed to train really did exist, Jamie stood. When she heard the slam of the car door, she started toward the front door. She was in the middle of the room when Dylan entered.

Almost dizzy with shock and hope, she said, "What are you doing back? Did you forget something?"

"Yeah . . . kind of."

"What?"

He came toward her and held out his hand. Her hopes soared, but, too afraid to believe that what she saw in his hand was real, she whispered, "What is it?"

Dylan was terrified; there was no other way to describe the feeling. He, who had faced some of the meanest and most vicious people in the world, was now trembling in fear. This beautiful, gutsy woman held his entire life in the palm of her hand.

After a sleepless night, his thoughts roiling like the ocean during a hurricane, he'd thrown every argument he could think of into his path, only to come to one final, inevitable conclusion: he couldn't live without her.

McCall had said that Samara's love made him a better man. Dylan didn't know if that was possible for him. He only knew that Jamie made him want to be the kind of man who deserved her love. She had accused him of being afraid to take a chance on them, and she had nailed it. But fear or no fear . . . he couldn't live without her. And if she said yes, he was going to make sure she never regretted her decision.

Wincing at the way his hands trembled, he opened the tiny box. "I wanted to surprise you in bed with it, but it took me a long time to pick it out."

"Dylan?" she breathed softly, her voice full of surprised wonder.

The diamond solitaire engagement ring sparkled like

sunshine—much like Jamie's smile. "If you don't like it, we can exchange it for—"

With a sob, she threw herself into his arms. As relief and a thousand other emotions almost swamped him, Dylan closed his arms around her and held her tight against his chest.

Raising her head to look up at him, she cupped his face in her hands. "I love you."

He swallowed around the giant lump in his throat, took a shaky breath, and, for the first time ever, said the words "I love you." Then, burying his face in her hair, he whispered, "God, how I love you."

Hours later, snuggled in front of the fire, her head on Dylan's chest, Jamie sighed with pure contentment. Never had she imagined she could be so happy. They hadn't talked about the future or the past; they'd just existed in a state of euphoric bliss.

Dylan's voice rumbled beneath her ear. "I need to tell you something."

"What's that?"

"Lance Reddington won't be hurting any more women . . . ever."

She lifted her head. "What do you mean?"

"I had a short but very frank talk with him. He's going to be looking over his shoulder for the rest of his life."

Dylan had known how much she wanted Lance to pay for what he'd done. That hadn't been possible, so instead, he had done the next best thing: he had made sure that Lance would never do to anyone else what he had done to her.

"Thank you." She kissed his lips softly and put her head back on his chest.

His arms tight around her again, he said gruffly, "I wish I could have done more."

"Knowing he's not going to do it again or be able to carry on his father's business is more than enough."

"I have a question to ask."

"What's that?"

"Swear that you'll be completely honest?"

Jamie lifted her head again. "The deceit between us is in the past. From now on, full disclosure . . . for both of us."

Pulling her close, he whispered, "Full disclosure," and covered her mouth for a long and tender kiss. Minutes later, when their lips finally parted, Jamie groaned at the hot, slumberous look in his eyes. Even though she knew he wanted to talk, it was all she could do not to jump his bones then and there.

As if he could tell exactly what she was thinking, a small knowing smile played around his lips. To have Dylan smile like that, to see him so relaxed and content, did something to her already full heart. She could barely believe that they were sitting here together, contemplating their future, and that she had the most beautiful engagement ring ever created on her finger.

"You keep looking at me like that and we'll have to put this discussion off for another hour or two."

Yes, she wanted to make love to him again, but having Dylan wanting to talk and share confidences with her was too exciting not to pursue. "Want me to move away so I won't be such a temptation?"

His arms tightened around her. "Don't you dare."

Tilting her head back, she said, "What did you want to ask?"

"I don't have to work for LCR."

Shocked and confused at the words, she pulled completely away to look up at him. "Why would you want to work somewhere else?"

"You have a right to have a say about the kind of life we're going to lead. If I stay with LCR, there'll still be danger, not to mention the weeks or months I'll be away from you when I'm on a job. I can ask McCall for fewer assignments, but—"

"But I still don't understand. Why would you think I'd want you to work somewhere else? You love your job, and you're damn good at it."

"But I love you more."

And she hadn't thought her heart could get any fuller. Pressing a tender kiss to his mouth, she said, "You're an LCR operative . . . a rescuer. I don't want you to be anything other than who you are."

"Who I am is the man who's going to love you for the rest of his life and make all your dreams come true."

Tears blurred her vision as she smiled up at him. "You've already done that."

Growling, "I love you," Dylan swooped down for a hard, devouring kiss. With a groan, Jamie gave herself up to the beauty of being held in the arms of the man she adored. Dylan—her rescuer, her lover, her life.

acknowledgments

I am so incredibly blessed to not only have a career I love, but to also have the support of so many. With special thanks to the following:

My loving and supportive family, especially my wonderful husband and my precious fur creatures.

My editor, Kate Collins, for her insight, kindness, and incredible patience. And to the entire Ballantine team, especially Junessa Viloria, Beth Pearson, Ted Allen, and Bonnie Thompson.

Kim Whalen, my fabulously supportive agent.

Special thanks to Kara Conrad for her patience in answering my endless questions about a multitude of topics.

Thank you to *all* the Reece's Peece's for your support, love, and laughter.

And to the readers of the Last Chance Rescue series, especially those who wrote asking about Dylan and Jamie, many, many thanks for wanting to read their story. I hope you enjoyed it!

Turn the page for a sneak peek at

SWEET REWARD,

the final novel
in Christy Reece's romantic suspense trilogy!

one

"Livingston, where the hell are you?"

As Noah McCall's terse words rang in his ears, Jared twisted his mouth into a wry grimace. His boss was pissed—not an unusual event. Couldn't do a damn thing about that . . . especially right now. Standing on a six-inch ledge twelve stories above the ground and only a few feet from a maniac with a gun impeded his ability to answer.

Plastered against the white brick wall, his concentration fierce, Jared focused on his destination—the half-open window ten feet to his right. Muscles strained as he extended his arms above him; his long fingers gripped the small overhang as his feet inched along the ledge of the building.

They'd been on the other side of the apartment door for over two hours trying to talk a nutcase into freeing a ten-year-old girl he'd snatched off the street. So far, all they'd gotten were threats to shoot the child if they tried to come in. Jared had gotten tired of waiting.

McCall had been in the midst of conversing with the man when Jared had walked away. The LCR leader was a good hostage negotiator, but hearing the child crying had turned Jared's stomach. He'd figured he had two choices: walk away and let the negotiations continue or do something to speed up the process.

"Livingston," McCall snarled softly, "if you fall, I swear I'll figure out a way to bring you back to life so I can kill you myself."

Apparently someone had alerted his boss that Jared had found an alternate entrance.

He was an avid climber, and at least once a year he went somewhere—lately Mont Blanc—and fed his need. Compared to that, hanging out on a ledge in downtown Agar wasn't that much of a challenge. Still, even just this high up, the air was fresher and the only creature around was a bored-looking pigeon that had barely acknowledged him.

A heavy gust of wind slammed him hard against the wall. His fingers tightened on the ledge. It was a good reminder that while a twelve-story building wasn't much of a challenge, it could still get dicey.

He inched closer to the window. Since they'd managed to slide a mirror beneath the door, he had a good idea what was going on inside. The creep faced the door; his back to the window, he held a gun to the girl's head. It seemed to Jared that the best option for a live rescue was to come in behind him.

At the edge of the window, Jared stopped. Barely easing his head over, he got his first real glimpse of what was going on inside. The man, known to them only as Bernard, stood about four feet from the window. A young girl sat on a stool in front of the man, her thin body shuddering in obvious terror, and with good reason—the gun was still pressed to her head.

Jared's eyes quickly took in the rest of the room. Sofa and chair to the left, small kitchen with a bar to the right. No one else in sight. Looked like the guy was on his own for this.

The window was open about half a foot, with no

screen, thankfully. Shooting the bastard was a temptation, but one Jared couldn't risk. Bernard's finger was on the trigger. One involuntary jerk and the child was dead.

A sudden flutter of wings was Jared's only warning as a pigeon dove toward him. As he instinctively ducked, his left foot slipped and he slid to one knee. His right hand latched on to the windowsill, saving him from plunging to the ground. A cooing sounded above him; Jared glared at the two birds sitting on the ledge. Not one whit intimidated, they continued their pecking and ignored him.

With a firmer grip on the windowsill, Jared pushed himself back to his feet. In that instant, Bernard whirled around. Wild, bloodshot eyes went wide as he stared at Jared. He swung his gun around, moving it away from the girl's head. Jared had a split second to make the decision. Without hesitation, he took the shot. A small hole appeared in Bernard's forehead and the man fell to the floor.

A flurry of people burst through the door. Jared slid the window open wider and slipped inside. Medics rushed to the girl; McCall stalked in after them. His boss's eyes went straight to Jared, and the expression on his face promised a future dressing down.

Jared mentally shrugged. He and McCall had a weekly "What the hell were you thinking?" meeting. He had gotten used to them. Sure, he had a deep respect for his boss and the work LCR performed, but Jared had told the man up front that following rules wasn't his strong point. McCall didn't always like Jared's methods, but he got the job done.

He moved across the room toward the lone Agar policeman, who also happened to be the police chief. A small town like Agar had only a skeleton force. LCR often helped out when small towns needed assistance. Though it had been a clean kill, that didn't mean there wouldn't be questions. In Jared's previous life, he'd been able to walk away with no one even knowing his existence, much less asking questions. Odd how he didn't miss those old ways.

Always aware of his surroundings, he knew McCall was bringing in the mother to console the sobbing child, who'd raced to the corner of the room the instant after the bullet hit Bernard. In the middle of the room, LCR operative Aidan Thorne stood over the dead man as a medical worker examined him.

The jaded, tired eyes of the police chief told Jared more than any words ever could. This was a man who'd been around the block a few times and had seen it all more than once. He'd probably moved to Agar from a larger city, expecting low crime and an opportunity to enjoy some peace and quiet. Problem was, evil had no respect for boundaries. It had a tendency to show up in the damnedest places these days.

In case those tired, knowing eyes had missed the obvious, Jared gave him the information. "It was a clean kill."

The older man nodded grimly, then proceeded to pepper him with questions, letting Jared know that even though he looked like he'd rather be anywhere else than here, he planned to do his job.

As Jared answered each carefully worded question with his own careful answers, his phone vibrated in his pocket. To most people, that wouldn't be a big deal. Phones rang 24/7 all over the world for all kinds of reasons. His phone didn't. He could count on one hand the number of friends he had, and on the other, he could count who else might need to get in touch with him. Either way, he wasn't going to ignore them.

Holding up his hand to stop the questions, Jared pulled his phone out and answered, "Yeah?"

"Jared?" A sobbing gasp and then, "Please . . . I need your help."

He was rarely surprised, but his ex-wife's frantic voice asking for his help came as close as anything had in years. Phone pressed to his ear, he turned and walked away for privacy. "What's wrong?"

"It's Misty. Oh God, Jared, my baby is missing."

The fact that both McCall and Aidan had stopped what they were doing and were staring intently at him told him they were aware of the importance of the call. A second later, McCall went over to the police chief. Knowing his boss would handle any further questions, Jared headed out the door. He stopped in the hallway at the entrance to the stairwell and said, "Tell me what happened."

"I went to her room this morning and she wasn't there."

"You called the police?"

"Yes, they're on the way. Carlson's outside waiting for them." She paused and then added, "Please, Jared, I'm begging—"

"I'll be there as soon as I can." He closed the phone on her plea. Damned if he wanted to hear her beg.

He turned to find McCall behind him. "I'm headed back to Paris. Lara's daughter has gone missing."

His boss's too-sharp eyes assessed him briefly and then he said, "Let me know if you want us involved."

Jared gave a stiff nod of thanks and strode to the elevator. The elevator, old and most likely unreliable, took its own sweet time getting to the ground floor. As soon as the doors opened, Jared took off at a run to the motorcycle he'd parked a couple of blocks away.

As he ran through midday pedestrian traffic, he thought about his boss's lack of questions—something he couldn't help but appreciate. Most people wouldn't have the same control. They would have wanted to know why

Jared cared about helping a woman who'd gone out of her way to let everyone know she despised the man she'd once been married to.

Most people didn't know the truth, and since it was no one's business, he kept his mouth shut. Lara had a reason to hate him, and while the feelings he'd once had for her were wisps of vaporous memories from another life, he owed her his help in any way he could provide it.

He spotted his Ducati half a block away. As usual, the cycle had attracted some admirers. His focus on getting out of town quickly, he moved through the small crowd and, without a word, jumped on the bike. Turning the switch, he revved the engine and was gone.

Paris, France

Two hours later, Jared stood at the entrance to the Dennisons' living room. Unnoticed by the occupants, he took in the scene. Lara, Jared's ex-wife, sat in a chair close to the fireplace. Her blond hair was pulled away from her pale face, and her slender frame seemed to have shrunk since the last time he'd seen her. The big, burly-looking man perched on the edge of an ottoman in front of her was her husband, Carlson Dennison. They were speaking in low, soothing tones to each other, and the affection and caring in their expressions were telling. This was a couple grieving and finding solace in each other.

The few who knew the truth behind Jared's failed marriage felt that Lara was at least partially responsible for their divorce. Jared disagreed. Watching Carlson and Lara together at such a stressful moment reinforced that opinion. For one thing, he and Lara wouldn't have had children together. They'd talked about it before they'd gotten married. Lara was focused on her career and couldn't take the time off; Jared hadn't seen the need to bring another child into the world when there were so many already here who needed good homes. Adoption had been in the future . . . until that future blew up in their faces.

And second, if their child had been abducted, he'd be out looking for her. Offering comfort and support wasn't part of his skill set. He was a doer, not a giver. Ask him to take out an evil dictator, and Jared was the go-to guy. Want a kitten rescued from a tree, he was more than happy to oblige. Rescue a child from a crazed lunatic? Sure, he'd be there in a flash. Open his arms and offer love and comfort? You'd better look to someone else, because Jared would be somewhere else.

Lara glanced up then and noticed him. The expression of relief on her face was a surprise. The last time he'd talked to her—the day their divorce was final—she'd called him a monster and told him to get the hell out of her life.

He had no hard feelings toward her. They'd had a few decent years, and when she'd found out the truth, he'd gotten out. She'd finally gotten a glimpse of the real Jared, hadn't liked what she saw, and wanted him gone. It wasn't as if he hadn't been down that road before.

"Jared, thank God you're here."

Before he could speak, she jumped from her chair and threw herself into his arms. When they'd been married, such spontaneous outbursts of emotion had rarely happened. In fact, the only time he'd ever seen Lara lose her composure was when she'd learned the truth and had demanded he leave. Her calm, no-nonsense demeanor had been one of the biggest reasons he'd thought they could make a go of it. She'd seemed a lot like him. Hell, maybe that had been the problem.

He extricated himself from his ex-wife's arms and held out his hand to Carlson Dennison. After the couple had married, they'd moved to Paris so they could work at the same hospital. Lara was an ER doctor; Carlson was a thoracic surgeon. Jared had met the man only once. He had been standing in a deli, waiting for take-out, when Lara and Carlson had walked in the door. It had been a brief and awkward meeting. Now, having a better understanding of his ex-wife, Jared thought she and Dennison made a good pair.

"Thank you for coming, Livingston," Dennison said. "Lara insists that you have the kind of skills that can bring our baby girl back home to us."

Jared shot a quick glance at Lara. He had never told her the full truth of his experience. When it became clear that the little information he had provided disgusted and shocked her, he'd seen no reason to go into more detail. If she couldn't handle the little things, she sure as hell didn't need to know more.

Apparently thinking she needed to explain, Lara said, "He knows you work for a rescue organization."

Her reticence to talk about her ex-husband to her present one didn't surprise him. Lara hadn't been one to talk that much. Another reason he'd thought they'd get along so well.

Jared nodded and jerked his head toward the couch. "Sit down and let's get started."

The couple seated themselves on the sofa, holding hands. Jared took a seat across from them and said, "When's the last time you saw Misty?"

"Last night I put her down around seven for the night. Then she woke me at three for a bottle. I fed her and put her back to bed. This morning, around six, I went to wake her . . ." She inhaled a trembling breath and finished, "And she wasn't there."

"Any sign of forced entry?"

Carlson shook his head. "The police checked every door and window. They took our fingerprints, and other than one set that belongs to our housekeeper, there were no others. No broken windows or doors."

As he took the parents through a series of questions, Jared kept a close eye on Dennison. Though he knew Lara well enough to be certain she would never endanger her own child, he didn't know enough about Dennison to say the same thing. The man's worried and grief-ravaged expression seemed sincere, but Jared knew better than anyone how easy it was to play a role.

"The police have any leads?"

Lara shook her head. "They're sending someone to ask more questions this afternoon." She straightened her shoulders, an expression of determination hardening her soft, attractive features. "I haven't told them about you, and I don't plan to." She leaned forward. "I want my baby girl found. No matter what you have to do, I want her back."

The message was clear: Do whatever it takes.

Now, that was one thing Jared knew how to do.

Ryker's Rescue
Chicago, Illinois

"I know I shouldn't have done it, but I didn't have any money to feed her. . . . They said they'd take good care of her."

Arms propped up on her desk, Mia Ryker leaned closer and tried to see the truth behind Sandi Winston's lies. The girl was pencil thin. Dark shadows beneath her eyes told of poor sleeping habits, her pallid complexion was an indication of bad health, and her black hair, limp and lifeless, proof of improper nutrition. She was scratching her arms almost frantically, which could be anything from severe dry skin or fleas to a side effect from her condition.

Mia had seen enough addicts to know the symptoms. Sandi said she'd given her daughter away because she couldn't feed her. More likely, it was in exchange for her drug of choice . . . whatever that was.

"When did this happen?" Mia asked.

"Two weeks ago."

Mia held back an infuriated sigh. The child could be halfway around the world by now.

"And you told the police everything?"

The flicker of her eyelids and slight dilation of her pupils gave Mia a warning before Sandi lied and said, "Yes . . . everything."

Mia would come back to that later. "And did these men say where they were going to take her?"

Sandi lifted a bony shoulder in a tired shrug. "They just said they would take her to a safe, warm place where she'd be fed and loved."

Keeping her expression as bland and nonjudgmental as she could, Mia asked, "How much did they pay you?"

Sandi's bloodshot eyes went wide with denial. "I didn't . . . They didn't . . ."

"I need to know as much as I can if I'm going to find your daughter."

Sandi chewed on her dry lips, apparently trying to decide whether Mia could be trusted. Mia reviewed her next steps. She had contacts—unofficial avenues—that the authorities wouldn't and couldn't pursue.

If the men were new, she might have more trouble tracking them down. But if they were some of the regular slime that dealt in human trafficking around the city, she should be able to locate them.

The two-week time delay was her biggest problem.

"When did you tell the police?"

"A couple of days after it happened. I got to thinking maybe they weren't legit . . . you know?"

Yes, she did know. Most likely, Sandi had woken from her drug-induced haze and realized what she had done. Screaming at the young woman who thought so little of the precious gift of a child was a temptation, but one Mia couldn't take. Finding the little girl trumped lecturing the mother.

That didn't include not putting Sandi on a major guilt trip, though. "Your daughter is depending on you. When a mother brings a child into this world, she gives her a promise that she's going to take care of her."

"But I did. I—"

Mia raised her hand to stop another lie. "If you really want to help her, you've got to tell me the truth."

Allowing the silence to eat into Sandi's guilt, Mia waited. She pushed aside the need to jump up from her desk, grab the woman by the shoulders, and shake her until she told the truth. At one time, that's exactly what would have happened. Experience had given Mia wisdom and, more important, patience. Pissing people off or scaring the hell out of them only worked sometimes, under certain circumstances. Patience would give her much better results.

Mia was almost to the point of reverting to her old ways when Sandi finally spoke. "Two thousand dollars."

Alarms went off inside Mia's brain. From a human-trafficking standpoint, two thousand wasn't a huge amount of cash for a healthy child. But if these were local lowlifes and they saw how desperate Sandi was, they should have known she would have taken much less. To give her that much made Mia think it was as much about buying Sandi's silence as it was about purchasing her child.

She picked up her pen and began to jot notes. "Describe them for me and how you met them."

"A friend hooked me up."

"And this friend's name would be . . . ?"

"Arnold, Ernie . . . something like that."

Mia ground her teeth together, the vague answers from Sandi putting her on edge. Again, she fought the need to shake the girl. "Sandi, look at me."

Startled and too-old eyes widened as Mia's stern voice shook Sandi from her lethargic state.

"You either give me all the information you have— answer *all* of my questions—or get up and leave with the knowledge that you'll probably never see your daughter again. Which is it?"

The girl released a shaky breath and said, "It was my friend Freddy. . . . I just didn't want to get him into trouble. He hooks me up with the good stuff sometimes. When I told him I didn't have any money, he told me about these men who might be willing to help me out. I called them."

"Describe them."

"There were two of them. They never told me their names."

"What did they look like?"

"One was real short and kind of fat. The other one had a foreign accent, was tall and thin and walked with a limp. They were both kind of old."

"Old? How old?"

"I don't know . . . maybe forties or something like that."

Though life experience had aged her considerably, Sandi was most likely still a teen. Forties probably *was* old to her.

"What about hair color?"

Sandi slowly began to describe the men. Once the girl warmed to her task, her descriptions were surprisingly vivid and detailed. Flipping to a clean piece of paper, Mia sketched the men. When Sandi stopped, Mia quickly finished her hasty drawing and then turned the paper for the girl to see. "Did they look anything like this?"

The gasp Sandi released told Mia she'd nailed the drawings. Not for the first time, she was grateful for the art classes her elite education had provided.

As Sandi suggested a few changes in the drawings, Mia absently made them while her mind zoomed toward what she needed to do. These men weren't any she'd seen or heard of before. Since setting up her rescue business, she'd become acquainted with the local slime that traded in people as if they were marketable merchandise instead of human beings. In some cases, she'd helped the police put the creeps away; others continued to evade detection. But she knew most of them by sight or reputation. These men were new.

What had they done with Sandi's one-year-old daughter? Was the child even still in Chicago, or had she been taken to another state already? Or another country?

"If I get your daughter back, Sandi, you're going to have to clean yourself up and be the mother your child deserves. You going to be able to do that?"

The emphatic nod seemed genuine, but Sandi's physical appearance indicated she was a longtime addict. Making promises and not following through was as habitual to her as the drug itself. Little did the girl know that Mia would make sure that either she cleaned herself up or the child would be taken away from her. She'd do all she could to help, but no way in hell was she going to put a kid back into her mother's arms if she was going to be endangered or sold again.

Mia opened a drawer in her desk, withdrew a disposable phone, and handed it to the younger woman. "I need to be able to get in touch with you. My number is already on speed dial. I'll call you if I have other questions, and if you think of something else, you can get in touch with me at any time."

The girl stood. "That's it? Is there anything else I can do?"

"Yeah. Clean up and get yourself some food. There's a restaurant on Eighteenth Street called Maxie's. Tell them Mia sent you. They'll feed you as many times as you need. Do you have a place to stay?"

"I'm staying with a friend."

"Is your friend using?"

"No. She's been trying to get me clean. She's the one who told me to come see you."

Eager to get started on the investigation, Mia stood and walked the girl to the door. "I'll call you as soon as I know something. And remember, if you think of anything, call me. Okay?"

Sandi nodded, her eyes filling with tears. "Do you think they're feeding and taking care of her?"

As much as she wanted to snarl at the girl that her motherly concern was too little too late, she wouldn't. Having Sandi's cooperation was imperative. Mia had learned long ago to keep judgment out of her tone and manner. Putting people on the defensive rarely helped a case.

However, neither would she lie. "I don't know what their plans are for your daughter, but I promise I'll do all I can to bring her home."

The instant Sandi cleared the door, Mia turned back to her desk. Even with a detailed description of the men, she had her work cut out for her.

She picked up her phone and began to make calls to the network of people she relied on daily for help. The little girl had been gone for two weeks. Finding her after such a long time was going to take everything she had, but she refused to believe it wasn't possible.

Having overcome impossible odds before, Mia was determined that this would be just one more thing she would conquer.